Thinking Out Loud

Grayson Long

Thinking Out Loud is a work of fiction.

Names, characters, places, and incidents are products of the author's imagination and intended to be used fictitiously. Any resemblance to actual events, locales, or persons, living or dead, is entirely coincidental.

Copyright © 2023 by Grayson Long

All rights reserved.

ISBN: 979-8-339-19500-9

No part of this publication may be reproduced, distributed, or transmitted in any form or by any means, including photocopying, recording, or other electronic or mechanical methods, without the prior written permission of the publisher, except as permitted by U.S. copyright law. For permission requests, contact Grayson Long.

Book Cover by Cindy Ras.

Editing and Proofreading by Caitlin Lengerich.

Formatting by Atticus Software.

To my husband,
For loving me, even in the dark moments.
For reminding me of the greatest love of all,
The One whom my soul loves.

Author's Note

To write a story, we must be true to ourselves, but also try to be respectful of those that may read it. In doing so, being tactful is a priority, especially when writing about mental health. With that, I want to inform you, reader, that even though this story is a romantic comedy, there are also real life struggles that are addressed. As you read, you will find on page descriptions of anger, anxiety, alcohol consumption, and physical contact. I hope you experience joy and excitement as you read this story, and that the on-page depictions have been done in a tasteful way. To those of you who have experienced mental health struggles, I hope you feel seen and supported by this story.

CHAPTER ONE

Ellie

"THAT'S UGLY."

A tiny goblin scowls at my notebook from across the table.

"You're ugly," I mumble under my breath before closing the notebook and shoving it into my bag.

The goblin sticks his tongue out at me before shoving a handful of Cheerios into his pie hole, his eyes penetrating into my soul. I take a long, slow sip of my coffee and stare back at him, intimidation factor on full blast as I squint and snarl behind my cup.

Another goblin comes flying past with no pants on.

"Boys! We have to go!" my sister yells from a different room.

A Cheerio hits me in the face as Goblin One sticks his tongue out at me and jumps out of his chair. I grit my teeth at my nephew, that I swear I love, and proceed to focus my attention on my phone.

Ms. Bailey,

Unfortunately, we are unable to offer you a refund as the deadline to submit a request has passed. We appreciate your business and hope you consider us for any social events you may have in the future.

Have a good day!

Abby Harper

Manager | Golden Valley Event Venue

I reread the email four times before slamming my phone down on the counter, resisting the urge to chuck it across the room.

"El, you ready?" I hear my sister wrangling her children near the front door.

I zip-up my bag, swing myself out of my chair and practically hear bubble wrap pop. The tin man has taken my body and replaced it with his rusty, old shell.

I stretch and twist until everything stops cracking—standing as slow as humanly possible in the process. I replay the last few week's events to find the culprit of the new aches and questionable noises. I haven't ran in a while, no new workouts or quick movements, nothing that could result in my bones screaming like they are.

It could just be a result of decreased activity—too many nights in bed, scrolling my phone. Or I just slept wrong. Or the reality that this past year has been so stressful, my body has no idea what's going on anymore. I guess it's decided to respond like an old man after a bad visit to the chiropractor.

The past year's events start to work their way across my mind, followed by a numbing fog as it starts to wander down a *what if, why me* spiral. I give each limb of my body a shake, jostling the thoughts until they're gone.

No time for *that* today.

I mosey through the kitchen and out the front door, climbing into my sister's SUV—the goblins seated directly behind me.

Wonderful.

This *should* be an exciting day, starting a new job and working with your sister—who is also your best friend—is usually something people look forward to. Yet, I feel like crawling under my bed and letting the effects of life's circumstances overtake me would be more fun.

It doesn't help that I can't stop thinking about my very cramped loft apartment in the attic of my sister's house—with unpacked moving boxes blocking the window, piles of letters and sticky notes covering my bed, and about ten different letters denying my refund for a multitude of wedding-related deposits.

Yep, just let me stay under my bed, please.

It's worth adding that today is the first day of my *third* new job this year.

I am *not* proud of this. Not at all.

It turns out that having a Ph.D. in Psychology doesn't actually make you more desirable in the job market. Especially when you have minimal life experience, and a very small client pool. I wish I could say it's hard to pinpoint why I'm not more sought after to help people with life's problems, but I would bet my inability to tackle my own issues could be one of the reasons. Leaving my clinic in New York wasn't easy, but I was confident I would find work.

Unfortunately, when applying for jobs in my field, a psychiatric evaluation is bound to happen. And the recent uptick in my intrusive thoughts were too much to hide from Larry, the evaluator.

Normally, I love my career choice.

I love working through problems with people, especially when I can relate on a personal level. But for the past four hundred and seventy-two days, I have been on a downward spiral, relating more than I probably should to clients, causing them to question if I'm really capable of helping them when I can't seem to help myself. And I can't blame them for that.

It turns out, being left at the altar really does something to one's mental health.

Shocker.

"How are you feeling? I am so excited!" Emma is overly giddy as she backs out of her driveway. She is a vibrant soul and, aside from my inability to stay at my job, she is one of the main reasons I left New York and came back to Oklahoma.

When we were kids, my sister and I would ride our bikes for miles, taking in the glimmers of sunshine peeking through oak trees down our street—the humid heat beating down on our windblown faces. Racing to the nearest pond and making mud cakes with red dirt and sticks. Borrowing—er, *stealing*—our dad's vintage Chevy pickup and speeding through cow pastures on the outskirts of town, practically flying through the roof when we ran over embankments we didn't see coming. Laughing so hard it was practically impossible to keep from spilling the truth of what really happened to the front fender. Oklahoma was home sweet home to me for most of my life, and after going off to college, I had every intention of coming back.

Staying halfway across the country never even crossed my mind until I was engaged.

Ugh, *was engaged.*

"I'm feeling fine. *So* ecstatic."

Her eye roll response is so strong next to me it practically reverberates in my ears.

"Really, I feel fine." I don't. "It feels good to be back."

It doesn't. But I keep that to myself.

She smiles at me as she pulls onto the road, glancing in her rearview mirror at the boys who have resorted to kicking each other. Thank God, they aren't kicking me.

Emma whips her hair over her shoulder and adjusts her mirror, looking like she belongs in an ad for the car we're riding in. She stands three inches taller, with long limbs and supermodel-like features without any cosmetic enhancements. Her rich brown hair is always smooth and frizz-free, giving no indication that she has two rascals climbing all over her everyday. And she almost always looks put together, whether it's at the park, at her job, or in the middle of a spin class, the woman embodies gracefulness. As for me . . . my hair requires daily washes, my skin needs monthly detox facials, and my attire? Well let's just say I teeter the line of a presentable member of society and homeless person daily. There is no in-between.

Emma is just as beautiful inside as she is on the outside too, which can be infuriating to some people. She was the person who rescued me from the altar when Liam announced to me, and my entire family, that he didn't love me anymore. She did what any elegant and graceful person would do, of course . . . flipping him the bird as she ushered me back down the aisle. She is a fiery force to be reckoned with at times and I feel sheepish knowing I might not have the guts to truly back her up the way she does me.

"So that's what you're wearing, huh?" She eyes me up and down as she drives, messing with the radio and simultaneously parenting the goblins.

"What's wrong with it?" I ask, curious if her tone is hinting at a compliment or insult.

"You look fantastic!" she assures me. "New York really sculpted you into a classy young lady. I am very impressed with this getup," she says, motioning to my wide-legged dress pants. "Can I borrow those?"

We both laugh knowing they will quickly change from pants to early 2000s gauchos if she wears them. Turning my attention to the visor, I smooth out my hair and adjust the angle for one last look of my outfit.

"Quit that," she says like she's reading my mind.

"What?" I shut the mirror and adjust the air vent on my side.

"Picking yourself apart—letting your mind run amuck."

I exhale, trying not to listen to her as she says, "Not that anything I say is going to change how you see yourself"—she shrugs—"but I think you look great and Glendale is lucky to have you."

Glendale. As in Glendale High School.

My new place of work for the next few months, smack dab in the middle of Oklahoma.

It was a culture shock coming back from New York—a place with millions of people, congested streets stretching from one end of the sun to the other, and subways filled to the brim with people, packed in like little sardines just praying to squeeze out of the sliding door and land on a platform packed with more sardines pushing their way into the can you just escaped.

It sounds awful, but I think I miss it.

I miss being swarmed with so much hustle and bustle you don't even have one moment of quiet to let your mind wander. This place was too quiet, and since being back my mind hadn't *stopped* wandering.

Glendale is a full forty-five minute car ride from Emma's house. And while I appreciated her driving, being accompanied by my twin nephews makes for a torturous ride. I would take navigating the subway system at four in the morning over this any day. It's not that I hate my nephews. I love them. I do. I just feel a slight detachment to them. Maybe it's because they look more like their dad than Emma. Or that they're loud and snotty. Or it's just the fact that children can be the worst. I love my nephews—a biological extension of my sweet sister—wholeheartedly, but in any other sense, not a fan.

Five-year-olds and I don't mesh well. Sure, we can tolerate each other, but we definitely thrive better when separated.

Preparing for the effects the rest of this car ride will have on my head, I swallow two ibuprofen pills and chase them with a swig of iced coffee.

"You're going to kill your liver," Emma says as she takes one of her way too expensive bottles of essential oils out of her center console, rolling it on her wrists. I assume it's some flippy-dippy hippie stuff you find inside a unicorn's rectum. That is the only justification for the amount of money she spends on it.

"You're going to kill *my* liver with that wretched stench you roll all over yourself."

The smell is a combination of old leather and citrus, and it practically singes my nose hairs as she waves her hand in my face. The motion wafts the smell even more forcefully into my olfactory nerves. I gag dramatically to accentuate the overpowering impact the oil stench has on me as she pulls onto the highway.

I lean my head back against the seat, watching other cars whizz past us as if we are at a stand still. I glance over at the speedometer and see Emma going ten under the speed limit.

She is usually a quick and efficient person—except when we're in the car. I bite my lip, sit on my hands, and refuse to point out the blatantly obvious fact that, at this point, snails are passing us. Normally I would be an enraged passenger in this situation, but I know my sister, and I know that her anxieties can be triggered by driving.

It's best I keep my thoughts about our speed to myself.

Emma glances at me before changing lanes—*slowly*. A mini van honks at us.

I'm honestly not sure what annoys me more, the fact that she refused to let me drive, or the fact that I might not get to work before Christmas.

Irritation swarms my head as we make our way down the road. The combination of leathery aroma and goblin farts only adds to my frustration, and, as a result, I'm so focused on my thoughts that I almost miss the view, namely a long stretch of Oklahoma interstate underneath a clear blue sky with streaks of pink and orange.

No clouds in sight and the sun has almost fully risen on our right.

I take a deep breath and focus on the colors. Letting the rising sun heat the side of my face as we drive.

It could be so peaceful . . . If I block out the kicking of my seat and the bullets of Cheerios being pelted at the back of my head.

Em is unphased—driving with a smile across her face, window down, humming to the radio we can't even hear over the screams of her husband's spawn. It's very hard to believe these hellions came from her considering they look exactly like their father, *Dr. Steven Jones*—it's infuriating.

I have nothing against Steven, except he takes my sister for granted about one *thousand* percent of the time and he's the one who introduced me to my ex . . .

Okay, maybe I am a little jaded.

Steven and Liam met in college, they were both pre-med and attended medical school together. When Emma and Steven got engaged, she was convinced I needed to marry a doctor too, hence introducing me to Liam.

"Just think of how amazing our lives would be! Sister-doctor-wives!"

I winced every time she used that phrase.

Steven, apparently, had suspicions about Liam's intentions weeks before the wedding and never told anyone. He only revealed these suspicions to Em a month after I moved all of Liam's stuff out and started my nightly spiral of Instagram stalking—a box of Franzia Sangria in hand. Apparently, calling my sister sobbing at 2 a.m. every morning to report there were still no new Liam updates was just too much for ole Steve to handle.

Of course, I can't blame him entirely for wanting to withhold this information. If I, too, learned someone I loved was about to be publicly humiliated and lose out on thousands of dollars worth of wedding deposits, and witness their entire life crumble before their eyes, I would also sit idly by and wait until I felt *so* inconvenienced that there was no other option than to share my dirty truth.

Again, *can't blame the guy...*

"Are you nervous?" Emma reels me back to the present and away from my disdain for her husband. I could never tell her how I felt about him. Not that I would want her to choose a side (although I fully expect her to choose mine), and I couldn't be the reason she had issues in her marriage. I wouldn't wish my emotional trauma and damage on my worst enemy, let alone my sister.

"A little," I answer—very delayed.

"Don't be. You will be great. You are exactly what these students need right now."

"Why did they rush to hire me anyway? This all happened so fast."

"Boys, please behave." The hellions are now rubbing their feet on the windows, whilst rubbing their boogers on each other and our seats. I probably have boogers in my hair now. "Did you not ask them that in your interview?" she questions, whipping the car to the right to avoid missing our exit.

Mindlessly scrolling Instagram I respond, "I wouldn't call what happened a very *thorough* interview."

The faculty at Glendale seemed to blindly trust my sister and her recommendation. I think I was asked a total of three questions for the entirety of the interview. I don't fully remember it really, except the fact that it was a panel interview over Zoom, and the only guy asking the questions actually had his camera turned off the entire time. His voice was almost hypnotizing on the other side of the screen—smooth and gentle. I felt so at ease listening to him talk I almost forgot to respond to even the simplest of questions. *"What do you do for fun?"* may as well have been a lullaby coming from his mouth. He seemed so focused on conducting the interview that he didn't even turn his camera on until the very end. Once it was over, I was pressing that sweet little red *leave* button without a second's hesitation, completely missing his face.

"Well . . ." She pauses to eye her boys in the backseat, still no rise in her emotions as they are now definitely wiping boogers in my hair. "Glendale is going through some administration changes. Budgets are being reallocated. Long-time teachers are retiring. All the usual politics in our education system are making a huge impact as well, but the biggest issue lately is the influx of students we have received after nearby schools closed their doors. Those homeschool cohorts and digital learning options really stuck after 2020 and a lot of parents were given a nice tax break when they continued sending their kids to a public school. So we practically doubled our student population, while also losing key faculty members—one of them being Ms. Patsy." She turns down a new road and rolls up her window. "You know Ms. Pat, she was our counselor for almost forty years. She has big shoes to fill but not a lot of time to fill them in. This term is a trial run, for you and for the school—to see if you can handle the variety of students we have and if you even want to stick around for a few months." She shrugs, again, ignoring the fact that I do not intend to be here any longer than I've already committed.

"I was very honest with our vice principal, and told him you would be a wonderful fit but that you may not enjoy staying here long-term."

"So what you're saying is . . ." I pause, careful to hide the glee I feel about the easy bailout I've been given. "I have a free pass to bail if this doesn't pan out?" I smirk at her.

I couldn't help it, she knows how I feel about this.

She huffs at me as she switches lanes.

I will hide my contempt for taking a job well below my pay grade from everyone and their dog . . . except for Emma. That's how our relationship is—we are brutally honest with each other even if it's regarding *her* place of employment.

She rolls her eyes as she adjusts the radio station a tad too aggressively. Her unspoken responses are louder than any words she could force out of her lungs. She thinks I will love this job, or at least she hopes I will. And more importantly, she wants me to treat it with respect.

Emma has been the art teacher at Glendale for three years and spends every family holiday raving about how they want her to be Mr. Clinton's replacement. Mr. Clinton, who is a dinosaur apparently, has been the principal at Glendale for about a century—per their school website. Emma tells us every year how the entire school sits on the edge of their seats waiting for that fateful day when he will announce his retirement. But every year Mr. Clinton closes his end-of-the-year rally speech with, "We'll see ya next year, folks!"

According to Em, it's both a sadness and a relief.

She would be a wonderful principal.

But with Dr. Steven taking on the odd shift work as the newest physician at the hospital, and the hellions still not old enough to go to school, the added responsibility would surely send her to the looney bin.

"I swear if one of you kicks my seat again . . ." I sneer loudly through my teeth. The boys cackle in response—snaggly, drooly smiles and all. How people find that cute, I'll never know. One of the twins sticks his tongue out at me then proceeds to eat a booger. Irritation boils through my veins as I watch them from the rearview mirror.

Would it be frowned upon to throw my shoe at them?

My sister gently grabs my clenched fist. Involuntary trembles move up my arms, my fingernails pinch the inside of my palm as I squeeze harder. Her touch is an attempt to soothe and prevent a rage-filled spiral.

From the outside looking in, a sudden reaction to two toddlers might seem normal. But for me, it's a quick reminder that my intrusive thoughts are not as under control as they should be, especially for a professional therapist.

Between my sister and I, I've always been the calm one. Em has always been patient and direct with her boys, but in other circumstances, her anxiety can be debilitating and destructive. Mom and Em were the reasons I went into psychology. Growing up, there was never a day where one of them didn't experience some sort of panic attack. Some were warranted, like my mother's anxiety regarding our water getting cut off, or my sister panicking when we were rear-ended by a semi-truck. Other times, it seemed to me their brains just weren't operating the way the rest of the world's brains were. Helping them process and stay grounded came natural to me. Just by talking to them, I was a key part in preventing their detrimental spirals. As a result, I found a passion for mental health.

My freshman year of high school, my English teacher, Ms. Walker, saw me talking a cheerleader out of a social crisis in the bathroom and she recommended I look into different counseling training programs after I graduated. And honestly, it was the perfect fit. Becoming a licensed therapist and finishing my doctorate in Psychology Research was the fuel to my fire of wanting to solve the world's mental health problem.

Marrying a psychiatrist by the name of Liam was the gasoline I needed to set it ablaze.

We were going to end the mental health stigma, bring about light in someone's darkest times, and show the world that our brains are nothing to be afraid of.

It was a good plan.

Was.

But even the strongest and most capable people can lose their way. Even with the right resources and education, some of the best professionals in our field can lose their cool. After last year, it's clear I've started losing mine. Now *I'm* the one who needs help staying grounded.

I catch myself hovering over Liam's text thread with my thumb—lost in the past—when we pull into Glendale's parking lot.

Glendale High School sits nestled behind a line of elm trees a few blocks away from the busy city streets. The sun shines through, speckling the pavement with gold shimmers and highlighting the red and gold Glendale emblem painted on the blacktop pavement.

I'm not sure if it was the feeling of anticipation or nerves, but something about Glendale sent flutters through my chest. We step out of the truck and the Oklahoma wind whips my hair around my face. An unexpected smile tugs at my lips as I survey the outskirts of my new place of employment.

Chapter Two

Benny

Today is orientation day and we have our new hire coming in.

I'm really looking forward to her joining our team. She seemed very elegant and professional in her interview, and I probably seemed like a dweeb for not even turning my camera on.

Filling my third cup of coffee this morning, I start to mentally go over today's to-do list. The summer flew by and I am ecstatic to be back. Yes, I'm the weird guy who loves their job and looks forward to summer break being over.

I never pictured myself working as a teacher, let alone becoming vice principal one day. Up until the age of thirteen I was convinced I'd be the next Eminem or the third member of Outkast. I had *dreams*.

Accepting a teaching job at my alma mater was an impulse. A way to pay the bills when I was right out of college—but it quickly turned into one of the best things I've ever done. Being at Glendale just feels right to me. I don't think I'm meant to do anything else—I love it here. Even though this job seems to put a lot of weight on my shoulders with the never-ending responsibilities, I wouldn't trade it for the world. But with all the changes coming up, this year is looking like it will be one of the most stressful years I've ever had as vice principal.

"It's going to be a great term!" Ms. Patsy walks into our breakroom, joining me at the back counter by the communal coffee pot. "Quit using that, you're ruining perfectly good coffee!" She motions at the container in my hand.

"What is so wrong with my flavored creamer?" I retort, setting my cinnamon creamer back in the refrigerator.

"Men are supposed to like black coffee. It's strong and simple. How a man takes his coffee can say a lot about their character." She laughs, patting me on the back a little too hard.

"I hope you don't view me any less for my creamer choice." I smile down at her.

"Oh, Benny, you know you're my favorite. Have all the creamer you want." She pinches my cheek before pouring herself a heaping cup of straight, black coffee—drinking it without hesitation.

I beam at her, ignoring how sad I am going to be when she leaves this place in favor of retirement next month. "Since I'm your favorite, be sure to put a good word in for me with this new hire."

We gaze out the large, double-paneled windows of our breakroom, over-looking a very overgrown football field to the left that backs up to steep hills, covered in deep emerald trees. Our staff parking lot sits just to the right of us. The sky is crisp and unobstructed by clouds as the sun beams across the field, shining through the windows and onto our faces.

This view has always been my favorite. So much so that I worked as a teacher's aide for three years before graduating just to have free access to it.

Getting coffee for Mr. Clinton from this very room was my primary job. He likes creamer too, but he is definitely *not* Patsy's favorite. I like Mr. Clinton—he has that stern, *my way or the highway* attitude, which Patsy has, but will deny. I always had fun witnessing them butt heads with each other as a teacher's aide, and now I get paid to witness it just about every day.

Mr. Clinton was the first one to approve me for the role as vice principal and went to bat for me in front of the school board when they questioned my ability to take on the job, considering my history and lack of experience. I owe a great deal to him, for many reasons, which is why I tend to suppress any overwhelming feelings that might surface regarding my ability to do the job well.

"Emma will be getting here soon with Ellie, the new hire," Patsy begins—going over today's agenda. "Her meet-and-greet is scheduled at 9 a.m. with bagels. Your cousin begged me to bring her vegan cream cheese. I tried to tell her we had everything covered but she is relentless," she scoffs. "She's already convinced Geer to switch from real milk to that nut stuff. I swear she won't rest until all of my favorite things are taken from this place!" Patsy continues down a rabbit trail of how things used to be, *back in her day*. When she gets feisty like this, I usually opt to play Sweden—stay neutral.

"Let Kate bring her spread." I throw an arm over Patsy's shoulders. "You only have one more week to put up with it, then you are off on your adventures, consuming every animal product you can get your hands on."

Her face softens, not in a happy way, as she continues staring out the window. She's sad to be leaving, and we're all sad to be losing her. Thirty-eight years is a long time to be in one place, let alone the same job. Patsy was here from the beginning—becoming a member of the staff when Glendale was still being built right outside city limits.

She always said, *"The future of public education is going to be here."* She believed Glendale would be a sought-after school, and the students here would go on to make a name for themselves. That's what made her the best guidance counselor—she's been a messenger of hope for our students and their future since the beginning. I mean, she even had hope for me when I was nothing but a class clown.

In my junior year of high school, Patsy pulled me aside and demanded I get a degree in education. I never understood why. The only thing I was good at teaching was the Melbourne Shuffle and a silly magic card trick that was definitely a dupe. But Patsy had faith in me, and when I lost my parents, she pushed me and stood by me in some of my darkest times. She saw the best in me when not many could, and the same goes for so many students that she's worked with for over thirty years.

She's leaving big shoes to fill and it's hard to imagine the new girl will be up to the task.

What if it doesn't work out?

"What if *what* doesn't work out?" Patsy snaps me out of my thoughts.

"How much of my thoughts did you just hear?" I pinch the bridge of my nose and groan.

"Ellie will be wonderful! She is more than qualified and she ain't got anything to lose! This will be good for her after everything she's gone through—"

"What has she gone through?" I ask abruptly, "Please don't tell me it will interfere with her work." I scratch the back of my head and mess with my hair before taking another big swig of coffee. The fear of hiring someone who can't provide these students stability and consistency puts me on edge.

"It will be fine"—Patsy grabs my elbow—"Relax."

I take a deep breath and nod. *Relax.*

Eleanor Bailey seems very fit for the job. Even a little overqualified. And I'm aware she doesn't intend to stay long, but I can't help but worry how invested she will be in her responsibilities. I just hope she doesn't have something going on that will hinder her ability to do the job well. These kids deserve someone who is fully present, even if it's for a short period.

"Plus, it's not everyday Glendale can say they have Columbia alumni on their staff." She takes a sip of her coffee, still looking out the window.

"That is a plus," I agree.

"And she's pretty." She smirks behind her mug.

It instantly feels twenty degrees hotter in our little break room. I clear my throat and avoid acknowledging her comment. I'm very aware of how attractive the new girl is, and I haven't even met her in person yet. Working with Emma for a few years, I've seen Ellie in photos—her delicate pink lips and striking eyes always make me do a double take. And seeing her on a computer screen in real time was enough to make my heart stop.

Hence, forgetting to turn on my camera.

"Will she—"

"They're here!" Patsy cuts me off as she practically pushes me through the glass when she barrels out of the breakroom, racing to meet Emma and her sister outside. I'm in awe as I stay planted in place, taking in what I see out of my favorite window.

A computer screen doesn't do justice to the in-person view of this new girl.

She's stunning.

And all of a sudden, my favorite view out of our large break room window isn't as appealing as it once was.

This new view—it's better.

CHAPTER THREE

Ellie

Patsy, a short Filipino woman with platinum white hair, plows through the doors to greet Emma and me for my first day.

Growing up, our grandma called her Pattie Cakes—they were best friends. She's been a high school counselor for what seems like an eternity and she's the reason Emma started working at Glendale in the first place.

Patsy seemed to be the matriarch of Glendale, having an unspoken authority over every faculty member who has come and gone during her years of reign. When the school started to have a terrible turnover rate with the faculty, Ms. Pat got word to our grandma about how desperate they were for fresh young faces to teach. So, of course, when she told the school to call a stay-at-home mom—with no experience—to fill in as a substitute teacher, they did. Pat has some magical influence around here. What she says, goes. And when she told the school board she thought Emma should become a full-time teacher, without any actual teaching experience, they didn't fight her on it.

It's probably that left eyebrow of hers. It's powerful. The higher it reaches, the more power it exudes.

I find myself staring at it as she races towards us in the parking lot and a rush of feeling overcomes me. I've missed this tiny, sassy woman.

"Ellie Belly!" My childhood nickname seems to echo across the lot as she engulfs me in a mighty, mama bear-like hug.

"Ms. Pat!" I exclaim, wiggling my arms free to return the hug. Her head fits snuggly under my chin—it's comforting. Somehow her tiny frame still feels strong enough to protect me from harm. I squeeze tight.

"We have been waiting for you! The whole staff is in the breakroom, they want to give you a warm welcome for your first day."

"Lucky me," I say, exaggerating my less-than-excited tone.

Patsy takes my hand in a death grip and leads me into the school. At first, I don't see anything special about the place Emma goes on and on about. It has simple white walls, with red lockers, and a giant helmet plastered across the floor. But the more I see, it becomes clear why she loves the place so much. It's quaint, and my heart warms as I take in the small details of school spirit sprinkled down the halls and on doors—old newspaper clippings, student photos, and flyers from the previous school year. Not to mention the Glendale Knights memorabilia encased in smudgy glass and flickering twinkle lights.

It doesn't hold a candle to the shrine to Oklahoma football glowing in my parent's front den, but theirs is an obnoxious obsession that I try not to focus on each family holiday.

"It's not much, but it really is the best place," Emma whispers to me as we follow chatty Patsy down the hall.

Emma drops the goblins off in the library with Margaret, a middle-aged woman with a slow pace and bad hip. And of course, chaos ensues as Emma shuts the door.

Poor Margaret.

They take me to a rather large break room, with big, beautiful windows on the back wall, and blinds pulled all the way up, allowing the sun to shine through.

I instantly regret agreeing to a meet-and-greet when I am swarmed by a pack of wild teachers.

As I'm bombarded by athleisure wear, surf shorts, flip flops, and sunglasses atop heads, I realize I am way overdressed for this *very* "informal" breakfast meeting. I was so concerned about my outfit this morning that I didn't pay attention to how Emma was dressed. I look over at her and my brain registers the attire: white linen shorts, sandals, and a t-shirt announcing, "Mom Life is the Best Life." That twerp let me ramble on and on about how I should look and didn't make a peep when I changed five different times.

I adjust my blazer, clearing my throat loudly in her direction. She giggles and leaves me in the mob of greetings, joining a man leaning against the refrigerator at the back of the room. He's attractive. Like *very* attractive. He leans so effortlessly and relaxed, like this chatty mob is something he experiences every day.

He smiles at me.

Or at least, I think he did? Maybe he just smiled at the wall?

Ugh, his smile.

The sun seems to bounce off of his perfectly straight teeth, and it's like his lips know the effect they have on a woman as they curl upward—*captivating*. They're plump, in a soft and subtle way. His cupid's bow twitches on one side, as if a muscle under stress holding its position too long. He's smiling . . . a lot. And the more he does, the more I *want* it to be directed at me.

Maybe he's just a friendly coworker, happy to see the new girl join the team.

I find myself stealing glances back at his lips a tad too many times, and each time leaves me a little dazed and disoriented. I try to refocus and muster up verbal responses for the teachers currently talking my ear off.

"We're so happy you're here! These students are the best and your sister is the best and this just feels like the icing on the cake for this term! Ah!"

I'm snapped out of the trance the gorgeous, dark-haired man has on me to see a short, bubbly woman standing directly in front of me—her curly hair bouncing in every direction.

"Thank you. It's nice to be here," I say, trying to sound convincingly happy, before I reach out to shake Jumpy's hand. "Eleanor Bailey."

"Kate! Kate Stanley, science teacher, and volleyball coach!" Her smile is big and friendly. "Seriously, we cannot thank you enough for joining us. These students need support and Emma has sung your praises for years. It's so nice to meet the amazing Ellie in person!" She practically shakes my arm out of the socket while she talks, "Please, sit, tell us about yourself."

"Oh, I don't think—"

"Let the woman get acquainted first. Don't smother her or we'll run her off." A surly man sitting at the round table in the center of the room joins the conversation.

He walks over and shakes my hand firmly. He smiles, but it's not as friendly as the others, and his beard is pristinely trimmed. "Eat a damn bagel already, Pat bought the store out for you. It's rude to let them go to waste." He holds his bagel choice up and heads for the door. "Malcolm Geer, math and football. Don't waste our time and we won't waste yours."

"Malcolm! Be nice!" Ms. Pat yells after him.

I watch as he saunters out of the breakroom, not looking back. No nonsense Malcolm, I like him.

"Don't mind him. He is the biggest teddy bear underneath all of that scruff." Kate walks with me over to the bagels.

I find myself staring at them, feeling a surge of tension run up my arms and into my chest. *Don't waste our time*. That's exactly what I'm doing. I don't want to be here. I told them in the interview that this would be temporary. So why are they making such a big deal about me being here? How obsessive are these people?

"I need some coffee." Quickly scanning the room, I find the coffee pot in the back of the room by Emma and the gorgeous man I have felt staring at me this entire time.

"The pot is over by Em and Benny. Creamer is in the fridge, but if you'd like, I have some vegan creamer in my classroom! I make it myself!" Kate offers.

Oh, God. She's one of *those* people.

I hear an audible sigh from Ms. Pat.

"Will it offend you if I use a creamer made from cows, today? I can promise to try the vegan one another time. Too much change in one day is a little overwhelming." I smile and try my best to avoid sounding absolutely disgusted at the idea of a vegan creamer. Kate seems pleased with my offer and nods.

I head over to meet Emma and *Benny*. As I'm walking, I swear I see Emma pretend to take a phone call and mosey her way out of the area, leaving just me and this *Benny* guy.

Heading straight for the coffee pot, my plan is to act like I haven't noticed him smiling at me and ignore what it does to the skin on the back of my neck. I don't have room in my emotionally damaged brain to humor an attractive man or his perfect teeth.

The coffee smells burnt and the pot is about ten pots of coffee past a thorough scrubbing. A violent chill moves down my neck over the thought of a dirty coffee pot. The image of smashing it into a dumpster flashes through my head.

Why don't people clean up after themselves?

I grab a pastel pink mug with a picture of a pug on it. Instinctively, I grab the one that is the cutest in an attempt to brighten the dread I have building in my stomach over the grimey pot.

"That's Mr. Geer's pot. He refuses to clean it," a whisper, smooth and gentle, swirls around my head and into my chest.

The voice is familiar.

Benny is watching me hover the pot over the pug mug. He must see the hesitation in my attempt to pour. Or, he can read my mind and is quite aware that I am having an internal crisis about dirty dishes.

Is he able to sense the intrusive thoughts I'm having? Is he completely aware that I'm feeling triggered by grimy coffee smudges and the smell of burnt glass?

Yes Ellie, this mysterious Benny is that intuitive.

I snort a laugh at myself and the absurdity of my thoughts.

I tend to forget that not everyone is used to sensing an imminent breakdown approaching.

Not everyone is a psychologist, Eleanor.

Gathering myself and putting the death pot back on its scorched burner, I respond with, "Why won't he clean it? Does everyone drink from this pot? Mr. Geer controls the community caffeine?" I fire off sentences faster than I intended.

I turn to face Benny, the pug mug still in hand. He's holding a glistening clean coffee pot, swirling with beautiful waves of coffee, smelling like a mix of coconut and mocha—*my favorite.*

"We keep a clean one in the corner so Malcolm can't tamper with it. You are free to use it anytime." I finally register his voice as he pours me a cup, effortlessly.

The Zoom guy. My new *boss.*

"You must hide the evidence or you will be banished from the clean pot island."

I feel a smile stretch across my face and sting my cheeks—he's funny.

"I'm Mr. Divata. It's nice to have you on board, Ms. Bailey." He shakes my hand and I pray he assumes my sweaty palms are from holding the coffee pot for so long.

"Ellie," I encourage, still shaking his hand and not letting go.

You can let go now.

His smile grows as I keep shaking his hand. His grip is steady and strong, but his thumb grazes the top of my hand tenderly, sending shivers up my arm and into my neck. His forearms are chiseled, with sleek, dark hair trickling across them. His arms look so welcoming . . . I could brush my cheek against that forearm. His hands were smooth and very slow to leave my hand when I *finally* stopped shaking it. I felt a tingle shoot up my arm and down to my stomach from his touch.

"Ellie, then." His eyes glisten and crinkle in the corners. "Is there anything I can do for you on your first day, Ellie?"

It's very noticeable that I'm gawking at him and his silhouette in the sunlight, but he doesn't say a word. He just continues watching me—an intriguing look in his eyes.

I blink and refocus. "Do you have coffee creamer?"

His eyes widen like a deer in headlights. *Please don't tell me I am the only one who drinks creamer around here.*

"In the fridge. Help yourself. Come find me after you get acquainted, I think Ms. Stanley is itching to give you a tour."

I see Kate practically bouncing out of her seat waiting for me to return to our conversation. I forgot she was here—I forgot *anyone* was here.

Benny leaves and I feel all of my dread for this day whittle away in an instant. His presence does something to my insides that I was *not* expecting. Scouring the creamers, I grab the best option and use the last few drops.

Mmm . . . cinnamon.

CHAPTER FOUR

Ellie

TODAY IS MY FIRST official day with students at Glendale High School and I am feeling a tad overwhelmed.

Over the weekend, Emma went on and on about how important my job is for these kids and how what I say to them could make or break their future. At first I thought she was just giving me that teacher-esque exaggeration to make me *pay attention,* but midway through the third conversation, she had a panic attack about the job, the responsibilities, and the idea that I may not be taking it seriously.

Her concerns were very valid, but I had to remind her that I only committed to this first term at Glendale. So for the next few months I will treat this job as if it is what I have spent the last eight years of my life working towards.

Ms. Pat spent the entire week preparing me—with a dash of micromanagement—for the role and helped move me into her office. It was bittersweet watching her choke up as she packed her little trinkets and knick-knacks away. Each of them held a small memory for her from the last thirty years.

I pulled up to the school a little before 7 a.m., and with only one other car in the parking lot I decided to stay in mine. Scrolling through my phone to pass the time, I reluctantly open every social media app to do a quick scan. Seeing Liam's life plastered all over my feed has been a less-than-stellar experience. Why I haven't just unfollowed him yet, I don't know.

I just like to self-sabotage, I guess.

Life with Liam flashes through my mind, landing on the God-awful wedding debacle, when I feel my car start to shake and realize it's because I am bouncing the balls of my feet. The bouncing moves up my legs and arms like jolts. Knowing exactly where this is going, I toss my phone and turn on the radio to focus on something else. Ever since the wedding, my intrusive thoughts have gone from controlled quiet moments to outbursts of rage.

The first outburst happened a month after Liam took his stuff. It was raining and I had left a window open. The floor was soaked when I got home and it was freezing. Instead of shutting the window, like a *rational* person, I started doing the dishes. Because a mentally stable person just leaves a window open on a rainy day to flood her house and starts cleaning plates, right?

The rain kept coming. The sink was on.

Drip.

Drip.

Drip.

The drips crawled up my spine and into my neck. I threw a plate. Then another. Then Liam's favorite mug from medical school. Before I knew it, all that was left standing was a skillet, ladle, and a set of plastic cups.

I knew what was happening, even when I was smashing things. I was triggered by the drops of water because it rained on our wedding day. I was acting on the intrusive thoughts surrounding a triggered memory.

Reactions to triggers aren't just emotional, they can be physical too. Which is something I teach my clients, and even helped some of them with when they were experiencing fits of rage or mania. My clients and my education are the only way I was able to pinpoint what was happening, *after the fact.* In the moment, of course, I was just feeling and acting like an uncontrollable lunatic. It's been over a year since the outbursts started and they are much less severe than in the beginning.

But they aren't gone.

I take a long, deep breath in and let it out through my nose, the bouncing in my legs starts to slow and fizzle away. I realize I'm also white knuckling the steering wheel, so with another deep breath I finally unclench and wipe my sweaty palms off on my skirt.

You have everything under control.

I pull down my visor to give myself one last look over. A truck pulls up beside me—in this enormous parking lot with at least fifty feet of space to the front door, and a plethora of other options than right next to me.

But no, this truck just had to park there.

And of course, out of the truck steps *Benny.*

Benny, whom I have been told by my sister, and new coworkers, is everyone's best friend—their go-to guy—the one you call if you need a ride. The guy that will bend over backward for his people. Benny hosts the game nights, and he always answers your phone calls. Benny is the guy that brings the dip to the potluck—the freaking dip.

Another thing about everyone's favorite boss—something my sister conveniently forgot to mention to me when I accepted this job—is that Benny is hot. And not just warm-your-face-in-the-summer-sun hot. *No.* Benny is the kind of hot that bakes you from head to toe, slowly melting you into a pile of ash.

He stands there, running his hand through his rich, dark hair before reaching for his bag in the backseat. I watch him out of the corner of my eye, heat moving up my neck at his swift movements.

He's practically glowing in the sun. As if his skin wanted to be sunburnt but the good genetics he has took over and created this creamy blend of olive and auburn. The color pops against the pale blue, linen button-up shirt he's wearing.

With the top button undone . . .

My heart pounds into my throat as my eyes note the small divot that lies in the center of his chest.

Excuse me, sir, this is a school.

Please cover yourself up . . . for my sake at least.

The shirt stretches taut across his chest and arms. It's so tight it looks like one perfect flex of his muscles underneath will cause the fabric to shred.

Is his shirt too small or something?

I squint subtly for a better look. Nope, the shirt is fine. It's loose around his waist—doing it's best not to cling too close to his abdomen. Probably to prevent lingering eyes . . . which is *exactly* what I am doing as he approaches my car window . . .

"Good morning!" he yells through my still closed window. *Roll it down, you idiot.*

"Morning," I say through the window, *still* not rolling it down.

"Can I walk you inside?" It's probably just my wishful thinking, but he seemed hopeful when he asked. But I can't walk in with him. Those broad shoulders and big arms swaying next to me? Too distracting. I won't be able to keep my eyes off him, and then I will face plant onto the pavement.

Unless . . . I follow behind him . . .

No, stop it.

"I'll be right in," I say through the window, gesturing that I need to make a phone call.

I dial Emma—anything to get him to go away. I have had the worst time this week trying to make small talk, feeling mushy and weak in the knees around him. The guy probably has no idea the effect he has on me. And walking fifty feet to the door with him will do me in.

I'm sure I seem a little closed off to him, running in the opposite direction when it was just the two of us in the hallway, or keeping my office door closed an abnormal amount. But there was something going on inside of me anytime he was around, and I had to shut it down immediately.

He nods as if I just shot him in the gut and heads for the door. I take in the view as he walks away. I might not be able to act on this sudden attraction, but I can at least admire him from afar. I silently thank the man upstairs for putting such a good-looking specimen on this Earth.

A few students yell and laugh as they race past my office windows when the tardy bell rings. The annoyance I feel is definitely plastered on my face as some of them make eye contact.

Children. They aren't my forte, teenagers especially.

They're too happy—and oblivious to the real world.

I shouldn't have assumed my office hours would be booked up within the first few weeks of class. None of these students know me. And most of the attempts I've made to click with any of them have failed. Aside from the faculty, the only person I seem to have connected with is the cafeteria lady, Gertrude.

Although, if all I have to do for the next few months is sit in my office and scroll on my phone all day, I really shouldn't complain.

But after a few hours of nothing *but* scrolling, I found myself praying for someone—anyone—to walk through my office door.

My client pool has only been adults, with the occasional nineteen-year-old who needed a psychiatric evaluation for some sort of job or enlistment. But at this very moment, as I stare at the clock ticking away on the wall, I would take all the children stampeding through the gates to talk about their weekend plans, or classes, or even their boy problems. Those conversations would most definitely be more stimulating than the ones I have been having with Mr. Geer at the coffee pot every morning.

"I brought tomatoes," he'd say without eye contact.

"Oh, thank you but I don't like—"

"You're welcome."

That's the entirety of our conversation *every* morning. He brings a new produce item for everyone to partake in. The generosity is sweet but as it seems to rotate through only tomatoes, potatoes, and every other vegetable I find unnecessary, I am caught sweating from guilt as I take whatever offering he has presented with absolutely no intention of consuming it.

I am incapable of telling any of these people "no."

Even Kate has started filling the fridge with soy creamer because I made the mistake of complimenting her diligence as she refrained from the whole milk Patsy brought in every morning. Their generosity is unmatched and I feel my Grinch heart swell just a tiny bit each time they direct their servitude towards me in any way.

"Hello, Miss Bailey." Emma appears in my doorway, holding two large iced coffees with *regular milk* marked on the cup.

"You're a lifesaver."

She laughs as she hands me the glorious bean water, and sits in the large gray loveseat—that has remained unoccupied all day—in front of my desk. "I like what you've done in here. Much cozier than what Patsy had. I begged her for years to get rid of those pink felt vintage chairs."

"They have history," we both say in unison, mimicking Ms. Pat.

"They're all rentals, I will send them back in a few months," I say as I check my phone. Emma snorts a sigh in rebuttal. "I'm sorry"—I pause and look at her earnestly—"would you prefer if I don't make statements like that?"

"You can say whatever you want." She waves her hand at me. "I just wish you wouldn't already be halfway out the door the first week you're here. I don't want to regret sticking my neck out to get you here." She rolls her eyes and sips her coffee.

"You're right, I'm so sorry."

She *is* right. I had been giving minimal effort my first week, and even if none of the students had willingly approached my office, I wasn't necessarily going out of my way to be a welcoming presence to them either. I wasn't even sure how to get this whole guidance counselor gig started. Ms. Pat left me folders of certain students who were required to meet with me per school policy, but those required sessions didn't start until next week. Anyone before then would be coming to me of their own volition, with the intention of actually opening up.

I shudder at the thought of listening to teenagers *share*. Someone has issues with their boyfriend? Sure, let's talk about it. *That* I can handle.

But real problems…emotional problems…I haven't listened to anyone share those in months. Am I even ready for that, again?

Surely their problems won't be as triggering to me as Brenda's infidelity, or Lorrie's continued relapse, or even the multitude of manic and schizoaffective disorders I encountered at my old clinic.

I thrived in that chaotic world for such a long time, trying to make sense of these dark thoughts people experience. The world of battling our innermost urges was, in a weird way, life-giving for me. It was jarring when all of a sudden I started feeling uneasy in sessions, like I wasn't maintaining healthy boundaries like I needed to.

Most of the time, in my client sessions, we could develop a plan to help their stability and implement strategies to prevent manifestations of their symptoms. But the battle in our brains is a constant battle. As much as I wish there was a quick fix for what someone has to wrestle through mentally, there isn't. Being a psychologist, I had to go alongside my clients in their battles, aware that we have to continuously be chipping away at the problem. And I had to accept that I would witness setbacks on a regular basis. A large majority of my clients would come to one session motivated and feeling *hopeful,* which in turn made me hopeful. But then in the next session, they could be the complete opposite. The pessimism was starting to impact me.

I was becoming so hyper-focused on solving my clients' issues that when it wasn't going as I expected I would spiral out of control.

My clients would decide they just wanted to live with their struggles, ignoring the need for treatment by convincing themselves they could reap some momentary benefit if they indulge in their darkness, rather than seek a lasting solution.

I was getting too attached and a little obsessed with their lack of compliance.

Dealing with noncompliance and the inability to disassociate from it was a tipping point. That, combined with a certain ex-fiancé I was working with, made me a poor choice as a therapist.

So here I am, a *high school guidance counselor.*

The idea that these students need someone like *me* to help guide them and work through life problems is laughable.

What could they possibly need regular sessions with a counselor for? Maybe to discuss grades or college applications, or just vent about the weekly locker room drama.

Ugh, locker rooms—football players.

The idea of having to listen to a kid named *Garrett* tell me about his game-ending injury and how his life is over makes me want to gag.

But I will do it, wholeheartedly. If that's what I have to do for the next three months, I may as well just leave my dignity at the door and accept my fate. Because my sister is the best person I know and I can't let her decision to go to bat for me be in vain. If the *Garretts* of this school need weekly pep talks, I will do it for *her*.

A knock at my window interrupts Emma's ramblings of her curriculum and art supply fiasco.

Benny stands on the other side of the large, glass window separating my office with the front office. With him, stands a wide-eyed teenager, looking a little too fidgety and uncomfortable with Benny patting her on the shoulder. He waves as he directs her into my office.

"Hi Sarah! How are you? How are your parents?" Emma jumps up, hugging the jittery girl standing in my doorway.

"Good, they're good. They are going to visit my grandparents this winter, so . . . happy," she responds, hugging Emma back uncomfortably.

"Ms. Bailey, this is Sarah Kim, one of our star students here at Glendale. She was just telling me how she wanted to find a mentor for the term and start working on college applications. I figured you were just the person for the job."

Benny penetrates my soul with his eager grin as he presents me with something to do. It was as if he knew I was dying a slow death of boredom between these four walls.

"Hello, Sarah. I'm Ms. Bailey," I say, reaching out to shake Sarah's hand. She shakes back, a little aggressively, and sits on the couch where Emma was. I look at Benny, my eyes lingering on his lips, seeing a smirk twitch on one side of his mouth. "Thank you, Mr. Divata." My voice cracks as his name leaves my lips—such a good name.

"Mr. Divata? So formal. Can I call you that now? Mr. B sounds immature compared to that," Sarah says, causing me and Benny to break our staring contest.

He laughs. "I think Mr. B suits me, don't you?" he asks Sarah, but is looking at me, running his hand through his black hair. It has a slight curl at the edges today, like he just let it air dry after stepping out of the shower and into the hot humid air. A very effortless look, but still sleek and put together too.

"I guess." She shrugs, opening her backpack and pulling out an extra-large, white binder, with a plethora of color-coded tabs lining its interior. I see I have my work cut out for me, already.

"I will leave you to it." He smiles amused at me, displaying his perfect, bright, creates-an-empty-pit-in-your-stomach smile.

The inability to verbally respond overtakes me as I clear my throat, desperate for water. I nod at him and Emma and take a long chug of iced coffee. They leave, but Benny definitely watches me through the window as he disappears down the hall. I watch him, with the straw of my coffee still in my mouth, tongue hanging out.

Drooling. I'm definitely drooling.

"He's hot, huh?" Sarah says, with a wry grin and mischievous eyes.

Choking on my coffee drool, I quickly recover, asking, "Um—what can I do for you today?" Directing my attention to the pile of binders, books, and manila envelopes now sitting on her lap.

"I need to get into Columbia. Or Yale. Princeton would even work." She sets the pile atop my desk with a thud. "I hear you can help me."

"Oh, well . . . I can certainly try. Do you have your transcripts?" I start to dissect her pile, quickly finding the manila envelope labeled: *Transcripts, 7th - 10th.* "So this is your junior year, correct?"

"Yes, I plan on skipping senior year. At this rate, I could be done by my first term of junior year, but my mom thinks I should at least finish it out and . . . *enjoy* myself." She rolls her eyes at the word.

"What's wrong with enjoying—"

"I have four years to get into medical school." She cuts me off. "This is the time for me to focus. Not the time to think about friends or boys or prom." Her nose wrinkles at the mention of boys and prom. "I don't have time to enjoy *anything*. Can you help me or not?" She looks at me with uncertainty, as if she's sizing me up, waiting to see what I have to offer her.

"I'm sure I can help you. But your acceptance is all on you, it will have very little to do with me. I can put in a good word"—I wave to my multiple degrees hanging on the wall behind me, one being *Magna Cum Laude* from Columbia University—"with Duncan in admissions. He's a long-time friend. But I will have to go over everything you have here and make sure you meet their standards. I don't recommend just anyone."

"Good." She sits back, obviously pleased with my answer.

This girl wants to earn it, I respect that.

"Now, let's discuss this upcoming year. I can tell you have everything prepared for applications, and a very strenuous term coming up." Noting a jam-packed class schedule for the fall, I start to read through her transcripts, doodling little pencils and talking points that I can use in casual conversation with her when she visits next. "Any fun plans you have to look forward to aside from school work?"

"No. Like I said, I have too much to do. Having *fun*"—she uses her hands to air quote the word for emphasis—"will set me back two whole weeks."

"If you intend for this year to be your last one, don't you want to make some memories?" I question, pen moving across my notepad.

"If I am to be a first-generation college graduate, I can't waste time making *memories*." She makes a yuck sound at that. I keep doodling.

"Noted. Well other than college applications, what else can I do for you?"

"Umm . . . I have some . . ." I hear the hesitancy in her voice and look up to see her twiddling her thumbs. The confident energy in the room has shifted.

I wait patiently for her to gather her thoughts. Without looking away from her, I reach for the box of tissues and walk over to sit next to her on the couch. "Anxiety." I hand her the tissue, stating a fact rather than posing a question.

Within moments of Sarah being in my office, my analytic brain started firing off physical signs of anxiety: jittery hands, cheek biting, stumbling on her words.

She nods. "I think so." Small tears bubbling up in the corners of her eyes.

We spent the rest of the hour dissecting her fears and recent stressors, and how she has been experiencing nausea, headaches, and loss of sleep, in addition to her overthinking and feelings of dread. All manifestations of anxiety. She shared with me how she feels immense pressure to succeed, and how the idea of going to medical school by the age of twenty is terrifying her but also fueling her. She also feels any ounce of confidence she has can be wiped away with just one small shred of doubt or panic. We talk about how her lack of sleep is inhibiting her from being more in control of her emotional response and after a lot of back and forth, she finally agrees to take one day a week to do something for herself—something not school related or even remotely close to the premise.

"You've never seen *The Princess Bride*?" I squeal at her, forgetting she is a student and I am not one of her besties having lunch with her in the school cafeteria. She giggles at me, either because she finds my reaction to her lack of knowledge of classical cinema funny, or because she realizes she is much cooler than the psychologist with a Ph.D. from Columbia.

"I'm more interested in documentaries—or reality TV. Did you know there was a documentary about reality television? I didn't leave my room for two days last summer!" She throws up both pointer fingers indicating two and slouches back onto the couch. She is much more relaxed with me now, and the anxiousness that was practically vibrating through her entire body an hour ago has slowed to a small hum.

I catch myself taking in this sweet, goal-oriented girl and quickly realize she is a lot like me.

Or . . . I'm a lot like her.

For obvious reasons, I know it is because we are both women, living in a man's world, with hopes and dreams of excelling in our desired fields. But more than that, we both feel insecure and anxious about letting the people we love down. Growing up, I felt the incessant need to be the mom of the family, especially when our mom was struggling. I viewed her and Emma's anxiety as a weakness that I just couldn't allow myself to crumble from. And for the majority of my life, I never experienced anxiety. Or depression. Or even minor intrusive thoughts. I always thought it was because I was meant to be the burden-bearer for all of them. Even when my dad was recovering from his heart attack, I told myself it was my job to take on some of his responsibilities. Case in point, I would have never willingly taught myself how to fix a leaky faucet or change the oil in my car unless I felt it was for the betterment and overall well-being of someone I loved.

It wasn't until Liam left me that my therapist told me I was suppressing too many of my own feelings to be empathetic to those around me, and one day it would all come crumbling down. Of course, I didn't listen to her. I actually fired her because she was dead wrong.

Until she wasn't.

A few weeks later, the kitchen incident happened.

"Well then, take a few hours this week to find a new documentary. Or watch one you've already seen. Do something that helps you de-stress and allows your brain some time away from these triggers. I will get in touch with some of the schools for your applications, and we can reconvene next week." I pry myself off the cozy couch. Stretching my arms overhead, hearing my back pop in about a million places, I ask, "How does that sound?"

Sarah hops up from the couch without any difficulty, back free of pops and pain. "Sounds like a plan! Thank you, Ms. Bailey." She gathers her bag and purple checkered cardigan and heads for the door.

I feel a fondness for her as she leaves and I remind myself to keep it under control—no getting attached to these kids.

Chapter Five

Benny

THE FIRST FEW WEEKS back to class went by incredibly smooth.

As great as this job is, the beginning of the term always has the power to make or break me. Something about being the one in charge of hormonal youth can really shake a man. And with the changes in faculty, and readjusting of schedules, I was preparing to be wrecked.

Pleased to report no wreckage has happened . . . thus far.

I can't help but think the newest addition to our staff has something to do with the smooth transition. Ms. Bailey has swooped in and stepped into her role with ease, even if it seems like it's the least fun she's had in her entire life.

"Alright, so we are all meeting at Wafflin' at six—Ms. Pat will be getting there at six-thirty! Kate, please leave the vegan cake at home, we don't want to give her a stroke." Emma sits in the overused leather recliner at the front of the teacher's lounge, directing our meeting today.

I'm grateful to her for that.

It's Patsy's official last day and she has been so busy spending time helping Ellie get familiar with her new job, I've barely seen her. Patsy usually spends most of her time in my office as we tackle the first of the year tasks. There were days I couldn't get the woman out of my office quick enough. Up until this morning, I hadn't considered I would be losing out on that time while she spends most of her day training the new girl.

I'm going to miss Patsy, a lot.

Today is going to be hard—emotionally.

And to add insult to injury—for reasons I can't seem to pinpoint—a small part of me is feeling jealous, wishing *I* was the one spending all of my time with the new girl.

Without coming across as too eager, I've tried making small talk with her every chance I get. She doesn't talk to any of us much, but definitely speaks the least amount to me. And most of the time, when I try to meet her in the hallway, she dips into the girl's restroom like she's trying to avoid me.

Maybe she feels weird around her new boss?

But even if she won't talk to me, I've spent a lot of my time these last few weeks watching Ellie.

God, I sound *creepy*.

In the most innocent way possible—a boss observing his new employee—kind of way.

Since I'm not leading the meeting this morning, I use it as an opportunity to take Ellie in a little more. I scan the room to make sure no one is watching me so I can let my eyes linger on her.

I feel entranced by her at times. The only time I've felt anything like this was when I watched the sun set over the Boracay Islands when I was eleven. The view was so mesmerizing that I forgot my family was waiting for me—they had to come drag me off the beach and back to our hotel. That was the last family vacation I had with my parents before they passed.

Her long brown hair is wavy today and she's pinned it back, displaying every inch of her face—it scrunches up when she smiles. She has a small scar above her left eyebrow and a few freckles on her cheeks. They look soft and delicate, and my fingers tingle at the thought of touching them.

She pushes a small piece of hair behind her ear and I instinctively take a deep breath. When she passed me in the hallway this morning, I got a hint of her coconut shampoo and was immediately transported back to the beach with my family.

Her eyes twinkle as she watches Emma. They are a shade of green that reminds me of a mix of emerald trees and palm trees. Both remind me of home, and family, and a nostalgia I haven't felt in a long time. I feel a sting in my chest every time she looks at anyone in this room but me.

My lingering has officially turned to staring, longing for her eyes to meet mine. When she does, a wave of *something* rushes over me. Something I haven't felt before.

It's a *weird* feeling—a desperate feeling.

Like she has the power to take a piece of my heart with her if she looks away.

I can sense the cringey, creeper smile my face decides to make when she smiles at me. Her cheeks go pink before she looks back at Emma.

I listen to Kate bicker with Emma about animal rights, and Malcolm is mumbling something about how, "These women will be the death of me."

I love my job and I love these people, but they really do feel like a dysfunctional family sometimes. I'm not sure Ellie knows what she's gotten herself into by joining it.

Ellie seems like the quieter type, but I can tell something is racing through her mind constantly. She is calculative—always carefully considering what she says and how it may affect the person she is responding to. Definitely not what anyone else does around here.

She sits next to Kate, smiling down at her notepad as everyone talks over one another. She doesn't talk much in these meetings, but I can tell she is listening.

And drawing—Ellie draws all the time.

"Most people can't even taste the difference if it's vegan! She'll never know," Kate says.

"Oh, she'll know," Malcolm grumbles.

"Kate, can we please just put our personal, moral dilemmas on the back burner? At least for today." I join the conversation before Malcolm can continue his retort. "Let's focus on Patsy. Then, come Monday morning you can smother all of us with your homemade creams." The words leave my mouth before my brain registers them.

"I won't be smothered in anyone's cream," Malcolm pipes in, chuckling at the ridiculousness of my statement.

"That's not . . . You know what I mean!" I pinch the bridge of my nose. "Let's focus on the task at hand." I groan as the group chuckles at me under their breath. "Patsy is leaving Glendale after almost *forty* years, she deserves to have whatever she wants—or doesn't want—at this party. Right?"

"You're right, I'm sorry." Kate puts her hands up in surrender.

"Perfect, now everyone here will be in attendance." Emma takes over the meeting again. "Minus Ellie. As well as Bill from janitorial—"

"You're not coming?" my voice comes out squeaky as I question Ellie, which of course results in more laughs from the room. My eyes pin Ellie's, the hopefulness of getting to see her outside of work hanging in the balance.

"Oh . . . no, unfortunately. Emma needs someone to watch the boys." I see the dread wash over her face at the task of babysitting her nephews.

I am *very* aware that she just tolerates them, and based on what I've seen so far, she doesn't seem like the children type—at least not the *little* children type. I love Emma's boys, they are hilarious, but every time Emma brought them in to work this week, I could see Ellie's body tense up whenever they so much as *looked* in her direction. It was quite comical watching her try and amuse them and their imaginations. I had a front-row seat to them duct-taping her to a chair, blasting her with Nerf bullets, and running away in an attempt to leave her for dead.

The idea of being taped to a chair is maddening, and I bet anyone else would have refused, but Ellie just let it happen. I could tell she had the worst time, but she never let them know, and those wildlings had the best time with her.

Ellie seems like that type of person—someone who gives more of herself so other people can feel happy. Just another beautiful thing I noticed about her.

"Can you bring them?" I ask abruptly, knowing full well that Wafflin' goes from diner to bar scene after seven p.m.

"Absolutely not," Emma answers before Ellie can. "Steven will be home by eight, and Ellie said she will try to join after, if we are still out." Emma gives me a side-eyed look I am unfamiliar with, but I ignore it.

"Oh good, we will definitely still be out."

"Says the grandpa who never stays out past nine," Kate counters with a raised eyebrow.

Ellie laughs so loud, I feel my stomach drop. Her laugh is bubbly and infectious, and I can't resist laughing with her. If mocking my grandpa-like behavior was the cost of hearing Ellie relax and laugh like that, I will pay it tenfold.

Kate leans to Ellie and whispers something I wish I had ultrasonic hearing for. Ellie laughs again, still staring at me with her green eyes.

I could get lost in them.

God, she is attractive. Beautiful, actually, and, unfortunately, *off limits*.

I have to keep reminding myself that it is against the rules to date my staff—and a girl who plans to only be here for one school term probably isn't the best choice to pine over anyway. But the more I'm around her, that reality becomes harder and harder to accept. She has quickly become someone I can't get enough of.

Ellie and Kate continue whispering and giggling, and my smile involuntarily stretches across my face as I witness it. Her smile is contagious, and her laugh bellows out of her like a smooth wave. The first time I made her laugh, it was after I said *pacifically* instead of *specifically*, and she lost it. I would usually run away in embarrassment over something like that, but it felt sacred to witness such a vulnerable moment for her, so I soaked it in.

Unfortunately, quickly after her bit of laughter, Ellie retreated down the hallway like she was one of the students late for class.

I want to be around her any chance I get—hear that laugh and see her smile, but I am learning quickly that Ellie isn't an open book. Or at least not to me—a complete stranger.

And her *boss.*

I have never had any issues building close relationships with my faculty. Not to brag, but I think I'm pretty welcoming and the faculty usually feel pretty comfortable around me. Even Malcolm—who is pretty much a drill sergeant who never smiles—opened up to me about his life after his first few weeks at Glendale.

But maybe I've been *too* welcoming to Ellie? Maybe too many "hi's" in the hallway? Too many attempts at break room small talk? A bead of sweat builds up on the back of my neck as I start to replay every interaction I've had with her since she got here.

Surely they all haven't been a disaster.

"So Wafflin' at six," Emma says again.

"Great, we have talked this plan up, down, and sideways, can we get back to class?" Malcolm starts to leave the breakroom, signifying the end of our meeting.

"Yes, good meeting everyone!" I call after them, trying to reiterate my authority.

Everyone follows Malcolm and they head to their own classrooms before the first bell rings. The break room is empty except for me . . . and Ellie.

She stays seated, drawing again, very unaware that I am just standing there silently watching her. Again, *creepy*, Ben.

I summon my acquired skills from those two improv lessons I took five years ago and plan to stifle a not-so-convincing cough.

But as I release the cough, Ellie stands from her chair. The two actions happen simultaneously and create a domino effect of startle, tumble, and crash.

Ellie yelps and falls back into her chair. But rather than staying upright, the chair fails at its *one* job and crumbles underneath her. Causing her to somersault backwards onto the ground.

Chapter Six

Ellie

"Oh geez, are you okay?" Benny is immediately by my side.

From what I can tell, I am in the most awkward and unattractive position. One leg is bent and twisted under me, my hair is draped across my face, and my other leg is caught on the toppled-over chair in front of me. I feel a slight breeze and am instantly aware that my skirt has ripped in the back, all the way up to my underwear. I feel . . . exposed.

"Here!" His big hands push the hair off my face and grab my arm to pull me up. His hand pauses on my back and I feel like I will combust from the heat that surges from where he is touching me.

He hoists me up as if I weigh nothing and puts his hands on my shoulders to keep me steady. "Are you alright, Ellie? Did you hit your head?" His eyes are filled with concern as he searches my face. I feel a tingle in my chest at the way he looks at me.

He *cares*.

"I'm fine, I'm fine," I say brushing down the front of my clothes.

"Maybe you should sit down? Here." He directs me over to the large leather chair, and I quickly cover my rear end rip with both hands as we walk.

I feel fine, but there's something about his protective hands all over me that has me wanting to fake a serious injury and demand he swoop me up in his arms and carry me away to safety.

He came to my rescue like it was second nature.

"Thank you," I whisper, feeling safe for a moment before the realization as to what just happened sears my brain.

Benny saw *everything*. I can't help but picture what it must have looked like from his point of view—although a mix of rag doll and wet mop comes to mind. My insanely attractive boss saw *everything*. I feel hot from embarrassment as he looks me over. I would rather Bill, the janitor, have been here pointing and laughing at the scene instead of *this*.

Humiliation starts to engulf me like a wave.

He reaches up and pulls my pen cap out of my tangled hair. His attempt to be gentle is thwarted at the obvious rats nest that has formed from the collision. He winces and mouths "*sorry*" as the cap comes free with pieces of my hair attached.

God. Just leave me here to *die*.

"I am so embarrassed," I say, my voice cracking as he hands me the cap.

"I'm going to throw that chair away first thing tomorrow. Justice will be served."

"My hero." I force a laugh.

He sits on the armrest of the chair and pushes a piece of my hair behind my ear. I feel my breath catch at the physical contact. I abruptly shove my hand up to my hair and smooth it out.

"Can I get you anything?" His voice is gentle as he smooths out a piece of hair I missed.

I can't seem to make words as I become fixated on how close his body is to mine. *Why do I feel so debilitated right now?* I stutter an attempt at words as he stares at me.

"Alright, twenty questions, let's see if you have a concussion," he says, placing his hand softly on my back. I nod in agreement, rubbing the back of my neck.

"Favorite color?"

"Yellow."

"Favorite food?"

"Tacos."

"Favorite movie?"

"Princess Bride."

"Dogs or cats?"

"Will this determine a concussion? Don't you need to know if the answer is correct or not?" I can't help but laugh at the sincerity of his medical evaluation.

"Ah, yes." He chuckles a hearty laugh that I feel all the way down to my toes. "What month is it?"

"September."

"Good. Where are we?"

I roll my eyes and giggle at the complexity of his questions. "Glendale."

"Correct! I think you will be okay." He grazes his fingertips against my back.

Is it me or is he *rubbing* my back?

I look back at him and see his jaw flex as he moves his hand to the back of my head. "Here, let me look." His fingers brush the nape of my neck and head as he checks for injuries. "Everything seems to be in order."

I bite back the audible reaction my body wants to make at the touch of his fingers in my hair. I smooth out my hair and attempt to shake off the fiery sensation his hands left. "Thank you, doctor."

We both laugh as he helps me stand. I feel lightheaded and dizzy when I'm on my feet and I instinctively grab his wrist for stability and he uses his free hand to grab mine.

Then . . . we just . . . stand there . . . staring at each other. His dark eyes seem to go darker as he looks from our wrists to my eyes. I let out a small sigh and his eyes drop to my lips at the sound. I try to make audible words but my mouth has dried up. I lick my lips and his jaw flexes again, eyes flickering back up to mine.

I feel a flushing sensation move across my cheeks as I stare at his lips, and the space between us feels oddly electric. I feel my knees give way a tiny bit the longer he stands there.

Careful, Ellie.

"I've, uh . . . been wanting to see how you're liking the job," he stutters, still staring at my lips.

Thank God. Talking about the students is a good buffer. My body relaxes from the physical tension as I let go of his wrist.

"It's not bad. Definitely a change of pace, but I'm sure it will grow on me," I say, twisting and rubbing my neck, a headache building. The heat Benny's hands left on me slowly evaporates as I focus on his question, and my pounding head.

Yes, definitely a good buffer.

"Do you want to get coffee after school and talk about it?" He slides his hands in his pockets.

"Sure, when works for you?" I start looking around the room to collect my things, being mindful of the tear in my skirt as I angle it *away* from my boss's eyes.

"Anytime you're available." His voice is cheery and excited—his smile, glowing and eager. "Tomorrow?"

"Sure." I squeeze the fabric of my skirt tighter behind me. "But if my concussed brain causes me to act ridiculous, just blame that guy." I chuckle and point at the turned-over chair.

"As you wish." He flashes a playful smile at me, making my heart flutter.

"You two done yet?"

Ms. Pat startles us—standing by the back door to the lounge, her arms crossed and a roguish grin extended across her face. God only knows how long she has been standing there—how much she saw. I'll never hear the end of it.

Benny clears his throat and stands up straighter. "Yes. We had a little fall."

"Well, Ms. Bailey seems to be in need of new pants." She chuckles as she eyes the back of my skirt.

Someone kill me now.

"Here." Benny pulls his Glendale windbreaker off of his bulgy shoulders and hands it to me. "To get down the hall."

Ugh, this guy is a *gentleman.*

"You are so chivalrous," I joke, tying the jacket around my waist and pulling it down to cover the ripped fabric.

"You bring it out of me." He gives me a sweet, playful smile then walks over to Ms. Pat.

I feel my heart racing at his words, "*You bring it out of me.*" How? Why? My mind is firing off a thousand questions as I watch him let Ms. Pat hook her arm around his.

"Ready for my final walk?" she asks him, holding her chin high. Her eyes are misty as she looks up at him.

A whimper of a sigh leaves his body as he looks down at Ms. Pat. He bows down and brings her hand up, pressing his forehead against it, as if it's something he does naturally. Ms. Pat's smile stretches across her face as he stands back up, hooking her arm around his. Then he leads her out of the break room and down the hall for her final day at Glendale High.

This place will never be the same.

"Hi, you've reached Emma Jones, I'm sorry I missed you. Please leave a message and I will get back to you pronto!" Beep.

"Emma, we have a hostage situation. I repeat, HOSTAGE SITUATION! I swear if you do not get back here and wrangle these psychotic ragamuffins you call offspring, I will give them the entire stash of Halloween candy I found in the pantry!" I growl through the phone. "And then, I will lock them in your *sacred* bathroom, with free reign of all of your expensive skincare and bath essentials!" I shriek at whisper level as I race down the stairs to a closet near the front door, squishing myself behind a pile of coats and boxes. "I am giving you ten minutes!"

I hang up, wishing I had a flip phone so I can aggressively slam it shut. I squeeze myself into a seated position behind the boxes, pulling my knees to my chest, and pray the gremlins don't find me.

I hear their footsteps upstairs, followed by giggles and childlike screams. It would sound cute, if I knew they weren't trying to *murder* me. I hear a loud thud and for a moment wonder if I should be concerned for their safety.

I shrug it off, settle in, and head to Instagram.

Quickly bored of seeing old friends and their New York life cover my feed, I go to Kate Stanley's page—my newest follower as of an hour ago.

Scrolling through I see some old selfies of her with a pug that oddly resembles the one on the pink mug from school. More recently on her feed I see a range of photos with a Golden Retriever, from puppyhood to full grown. I double tap a few old photos, making it evident I'm creeping.

As I return to my main feed I notice she has posted a new photo, with a group of familiar faces, just seconds ago—the Glendale group. Everyone is gathered around a very smiley Ms. Pat, who is wearing a very large hat atop her head that says, *"THIS CHICK IS RETIRED"* with chickens painted all over it.

Emma's doing, for sure.

They all look so happy, with big smiles, slightly glassy eyes, and drinks in their hands. Except for Benny. He stands to the far left, smiling, but not as bright as he usually is—maybe it is a little past his bedtime. I chuckle at the thought of him yawning in the middle of a party as everyone around him rages.

I gaze at the photo, feeling a heat creep its way up my chest and to my cheeks—warming me down to the cells in my body.

I like these people, and I like seeing them at work—even Malcolm and his vegetables.

I stare at Benny, and his much more visible chest in the photo. He's wearing a white button-up with little birds all over it. The top two buttons are undone—a much more relaxed look that suits him *very* well. A few tiny chest hairs peek out above the first clasped button, and his skin is a warm, creamy color, glistening with what I'm going to assume is sweat. I pinch my screen to zoom in and follow the traces of sweat up over his protruding collarbone, along his thick neck, leading the way to his plump, pink lips. His smirk is sultry . . . sexy, even.

Why am I staring at this photo? And why is it making me feel all hot and heavy?

And why was he sweating? Why are they *all* sweating? The more I look the more I realize this photo was snapped quickly, in the middle of conversation and dancing, probably.

In the middle of *fun*.

I feel myself getting major FOMO and am slightly irritated that I am stuck hiding in a coat closet from the two junior Rambo's instead of out with my new colleagues.

Double tapping the photo, I comment, "Looks like a fun crew!" Accompanied by a heart emoji.

It is no less than ten seconds after I commented that Kate liked my comment and texted me directly.

Before I can reply, I hear tiny voices snickering and giggling as they trample down the stairs.

"Where is she? She's too big to hide! We will avenge the princess's death!"

Holding my breath, I pray they don't look in the blatantly obvious hiding spot near the front door. Not that it hasn't been fun to be the princess they were rescuing, *then* a jester they were torturing, *then* ending up the dragon zombie that killed said princess. I gave up making sense of the roles when they forced me to flee their tower.

That was when they decided to become tactical G.I. Joe's with an arsenal of Nerf guns and ping pong balls. I rub the red spot on my arm from a Nerf bullet, concerned they could be encased with metal instead of foam.

Feeling overstimulated by the footsteps, arm pain, and invite out, I text Kate rejecting the invite.

The idea of going out sounds appealing, and I haven't been out with friends in so long, let alone my peers. And I really don't want to play into the reputation that has followed me around for the last few years anymore—a person who doesn't have time for meaningful friendships. *Thank you, Liam for that one.* But I know full well I won't be as fun to be around as I would like after being with the boys all night.

"Boys, I'm home!"

Interrupting my reflective pity party, I hear Steven's voice come from the other side of the closet, followed by a loud thud and tumbles down the hall. I hear the boys run and an audible gust of air come out of Steven's windpipe as they tackle their dad to the floor.

Climbing out of the closet, I see Steven flat on the floor and the two goblins climbing all over him. It would be a sweet sight to witness, if I didn't have unresolved issues with *Steven* and hadn't spent half the night imagining the boys as feral kittens that I wished I could let loose outside.

"Welcome home." I can't help but laugh as I watch Steven wrestle the boys off of himself and drag them into the living room.

"Did you guys have fun with Aunt Ellie?"

He practically hurls them onto the couch and they bounce off, unphased, before running upstairs shouting, "AVENGERS, ASSEMBLE!"

Steven smirks at them and begins cleaning up the living room.

"Do you want help with that?" I offer reluctantly and he nods, gratefully.

Watching where I step so as to avoid the shrapnel of Legos left scattered across the living room, I help Steve tidy up.

We clean in silence—it's been this way since I moved in. Steve isn't a talker, especially with me. I never expect much from our interactions, so I haven't made any effort to go much further than my usual one-word lead ups like, "*Hello,*" "*Hi,*" or the occasional, "*Sup.*"

But just as I gather the last of the Legos and Nerf bullets, Steven intentionally clears his throat. I look up to see him standing there, awkwardly. "Yes?" I respond, making it clear that I heard him but his awkwardness doesn't phase me.

It does, but I've gone to extreme lengths to act unbothered around Steven ever since the Liam betrayal. Now I have to keep up the charade no matter how weird he acts around me.

"So, I um . . ." the long pause draws a bead of sweat from my temple. I have a feeling I know where this is headed. "I talked to Liam today." There it is.

If there were ever a time I wanted the goblins to come knock me out with their T-ball bats, now would be the time.

"Oh, yeah? How is he?" Ignoring the crack in my voice as I scurry off to the kitchen. Their house is an open floor plan, so I literally have nowhere to hide when a conversation like this is thrown at me.

"He's doing fine. Working long hours in the clinic with the new case—" he cuts himself off, realizing what he's saying and whom he is saying it to.

Liam's *heavy caseload* is because of my absence.

I never had any doubt or hesitation when I took a job at the clinic my then-fiancé was a locum resident at. It never crossed my mind that there could be complications to working with your significant other. Liam was only part-time when I started seeing clients, and he was mostly at the hospital anyway so it worked out well, even when he decided to call it quits moments before we exchanged vows. I wasn't going to leave my clients just because my own life seemed to be in shambles, so he was going to offset his clinic days with my office hours, ensuring we never interacted one-on-one.

We had a plan, and it was working . . . until it wasn't.

Liam started coming into the clinic more often, most likely to check on me. I was barely holding myself together as it was, and him breathing down my neck, checking my charts, and overriding my care plans was *not* helping.

"Yeah? How *is* that case load?" I snap back, emphasizing the irritation in my tone.

Steven clears his throat. "I'm sorry, I wasn't thinking."

"Why are we talking about Liam?" I grit my teeth, picking up the rest of the toys.

He puts his hands in his scrub pockets. "He, umm . . ." He stares at me then averts his gaze to the window. Steven is not a confrontational person, he usually avoids conflict whenever possible. This situation had to be killing him, which tells me it's important to him. I take a deep breath and turn to face him directly, providing softer, more open body language to encourage that, while I'm not thrilled about the current conversation, this is a safe space to speak.

Steven notices my posture change, letting out a sigh he says, "He asked about joining for Halloween."

I feel an instant ache in my chest. I blink at him.

Blink.

Blink.

"I told him I wasn't sure if that was a good idea. I tried to remind him where we all stood on things and he wasn't allowed to just partake in our family events anymore". Steven's response was rapid, attempting to put out the fire he just set in my brain.

"I appreciate that." My voice felt thick, still feeling stunned and a little insulted that Liam would even consider asking to come to Halloween.

Halloween was *my* thing.

My favorite.

My party.

My family.

MINE.

Liam doesn't even like the holiday. Pumpkins with faces freak him out and he always dresses up as the same thing every year—a psychiatrist on holiday—because for some reason that was the funniest thing he had ever heard of and, *"Why mess with perfection."*

"It's just . . . he's been really down. Really lonely." Steven looks down at his shoes. "We talked for a really long time today and he just thinks being around family would be good for him."

I gawk at him. "Steven, you are *my* family! He has a family! He can go see them for Halloween! He has no right to be here!" I felt myself getting louder by the second. Steven was nodding nervously in response, bracing himself for the inevitable impact of my impending breakdown that was sure to follow this conversation.

"Knock, knock! Hello!" Emma walks through the front door in time to witness the tension building in the middle of her living room. Looking between me and Steven, her eyes go wide. "What's going on?"

"Steven, here, was just telling me someone's idea for Halloween this year!" My voice is shrill as I grit a smile across my face. "Go ahead, tell her this brilliant idea, *Steven*!"

I storm past him, yanking the car keys from my sisters' hand and storm out the front door. I climb into my sister's car, texting Kate:

Me

On second thought, a drink would be great!!!

Then peel out of the driveway.

Chapter Seven

Benny

IF I WAS FLEXIBLE enough to kick myself in the head, I would have done it a hundred times by now.

Going home early from the party the other night was the worst idea I have ever had.

I am a dumb, silly boy.

Because now, I have to sit here and listen to Kate tell me all about how she spent the night eating waffles with Ellie, laughing and having a grand ole time.

Hooray. Good for her.

"Did you know she graduated Magna Cum Laude from Columbia? The girl is brilliant! I still can't get over her coming here." We were supposed to be discussing the fall campus visits, but instead I was being forced to listen to her recap how amazing her night was.

"Yes, I knew that. I did actually see her resume before hiring her, ya know," I say, with more of a bite to my tone than I intended.

"What's wrong with you?" She raises an eyebrow at me. She refuses to ask me directly what's going on until she has tried to get it out of me with kind gestures. She is sweet, but also sneaky. Even when we were little, she would bring me a pet rock and encourage me to share my feelings with the rock. It worked . . . until I was thirteen and realized her strategy.

So all morning she's been buttering me up. She even brought me a hot coffee, with full dairy creamer in hand, which was a sure sign that she could tell something was off. And knowing I missed an opportunity to get to know Ellie a little bit better the other night really isn't helping my poor mood.

"I'm just tired. Frankie kept me up all night." If I don't give Kate any information she will keep force-feeding me the homemade bagels she brought.

"Is she sick again?"

"Most likely. But the sitter didn't give her her medication the other night, and I didn't realize it until the next day, so that didn't help."

Kate laughs. "I still can't believe you won't leave her home alone."

"How can I? She's only nine! That's absurd."

"Benny . . ." Kate looks at me with judgy eyes. "It's a *cat*. It probably wants to be home alone!"

"Frankie"—I remind her the "*it*" we are discussing has a name that *she* helped pick out—"does not like to be alone. Plus, with how often she needs medicine she can't be left alone for too long anyway. Which reminds me . . . I need to text her daycare."

Kate lets out a loud annoyed groan and proceeds to leave my office. It amuses me how annoyed she gets about Frankie, considering she was there when I adopted her two years ago and she's the one who told me to, "*Get the ugly one.*"

I had no idea she was being sarcastic until I paid the adoption lady two-hundred dollars to rehome a hairless cat with a fear of all living creatures and uncontrolled Diabetes.

I check-in with her daycare to confirm she was given her medication, and they respond quickly with a picture of Frankie sitting on top of the cat tower with the goofiest squint across her face. The photo makes me laugh out loud.

I try to bring my attention back to my phone when I notice Ellie across the hall, standing in her doorway, smiling at me. The sight of her jolts me out of my laughter.

She's gorgeous. My new employee is my dream girl made real. Her brown hair flows down one side of her face, the other side, bare. It looks soft . . . her cheek . . . her neck . . . My throat goes dry when they land on her lips. They turn up on one side, a peek of her tongue sticking out in the corner. I gulp and try to focus on something else, something less *distracting*.

Why is she looking at me?

What should I do?

Wave—yes, waving is good.

I wave the most nonchalant way I know how, lifting my arm up like a limp noodle, which of course causes me to drop my phone and knock over my coffee. *Perfect.*

"Are you okay?" Ellie rushes in here quick enough to see the coffee all over my shirt. Thank God, it's this morning's coffee and has already gotten cold.

"Just a little clumsy today. Sorry if I startled you," I say, wiping the droplets of coffee off my desk into the trash can, avoiding eye contact with her. I *am* the clumsy nerd who will burst into flames if she looks at me with pity in her eyes.

"I'm more concerned about what was so funny that it had a ripple effect in here." She giggles as she helps clean my desk.

I stop with my hands on top of my desk and look at her.

"What?" she asks, her soft eyes punching me in the heart.

"You're just so . . ." My words linger in the air, everything I want to say will freak her out. Don't be weird, Ben. *Play it cool.* "Alluring . . . ?" My brain has failed me.

She bites her lip and looks away.

Smooth, Benny.

"I just mean . . . ugh that was weird." My face is hot. "Sorry! I meant you're just delightful—er, pleasant—no, you're—" I am spitting out every other word that is not normal.

Somebody please come punch me square in the face.

"Thank you." Her green eyes disorient me for a moment. She bites her lip, *again*.

I can't help but stare at her lips, then back to her eyes, now at her neck—she's wearing a black turtleneck that clings in all the places I don't need to be looking.

"So . . ." I clear my throat while erratically grabbing a pile of papers. *Make yourself look busy, Ben.* "How are things? Has Devon made it over to meet with you yet?"

"Not yet. I was actually hoping to talk to you about that. Do you have time to meet after school today? His mom came by yesterday and I just want to chat with you about the situation. She gave me permission to do so, said you were the only one she trusted to involve," she says sitting down on the edge of my desk—a loaner desk from Malcolm actually. She crosses her legs, smoothing out her skirt, blessing the surface of the desk with a beautiful curve I have to shield my wandering eyes from.

Be a gentleman, focus on the conversation.

"Yes, of course." I focus my attention on my computer screen, palms planted firmly on my desk. "Ms. Johnson is a longtime friend, I would be happy to meet him with you. Do you want to meet in the breakroom?"

"Actually, I was wanting to take you to Wafflin'. I'll buy!" She reaches over and touches my hand. Surely just a friendly gesture, nothing to overthink Divata. Just the most stunning woman you've ever seen gently grasping your grubby hand.

Her hand feels like a soft blanket on top of a pile of wet sand, because I am sweating now. She definitely feels the sweat, no way she can't.

I stare at her hand on top of mine, not moving it an inch. "Sure, that would be good. I will see you there."

She gives a gentle squeeze then the hand is gone.

"Great! See you!" She slides off the desk and floats out of my office.

My throat feels dry as I slam my mouth shut. *Was it open this entire time?* Running my hand down my face, I collect myself, hearing snickers on the other side of my office windows.

"If you have something to say, please get it over with." I roll my eyes as one of my students limps in, my dignity gone. Despite the walking boot on one leg, he's refusing to use his crutches as instructed. "Hi, Garrett. How are we this morning?"

Garrett maneuvers himself into a chair by my door and drops his bag to the ground. "Mr. B! What's going on with you and the new chick?"

"That is Ms. Bailey to you." I eye him. "We've talked about how we should refer to women."

"Right, right. My bad," His tone is always chill and *bro-ish*. "What's up with you two?"

"Nothing, we just work together."

"She wants to work with you alright." He wiggles his eyebrows up and down.

I ignore his innuendos and refuse to let my mind wonder why he would think that. "What can I do for you this morning, Mr. Connors?"

"Oof last naming me, alright then. I need to change my classes." He hands me a pop quiz with a large red "F" marked at the top.

"I see. Well, Mr. Connors, if you are wanting to drop a class you will have to set up a meeting with Ms. Bailey. I can't bail you out this time."

"Come on! Aren't you her boss? You can't just use your authority to put me in an easier class?" He groans as he slides down the chair into a lounging stupor.

"Not that I would do that anyway, but no, I cannot." I shuffle through my agenda for the day. "You will need to set up a counseling meeting and she will go over your classes with you. She can find alternatives, or she can assist you in study hours."

"Please don't make me." He drops his head back against the wall and points at me without looking. "You got coffee on your shirt by the way."

I quickly pull my Glendale windbreaker over my stained shirt and take a seat next to Garrett. "Look, this is only the first term. Let's meet with Ms. Bailey, develop a plan, and fix this. You have one year left to pull it together so you can get into college."

"That's not gonna happen. Nobody wants a washed-up quarterback with a bum leg, I'm done." He crumples up the pop quiz and tosses it into the trash can. *Swish.*

"Let's just try, alright? I can still help you and so can Ms. Bailey. We have time." I pat him on the shoulder. "You have just as much of a chance to get into college as the next guy."

He gives me a half-hearted smile and stands on his wobbly leg. He towers over me with his six-foot-plus height. "Fine, I'll figure it out. But if I don't get in, you have to give me a job here because I don't know what else to do." He jokes, but there's worry in his tone.

"Sure thing. Bill could always use some help." I give him a wink and shake his hand.

He rolls his eyes at me and starts to leave. "She's totally into you by the way." He motions towards Ellie's closed office door. "You should ask her out."

"I am not at liberty to date my faculty," I say, walking back to the other side of my desk—the school policy hovering over me like a dark sad cloud.

"She's not staying here long though, right?" He winks at me. "Just sayin'!"

"I appreciate your concern, Mr. Connors."

The kids know when I use their last name I mean it in a finality kind of way. I was hoping the emphasis on his name would remind him of that so he would drop it. I was already aware of the rules and my physical attraction to Ellie was pushing those limits to the max. I didn't really need Garrett Connors encouraging anything, even if I did want him to be right.

Chapter Eight

Ellie

"He didn't mean to upset you. He just doesn't know what to say . . . and what *not* to say sometimes." Emma had been trying to smooth the tension between Steven and I for almost a week now.

"Please just let it go. It's fine, it's over." I was packing up for the day and did not feel like staying late to reiterate how *over* the Steven situation I was. I really was over it, I couldn't control Steven's guilty conscience. That was all him.

"So, does this mean you're throwing a Halloween party? Can I help?!" Kate inserts herself into the conversation.

She was very involved in this situation now, since I told her everything that happened in a hot rage after leaving the house the other night. She's quickly becoming a strong companion around here. It's unfortunate I still don't plan to stay here long term though, she would be a good friend to keep around.

"Yes!" Emma says at the same time I say, "No."

"No, we aren't having one," I say. "The last one was a dud anyway."

The idea of having a party was the least of my concerns right now. Plus, the last one I had was . . . underwhelming. It was the first annual Halloween party I threw without Liam. Our friends felt conflicted on whose party to go to, so they either tried to attend both or just bailed altogether. These are also the *friends* I haven't talked to in almost three months.

"Other than everyone here, I wouldn't know who to invite." Making it clear I didn't have any close friends at the moment.

"That's all you need! We are a blast! And I'm sure Steven has some cute doctor friends he can invite, right Em?" Kate wiggles her eyebrows and shimmies her arms. She's a saucy one.

"He definitely can. Come on El, it will be fun and you know it." Emma smiles expectantly at me. "And if I have anything to do with it, no exes of any kind will be at this party."

I look back and forth between them, both pouting and silently pleading with prayer hands. I know I won't be able to tell their puppy dog eyes no.

"I'll think about it." I smirk.

I already know what my answer is going to be, but I can let them stew just a little bit longer.

They can tell I'm playing them because as I go to leave the breakroom, they start discussing decorations, food items, and group costume ideas. I swear if they try to make me a Spice Girl, I will lose it. There are only three of us, there's no way we could do that. An incomplete group costume seems like no big deal, except my brain will trigger on all cylinders about why we couldn't be something else or what other people will think of it.

Spiraling thoughts start to ensue.

Who is going to decorate? What food will we have? Are we really inviting the entire faculty? I fire off questions in my head, feeling more irritated by the minute. My mind flashes with images of shopping for supplies and decorations, and not finding the right costume.

I feel the urge to crack my neck as an irrational feeling of anger swarms inside my brain over this entire debacle. I can feel the anger trickle down my neck and into my hands. God, Eleanor, *calm down*. I shake them out as I make my way down the hallway.

Class just ended and the hall is jam packed with students moving in every direction. Most of the kids are dressed in the school colors: red, gold, and blue. Tonight was the first football game of the season and everyone was getting excited for it.

Football is a religion around here.

Walking down the halls, I see some familiar faces and some unfamiliar. It was nice to see the kids smiling and laughing, especially the ones I see as clients. I never had the opportunity to see my clients outside of their sessions in New York—there was never any likelihood that I would run into them on the street or see them at a book club. I just had to go home and hope they were doing well, and when I saw them next I might get to see improvement.

But I have to say, it's nice to see some of my clients out of the office, showing signs of stability and joy.

Passing by the principal's office, I peek in to see if Benny is still here and feel a twinge of disappointment when I see his office light is off. Sarah is standing by her locker with one of her friends as I pass by. She smiles at me, but continues talking to her friend. My goal with interactions outside of sessions is to be discrete. I have no idea how much these students share with one another and it feels like a breach of confidentiality to acknowledge them unless they approach me. So I return the smile and head to the front doors.

The disappointment I was feeling about missing Benny fizzles immediately as I step outside and see him, standing by my car. He waves at me earnestly, like he's happy to see me.

I walk up to him, fighting the smile tugging at my cheeks. Why did I feel so happy being around this guy? He *does* radiate positivity, like happiness is just second nature to him. Which is the exact opposite of me lately. Maybe that's what it was—my soul wants to be that again. Positive. Happy. So maybe it's just drawn to positivity and sunshiney-ness.

Or it was drawn to Benny specifically. I still wasn't sure.

It was definitely confusing to my heart to see how excited he always was anytime he was around me.

"Well hello, Ms. Bailey! Long time no see!"

He stands next to my car, with his hands stuffed deeply in his pockets. Probably to indicate a barrier between us—*boss* and *employee.*

"Hi, I thought we were meeting at Wafflin'?" I go to unlock my car.

"I figured we could walk. It's so nice out, and I have to make a stop on the way." He puts his hand on the hood of my car, leaning in closer to me as I open my door—barrier gone.

"Oh, that sounds great! Can I change shoes?" I wiggle the brown leather clogs on my feet in his direction.

He laughs. "Why? Those are the perfect walking shoes."

He was joking. I liked when he joked.

Most of the time his joking was unintentional, like he didn't think before he spoke. Which made him even funnier to me. But occasionally there were fun moments where he made the extra effort to make someone laugh. And when it was for me, it felt sweet.

"Perfect for you, maybe. What size are you? Maybe we can trade!" I laugh and reach in my car for my spare Hokas and swap them out.

I see Benny staring at me when I finish tying my laces. "What? Do I look weird?"

"So weird. I had my heart set on the clogs." He winks and shuts my car door for me. He keeps his hand on the doorframe as he surveys my shoes, his eyes crinkling in the corners when he looks back up to me.

"Cute." He gives me a playful smile.

I shove his shoulder as we start to walk down the sidewalk to Wafflin'. He winces sarcastically, rubbing his incredibly muscular arm like I made a dent. His arm was solid, and I found it very difficult to not just caress it.

We walk in silence for a few minutes. It was kind of nice—natural even. The urge I usually have to fill the silence wasn't there. I didn't get many quiet moments these days, and definitely not when I was in New York, the city that never sleeps. Even in my job, it was important for my client to feel safe enough to share *everything*.

It's my job to study and interpret someone's mind and behavior. Allowing someone the space to be open and vulnerable was an integral part of a successful client-therapist relationship and if I ever wished for a client to be *quiet* I was doing them a disservice. Also knowing our minds are always working, always *thinking*, I needed my clients to talk.

A quiet session is never a good thing.

On top of that, being engaged to a psychiatrist never allowed for silence. Both of us were guilty of always interpreting the others' feelings or emotions, then constructing a one-sided conversation to handle any and all conflict.

At the beginning of our relationship, I wished for a mute button in our conversations just to have a moment of silence to myself. Then it became a battle between us . . . who could psychoanalyze the most? It wasn't until Liam moved out that I started noticing the quiet again.

It was scary how quiet my mind became.

I was quiet and alone in my own thoughts.

But right now, in this moment, walking on the sidewalk next to Benny, the quiet is different.

The quiet isn't scary.

"So, how are you?" Benny asks as we approach an intersection.

"Good." *Ugh*, I am terrible at small talk.

"You don't feel overwhelmed with the students, yet?" He kicks a stick out of our path as we cross the road.

"Definitely not. It's actually been refreshing to not have to sit and analyze a person's emotional or mental issues for an hour. The majority of my sessions have been discussing grades, college, or summer plans." I look both ways as we cross. "Not that these kids don't have real issues—just not what

I'm used to. Life's disappointments haven't tarnished their dreams . . ." I feel his eyes on me as I trail off. I let out a sigh, thinking about the burden of my own life's disappointments weighing me down.

Without intending to, I stop walking and take in the sight.

It's the end of September—still warm but the leaves are slowly starting to change. A mixture of green and orange hang like a tapestry above the power lines on one side of the street.

Down the street I can see different colored brick buildings attached to each other, different establishments in each one, all busy with people. Wafflin' is nestled on the end of the street, with a large window. Inside is filled with a handful of people, a calm environment for an early dinner. It looks so different from the picture I saw Kate post the other night. The excessive luau decorations and strobing lights are gone. And there definitely aren't any red-eyed teachers dancing in the middle of the floor. My gaze follows the sidewalk and lands on a pet daycare. A quaint little place, with a gray cat lying in the window.

On the block across the street are tall city buildings. A combination of concrete and steel stretching down the block. The people coming and going were dressed to impress in their business suits. It was giving New York vibes without even trying, which was a slight contrast to the laidback side of the street we were standing on.

Something inside me was telling me I belonged on the other side of the street. It felt familiar to watch them rush in and out of their respective buildings, so completely consumed with their work that they're missing the sky directly above them.

I look up and let the sun bake on my face through the trees.

It's invigorating and peaceful. And I wonder to myself how many times I was so preoccupied with life that I missed a view like this.

Without realizing, Benny shuts my over-analytical brain down and asks, "Is that something you needed?"

"Hmm?" I look at him.

"Do you think you needed something refreshing?" Benny stops walking and stands by my side. He's watching me intently, his eyes flickering a shade darker as they move across my face.

"Not at first. But now that I have it, yes." I turn to face back down the street. "It's a good break to have for a short while."

"Good, I'm glad you can have that while you're here. These students might not have experienced life yet, but they can be life-giving if you let them." There was a smile in his voice anytime he talked about the students and it warmed my heart to know these kids had this guy in their corner.

We continued walking down the street. "What about you?" I ask him.

"What about me?"

"Do you need something new? *Refreshing? Life-giving?*" I motion the-atrically for emphasis.

He puts a finger to his chin in contemplation. "Maybe. I just don't know what."

"Or who?" Drawing out the "*oooo*" sound.

"What do you mean?" His eyes widen so much they might pop out.

Laughing I say, "You said the students could be my life-givers. Who is yours?"

"Oh." I feel his eyes on me, I take a deep breath preparing to hear about some lady friend of his that fills his life with all these good things. About how they are perfect for each other and how she is so different from me. Making it painfully obvious I would never stand a chance.

Not that it matters, *Eleanor*. He is your *boss*.

"Frankie," he responds with a huge smile.

"Oh? Frankie, huh?" I say through my teeth.

"Yes! She is my life-giver."

"What's she like?" Please don't tell me.

"She's a homebody. Not big on people. Has some health issues, but we manage. And she's hilarious!" he says in one breath, like he couldn't tell me about her quick enough.

"She sounds . . . lovely . . ."

I hate her.

Why did I care? Benny Divata is my boss. He's off limits—thanks to some school policy or something absurd last I heard. And I won't be here long anyway.

There are so many clear reasons why he and I won't be a thing, so why let myself feel even an inkling of intrigue for someone who is a "no" from the start? I know the rules and am an avid rule follower. But there was something about this guy that was drawing me in little by little.

Spend time around someone as attractive as Benny, and you're bound to feel something. Hot people have that effect, even when they don't intend to. Now when they *know* they're hot and use it for evil, those feelings are bound for destruction.

But Benny doesn't use his looks for evil. I mean, there is no way he doesn't know how handsome he is, but you can tell he doesn't play into it for his own personal gain. He's a babe magnet in all aspects.

Even right now, as he laughs uncontrollably about the hilarity of this "Frankie" girl. His mouth is open as wide as possible, shoulders shaking, his hands on his hips to steady himself. It's a charming sight that I could watch for hours.

But why was he laughing so hard? Was Frankie *that* funny?

He kept laughing as he crossed the street. I watched as he jogged the last few steps, his back muscles flexing through his shirt as he runs his fingers through his hair and reaches for the door. He waves at me to follow him as he walks into the pet daycare.

I cross the street and get to the door, seeing, through the window, complete and utter chaos.

From afar, I expected this charming little shop would house a quiet group of sleeping cats like the one I saw in the window. Unfortunately that cat isn't even real, it's a statue, in memorandum to Mr. Lebron Fluffy James. And he is nowhere near a clear representation of what I see happening inside right now.

Pulling open the door and stepping inside, I see no less than a dozen cats chasing after each other, running across the floor, climbing up the registration counter, and jumping on top of the kid hiding behind said counter. He was crying and yelling on his cell phone, "Come get me! This isn't worth it!" I close the door behind me and stay pressed up against it, keeping as much distance between me and the mayhem as possible.

Benny runs over to him. "What happened? Where's Frankie?" He's looking around frantically. *Does Frankie work here?*

The cats finally notice me and all come running after me—meowing and pawing at my legs. I try to gently shoo them away with my foot but it's no use. I'm *cornered.* Even after gently tossing a gangly brown one to the side, he comes scurrying back. One is weaving in and out of my legs, brushing up against me. Another is rolling around in front of me as if to show me how agile it is. They start to lick my legs, literal sandpaper tongues all over my shins. No amount of shooing and hissing I do gets them to stop—it just spurs them on.

They have me trapped against the door. I could make a run for it, but then I'd be the numbskull who let a herd of cats out into the street.

A rather large reddish orange one, who seemed to be the leader of the pack based on how it was perched on the counter, was staring at me. Not blinking, just . . . *staring.* Watching as I squirmed and his little minions kept me surrounded. Any movement and they swarmed me even more, brushing, pawing, *licking* me—Big Red watching the entire time.

This is my nightmare.

"What is going on?" I yell over the feline orchestra at my feet.

"They got out, I don't know how! And I'm allergic! I can't touch them!" The kid behind the counter was sobbing as he cowered as far from the cats as he could manage.

Why would he work here? I resist the urge to psychoanalyze and table the thought.

"Where is Frankie?" Benny was scooping up cat after cat and carrying them through a door behind the counter. He seemed nervous and a little agitated, but was roping the cats up with ease.

"She's supposed to be in the back!" The kid screamed through his tears.

Benny scooped up the rest of the cats at my feet and looked at me. "Are you alright?"

"Fine, just . . . you know . . . didn't expect to be a feline's snack today." The cats in his arms look at me with beady eyes.

He belts out a laugh. "I think they like you!" He laughs again at my eye roll. "Come on, let's meet Frankie."

He leads me through the door, cats in hand as we enter an oasis. Elegant cat trees sit in every corner of the room, with plush pillows spread out across the floor, and boxes of cat toys lining the walls. I also note the glass treat jar placed by the door. The lights were dimmed and a white plush sofa was in the center of the room, a black cat with white paws laying across it. She didn't budge when we walked in, and seemed to care less that I was around. Why can't the others be like her?

Benny places the cats in little pods on the back wall. Each one was filled with a variety of toys, pillows, bowls—all the things a cat may need to entertain itself I presume. Each one was labeled with a name tag indicating that was *their* spot. There was Smudge (the brown one), Oscar (the one with tricks), Nana (her kennel was empty, probably the one on the couch), and Roger (Big Red). I scanned over the names giggling at the absurdity of some before finally landing on the final pod to the far right . . . *Frankie.*

"Frankie . . . is a cat?" I feel sheepish when I see Benny smirking at me as if he had pulled the best prank possible. Real cute. "Wow, you had me thinking it was your girlfriend or something!"

"Don't be jealous, what Frankie and I have is totally platonic." He chuckles again.

"Ha. Ha." I smile at him, then looking in Frankie's kennel I realize she isn't there. "Where is she?"

Benny starts scanning the room, growing more nervous by the second. Picking up pillows, looking in each kennel, looking under the couch, behind it, then under it again.

"Where is Frankie?" he asks me frantically then yells, "Carl! Where is Frankie?"

Carl runs in sweating and gasping for air, inhaler in hand. "I don't know! I looked everywhere for her but she's not here. I think she may have ran through the front door when I went to put the sign out."

"Carl, come on! You know she's a runner! Did you give her her medicine?"

Carl looks down at his feet, a thin line forming on his face. His response is enough of an answer for Benny, who spins on his heels, frustration pinching at the center of his forehead.

"Come on, we have to find her!" Benny grabs me by the hand and pulls me out of the pet oasis and into the street. "She couldn't have gone too far, let's hurry!"

We spend the better part of an hour searching high and low for Frankie. Benny took me to her favorite spots: the park, the bench by the donut shop, back to the school, even to Kate's house. Kate hadn't seen her and decided to help us look. "If we split up we can find her faster!"

"Ellie can stay with me," Benny said, tugging me along by the tips of my fingers. I tried to stay focused on our search and rescue mission, but something about feeling his thick, strong grip move along my fingers and settle around my hand so tenderly was enough to discombobulate my brain.

We kept looking all the way to sunset. I found myself calling out for Frankie, even whistling for her. This was so out of character for me—I have never been a pet person. Or a kid person. Hell, my shriveled up succulent farm would indicate I'm not even a plant person.

Why does anyone get a pet anyway? To have something listen to you and cost you money? I listen to people for a living, that's enough for me.

But here I was, so guilt-ridden that something could have happened to Frankie and Benny lost her for good. He seemed a lot calmer than I expected him to be, but I kept the conversation light just in case. We talked about our favorites and our least favorites.

"If I had to choose, it would have to be a burger. Can't beat the perfect burger." He licks his lips, and I feel the air leave my lungs at the sight.

"You'll never see me eat onions though, not for a million dollars."

"What about world peace? Would you eat an onion to bring peace to this dark and cruel world, Mr. Divata?" I laugh, gesturing a big circle with my hands.

The corners of his eyes twitch up for a small second before he forces a sad look at me, shaking his head at my audacity. "That's low, Ms. Bailey."

"A rapper or a cowboy, or both." His voice is a whisper as he admits the embarrassing truth of his childhood dreams.

"Definitely The Jonas Brothers," I say with pride, revealing my childhood crush. I refuse to acknowledge the minor obsession I *still* have for them.

"Which one?" He eyes me.

"All of them." I shrug as if this was a normal answer.

"You would've married all three?" When I nod, he cocks his head back and a laugh so big and breathy escapes him, his chest puffing up and out as he laughs. The sound was invigorating and cozy all at once. We found ourselves heaving and cackling together like a couple of old friends as we continued sharing.

"My cheeks hurt," I say with a breath, rubbing the sides of my face as we walk.

"I haven't laughed this much in a long time." He grins from ear to ear, the joy of the moment illuminating his face, and rubs his jaw.

After a couple hours of surface level discussion, it became clear the next step was going deeper and neither of us initiated. We began a quiet stroll into a neighborhood down the street from the school.

"Why don't you go by Eleanor?" he asks after a few minutes of silence.

"I've always gone by Ellie, I guess. My mom called me that as a kid and it just stuck."

I didn't really want to tell him that I love Eleanor—that it feels elegant and timeless, and when someone calls me Eleanor it makes my heart flutter. I have always been Ellie, the quirky girl who uses humor as a coping mechanism. The therapist girl who fixes other people's problems and leaves her own by the wayside. Ellie, who suffers from angry intrusive thoughts and doodles about them. Ellie, who is so unlovable she was left at the altar.

Eleanor is not that. Eleanor is sophisticated—distinguished. Eleanor reads instead of doodles. Eleanor shares her feelings without hesitation. She has gifts and she uses them to serve others. She extends grace freely because she wants that in return. She isn't closed off to people who are different from her or view the world differently than she does.

Ellie isn't any of *those* things.

Ellie feels distant and guarded—letting her own trials overshadow the good and beautiful things in life.

Eleanor seeks out the beauty in this world. She delights in it, knowing that there is something out there worth clinging to—something that makes all of the brokenness and disappointment in the world worth enduring. Ellie and Eleanor are two different people.

And I felt *stuck* as Ellie.

I want to be Eleanor again. She has hope, and I need that back.

"I like Eleanor," Benny says softly.

I can't fight the giddy, bashful smile that works its way across my face. "Thanks."

"What about you? You don't seem like a Benny to me."

He laughs that contagious laugh and I let it surround me like a warm hug.

"It's actually Bayani—it's Filipino. My parents wanted me to fit in as a kid, as much as an Asian American kid in a small Oklahoma town could fit in, so they nicknamed me Benny. It stuck." He shrugs matter-of-factly.

"What do you like to be called?"

"I like Benny, actually. Bayani was my grandfather's name. I think it sounds old."

"So when you're old and senile, call you Bayani. Got it."

Laughing again he says, "Definitely."

"So . . . Do you have a girlfriend, *Benny*?"

"Is this an appropriate boss-employee conversation?" He leers at me.

"We're off the clock." I bump my hip into his playfully. I was definitely feeling more comfortable with him—and a little more flirtatious. It was harmless, really. I've flirted with guys since Liam, and Benny was very clearly unavailable to me so what harm could a little playful touch and banter do? Plus, he made me smile, and I hadn't smiled this much in years.

Again, harmless.

Right?

And I need to know if he's off the market if I want to keep indulging in these flirtatious desires.

He bumps me back, playing along. "No girlfriend right now. There was someone a few years ago but it was just a summer fling."

"Mr. Benny Divata had a fling? Whaaaaaaaaat?"

"Hardy har. It wasn't anything serious, just a few dates. I haven't been with anyone in a serious sense for quite some time." He looks at the ground as we walk.

"Why? Is there something wrong with you?" I joke, trying to make light of the topic. I can't tell if he feels embarrassed, or shy for sharing this information with me.

"Hmm, maybe. Just don't seem like the dateable type, I guess." He shrugs and kicks at a rock on the sidewalk.

"I doubt that's the case. You seem very dateable to me."

"Would you date me?" His voice is relaxed and casual as he lingers on the question. "You know, friend to friend."

I pause for effect, and to gather my thoughts. I've never been a dishonest person, but right now may have been a good time to try being a liar for once. Of course I would date him, *look at him*. His black hair was windblown and curling at the ends, his cheeks were smooth, like they were freshly shaven. I had to fight the urge to press my fingers against the subtle indentation at the top of his cheek and trace it. His eyes were practically twinkling, moving up, down, and all around me. He bites his lip, and I instinctively bite mine. I feel heat move across my chest and up my neck as I take in the view.

My mind starts to drift into a *what if* cloud, making me feel flustered at his question. Too flustered to be a liar now.

"I would." My voice cracks. "*Friend.*"

He nods, smiling more to himself than to me. Then he takes his foot and gently taps it on top of mine. "Same, *friend.*"

The heat moved down my entire body and I was spinning. My stomach was fluttering and a tickle ran up my spine, leaving me a little stunned and perplexed.

Was he saying he would date someone *like* me? Or that he would date *me*?

I hadn't thought about actually dating Benny. I've definitely thought about other things, like what his lips might taste like, or what he might look like getting out of a swimming pool—just innocent thoughts, of course. The idea of dating anyone had been so far in the back of my mind I forgot that desire even existed. I've gone on dates since Liam, yes, but free food speaks for itself. And it was never more than a free meal. I mentally sabotaged any physical attraction I may have had with any of them—one guy chewed with his mouth open, another had a wrinkly shirt, another had a mullet and a goatee . . . at the same time.

But tonight felt different.

Like the possibility of dating Benny would be bearable. More than bearable actually, it would be wonderful. He was a total catch and I felt lucky enough to be in his presence. Just sucks it won't ever happen.

Chapter Nine

Benny

IT WAS ALMOST EIGHT o'clock when we made it to the cul-de-sac of my neighborhood–my tiny house nestled in the back.

I didn't intend for Ellie to follow me to my *house*, at *night*. But she didn't say anything, she just stayed with me and helped look for Frankie. The house had already been checked earlier, but I needed to turn the lights on, just in case she came back.

"You don't have to come in, I'll be quick," I tell her as I open my front door.

I needed some space to get my bearings anyway. This night was throwing me for a loop.

Being around Ellie had already been difficult at work. My attraction to her has been hard to contain as it is. But now . . . spending all of this time with her was making it near impossible. I couldn't get enough. Every new thing I learned about her, I needed more, *wanted* more.

I feel pulled to every piece of her—like a magnet. And the fact that I can't do anything about it is physically frustrating.

I go inside to collect myself—pacing across the floor, stretching my arms, flexing my hands, rolling my neck in circles—anything I can do to get rid of the tension that has built up and ached my muscles. I even splash water across my face and give myself a mental pep talk.

No more awkward comments, Ben.

No more lingering eyes, Ben.

And please, for the love of God, stop saying everything that crosses your mind. You will creep her out.

"Benny!" Ellie yells from my front lawn.

I run outside and find Ellie holding a cat—a naked cat—with her red sweater vest.

Frankie.

"Frankie! Where have you been?" Scooping Frankie out of Ellie's hands, I carry her inside and Ellie follows.

"Maybe she just needed a night on the town." She giggles and I watch as her eyes sweep over my place, looking at my photos, books, and *mess.* I left a coffee cup on my table, my gym bag is wide open on the floor, and my socks are in the hallway.

You are a slob, Benny.

I kick my gym bag underneath the couch and throw a towel over the dishes in my sink as I walk Frankie into the kitchen. I immediately check her blood sugar and give her the medication she missed earlier. I look her over for injuries and then set her on her cat tower in the corner of my living room.

"I'm sorry Frankie took away your entire evening." I rub the back of my neck. "And for messing up our meeting. Can we try another time?" I swallow my disappointment about needing to reschedule. Spending the evening walking with Ellie was the most fun I've had in a long time, but I doubt it was what she had in mind for our after school meeting.

"Well . . . what if we do it now?" She smiles at me.

"Really?" My confusion is blatantly obvious—surely she wants to go home now. "Do you want to just reschedule?"

"Seeing as we're already together"—her smile widens—"I figured we could go ahead and knock it out."

I fight back my eagerness over spending more time with her. "Do you still want Wafflin'? I know breakfast for dinner is weird but they have a few dinner options, too."

"I love that idea!" She looks genuinely excited about my suggestion and it feels good to be the one to make her excited.

We trek back into town and make it to Wafflin'. It's a weeknight so the usual busyness of the late night bar-diner vibe had fizzled out before we even got here—an hour before closing. I had every intention of discussing work.

We spent that entire hour discussing everything *but*.

"Ben, you wanna close up for me?" Sam, the owner, had been taking his time closing out the register before he finally gave in and approached us—wanting to leave.

"Oh, we can go ahead and go if you need us to!" Ellie starts to get up from the table. I don't budge—I don't want this night to end yet.

"Not a problem, Benny knows what to do. Just leave a good tip on your way out!" He winks at me before leaving us in the dim lighting of the diner.

Looking at her phone, Ellie says, "It is getting pretty late, maybe we should wrap up?"

"You're probably right," I say reluctantly.

But instead of getting up to leave, we sit there and just look at each other. It takes me a moment to come back to Earth and gather my thoughts. She is mesmerizing and I could probably spend every waking moment of my life looking at her.

Clearing her throat, she messes with her napkin. "So, about Devon Johnson." She pauses, probably waiting for me to respond. "His mom came in this morning and was very concerned with whom he has been hanging out with outside of school. I, obviously, am very unfamiliar with who these other students are. So I thought maybe you could help me . . . approach the situation gently."

"Did she say whom he has been hanging out with?" I had an idea who, but hate assuming the worst about our students.

"Travis and Ethan?"

I nodded—exactly who I thought it was. "Yes, they can get themselves into trouble, but overall they are harmless."

"So no drugs or criminal records?"

"Maybe a few warnings from the local police, or Johnny from security, but nothing severe." I couldn't help but laugh at the memory of Travis and Ethan in my office one morning after attempting to break into the theater room and steal the costumes from the Hamilton project. They swore to me they felt *inspired* after watching rehearsals. They wanted to try them on for size. I had a hunch they planned on giving them the ole E.T. makeover—their trademark title.

"Why would Ms. Johnson be so concerned then? If they are harmless?" She takes a sip of her decaf coffee. "And isn't Devon an adult?"

"He's seventeen. Devon is a really good kid, with a very promising future. He has surpassed everyone's expectations and trumped their assumptions. There is no doubt he will go on to make a name for himself, but after all Ms. Johnson has done for her boys, I can't blame her for worrying about whom he spends his time with. A mother knows best, right?" I ask as I finish my cup of regularly caffeinated coffee—a decision I'm sure I'll regret considering it's eleven at night.

"Do you know them personally?" She fiddles with her napkin.

"Naomi—er, Ms. Johnson—and I went to school together. She was good friends with Kate—they were a second family to us. I watched DJ grow up."

"Devon?" she asks, referring to the nickname. I nod as I wipe my lips with my napkin.

"Could you talk to him then? I'm sure if he has an already-established relationship with you, he would feel more comfortable."

"What exactly does Naomi want you to do?"

"Find out why he is hanging out with them. Convince him not to. Keep tabs on him." She looks out the window next to our booth—it's pitch black with only a few street lamps lighting the street.

"But you can't do that, right?" I rest my hands on the table between us.

"Right. Client confidentiality." She looks back at me. "There are only a few things I can discuss with the parent, and if Devon isn't endangering himself, or someone else, then it stays between us. But if she wants information . . ." She pauses and stares at me with *"you could do it"* eyes.

"I wish it was that simple, but we should also give Devon the benefit of the doubt. I can talk to Naomi and try to put her mind at ease. But you might still need to meet with Devon and help *guide* him." I wiggle my eyebrows at my pun, Ellie rolls her eyes.

"I'm not cut out for this," she responds, her voice sounding defeated.

"I don't believe that for a minute."

"These kids don't know me. They need someone like you, or like Ms. Pat. Hell, even Emma would be better suited! I met with one girl, Birdie something? And it took everything in me to get through discussing her social dilemma of *winter formal*," Ellie says this with disgust and I bite back a laugh. "Should she wear red? She likes red but it might clash with her hair. And Claire likes red so maybe she will wear red, and you definitely can't have two people wearing red. It won't look good in the group photos, right? And who should she go with? There are five prospects. Whomever should she choose?" Her voice is getting more animated and dramatic as she continues her story. I couldn't resist laughing.

I know Birdie. Everyone knows Birdie. So I can only imagine the torture this conversation was for her.

"She compared each of these boys to me for over an hour. Coming to the final conclusion that she should go with her *gals* because she is a woman—a woman who doesn't need to be paraded around by a prepubescent boy."

I am laughing way too hard at her point as she continues. "But here's the kicker"—she points a finger at me—"she will still go to the after party with one of them so she doesn't look *'too available.'*" Her hands go up to give air quotes, "What does that mean, you ask? Apparently going to the after party alone is *sad*. But going with someone you're *actually* dating is sadder. So you have to meet in the middle—go with someone you wouldn't mind being seen with, but also could care less about actually making out with."

Ellie throws her arms up in the air, rolling her big green eyes, clearly annoyed.

I try to catch my breath from laughing. "That sounds like Birdie. Her priorities might be a little . . . skewed." I laugh again.

"Try *a lot*. It was very hard to sit through, and now she wants to meet weekly?" She groans. "I have no earthly idea why! I can't endure this week to week." She puts her head in her hands in a very dramatic way. She's adorable.

I take a moment and look at her, no more laughing. Reaching over and pulling her hands away from her face I say, "Because you are good at what you do. Even if you don't know it at the moment, you are. And these kids are lucky to have you."

"How could you know that? You can't see me do my job, that's illegal." She rolls her eyes at me and looks down at her hands.

"I just know." And that's the truth. I can't explain it, but there is something about Ellie. My infatuated feelings aside, I can sense she's not just good at this job, she's *great* at it.

She blows breath out of her lips and deflates in her seat.

"I just have a good feeling we chose the right person for the job." She doesn't look up so I keep going. "You are compassionate without even trying. You stay engaged when you could easily zone out, *and* you make people laugh." Her smile pulls up on one side of her mouth.

"When Kate brings her vegan food, you partake without hesitation when I know for a *fact* you would rather down a double bacon cheeseburger with a fried egg on top." She lets out an *"mmm"* sound. "When Malcolm called in sick, you offered to sub for his class—a math class—and you've barely been here two months! Some people have been here for over ten years and they *refuse* to sub." I scowl at the stubbornness of my faculty. "You advocate, making sure we feel encouraged to share rather than discouraged. In our meetings, you sit quietly and patiently, letting everyone around you share their troubles. And you doodle shorthand in your notebook so you can remember what everyone shares." I was aware that I didn't need to continue with this rant but something in me didn't want to stop reminding her of how valuable she is.

"And I can tell not all of your doodles are in that therapist-taking-notes sort of way. They're in a thoughtful way, so you can remember the little things. I know this because Bill, who *never* comes to our meetings, came in one day to complain about his mop bucket being broken. I *saw* you listening, then you started doodling. The next week Bill had a new mop bucket. Now who did that?" She gives an innocent shrug at my question. "Well it sure wasn't me, and *I'm* the one he was talking to."

She gnaws on her lip as she looks down at the table.

I take a deep breath and continue, "Everything is warmer and brighter around you. Like the sun or something hotter, if that's possible. You're this bright light. And I just think if you can be *that* with these ridiculous teenager situations, then *when* these students have real issues, because they *will* . . . you will be the one to help them."

I was looking down at my hands at this point, nervous that I may have said too much. But instead of running out the door like a sane person, Ellie got up from her side of the booth, and sat next to me. She leaned her head on my shoulder and hooked her pinky finger around mine.

"Thank you." Her voice was a whisper.

"You're welcome." I can't control myself when I look down at her. I brush her cheek with my thumb, wiping away a small tear before it falls to her lap.

"You're something else, Benny." Her voice is tender and the taste of her sweet breath hits me as she looks up at me—our faces almost touching.

I gaze down at her, taking in her soft skin and dark hair. Committing what I see to memory, refusing to blink so I don't miss a thing.

The next morning faculty meeting was a little tense, to say the least.

The events of last night kept swirling through my head. One moment Ellie and I were looking for Frankie, the next we were holding pinkies?! And *then* we walked back to the car, and I *hugged* her?

What was I thinking?

I am *insane*.

We were in dangerous territory and I felt so out of control of my actions, I can't imagine what I might do next. I was putting her job and mine at risk.

Malcolm was leading the meeting, going over the next month's events. My head was spinning as I tried to focus on what he was saying to the group.

"I'm tired of being the only coach. I want to work in my garden and feed my chickens, and I can't do that when I'm stuck at practice all night." Malcolm was pacing back and forth, grimey coffee pot in hand.

"I know, we're working on it. We have the job posted—" I stop talking mid-sentence when I see Ellie walk into the break room. I stare at her like a madman, and everyone looks in her direction, making her blush. She looks at me with big eyes and rushes to sit down. I'm still not talking and now everyone is looking back at me, then at her, then back at me.

"So . . . you said the job has been posted?" Emma joins the conversation, saving me.

Blinking a million times a minute, I respond with, "Yes . . . Yep . . . The job is posted and we are waiting for applicants." I feel myself glancing back at Ellie every few seconds. She's sitting there giggling at me as I stumble on my words.

"Good, find someone . . . fast," Malcolm snaps at me.

"What if I help coach so it's not all on you? We can split the games too?" This was good, it would keep me busy after school so I wouldn't be tempted by Ellie. I needed time to figure things out, set healthy boundaries, and there was no way that was happening with her around me.

Malcolm seemed pleased with my offer because he nodded in his "*I approve*" way, which doesn't happen often.

"On an unrelated note, I would like to invite everyone to our Halloween party this year! Details have been sent to your emails, and sign-ups for food are attached . . ." Emma trailed off into party planning mode and I went to the back of the room to collect myself.

"Mr. B?" I look up from my coffee to see Garrett standing in the doorway, leaning against his crutches.

"Mr. Connors, what can I do for you?" I walk over to him.

"I was, umm . . ." He looks around the room. "Wondering if I could meet with Ms. Bailey now?" He nods in Ellie's direction.

As if Ellie could sense Garrett's need to interrupt and demand a room's attention in any scenario, she quickly gets up and meets him in the doorway.

"I'm Ms. Bailey." She reaches out to shake his hand.

"Sup, Ms. B!" He high fives her hand instead of shaking it and I'm immediately embarrassed for him. "I'm Garrett!"

And then, for some reason, Ellie stares daggers at me.

Chapter Ten

Ellie

"WHY CAN'T I SEE the inside of my eyelids?"

Garrett asks me as he lounges in my office, feet propped up like he was on his own couch. We had somehow entered into twenty questions territory instead of *actual* counseling territory.

I don't know how this happened, but I was doing exactly what I had hoped I wouldn't have to do . . . waste time, humoring a teenage football player instead of helping the world's mental health crisis. As he continues spouting off answers to his own questions, I squeeze my pencil under my desk so tight it snaps. It's very hard for me to play along with these ridiculous posings when I have students who genuinely need help.

Maybe Garrett has actual issues he needs to work through, but for the last thirty minutes, we haven't even come close to them in conversation. Instead, he has talked about his haircut, the new cafeteria lunch options, and has shared with me his senior-year prank ideas.

I realize I have zoned-out when Garrett asks me, "What do you think I should do?"

Staring blankly at him, afraid to admit I don't know what we're talking about anymore, I ask, "What do *you* think you should do?"

"Well, I obviously can't fix my knee any faster, and I for sure can't not graduate. None of the colleges will even look at a gap year student, and my family can't pay for me to go to school. It has to be a scholarship." He was sitting up now, looking down at his leg nestled in a knee-high walking boot, and a large bandage wrapped around his knee.

He's sharing a *real* problem. Now we're getting somewhere.

I could sense the sadness in his voice and the fear of the unknown, a side of Garrett he has been trying to hide with jokes. Using humor as a coping mechanism is something I can relate to.

"Those are all very real concerns. Have you discussed this with your family?"

"Nah . . . I think they just think I won't go to college now because of the leg."

Suddenly, the happy, goofy, six-foot-two football player looks half his size. My heart softens for him a little.

"Have you shared these feelings with anyone?"

He shakes his head.

"Would you like to share with me?"

"I don't know what to say." He shrugs.

Approaches in counseling can vary. A lot of sessions are geared more towards cognitive behavior—implementing cognitive restructuring, challenge thinking, or even physical strategies like controlled breathing or muscle relaxation to solve the problem. But sometimes those strategies don't work any better than just *listening* to the person. In this situation, I realize the best thing I can do for Garrett is just that, listen.

I try to think of something profound or clever to get the ball rolling and his brain turning, but I'm coming up blank.

So I settle on the only thing that seems to make sense at the moment and say, "Just . . . think out loud."

And then . . . he does.

Garrett *shares.*

We go back and forth, talking about his childhood and his family, how they left Kansas and ended up at Glendale. He shares his hopes and his dreams—he even chokes back a few tears thinking about how they might not happen. We discuss the possibility of new dreams, and his eyes light up and shoulders relax. We discuss football and how the sport brings him purpose. And finally, he shares his fears of the future and admits to using jokes to make himself feel better.

All the while, I jot down notes and doodle little footballs and crutches—with my broken pencil.

"What about you, Ms. B?" Garrett asks me after sharing about his childhood crush on the Pink Power Ranger and his obsession with Dora the Explorer.

"I wouldn't say I had a Power Ranger crush, but Dora was always cool. She helped me learn what *vamanos* means." I chuckle.

"Nah, I mean do you have any crushes?" He was wiggling his eyebrows at me.

"Oh, umm . . . that is not an appropriate question to ask." Heat moves up my neck at the sheer audacity of a teenager asking about my love life. The only real *crush* I've had recently left me at the altar. My defense mechanisms start firing, the instinct to slam my notebook shut strong. "I think that's all the—"

"I'm sorry, Ms. B." He stops me, a gentle tone in his voice. "Just trying to make conversation."

I study him, feelings swarming my brain as he shrugs his shoulders. *Harmless.* "Gotcha, well . . . regardless, I shouldn't be discussing my personal life in that way with a client—let alone a student."

He puts his hands up in surrender. "I get it, I get it. I was just asking because I think I know of someone who might have eyes for you." He winks at me and bobs his head towards the closed office door across the hall. Benny's office.

Looking at the door for a little longer than I should, I snap my head back to see Garrett smiling at me—a wide, kind of devious smile.

"Alright then," I say abruptly, "same time next week?"

He's still smiling, not speaking. I choose to ignore what is being said in the silence.

"Mr. Connors . . ." I say, trying to have a stern tone, "next week then?"

"Oh, absolutely. I look forward to it." He stands in the most ungraceful way, balancing on his booted leg. He has this suave-ness about him that overshadows the limp as he moves towards the door.

In the same moment, the door across the hall swings open and a stocky teenager walks out of the office. His face is pinched as he makes eye contact with me.

"Sup, Devon!" Garrett meets him in the hallway. "See ya, Ms. B, it was fun!" They walk off together and head to class.

I start doodling on my paper again, making mental notes of the session, when I hear a knock at the door. Benny is there, leaning against the open door. I feel the air escape my windpipe at the sight of him.

"Doodling again?" He nods at my paper.

"It helps me think, and remember. Plus it's fun, thank you very much," I retort and set the broken pencil down on my desk.

"What'd he do to you?" Benny asks, eyeing the jagged pencil in pity.

I frown, embarrassed at the truth. "Just a moment of weakness."

Benny makes a silent *"ah"* and nods like he *gets* it. But does he get it? Does he understand having the angry impulse to just break something?

"What can I do for you?" I ask him.

"I met with Devon just now. I was wondering if we could chat about it."

Waving to the open chair. "Of course, please sit."

Just as Benny sits down, Sarah comes running into my office.

"I need you!" She's panting, looking frazzled and anxious.

Benny stands quickly. "Ms. Kim, is everything alright?"

She looks back and forth between Benny and I. "Uhh yes. It's a . . . girl situation . . ."

Benny nods, smiling as he hurries out of the office. Sarah slams my door shut behind him.

"What's going on, Sarah?" I watch her clench and shake her hands, looking all around my office as she paces back and forth.

"It's Ethan Blake!" she growls. "He's told every guy on the football team that I made out with him under the bleachers and that is *not* what happened! He cornered me!"

Feeling instantly protective, I interrupt. "Did he force himself—"

"No, no!" she interjects. "He just cornered me . . . with his sexy eyes . . ." She stops pacing and looks at me with her own pitiful, love struck eyes.

"Ahh." I nod in understanding. "I see. Go on."

"He told everyone on the football team, and now they all think I'm easy or something. It was *just* a kiss—an unexpected one, especially from me. I'm the smartest kid in school—he's the hottest. It's disrupting the status quo! We threw homeostasis off balance and now they are rioting! It's everywhere. People are *looking* at me. Texting me. Birdie hates me!"

Birdie was Queen Bee, apparently. Everyone knew it, and I'm assuming Ethan was "hers," because in high school, of course we look at our partners as property and not humans with individual thoughts or opinions.

I try not to wonder if she had listed Ethan as one of her prospective formal dates and focus on Sarah.

"She has the entire cheer squad whispering about me! It got all the way to Ms. Simmons before debate practice and she never knows anything! The woman is oblivious to the social norms. I couldn't even finish my defense on subsidization of renewable energy production!"

Sarah kept going—even going as far back as the third grade when Birdie moved here and how they were best friends for years. Then comparing how different they were now: Birdie got boobs, Sarah got brains. Then on to Ethan—how she's loved him since she knew what love was and decided pursuing him was like grasping at the wind. And of course, how she thought loving Ethan would fade but it has grown into something she can't run or hide from, and now she has to watch this person she wants to be hers, be with someone else—someone who doesn't appreciate him like she does.

Her words, not mine.

She became very poetic, and a twinge snarky, which I am thoroughly enjoying.

Sarah is in love with Ethan. Even if she is a teenager, what she feels . . . is love.

I remember my first love in school—he went on to be assistant manager of a Best Buy.

I start to doodle little tweety birds and reading glasses. It may seem silly to someone on the outside—this teenage drama—but the reality that these years are extremely formative for a person is at the center of my mind. I think back to my conversation with Benny the other night, and focus on Sarah's situation.

As much as I want to grab her by the shoulders and shake her senseless, I have to fight that feeling and remind myself of her heightened emotional capacity and the continued development of her brain. It is essential, as someone she confides in, for me to listen well and validate her feelings as being normal, even if I know, in the depths of my soul, that she can do *way* better than Ethan Blake.

"What I need to do is find a super hot date to prom!" She finally stops pacing to share this revelatory solution.

"Do you think that will improve this situation?"

I know exactly why she thinks this is a good idea, and I won't lie, it would definitely get heads turning and provide her that confidence boost she desperately wants, but is it the most logical, and emotionally mature option? Absolutely not.

"Maybe! It might at least clear my name from the hallway whispers, it will get Birdie off my back, her minions will find someone else to gawk at, and it will definitely make Ethan jealous."

"Prom isn't until next term though," I say.

"I know, but what other option do I have?"

"Does the only solution involve another person?"

"Yes, that's the only way. Unless I started a rumor that I made out with someone else? Or left someone on read! Oo! I could say I was dating a guy in college!"

"Or!" I jump in, quickly interrupting her last idea. "Now hear me out . . . what if you actually dated someone, for real?" If her only solution involves another person, I will go along with it to at least avoid her trying to date a scrubby college boy.

"Like a boyfriend?" she asks, rather stunned by my idea.

"Yes. A boyfriend. A *real* one."

"Don't be insane! There's no way!"

"Why not? You have so much to offer! Brains, beauty, sassiness—boys like that."

"Don't you think if boys liked what I had to offer they would have asked me out already? Who cares if I'm smart or sassy if I can't even get a guy's number!"

I study her for a second then redirect. "Well, if that's not an option, then maybe we can find a different solution that focuses on you."

She looks at me with a shrug, like, "*What about me?*"

"What will finding a solution do for *you*?"

She slouches down in the chair and leans her head back on the wall. With a big sigh she says, "Hide my heartbreak."

She starts to tear up, her anxiety building up again. I get up and sit beside her, bringing her in for a hug. As soon as I do, she lets it all out.

The tears of her first heartbreak, right here in my office at three thirty in the afternoon.

And for a moment, as she hugged me back, I didn't feel truly alone. We were all hurting from something or someone, reeling from the emotional roller coaster of life. Sarah's reactions may seem over the top to any other adult, but to me, it felt like a mirror image of the feelings I've been bottling up lately.

If Sarah's teenage hormones are the natural cause of her emotional reactions, then what was causing mine? Why do I feel the instinct to break something anytime I let myself feel anything but put together? I couldn't use the excuse of teenage hormones for my actions.

The feeling of abandonment is a trigger for me. And the fact that my fight-or-flight response seems to be very fickle lately could also be at fault. But the real reason for my lack of control—the one I've been reluctant to admit to anyone, even myself—I'm hurt.

And lately it seems the only way I'm letting myself get over the hurt is by getting angry.

Love is a complex thing. It intertwines itself deep within our hearts. It's a sacrificial and intentional choice to put someone above yourself. It's a messy and beautiful choice to love someone—and when you feel that love in return, the feeling penetrates deep within you, filling you with desire and hope for a future filled with that love.

But when that love breaks you . . . getting angry feels like the only way to survive it.

Wiping the corners of my eyes I ask Sarah, "What do you say we let some of this anger out, huh?"

She wipes her own tears and stares at me. "Okay . . ." Her voice full of concern.

We leave my office and make our way to the opposite side of the school.

Emma is standing at her high top desk, talking to Steven on the phone. "Well, honey, I thought it would be nice to have you home for dinner tonight."

He was bailing on dinner *again*.

That was the third family dinner he's had scheduling conflicts with and I couldn't help but assume it was because I was in attendance. Ever since the Halloween discussion, Steven had been very standoff-ish. I wish I could say I didn't blame him, maybe I did act a little psychotic and irrational when I sped off in his wife's car.

It's not like I went on a rampage across the city. I just went for drinks and dairy-free ice cream with Kate. Then I slept with Dolly Parton, her Golden Retriever, on her couch. Being out all night may have sent Steven over the edge, but I will die on the hill of justification.

Yes, he is guilty by association. But I have no intention of addressing this with the person responsible. So being angry at Steven is the next best thing. Plus, my actions were very mild compared to what I really wanted to do, which was shove Dr. Steven's face in the toilet and give him a good ole fashion swirlie . . . but I took the high road, emptying his gas tank along the way.

"No, I understand it's been busy, I'm sorry. We just miss you," Emma whispers before noticing Sarah and I in the doorway. "I'll talk to you later, I love you."

Hanging the phone up, I see her go from gloomy wife to cheerful teacher in a millisecond. "Hi ladies! What can I do for you guys?"

I rush to her and give her a big hug, quick as to not make Sarah feel awkward, but hoping to remind her I see her and am here for her. She squeezes tight.

"We want to smash some things," I say with a big grin, wiggling my eyebrows.

"Wait, what? We're doing what now?" Sarah interjects. "Ms. Jones, I don't want to—"

"Trust me, you do!" I wink at her.

Emma leads us to the back of her studio classroom. Behind a partition we see a wall of sledgehammers, axes, mallets, and the like. It's the angry ex-girlfriend's armory on full display. In the corner are piles of broken art pieces: wood, clay, cement, even a giant plush teddy bear with an emo aesthetic, donning a *Panic! At the Disco* t-shirt. Sarah looks over the wall and back to me, suspicious uncertainty all over her face.

"You can choose any tool you want. Only hit the scraps, don't go rogue and trash one of my tables. Keep safety goggles on at all times, and please sign a waiver before you start."

"What is the purpose of this?" Sarah asks, still uncertain.

"To let out your anger!" I say as I grab a mallet.

"The purpose, *actually*, is to make art," Emma says, correcting me.

"With trash?" Sarah makes a face looking at the pile of scraps. Maybe this wasn't my best idea.

"These were art"—she gestures to the pile—"and they can actually be art again. They were broken off during someone's art process. Whether it's rebuilding, restructuring, or just tweaking small details, it never looks the way you pictured it would in the beginning. The process changes and adapts with the artist. It's a way to express, or calm, their emotions in a tangible way. It's amazing what we can say with shapes and colors that we can't say with words. It can be a healing process, and the pieces you see here may be leftover from someone else, but they can also be reused in another person's process. What we leave behind may even help the next person."

Emma is beaming as she imparts beautiful wisdom and emphasizes the power of art to Sarah. I feel so fortunate to witness Emma's heart in many different ways, but getting to witness her passion for art, and how it has impacted her, is truly wonderful.

"I see." Sarah is still staring at the wall, probably unsure about what she is getting into.

"Or you can just break some stuff," Emma says with a shrug.

"Okay, cool!" Sarah perks up and grabs the goggles.

Teenagers.

I smile at Emma and hand her a mallet. She hesitates at first, unsure if she should partake in the releasing-of-anger-activity with a *student*. Then after a moment, she smiles and takes the mallet. "Oh, what the heck!"

Turning on the bluetooth speaker and blaring Taylor Swift, we all take turns smashing different pieces of art—with safety goggles on, of course. Big swings with a hammer, followed with hands on our knees laughing, then gasping for air only to rear back and swing again. Once the tall, clay sculpture is pummeled into a pile of broken shards, a sudden sense of calm moves through my body—as if the pile of clay statues now lying on the floor was a tangible representation of my anger being dissipated by my own hands. It felt good and therapeutic to break something, and this time I didn't feel shame about it.

We all slide down to the floor to catch our breath and whip our safety goggles off.

"I can officially say you guys are the coolest grown-ups I know!"

I smile at Emma, feeling very grateful for her and this job, and the memories we are making together, even if it is just for a short time.

Chapter Eleven

Benny

"What do you want from me? I'm doing everything I'm supposed to and she's still hounding me. Why can't I have some time to myself and hang with my team? We aren't even doing anything wrong!"

Devon is in my office for the third time this week, and he's fuming. And there really isn't a reason for him to be in here. He's right, he isn't doing anything wrong, but Naomi has been rather persistent regarding his whereabouts lately and the best way to keep her off campus, *every* hour of the day, is to start meeting with Devon regularly. He's not happy about it, but this is my attempt at a compromise. And my attempt to prevent his mother from circling my school like a crazy mother goose.

"I know, but you're her son, she's just being a mom."

"Yeah, an annoying one. She's the worst."

"Moms just worry, it's a weird neurotic way of showing they love you," Ellie says from the corner where she is currently sitting.

Ellie was supposed to be meeting with Devon one-on-one but he refused to meet with her, and of course, Naomi insisted. So we came to an agreement, we would have a group meeting. It was going as I expected, Ellie sitting and observing and . . . drawing, Devon resisting, and me, trying to keep the peace.

He was standing across from me, refusing to sit, for the entirety of our thirty-minute meeting—arms crossed, feet planted in place. I couldn't help but wonder if this five-foot-eleven tank of a young man was attempting to fool me with his tough guy stance, but all I could do was smile inside, picturing the little six-year-old that used to sit on my shoulders to see the Fourth of July fireworks. I kept having to correct myself when I would accidentally refer to him as DJ in front of Ellie.

Devon is a fantastic kid, and the youngest of four. I feel very fortunate to be someone who has watched him grow into the young man he is. Naomi was best friends with Kate growing up, and after I lost my parents, her family took me in as their own—spending every family holiday and summer breaks together. We were all inseparable. Falling in love and getting pregnant at sixteen was not in the plan for Naomi, but she and Devon's dad made it work. They have shown such resilience and perseverance raising their kids.

Even though he's the youngest, Devon took on extra responsibilities to lighten his mother's load—he excels in school and sports, and has multiple, full-ride, football scholarships awaiting his decision. But when his sister moved away last year, leaving him to be the last child at home, he started slacking off and it was enough to lose a few scholarship offers. As a result, this, in addition to his recent late night adventures with a few other football players, has put Naomi on high alert. Which puts *me* on high alert. Naomi can teeter between worried and downright psychotic when it comes to her kids. And her hourly texts and phone calls to the school lately are an indicator the line between the two is close to being crossed.

"You don't mean that. She just wants what's best for you. We all do," I say, crossing my arms to match his tough guy energy.

"Whatever, I still have scholarships. There's nothing to worry about."

Ellie sits quietly, another doodle drawn. I see a *dollar sign* doodle.

"Actually, there is. I spoke with Mr. Geer this morning and he informed me that you are at risk of failing Calculus this term."

Devon's eyes go big—he didn't know it was *that* bad.

I see Ellie draw a calculator.

"Yep. So I think the best thing to do now is take a little extra time to meet with Ms. Bailey and develop a plan of action to prevent a failing grade from ending up on your transcript." I keep my tone stern and serious.

Devon rolls his eyes. "Why do I have to keep meeting with her?"

Dude, she's right there. "It's for your benefit."

"Can't you just meet with me to keep mom off my back? And talk to Geer?"

I sigh. "You know I would, but this is how it is now. I can't let our personal relationship interfere with your success in school, Devon."

He rolls his eyes and looks at his watch. "Fine, whatever. I gotta go."

"Same time next week?" Ellie stands and smiles at him.

"Yeah, okay."

I reach out to shake his hand. He looks at it like it's a foreign object, then shakes reluctantly before leaving.

"It feels weird to be acting so professional around him lately," I say to Ellie. "I know how much pressure he is under, but he's still just 'little DJ' in my mind. I'm having a hard time keeping Uncle Benny and Mr. B separate." I open my office blinds.

"That can be hard—separating work from your personal life—even for me, and I'm a therapist." She shakes her head at herself. "You can really grow to love your clients, then it becomes increasingly difficult to avoid blurring those lines. Transference can happen on both sides," she says, putting her notebook away.

"Transference?" I question, sitting back at my desk.

"Well for me, it would be countertransference, but yeah!" The attempt to hide the confusion on my face fails as she continues, "It's a psychological phenomenon."

"Oo, please tell me more. I love phenomena." I wiggle my eyebrows and place my chin on my hand.

She smirks at me. "Essentially, it is an unconscious projection of emotions from one person onto another."

"Tell me more." I lean and rest my arms on my desk, giving her my full attention.

"It happens when someone experiences feelings caused by one person and projects those onto someone else entirely. These feelings are usually about a person who may have made a significant impact on them—positive or negative. As a psychologist, transference may be done on me because I am the one they share these impacts and emotions with." She relaxes as she keeps going. "The concept emerged from Freud and has been a method for identifying conflict resolutions for ages. Did you know, he believed that our development and adult personality was heavily impacted by our conflicts? Freud, I mean." I could see she was starting to get excited about sharing this information with me.

Her face is lighting up as she talks and I am hooked. She's nerding out and it's adorable.

I feel genuinely interested in what she's talking about. Even if she is using big words that make me feel a little dumb, she is trusting me enough to open up and share. And I want her to feel safe enough to share with me.

"This is probably boring. Psychoanalytics isn't everyone's cup of tea." She looks around my office without meeting my eyes.

"No, please go on. You have me intrigued," I say, looking her in the eye.

She continues, slowly relaxing and talking fast, like a child sharing their secret prized possession—bug eyed and excited, unaware of how insignificant it is to someone else because it's the most important thing in the world to them. A smile stretches across my face as I listen to her.

She stops talking for a second and gives me a look, a different look than I've seen. Her eyes are softer and searching my face for something.

What is it, Eleanor?

Clearing her throat she continues, "Anyway, transference usually happens in a clinical setting. But it is possible that it can happen in everyday life. If you feel an attachment to Devon's family, it is only natural to project all of those emotions and memories onto him involuntarily. And if you have a relationship with Naomi—"

"It's not that kind of relationship," I cut her off. I feel the immediate urge to clarify that I am in no way, shape, or form anything more than a friend to Naomi. Aside from the fact that I've known her since diapers, her six-foot-tall husband is a big enough deterrent to that possibility.

"Oh, I don't mean that way, I'm sorry," she whispers.

"I just want to make it clear, I don't have a relationship with Naomi outside of close friendship. I don't have a relationship at all in *that* sense," I say hoarsely, a twinge of embarrassment karate chopping me in the throat.

"Right. Well, if you have a close friendship with Naomi, even if you know Devon personally, you could naturally project your feelings for his mom onto him because he might remind you of her and she's important to you. Countertransference." She stifles a laugh. "It can be difficult to separate that from here. But I think you're doing a great job, and he obviously trusts you to agree to meet with me just because you asked him to."

Relaxing into my chair I ask, "Have you experienced this countertransference thing?"

"That discussion calls for more coffee." She smirks at me.

Eager to hear more from that nerdy brain of hers, I slap my knees and stand. "Then let's go."

We walk out of my office together and head to the lounge for our morning cream with a splash of coffee. I was growing very fond of my morning coffee with Ellie, and the fact that we took our coffee the same was doing something to my heart that I couldn't explain.

It's now the beginning of October and the school is entering into their Harry Potter decor phase—red and gold colors everywhere, fake candles hanging from lockers, pumpkins on the floor, and there's an attempt at an enchanted sky with old rusted twinkle lights from Bill's janitorial closet.

We walk instep and I tell her about my morning dealing with Frankie and her attitude towards the change in weather.

"I guess it's colder for a hairless cat." She chuckles.

"Frankie was meow-screaming at me because all she had on was a vest. I finally swapped it for her black hoodie with a pink bow on the front. Dressing up a cat . . ." I shake my head as I ramble out loud and she laughs louder. "Am I a cat man? Is a cat man a thing? Not to be confused with Batman, *obviously*."

"Obviously." Her confident response reaffirms my weird train of thought. Ellie does that a lot—reaffirms me. It feels nice.

"I bet if Batman dressed up a hairless cat it would actually look cool." I laugh, mostly at myself.

"You are super cool." She places her hand on my arm.

"God, I really sound sad, don't I?" I run my hand down my face.

She laughs at me. "I think it's endearing."

"I seem to ramble a lot when we're together."

"I don't mind it. You're easy to listen to, even if it's *nonsense*." She gives me a wink.

I chuckle. "Thanks for the reassurance."

"Really, it's like you trust me to be your completely, unfiltered self. It feels special." Her shoulders raise as she wraps her arms around her waist, snuggling into her cardigan.

I stop walking to face her. "I just really like talking to you."

Ellie touches the side of her cheek, her eyes moving across my face. I can't tell if what I said was a good thing or if it made this entire moment awkward. And then, she grins that soft, sweet smile at me. A smile that is ingrained forever in my memory.

I smile down at her, taking her all in. Her dark hair is pulled into a high bun, green eyes sparkling from the twinkle lights. Her pink lips are shiny today, filling me with a teenage urge to meet her under the bleachers.

I shake the forbidden image out of my head and force my eyes away. *Not allowed.*

We walk into our break room, instantly hit with the smell of scorching coffee grounds—the strong stuff. I practically choke on the air, the fumes potent. Malcolm is the only one in the room, sitting in complete darkness with his personal pot within arms reach.

I whisper to Ellie, "Don't mention my Catman spiral."

Flipping on the light, Malcolm lets out a grunt.

"Good morning, Mr. Geer!" I pat Malcolm on the back.

Another grunt response.

I head to the coffee pot to brew a lighter pot than Malcolm's gasoline, and scope out the produce he's brought in: eggplants, apples, and some squash. I grin at his generosity.

"Fall is Malcolm's favorite," I say motioning to the fresh goods he's provided.

"No it's not," Malcolm growls over his shoulder.

"He will never admit to having a favorite anything," I fake whisper, "but I know it is. He always brings more produce in the fall, stays at the school longer, and he *always* agrees to participate in the classroom decorating contest."

Ellie gasps. "You do not!"

"He's lying," Malcolm mumbles into his mug.

"Granted his decoration is a single pumpkin sticker on the center of his door." I shrug, pulling out a mug for Ellie and myself. "It's more than we would expect at any other time of year from Mr. Geer."

The coffee finishes brewing and I fill our mugs the same way, a fourth cinnamon creamer, the rest with coffee, and a spoon to stir. She watches me and I can't make out the look on her face as I hand her the cup. We linger by the pot for a moment before I walk over and sit next to Malcolm.

I ask him, "So how is Devon doing in your class?"

Malcolm rolls his eyes. "Could be doing better. Kid won't even try."

"It seems that way, huh?"

"It's a shame to just quit trying when you're so close. Makes no sense." He lets out an exasperated sigh, Malcolm doesn't have the patience for laziness.

"Maybe he just wants some freedom—enjoy his childhood before going off to college." I force an optimistic tone, afraid my feelings towards DJ are becoming anything but.

We start discussing Devon and some of the other football players and I see Ellie pull out her notebook and start doodling. I try to respect her privacy, but I also want to know every little thing about her.

I steal glances of the paper. Surely if it was private she wouldn't have it out in the open, right?

Malcolm goes on about the season and the need to find an assistant coach—something I was definitely putting on the back burner.

"I know, we will figure that out." I glance at the notebook again.

Fall leaves.

Pumpkins.

Eggplants.

She erases the eggplant forcefully and peeks up at me embarrassed. Probably because it resembles something one shouldn't doodle in a public school.

I can't help but grin at her. Her cheeks go red and she shuts the notebook.

"I'm tired of being the only one in charge of those kids."

Malcolm was only supposed to be an interim head coach until we filled Eric's spot. But the applicants recently have been less than optimal and

Malcolm was doing such a fantastic job, it was hard for me to push for a replacement. He finally agreed to stay head coach, as long as I found him an adequate assistant.

"He wants to act like a child. They all do. A child can't handle college."

I guess we are back to Devon.

"Surely he will come to his senses and learn how to handle everything. He's done so much already, one more year of child-like fun won't be terrible."

"We'll see."

Malcolm doesn't have as much hope for the students as I do. But he is a good teacher and he always does what's right. Right now, that might be letting a student fail so they will learn the principles of discipline and perseverance—even if it affects his faculty performance review.

"Did you get the invite to the Halloween party?" I ask him, nudging Ellie with my elbow. Grasping at straws for a subject change.

He holds up his cup of coffee. "Nothing excites me before coffee."

Nodding, I smile at Ellie. We all sip in silence until our cups are empty.

After a few moments, Malcolm sets his cup down and looks at Ellie. "There, now you can ask."

"Umm . . . are you excited about the Halloween party?" She recoils with her own question.

"No."

"What do you mean you aren't excited?" Kate yells in our general direction. She had come into the break room mid-conversation and was now stomping towards Malcolm. I leave the table to avoid the ambush that is little Kate Stanley. She is a fireball.

"I'm not going to a party unless it's to celebrate someone retiring or dying."

"Celebrate someone dying?" Kate asks in horror.

"We don't *celebrate* someone dying," I say over my shoulder.

"I said what I said."

"You have to come! All of us do! This is the first party I'm getting to throw with Ellie and I need it to be perfect."

Ellie was blushing, definitely not enjoying being the center of attention.

"Nah, I'm good." Malcolm starts to pour another cup.

"Just come for an hour. Eat the *free* food, drink, and be merry!"

"Merry is for Christmas," Malcolm grumbles.

"You know what I mean! This has to be great, and it will be a success if you come, Malcolm! Please, please, please." Kate is clasping her hands in front of her chest, begging.

"No."

"Please."

"Nope."

Kate stares at Malcolm for a while, then sits down with quivering lips and lets out a deep, shaky breath with force.

Here we go.

"Don't do that." Malcolm's eyes were pinned on Kate.

"Do what?" Her voice cracked as she blinked her sad eyes at him.

"Don't cry." He leans back in his chair with a pained look across his face, bracing for impact.

She blinks again. "I'm not going to cry."

She started crying.

"Dammit, Stanley. Fine, I'll go. Just don't cry, stop that right now," he says, pointing his finger at her. Kate grabs it and starts shaking it like it was his hand.

"Perfect." She was smiling ear to ear, tears miraculously evaporating as she kept shaking his finger. "This is binding in the school of Glendale."

"You little punk."

Malcolm hated to see a lady cry, and he hated even more to see *his* ladies cry. He would deny it, but he loves this faculty and would fall on a sword for any of us. As much as he tries to convince us he is just a stubborn, old, grandpa inside—underneath that grumpy facade, and fishing shirt, was a big heart for his Glendale family.

Kate jumps up and kisses the top of his head. "You love me."

"I'm not dressing up though."

Malcolm pushes out from the table, screeching his chair legs across the floor—grumbling under his breath as he leaves.

"You're going to be the death of that man," I tell Kate.

"Dying for the cause isn't such a bad thing," she says, laughing.

"So how is the party planning going? Anything I can do?" I ask her.

"Nope, we have it all covered! Just show up, dress up, and get crazy!"

"Oh you know I am the *definition* of crazy," I say dryly.

"Or just come and sit idly by while we all embrace the best holiday of the year! Besides Christmas, nothing beats Christmas."

"I respectfully disagree," Ellie pipes in.

"Spooky season is the best, hands down," I say in agreement as I head for the door.

"Where are you going?" Ellie asks me.

"Just to do vice principal things, don't let me interrupt the planning."

"You don't want to help?"

"Ugh, please no! Benny can't help with this. His ideas will literally turn this into a wake from how dead the party will become!" Kate groans.

My ideas aren't *that* bad . . . I don't think.

"Kate and I just party differently. I can throw some bangers, let me tell ya."

Kate snorts. "A Mario Kart party is not a banger."

"I'm sure we could find him something to do. We need plates and cups! Benny, do you want to be in charge of that?" Ellie asks me with a pitiful smile. She's trying to make the task seem cooler than it is.

"Don't screw it up. This is your one chance," Kate says, staring at me as if this mission was life or death.

"You can count on me," I say with a forced smile and a finger salute.

Plates and cups? *Lame.*

"Great, thank you." Ellie smiles back at me.

I quickly shove the feeling her smile gives me deep down and lock it up tight.

Not allowed.

"Alright, thank you for your contribution. You are free to go." Kate waves me off.

I blink. "I'm in no rush."

"We have more party planning to discuss and I don't want you getting any more ideas on how you can help."

Chapter Twelve

Ellie

Benny looks at me with a soft, pouty smile as he leaves the break room. Ugh, that smile . . . those lips. I have this itching desire to press my face up against them. I feel myself staring at the door frame he was just leaning against.

"So . . ." Kate crosses her arms in front of me. "What's going on there?"

"Hmm? What?" I drag my eyes from the door to hers—caught red-handed.

"Oh, come on! With you and Ben, what's going on with *that?*" She waves her hand in a circle.

"Umm . . ." I bite my lip, and my cheeks flush at *that.* Maybe it wasn't too obvious. I've just about mastered my friendly work smile. I doubt it's any different than how I smile at Benny . . . like he just rescued a lonely, stranded sea turtle. "We're just becoming friends, I think."

"No way that's it. Benny doesn't linger like that with *anyone.*"

"I think he's just trying to be welcoming since I'm new." I give her an innocent grin, trying not to fixate on the knowledge that he doesn't *linger* with anyone else, but I've definitely noticed his lingering with me.

"You've been here two months." She raises an eyebrow at me.

"New-ish?" I give an unconvincing smile.

She laughs. "Whatever, I'll find out if you're hiding something! Ask anyone, you can't keep these things from me. Especially when it has to do with *that!*" Waving her hand again.

"*That* was just friendly smiling," I say, waving my hand the same way.

"*Thaaaaaat*"—another   wave—"was   flirty-longing-pining-wish-I-was-yours kind of smiling!"

"Oh, please! It was not!"

Was it?

The center of my chest aches at the thought of his smile. The fact that nothing could happen between us, and the sheer disappointment I felt about it, was forcing itself to the forefront of my mind.

"Yes, it was! And what's this? Doodling about him?" She snags the notebook I was mindlessly drawing in off the table.

"Not about *him*." Not the full truth. "It's about everything. I just doodle." I look down at the smile doodles and differently shaped cups I drew mindlessly—a coffee cup with a small heart in the center is in plain sight for Kate to see. I shut my notebook to emphasize that it's private.

"You doodle a lot." She gives an astute observation.

"I do."

"They're cute."

"Thanks."

"Is it for fun?"

"It started that way, but over time, it became a way for me to deal with certain things, and concentrate on my clients."

"Really? That's cool!" She pulls out her Halloween binder, indicating to me we don't have to continue the conversation if I don't want to.

I'm grateful.

I haven't shared my doodles with anyone—except Liam.

Doodling was for fun in college—when I was in a mind-numbingly dull class and needed a fun way to take notes. Liam encouraged me to keep doing it, as a stress reliever, and even after everything he did, I kept doodling. My dissertation in college was a research study on the benefits of drawing, and how it positively impacts recollection and the retention of information.

I loved it so much that I implemented it in my process as a psychologist. Doodling while a client opens up is an easy way to remember what they share without feeling the pressure to jot down as many notes as possible. And avoid cramping in my hand.

"You know, doodling is actually an effortless stimulation that increases the brain's attentional capacity." I hear the nerdiness and instantly regret my babbling words.

"Interesting, like a brain exercise with your hands?" Kate asks, sounding intrigued.

"Pretty much, yeah! It's also good for stress."

"Is that another reason you do it?" she asks in a whisper.

I feel myself gawking at her unintentionally. It has been a long time since anyone asked me about my stress.

"I'm sorry, I know you don't like to share. You don't have to answer," she says quickly.

"No, it's okay." I bite my lip and click my pen a few times.

Not only are the doodles shorthand, they are my thoughts—doodled thoughts. Thoughts I am too scared to voice out loud, or accept are actually coming from my brain sometimes. They're not all bad, but when they are, the doodling is a way to put the intrusive things out there—without anyone knowing how bad they are.

Sometimes my thoughts can be hard to digest, even for myself. The scary thing about our brains and its intrusive thoughts are we don't know which thoughts will leave a lasting impression. I learned early on that something I could do to combat those dark thoughts was to create a tangible way to get rid of them. We hear about people writing letters to those they are angry at then burning them in some symbolic fashion. My doodles are like an angry letter to my brain, and instead of burning them, I doodle on sticky notes and throw them in the trash.

I decide to be brave. "I feel more at peace with my thoughts when I doodle them."

"Hey, that's great! Multipurpose doodles!"

"Exactly, it's fascinating what these little doodles do for the brain."

"Brain empowering!"

I laugh. "Definitely!"

"With how much you doodle, you probably have an Einstein-level IQ!"

We both giggle and Kate begins discussing the party planning to-do list. Is it just me or are the people here at Glendale overly nice and accepting? It has been a long time since I've felt any sense of peace around other people—specifically people who may not have mental struggles like I do. More times than not, I encounter someone who denies their own struggles or has zero interest in me sharing about mine. The stigma surrounding mental health is toxic and creates an involuntary barrier around my heart. My doodle statistics and how they help me combat my own issues are something very close to my heart and I was slowly starting to feel safe enough to share them.

"So we have two weeks until the party and you have yet to commit to a costume! Are we going as Thing 1 and 2 or what?" Kate looks at me, all business.

"Is that my only option?" I suppress the disgust that is surely creeping across my face.

I have a hunch I will be required to paint my hair blue and I am not a fan.

"That, or you dress up by yourself! I can get Malcolm to be Thing 2 no problem. I just wanted to give you the option to do it with me."

"How will you get him to dress up?" I smirk at her.

"Like this . . ." She proceeds to form tears in her eyes and look at me like I just ran over her puppy.

"Wow, bravo!" I applaud her.

"Thank you, thank you!" She gives a bow. "But seriously, do you have any ideas on what you want to be yet?"

"Not really." My mind flashes with a montage of past Halloweens—my attempts to do couples costumes and Liam refusing. Him making me fight back angry tears as he blabbers on about his disdain for the holiday and anything that resembles pumpkins.

As if she can read my mind Kate says, "He can't ruin this holiday for you anymore."

"I know." I pause and look out the window. Orange and yellow leaves are falling from the trees—the wind blowing and rustling them into sporadic piles over the school parking lot. "It's just hard to convince your brain things will be different after enduring the same experience repeatedly. Our brains predict what is going to happen based on repeated stimuli. It takes these perceptions and sets behaviors in motion based on what has happened in the past."

I stop, realizing this might not be a very fun topic for Kate. Her mantra was practically *Live, Laugh, Love* and my over-analytical brain was sure to put a damper on that.

"I'm sorry, this is such a boring conversation." I force a laugh.

"Not at all, keep going," she encourages.

"Essentially, when our brain experiences a repeated stressful event, it assumes that event will continue happening. Even if it hasn't happened in years. So for me"—I take a deep breath—"my brain correlates this time of year with the parts of a past relationship that were less than ideal."

"Like . . . PTSD?" she whispers the question like it's a secret.

"In a sense, yes. And it's hard to share that with someone because having an argumentative fiancé and broken off wedding may sound like *heaven* to someone else. Someone who may have had much worse experiences than me. It feels silly for me to put it in the same category."

"But . . . it *is* in the same category, right? Like how it affects the brain and what not?"

"Precisely. No matter how big or small the distressing experience was, our brain registers it and does everything in its power to protect us. So something as small as yearly fights at Halloween can still cause my brain to go down a crazy, never ending spiral of intrusive thoughts."

"Well maybe you need to experience something new so those old memories can fade away." She shrugs like *obviously* that will fix everything.

"Maybe."

"Maybeeeeeee, you can experience something new with a certain someone . . ." She winks and shimmies her shoulders at me.

"I know what you're getting at and I think that is the worst idea possible."

"Why? He's a great guy—the best actually!" Her affirmations about how wonderful Benny is not good for the little crush I have forming. "Party planning abilities aside, he's a nine out of ten!"

"Why not a ten?" I laugh.

"Only one man in this world is a ten, and that is Henry Cavill. Benny may be *swoony* for some, but he is no Superman."

"You make a strong case." I laugh, and a picture of Benny in a Superman suit flashes across my mind.

Quit that, Ellie.

"But really, what's wrong with seeing him outside of work?"

"I do see him outside of work! Quite often, actually."

"Not on a date, though."

"Isn't it against the rules?"

"Meh, no one will ever know!"

I roll my eyes, with how chatty the people in this school can be left me unconvinced. There is no way a date with Benny Divata would go unnoticed around here. "I highly doubt that."

"Well . . ." She pauses, a studious look in her eyes. "If you really don't plan to *work* here for much longer, what's the harm?"

She has a point.

Chapter Thirteen

Benny

Frankie is attacking my feet and meowing at me an octave higher than normal while I cook dinner—her extremely annoying and clingy nighttime routine.

Chicken adobo, my parents' recipe, is sizzling in the skillet. I'm not sure what's going on with me lately, but I feel lonely, and I miss them a little more than usual. But instead of resorting to sad takeout, I figure handling my emotions like an adult and cooking my own dinner would be the way to go.

Frankie keeps pawing and scratching my feet, completely ignoring her insanely huge cat tower standing in the living room. She knows I'm making something she isn't supposed to have and, per usual, is awaiting her offerings.

I take a piece of unseasoned chicken and toss it into the living room. "There, you naked vulture."

She scurries after it and I return to my sizzling chicken, stirring it around the pan. This is the only dish I know how to make well, aside from spaghetti, but knowing how to cook spaghetti should be a survival skill. Nothing to write home about.

I try to glaze over the pity that befalls me as I cook dinner for one, on a Friday night, for the one thousandth Friday in a row.

As I prepare my plate, a notification *dings* on my phone. Of course, Frankie is laying her fat gut on top of my phone so I ignore the sound and continue focusing on dinner. Then I hear another *ding*.

Then another.

Then it starts to ring.

It's almost 11 p.m., who is calling me?

"Hello? Hellooooo?" A voice comes from the phone.

I pray it's not Facetime and they aren't getting a big fat view of Frankie's underside as she stays plopped atop the screen.

I walk over to the voice and reach to move Frankie off the phone, getting attacked and hissed at in doing so. "Will you get off?" I nudge her over and snag the phone before she stretches her huge stomach back over it.

"Hello?" I say, answering the unknown number.

"Mr. B? It's Garrett." His voice is shaky.

"Mr. Connors, why are you calling me so late? What's going on?"

"Mr. B, it's Devon. You need to get here fast!"

At the same time Garrett is talking to me, I get a notification from Kate.

Kate

Heard there was a busted party at Charlie Hender's house. Devon was there???

"Garrett, send me the address and I'll head that way." I hang up the phone, turn the stove off, and throw on my jacket. I text Kate back and head to my truck.

Connors called, I'm heading there now.

Kate

Need me to come?

I don't think so

Kate

Will you be ok?

Yeah, just stay by your phone

The drive is going to take me about thirty minutes and for the first time in a long time I feel a surge of worry. It all looks a little too familiar, a time I drove late at night from a party flashes across my mind.

Sir, have you been drinking?

Why don't you step out of the car?

It's been five years since the accident and yet, I feel weighed down in my truck thinking about it.

I've broken up underage parties in the past. These kids are ruthless, and I seem to be the one they would always call when it got out of hand. It's nice to feel trusted, but I am very aware of the lack of boundaries I have set for myself since they think they can call me to bail them out.

I'm still a few miles away when my phone starts to ring . . . Ellie is calling.

"This is Benny," I answer, assuming she knows what's going on.

"Hey! What are you doing?"

Did she not know? If she didn't, why was she calling me this late?

"I'm headed to break up a party. What are you doing?"

"Oh really? Kate said there was something going on. I didn't know you were the one they called." Her voice sounds quiet, and soothing. The tension in my back loosens and my grip on the steering wheel releases as I listen to her. She has this grounding power for me and I didn't even realize I needed it.

"It seems I am. Lucky me, huh?" I laugh.

"Do the cops get called?"

"Sometimes, only when it gets really bad. They figure they can call me before it gets too far, I guess."

"Do you need any company?"

"That's alright, I'm almost there." I refrain from telling her I want her company more than anything.

"Okay, well keep me updated. I can come out there if you need me."

"Thanks. Talk tomorrow?"

"Tonight. Call me after, I want to talk to you." It might be my wishful thinking, but I hear a smile in her voice as she says *"you."*

The smile stretches across my face like a child at Christmas at the thought of talking to her more.

"As you wish," I say before hanging up the phone.

The split-second phone call has me in a whimsical haze. Just hearing her voice for a moment lifts my spirits. This is either a very good thing, or a very bad thing, and I'm afraid to think too much about it.

Pulling down a long gravel driveway, on a large acre of land, I see a large brick house with kids everywhere. Cars are parked every which way in the yard and beer bottles, red solo cups, and other paraphernalia are scattered on the ground.

Meanwhile, the kids are drinking, laughing, some dancing, and acting like this night was never going to end.

"It's almost midnight," I grumble to myself.

The party usually disperses when they know an adult shows up, but they are unphased when I pull up.

Do they know I was called?

I sit in my truck for a moment, scanning the crowd to see who's here. Birdie and her cheerleader friends are standing on the deck, a group of baseball players are playing cornhole, Ethan Blake is standing by a keg with the other football players, but I don't see Garrett anywhere, or Devon.

I climb out of the truck and Birdie clocks me fast.

As if I didn't witness everything, she throws her drink over to the side of the house and yells, "Mr. B, what's up!" Signaling my arrival to the others.

In an instant, the students simultaneously pour drinks out, stomp out their rolls, and kick trash away from their path in an attempt to hide the evidence. Some even mosey on to their cars and go to leave.

"Where's Garrett?"

A few of them look around like they are hiding something, and no one answers my question.

"Alright, we can make this easy. Someone tell me where Garrett is, and I don't need to make a phone call."

"Man, we don't know where they went," Ethan says with a shrug.

"How long have they been gone?"

"Devon got into it with Travis, bad. Garrett broke it up and they left!" Birdie yells at me—the cheerleaders all nod in agreement.

I walk over to Ethan, knowing he will know what happened. He looks at me with a smug smile and I feel the very rare urge to punch one of my students in the face.

"Where are they?" I resist the urge to clench my fists and try to maintain my composure while he just smirks at me in response. I look at the other guys standing with him and throw my arms out to the side, silently asking, "*Well?*"

"Travis pissed him off . . ." Charlie, one of the baseball players, walks over and whispers, "They loaded him in the car and left. I think to take him home."

I pat Charlie on the shoulder as a thanks and pull my phone out, dialing a number. I have a hunch I know where they are going. "I'm giving you all an hour to get this cleaned up and go home, then I'm calling the cops. Got it?" I shout at all of them, but fix my gaze on Ethan, the instigator and obvious leader of this pack. Most of these kids are eighteen or older or hit this party scene often so my threat probably wasn't effective.

But I'm going to call the cops anyway.

Heading back to my truck, I press call on the number I dialed.

The call is answered after one ring. "They just got here, hurry up."

"I'm on my way."

Driving away from the house, I text Ellie:

> Things are worse than I thought, raincheck on the call?

Eleanor

> Of course, do you need anything?

> Just a prayer I don't strangle any of these kids

Eleanor

> I'm here if you need me!

> <3

I'm speeding now and don't have time to overthink the fact that I just sent Ellie a heart emoji. Or that I want to fill her in on every little thing that has run through my mind today, and how she's one of the things primarily keeping my mind occupied. I'm also trying not to think about the fact that this night is bringing back some dark memories for me and I want her to hold my hand and help me through it.

And I'm definitely *not* thinking about how I want her here with me more than anyone.

Denial only gets us so far though, and the drive isn't nearly enough time to finally admit to myself that I really like this girl. It's about five minutes into the drive that I accept this isn't just a small crush, but that I really like her.

I resist the urge to text her, while I'm speeding ten over the speed limit, to tell her I want her to meet me, but there's the whole I'm-her-boss thing I have to figure out. I like her, yes, but do I like her enough to lose my job? Or cost her hers? No.

But, isn't she planning on leaving in a few months, anyway?

Yes. She's still leaving.

Wait, that's not good. I don't want her to leave. I want her here with me.

What if she doesn't like me that way? And she still plans to leave? I can't admit my feelings, make it awkward, then get no time with her before she goes back to her life. No way. I would rather have every second with her before that than none at all. I'd rather be close enough to Eleanor to just have her in my life than on the outside and not have her in any part of it. Admitting my feelings could push her away.

Sometime along the drive my internal thoughts became actual words and I find that I'm talking to myself like a crazy person. "*Thinking out loud*," as my mom used to call it. I was so enraptured with my own thoughts that I didn't see the car behind me as I back into the spot.

I rear end the bumper, *hard*, and bend it in.

I mumble profanities as I climb out of my truck.

It's an overly nice sports car parked right in front of Wafflin'.

Fantastic.

I throw my head back in frustration, feeling way too frazzled to leave a note. I snap a picture of the license plate and run inside the diner. I'll look up the owner later.

It's the active bar scene now—legal-drinking-age people chatting and laughing. I weave my way through the booths and meet Sam, the owner, at the bar.

"Thanks for coming, they're in the back."

"Thank you, Sam." I pat his back and cross behind the bar into the back room.

The back-room light flickering, barely lighting the room. In the center there is a couch where I see Travis—laying there, knocked out—his face bloodied and eyes starting to swell. Garrett's sitting on the floor next to the couch, Devon is in the back of the room pacing.

"About time." Malcolm meets me at the door.

"What happened?" I whisper.

"The two got into it over something. Travis was drunk. I was heading home when I saw them pull-up in the back."

"Thank you, Malcolm. Has anyone called Naomi?"

"No!" Devon yelled at us.

"DJ, we have to call your mom. You are a minor, and you assaulted someone."

"He got mouthy and tried hitting me first! And he was *drunk*, what was I supposed to do?"

"Travis started it, Mr. B. I saw the whole thing. And D hasn't drank anything, we're sober! Travis is drunk off his ass," Garrett says, using the couch to stand on his bad leg.

"I don't care who did what. You are all underage, at a party with *alcohol*, it is my responsibility to call someone."

"I already called her, no answer," Malcolm says.

Sam walks in from the bar. "The doc is here. He'll look over Travis."

Dr. Steven Jones walks in behind Sam, wearing scrubs and carrying a dark green backpack, with a stethoscope draped over one shoulder. He walks over to Malcolm and I, shaking our hands.

"Long time, no see, Mr. Divata, Mr. Geer."

"Thanks for coming," Sam says. "I need you to check him out. Make sure he's not dying so I can kill him myself."

Steven laughs. "Please wait until I leave. I don't want to be an accomplice."

"Same," Malcolm grumbles.

Steven walks over to Travis before putting on gloves, and then starts examining him—opening his eyes, checking his pulse, listening to his chest. Garrett hovers over the couch, balancing on his good leg while Devon backs up against the wall, arms crossed. They both watch anxiously as Steven does different maneuvers to assess the state of Travis.

"He's going to be fine. He may have re-broken his nose though," Steven says, taking off his gloves. Devon and Garrett both let out a big sigh of relief.

"I'm not paying to fix it this time," Sam says standing in the doorway.

"You're his guardian, correct?" Steven asks.

"Unfortunately." Sam rolls his eyes. "Fart wad's my nephew."

"He may have a concussion. You'll need to monitor for vomiting and confusion. Ice his face and tell him to lay off the peppermint vodka."

"Seriously, I can smell it from here." Malcolm rubs his nose.

"Thanks for coming, Dr. Jones," I say, shaking his hand.

"Not a problem, and please, call me Steven." He grins.

Malcolm rolls his eyes. I smile and nod as he leaves.

"Alright, are you guys good? You need a ride?" Sam asks Garrett and Devon.

"I think we're okay, I can drop him off on my way home." Garrett starts putting on his jacket. "Sorry about all of this."

"You're not the one who needs to apologize," Malcolm says, staring at Devon.

Devon doesn't say anything as he walks up to Sam and shakes his hand. Sam accepts it and nods—a mutual understanding in their unspoken words. Devon rushes out the door, without saying a word to Malcolm or I. Garrett fist bumps my arm as they leave.

"Sam, I'm so sorry—"

"Ben, don't. You are not responsible for these boys. They make their own decisions and they gotta deal with the consequences. I try to tell this idiot that all time," Sam says, throwing a blanket on top of Travis.

"He's right." Malcolm pipes in. "You gotta quit letting these kids make you feel like you owe them anything."

"I know, I just remember being a dumb kid and making one mistake that had a lasting impact. I hate to see that happen to them." My voice cracks at my own memories.

"That was a long time ago, Ben. You've paid your dues." Sam pats me on the shoulder. "You learned from your mistakes, they will too. They have to."

Malcolm and I say our goodbyes to Sam and weave back through the crowd. "What are we going to do about DJ? He won't listen to any of us," I say.

"He'll come to his senses eventually, they always do. Use this as a teachable moment."

"How can it be a teachable moment if he doesn't want to learn?" I ask, irritated. "You're the *teacher*, help me figure this out!"

"Coming from a teacher-turned-vice principal? You don't need my help."

We walk out of Wafflin' to the parking lot. As we approach our cars, I see a note left on my windshield. I pinch the bridge of my nose, probably hate mail from the car I hit.

"Looks like someone left ya somethin'," Malcolm says, grabbing the note. "Secret admirer, huh?"

"Doubtful." I snag the note from his hands. "I'll see you in the morning."

Malcolm chuckles and heads to his truck. I wince at the piece of paper in my hand, afraid to read the angry words someone more than likely left behind for me. I probably deserve it though. Should've left a note or insurance information but these kids had me flustered. Now I'm the jerk who hit a car and ran.

Relief washes over me when I read the note:

You owe me a bumper. Come over for dinner sometime and we'll call it even. – Steven

Chapter Fourteen

Ellie

"What do you mean, you got rear-ended?" Emma's pacing the kitchen floor in her classy silk pajamas and fuzzy robe. The contrast to my oversized t-shirt and plaid fleece pants was astounding. She truly is a doctor's wife, and I am a potato.

"Why were you at Wafflin' after work anyway?" She's visibly irritated at Steven, but I also sense some anxiety peeking through.

"Em, sit down. Let him explain." I pat the seat next to me.

Steven looks at me with grateful eyes and I fight back the urge to snap at him. *I'm doing this for her, not you.*

I just smile instead. "Go on."

"I got a call about someone needing to be checked out. It was on my way home from the hospital. It was late on a Friday night, anything is bound to happen." He shrugs off her anxiety.

"That's my point! Anything can happen! *You* could have been hit"—*stretching here, Em*—"not just the bumper," she whispers, bouncing her leg and fidgeting with the tie on her robe.

"But honey, I wasn't. I'm fine." Steven sits across from Em, reaching out his hand. She takes it and her legs stop bouncing. I may have my issues with Steven, but he does have a knack for keeping her anxiety at bay. "And I left the driver a note to come by sometime."

"What?" she says, incredulously.

Alright, maybe Steven is also a *trigger* for her anxiety sometimes.

"Why would you invite a stranger who *hit* your *car* to our house? What if it was intentional?" She stands up, pacing again—hysterical.

"I promise you, it wasn't intentional. I think the gentleman will be by this evening," he says, smiling. I'm not sure what Steven is scheming but there must be other ways to do whatever he's planning, without throwing my sister into a fit.

"Why would I want a complete stranger in my house? What are you going to do, exchange insurance in our *driveway*?"

"No, I figured he could stay for dinner."

"Dinner?" I ask.

"Why not?" Steven shrugs.

"You are a crazy man!" Emma yells and storms out.

"Honey . . ." He follows her.

Part of me is surprised Steven would invite a complete stranger over for dinner. The people he encounters at his job, working in the biggest emergency room in the city, can be quite alarming. Why risk a stranger coming to your home? He told me about a schizophrenic patient who ripped out his IV, ran from his room to where he was seated, and tried pinning him to the ground. The man was off his medications and homicidal, it was a miracle he wasn't injured. Luckily Steven is a big guy, with a lineman stature, so he can definitely hold his own. Emma, of course, has no idea this happened. This was one of those rare occurrences where Steven felt compelled to share a work story with me based on the common denominator of mental health concerns. I've had my fair share of patients with uncontrolled schizophrenia, and sharing in those traumatic instances with my brother-in-law eases the blow that is our rocky relationship.

I sit in the kitchen, taking in the calmness of the morning. It's a rare sight in the Jones home. Their kitchen is your stereotypical modernized kitchen, with wood cabinets painted off-white, gray marble countertops, and a variety of cheesy kitchen decor that reminds you of your grandma.

Plus, there's scattered fall decorations in each corner, pumpkin-scented candles, and a lettered sign that says, *"72 days until Christmas."* It isn't really my style but it is my sister's through and through.

"Ellie! Ellie! Do you want to see my new dinosaur?" Gargoyle One yells as he plows into the kitchen.

"Sure." *This better be a realistic dinosaur.*

He holds up an orange, spotted dinosaur with googly eyes—it's hideous.

"How cool!" I say in the most unconvincing tone.

He runs off snickering and collides with Gargoyle Two in another room. I take a deep breath, reminding myself to be patient with the small, innocent humans who drive me bananas.

A notification pops up on my phone . . . *Benny.*

Benny

> Hey! Sorry I didn't get back to you yesterday. Did you still need to talk?

My cheeks feel tight as I try to suppress a smile. Seeing his name pop up on my phone makes me feel some type of way. I shake my body out at the giddiness trying to bubble up and shove those feelings to the back of my mind.

> Hey! That's ok!

Benny

> Did you want to talk today?

I really do—about what though? Where is this persistent desire to talk to Benny coming from? Why am I picturing his face every time I see something that makes me happy? And why am I feeling this weird weight in my chest over the realization that I won't be around him every day in a few months? Yes, he is attractive. And kind. And funny. And his lips—God, I want to press them against my lips. But it feels more than that.

My boundaries are usually pretty solid, and even when I find someone attractive, I've had no issue finding something wrong with them.

But for some reason, with Benny, I can't. Which is *not* a good thing. I can't catch feelings for my *boss*.

> Yes! Are you free tonight?

Benny

> I'll be at dinner, maybe we can find a time to chat after?

> Oh gotcha! Maybe another time!

Benny

> Fingers crossed :)

Dinner? Did he have a date? *Not that it matters, Eleanor.*

Ending the conversation with Benny, I stare out the window and take in the view. The tapestry of green and yellow leaves hovering over the side of the house, a slight crispness in the air. Fall really is a magical time—a season of transition. This time of year was always a positive one at the clinic, witnessing substantial progress with a client and their healing journey before the gloomy winter hits. Seasonal changes have such a profound impact on our brains.

But unfortunately, during this particular season at Glendale, the progress was minimal. It's understandable, these students don't know me and they're aware I won't be here long.

I remind myself of the potential job openings back in New York, open my phone, and start scrolling. Some viable options pop-up and I email myself the link so I can look at them later. Checking for the email from myself, I scroll through my inbox to start deleting junk mail when I see one from a recognizable user . . .

drliam.peters@outlook.com

A hot rage boils in my chest and without even thinking I chuck my phone across the kitchen, watching it hit the side of a cabinet, before shattering, and falling to the floor in multiple pieces. I drop myself to the floor, feeling like gravity has pulled me down by my shoulders. I stare at the mess, internally screaming every profanity I can think of.

"Is everything alright?" Steven comes rushing into the kitchen. "I heard something."

He walks towards me, stepping on phone pieces as he kneels so he's eye level with me.

"Ellie, what's wrong?" He hands me a napkin and in that moment I realize I'm crying. For the first time in almost a year, my body is creating a physical response to emotional stimuli that isn't *only* breaking something. My tears are faint at first, then realization washes over me and I start to sob—uncontrollable, body heaving, sobs. I've been highly aware of my lack of emotional response lately and the inability to cry has been concerning. I have done everything I can think of to have a good cry, I even watched *Marley and Me* and . . . nothing. Crying is a safety valve, and mine has been broken. Not only does it alleviate stress, it maintains homeostasis and, based on my constant doodling and breaking stuff, my homeostasis is out of whack. Crying is an essential coping mechanism and I'm actually doing it.

I sob for a few more minutes, and gradually start to slow down my thoughts.

Why am I crying? *Because I'm mad.*

Why am I mad? *Because Liam emailed me.*

Why did he email me? *I don't know, my phone is broken.*

I work through the question train I use with my clients, timed breathing on each answer. My sobs slow back down and I compose myself enough to speak.

"Liam . . ." I quiver. "Emailed me."

"Oh." Steven sits on the ground beside me. "What did he say?"

"I don't know . . ." *Sniff.* "I threw my phone."

"I see." He wraps an arm around my shoulders and squeezes once.

"Have you talked to him?" I wipe my nose and hide the snot rag in my hand.

"Not in a few weeks, no."

Emma walks in, noting the massacre to my phone and the dent it left in her cabinet. "What's going on?" she asks, her eyebrows furrowing at the mess.

"Liam emailed Ellie," Steven says solemnly, patting my back as he hands me another tissue.

"What! Why? What did he say?" She rushes to my side and pulls me in for a hug.

"I don't know, I threw my phone before opening it," I say, hugging her back.

"Are you alright?"

"I am. Had myself a good cry about it," I say, giving Steven a smile.

He smiles back, with a hint of sadness in his eyes. I chalk that up to the damage I have caused to his precious oak cabinet and refuse to think it's because he feels bad for me. *Don't pity me. I am handling all of this fine.*

"I see. Well, let's refrain from breaking anything else, alright? That's what the art is for."

"Of course, the *healing* art," I joke.

We both laugh as Steven leaves to check on his spawn—*children.*

"Are you sure you're okay? Breaking your phone seems a bit . . ." Emma trails off as she pushes a hair out of my face.

"Psychotic . . ." I whisper, confirming what she's thinking. "I know. I'm working on it."

"I know you are. How can I help?"

"Hide all your glassware?" Wincing at my painful attempt at a joke.

"Not a chance, it's a focal point in here." She waves at her kitchen. The space was so bright, with monochromatic tones of white and gray—a very minimalistic look. But the glassware that sits in the open view cabinets is a vintage china set with purple flowers and gold trim. In any other home, it might seem like it clashes with the space, but Emma is an artistic master-mind. She combines things you wouldn't consider working well together and turns them into something beautiful and authentic. It's why she's such a good art teacher, she encourages her students to go against the grain and push limits with what is expected in art—bringing their own originality to it.

"Of course," I say waving towards the kitchen the same way.

"Do you want to run to the store with me? I have to get stuff for dinner tonight," she says, standing to her feet.

"Ah, dinner with the stranger, huh?"

"Not really a stranger," she says, smiling. "You can come with me to get stuff."

"Do I *have* to?" Not that I don't want to help Emma prepare dinner for this mystery person, I have a long list of things to do—getting a new phone now at the top of the list.

"No, you do not." She chuckles.

"Great, then no. But I would love to help tonight!"

"You better, or you get scraps." She pats my hand and turns to clean up the phone pieces. "Do yourself a favor and get a sturdy case for next time."

"Sure hope there won't be a next time." I laugh.

Scouring the internet for jobs isn't all it's cracked up to be. I spend a few hours going through the repetitive motions of filling out the application, attaching a resume, and questioning if the job is even worth the hassle, then deleting the thing all together. After the revolving door of tasks, I end up applying to only one prospective job.

I'm so productive.

Closing my laptop, I take that single application as a win that I actually applied to something. For some reason, I have kept putting the job search off. A few months ago I was itching to get back to New York, but the more time I spend here, at Glendale specifically, the more hesitancy I have to go back.

Did I intend on the time and money I spent on my education to be used for a guidance counselor position? No.

But am I starting to enjoy the job, and the people it has put in my life? A little.

At that, I pull up my email, and completely disregard the email from *drliam.peters@outlook.com.*

I'll tackle that when I feel more stable.

I see an email informing me that I have missed notifications from the faculty group messenger. Opening it, I see the topic of discussion:

End of Term Block Party

Another party? How many does this school need? It's not a fraternity.

Glendale Faculty
End of Term Block Party!!

8:28am

MGeer:
I refuse to do the dunk tank again. It's Divata's turn.

BDivata:
You know I'll do it. But that leaves an opening
for the pie throwing (:

KStanley:
Just do both, Ben. Malcolm will be busy judging
the bake sale.

MGeer:
The most important job.

EJones:
Is Patsy going to make it back? She said she will do the bake sale!
- Emma

MGeer:
NO, bake sale is mine

KStanley:
FIGHT TO THE DEATH

BDivata:
Malcolm, you and Pat can both do the bake sale. It's probably
best for your blood sugar anyway (:

MGeer:
Keep my health outta this. You got a cat for that

KStanley:
BAHAHAHA!!

EJones:
Lol!
- Emma

Let it be said, Glendale has a faculty of over forty teachers and this thread has every single one of them attached, with only these four knuckle heads responding. With an occasional smiley face from Bill, the Janitor.

Glendale Faculty
End of Term Block Party!!

9:17am

EBailey:
I'll do the pie contest if you need someone :)

KStanley:
Girlllllll, you are the BEST!

BDivata:
You are too kind, Ellie (:

MGeer:
Sucker.

EBailey:
Consider it a farewell gift!

KStanley:
:(

EBailey:
Sorry! :(

KStanley:
Why haven't you texted me back?!

EBailey:
Phone broke!

EJones:
Ha!
- Emma

KStanley:
Well come over on your way to get a new one! Dolly misses ya!

EBailey:
I miss her!

The affection I have for the kooky people of Glendale High fills me with some comfort. It's been a long time since I felt this way about friends. Not that my New York friends aren't great, because they are . . . in their own way. There is just a vast difference between the people I willingly left in New York, and the people here that have seemed to wedge themselves into my life. Something in my stomach churns when the thought of leaving them crosses my mind.

Leaving New York was one of the easiest things I had done in a while, and not speaking to those old friends hasn't even phased me. I can't even remember the last time I had a full conversation with one of them, and their attempts at maintaining a friendship with me fizzled quickly after the move. That's probably my own fault, but a part of me isn't even sad about it. But the sadness I feel over leaving Glendale . . . Kate, her constant meme sharing in three different conversations, Malcolm and his courtesy vegetables, and not being this physically close to Emma anymore.

Benny . . . My breath catches at the thought of not seeing him every day.

I start doodling their faces. Amateur level of course, I'm no Picasso or Cindy Ras.

Kate with her bouncy curls and cheek dimples, Malcolm with his pristine beard and scowl, Emma and her sleek ponytail, art brush behind her ear, and Benny . . . his dark, kind eyes, and joyful smile. I draw and erase his hair a million different times—giving up because it's impossible to recreate the soft curl on the edge. I draw a backwards cap and my insides melt.

A direct message pops up on my screen from BDivata.

 **Direct Messenger**

9:21 am

BDivata:
No phone, huh?

EBailey:
Just for now. Going to get a new one!

BDivata:
Good! Can't imagine not being able to reach you outside of school (:

EBailey:
That would be devastating, huh? Haha!

BDivata:
You have no idea.

EBailey:
Gotta run, text you later?

BDivata:
Please do (:

EBailey:
Send me something to look forward to!

BDivata:
As you wish (:

EBailey:
Words after my own heart 🤍

Smiling, I exit the messenger and play the movie *Princess Bride* in my head. Scrolling through the rest of my emails, I finally land on Liam's—hesitancy prickling at my fingertips as I open it.

Eleanor,

Can we talk?

Dr. Liam Peters, DO
Psychiatry Associates, LLC
New York, New York

The hesitation is gone quicker than it came as I delete the email. Why would he want to talk to me? Hasn't he done enough to me? I uprooted my life because of him and he has the audacity to reach out to me? He of all people should know the kind of trigger he can be to someone's mental state after what he pulled. The hot, boiling rage is back as I slam my laptop.

I feel my thoughts spiraling and suppress the urge to frisbee throw my laptop across the loft. I only have the margin to buy one new electronic device today.

I work through the exercises I have with clients.

I already identified the emotion I'm feeling: burning fury.

I know what made me feel this way: Liam's email.

And I know my response: not responding.

The questions that hover in my mind over his email are pushed to the back and locked up. I recite to myself, *nothing good comes from overthinking,* out loud. I use this phrase with my clients when they demand answers, whether it be from a partner or an assailant, or just their own minds. When we are emotionally taxed and going down a path of toxic thoughts, nothing good comes when we overthink every aspect. Why does a partner want to confront a situation? Why does the assailant want to seek retribution? Why is our brain questioning our ability to handle the situation? It's easiest to spiral down with negative assumptions—the partner wants to validate themselves, the assailant feels no remorse and wants you to know it—your spiraling brain doesn't always operate in favor of your benefit. The hope we have for resolution, in any scenario, is thwarted by our own thoughts. Overthinking kills hope.

Overthinking and refusing to hone in on what I could do to let it go, I crumple up my doodles and leave.

My anger was so pent up and I felt like a hawk, refusing to release it from my talons as I swirled in the sky looking down at my future. Just holding on tight to what is hindering me from looking forward to the what if's. Good or bad, I don't know what is ahead of me, and I'm not allowing myself to be open-handed with the possibilities. I know this, yet I'm still refusing to just *try* and work through my anger—like a temperamental child. I am no better than my nephew-minions when they get told they can't jump out of a moving vehicle.

I also haven't found a therapist locally, yet. That would probably help but I may as well keep on with my self-sabotaging, *right?*

On the way back from the phone store, I power up my phone and a slew of messages come through. Multiple from Emma, a couple from Kate, and then Benny. Ignoring the gals' texts, I open Benny's immediately.

The thread is welcomed with a funny meme with Inigo Montoya, another with Westley, a picture of Frankie napping, a picture of Frankie stretching, and then, my favorite of all, a selfie of himself with Frankie peeking behind his shoulder. There's no way I can hide the smile that's plastered on my face. I set the last picture as his contact photo, then tell him how good Frankie looks in the sunlight—resting on his shoulder like he's her personal human perch.

He texts back immediately and the giddy feeling it gives me is borderline gross. I think about my students and the recent scenarios I've had to endure in our sessions. *Does he like me? Does he like me not? Why would they do this if they felt this?* On and on and on. It's maddening at times.

But now . . . those questions are circling my own brain as I text Benny. I am hyper-focused on each punctuation, response time, even the tone of a text. The tone. As if I can fully interpret each minuet detail within the little words on my screen. My responses are just as bad. Overthinking each word or phrase. *Am I being funny? Flirty? Annoying?*

I don't even know anymore. But I do know for sure one thing I'm being . . . a hypocrite.

No . . . worse.

I'm being a teenager. *God, help me.*

A very, tiny part of me is being rational, questioning why I am allowing this to continue. But that teeny part is shoved out of the way by the large, pulsing part of my brain that likes this guy.

We text back and forth throughout the day, sharing memes, gifs, and being flat out flirtatious. I just have to call it what it is, Benny has been flirting with me and I have been more than reciprocating. It feels easy and natural to be on this level with him, and I have a strong gut feeling that he isn't this way with just anyone. I mean, Kate made it apparent that the man is practically a monk with how rarely he dates. Even Sarah Kim was telling me he's been single for "like a century," although it's hard to imagine why.

I have my phone attached to my hip until it's time for dinner with our mystery hit-and-run guest. Instead of helping set the table, I am leaning against it, giggling at my phone. Again, like a child.

Meanwhile, Emma is rushing around the kitchen like her life depends on it when she snaps at me, "Either help or get out of my kitchen!"

Startled and terrified, I shove my phone in my pocket and begin setting the table. "I'm sorry! What else can I do?"

"Go get dressed."

Looking down at my high waisted black jeans and oversized Halloween-town t-shirt I've tucked in I say, "I am dressed. Do you not like it?"

"Trust me, you'll want to freshen up," she says as she pulls a dish out of the oven.

"I don't think I need to impress this mystery hit-and-run driver, but thanks."

"Just change! At least put on a different shirt." She rolls her eyes so far back I was afraid she'd lose them back there.

"Alright, fine . . ."

I rush upstairs and ransack my room to try and find a suitable top that would meet Emma's approval. With no luck, I ransack *her* closet and find a red, off-the-shoulder sweater. Cutting my losses, I throw it on praying it fits, and it does. One last touch up in the mirror and I hear the doorbell. Maybe it was the spooky season, or the loss of sunlight, or the dinner situation as a whole, but panic runs through my veins with the idea of a complete stranger coming into our home. On instinct, as I head downstairs to meet the guest, I grab a small metal bookend from a hallway shelf and hold it tight against my back. *Always be prepared.*

Another doorbell ding. *Impatient much?*

"Ellie, can you get that?" Emma yells from the kitchen.

Heading to the front door, I grip the bookend tight against my side ready to strike and swing the door open.

CHAPTER FIFTEEN

Benny

It's not every night I'm greeted at the door by a charming, beautiful woman, holding a metal triangle over her head, yelling, "Back off, bozo!"

If I could have snapped a picture without seeming too weird, I would have done it.

Usually, this would be alarming and I probably would have high-tailed it back to the truck. But I just stood there, gaping at Ellie and her adorable attempt at intimidation.

"Oh my gosh, Benny!" She drops the weapon. "I'm sorry, I thought you were the hit-and-runner."

Her face is as red as her sweater as she bites her lip in embarrassment. Again, *adorable*.

"Umm . . . I am, actually." Biting my own lip in embarrassment. "I brought these as a peace offering!" Holding up the bouquet of flowers and bottle of wine. They were last minute decisions on the drive over and by the looks of the wilted leaves and flaky wrapping paper, Ellie can probably tell. But she doesn't say anything.

"They're beautiful!" She takes them and hugs me.

I hug her back and refuse to be the first one to release. So we just stand there, hugging. It's just a moment, hugging in the cool air under a porch light, but I feel it happen in slow motion. My heartbeat picks up, feeling hers against my chest, the wind blowing her long hair into my face. The smell is intoxicating.

"Benny! You made it!" Steven says, coming to the door.

Ellie releases from our hug, but lingers at my side. Like she wants to stay there.

"Steven, hey. This is for you." I hand him the bottle of wine, hoping it's up to a doctor's standards.

He takes the bottle and shakes my hand. "Thanks, man! Come on in, dinner is ready."

We follow Steven inside and Ellie whispers, "Don't worry, you picked a good wine, and they're big wine people."

I jokingly wipe my forehead. "Whew, thank God. If not I may as well just leave now."

She laughs. "Please don't! Oh, and Emma will love the flowers."

"They're for you, actually." My face gets warm, unsure if admitting that was the right move.

"Really?" She stops to look at me, then looks down at the flowers. "They're perfect."

I deflate with relief. "It isn't too weird that I brought my employee flowers?"

"Just a normal amount of weird." She winks.

"Benny! Welcome! We're so glad you could make it," Emma says, hugging me in the kitchen.

"It was the least I could do since Steven isn't suing me."

"Nonsense, it was barely anything. Easy fix," Steven says.

"Here, have a seat, I have plates ready!" Emma says, directing me to the kitchen table.

Ellie hooks her arm around mine and guides me to the table, sitting right next to me. It feels like she's shaking under my arm, but she's warm so it's not because she's cold. Is she *nervous?* I'm the one who should be nervous. I'm having dinner with her and her family. This is more than coworker territory. I'm not upset about the closeness by any means but what does it *mean*? Is she just being friendly? Maybe this is how she is around all of her friends and I'm too smitten to think of it as anything but attracted affection. Because surely she isn't interested in me . . . *that* way. I am suffocating in my own feelings. Beads of sweat start to build-up on the back of my neck as I start to overthink everything I have ever done that has led me to this point in my life.

"So, how's the kid doing? Talk to Sam today?" Steven asks, sitting across from us.

A topic to focus on, good. "He's doing okay, Sam said he woke up with a headache and two black eyes but nothing out of the ordinary." I shift in my seat to not lean in towards Ellie too much.

She shifts her legs toward me. *What do I do?*

"That's good. Did Ms. Johnson get a hold of Devon?" Steven chuckles.

"Haven't heard, but I wouldn't be surprised if she did. I'm sure we will find out Monday." We both laugh, as Emma pours us water.

"Honey, can you help me with the plates?" she asks Steven as she walks back to the kitchen island. He follows her and leaves me sitting with Ellie.

I glance towards her out of the corner of my eye and she does the same. I readjust to face her, setting my arm on the back of her chair. I can't help but turn my body towards her, she's like a magnet, pulling me in. She leans against my arm, turning her body towards me, our knees touching, jolting a shock through my body. I let out a sigh and her pupils dilate in response.

Breathtaking.

"Your eyes remind me of palm trees," I say, staring at them.

She smiles. "Is that a good thing?"

"I think so. I love palm trees."

Her cheeks flush and bunch up at my words. "They are pretty green aren't they?" She tilts her head back, playfully widening her eyes and fluttering her eyelashes at me.

"Very pretty."

I gaze over every inch of her face, mesmerized. I don't know why but I feel the need to commit everything I see to memory. Her eyes, the little wrinkles at the corners, the faint freckles on her nose, the way her eyebrow twitches slightly when she smiles.

Attempting to be subtle fails me when my eyes drift down to her lips and linger. She's not wearing anything on them and they're perfect. They look delicate . . . and soft . . . She bites her lip, very aware that I am staring at them. I could kiss her right now and have no regrets.

Except maybe the fact that she won't reciprocate.

And then it's weird.

And then I'm that creepy boss who kissed his employee.

Then I'm fired.

I let out a sigh and it sounds like a whimper. Unsure how to respond, sending unease surging through my body. I need to reorient my focus so I don't lean down and kiss her right here in the middle of her sister's kitchen . . .

"Food's ready!" Emma calls from the kitchen.

Thank God.

Ellie smiles and pats my knee before heading to the kitchen. I take a second, breathe in slowly, and rub the tension out of the back of my neck as I follow.

Dinner ends up being one of the best nights I've had outside of work—with work people—in a long time. Emma and Ellie share childhood memories and embarrassing stories. Steven and I talk about sports and my current search for an assistant football coach. It felt natural, which was interesting since Steven always seemed very closed-off every other time I've been around him.

About half way through the night, we migrated to their back porch and lit a fire on a fancy stone table. Their house backs up to a large wooded area, no other houses in sight. Emma and Steven started sipping wine and eventually found themselves to be a little tipsy and giggling. The realization that her boss was sitting across from her was lost when she toppled herself onto her husband's lap and planted one on him. And he didn't seem to care that I was there either. They were so consumed with each other for a bit, I felt the need to give them some privacy. Leaning back against the couch I've been sitting on, I tilt my head up and watch the stars.

"If this makes you uncomfy, wait until they turn the music on," Ellie's whisper comes from behind, her sweet breath tickling a soft spot on my neck. Didn't realize that was a sensitive area until now, thanks to the pulsing sensation it sent down my body.

"Just signal to me when it's coming and I'll fake an emergency," I whisper.

"Emergency enough for both of us, right?"

I turn to face her, stunned by her smile sparkling in the firelight. "Of course."

She beams at me, and I summon the courage to pat the seat next to me. She sits next to me, pulling a blanket with her and draping it over our legs.

"You know, it's nice to have another guy around here!" Steven shouts coming up for air from his Emma bubble.

"Isn't it? And it sure has made Ellie happy! She has been such a downer lately too!" Emma says laughing.

"I have not," Ellie whispers next to me.

"Yes, you have! Liam messed you up big time! Like he sucked all of the life out of you when he left."

I take a sip of my water as I glance down at Ellie. Her leg bouncing up and down next to mine. I can tell she's uncomfortable as she fidgets with the tag on the blanket.

"Can we not?" She eyes her sister then back to the blanket. There's a sadness to her voice and it guts me.

"I'm just saying, he was a douche and he wrecked you!" Emma says, shrugging.

The bouncing in her leg speeds up as Emma and Steven start talking about Liam, whoever that is. I impulsively reach over to place my hand on her knee and look at her . . . *You're okay* . . . I hold it there, tracing the inseam of her jeans with my thumb. *I'm here.* Her knee slows down as she looks at my hand then at me, a "thank you" in her eyes, I think.

I pull the blanket up and wrap us both up. Trying to respect her boundaries, I leave a small space between us, but she closes it without hesitation. I let out a breath of relief and lean back on the couch, the rigidness of my shoulders softening. And as if Ellie was tightened up like a spring too, she uncoils, relaxing herself into me as she leans over and rests her head on my shoulder.

"He is a douche, El. And I'm sorry," Steven says sitting up straight. "I really am."

Ellie nods at him as they say their goodnights and head back inside. I glance at my watch, it's past midnight and the exhaustion hits me. I'm never up this late.

"You probably want to get to bed, huh?" Ellie says, still leaning against my shoulder.

"Not yet," I say, resting my head on hers.

"Can we talk?"

She sits up to look at me, her face serious. I look away, afraid of having a *talk*. Talks are never good, especially when she's looking at me so seriously. I nod, staring at the flames spark and flicker. Focusing on the heat hitting my face instead of the heat I feel everywhere else because of Ellie.

"What is this?" she asks plainly.

I know I can't keep looking at the flames now, so I sit up to face her.

"What do you mean?"

Rolling her eyes. "*This.*" She waves her hand in a circle.

"Friends sitting by a fire?"

"Friends, huh?"

"Right, yes, a boss and his employee sitting by a fire." I smirk.

"Oh, please!" She hits my arm, throwing herself back into a slouch, crossing her arms. She is even cuter grumpy.

I rest my arm behind her slumped head. Because I am smitten, I can't resist the chance to play with her hair. Twirling the end of a dark wave around my finger I ask, "What do you want this to be, Eleanor?"

"I think . . ." She pauses, leaning in closer. "I think, I want to be *more* than coworkers."

"Boss and employee," I joke, choosing a terrible time to be a punk.

"Alright, boss man." She pokes me in the ribs. The physical violence of this woman. "I'm serious."

I stop twirling her hair and take both of her hands in mine. She's right, this is serious. Something like this has never felt more serious, but what can I do? It's against the rules to pursue anything serious with her.

Unless we decided to date . . . in secret? Lord knows I can't keep a secret to save my life. That would last a day then everyone at the school would know.

"Tell me what you're thinking," she says, waiting patiently.

I take a beat. "I'm thinking I feel the same way. I like you." Her smile stretches across her face in response. "I don't know how else to put into words what I'm thinking."

"Just try thinking out loud."

I stare at her, unable to form words at her statement. A phrase my mom told me growing up anytime I was unable to communicate—*think out loud, Bayani*. She would sit beside me, and wait as her seven-year-old son would fumble over his thoughts and emotions, not making sense, backtracking, and second guessing his feelings, until finally making sense of what was going on in his brain. The simple task of just saying exactly what was crossing my mind *out loud*. And it always worked.

Except now, of course.

Now I was stunned over what Eleanor just said—what my mom used to say. My feelings are tangled like wires and I don't know which one to pull at to start untying them.

"I don't think I can," I say looking down at our hands gripping the other's.

"Do you want to try?"

Clearing my throat. "My mom used to say that . . . 'Think out loud.'" I pause and Ellie watches me, no pressure, no ulterior motive, just listening. There's a reason she's good at her job, but in this moment, I know she's not viewing me like one of her students or someone sharing their dirty secrets. She's here for *me*, letting me be heard. It's been a long time since anyone has seemed even a tiny bit interested in hearing me talk—people usually like to hear themselves talk. I've grown to accept that I have this reputation of being a good listener, the one everyone goes to when they need reassurance or affirmation. I don't mind doing it, but over time you can't help but hope for someone to be that for you.

After I lost my parents, Patsy was my listener. Patsy was there for everything. Until last year when she planned her retirement and I took on more responsibilities. I don't blame her, it's not her job to make me feel better about myself. But there is only so much a person can give of themselves without anything in return, before they start to feel empty and hollow. It wasn't until this moment that I realized I've been hollowed out. Words evade me again as this awareness clouds my brain.

"Tell me about your mom and dad, what were they like?" she says after a beat. Her eyes are genuine, and without pity. Saving a man's dignity as she asks him about his dead parents.

"They died when I was thirteen." I clear my throat, my eyes feel blurry. "I haven't talked about them in a long time."

I pause, words gone . . . again.

She squeezes my hands, drawing circles with her thumbs.

"Think out loud," I whisper, chuckling at myself.

"Well . . ." She pauses, letting go of my hands and I feel an ache at the emptiness it leaves. "I know sharing feelings can be difficult and I don't want you to feel pressured to share with me. But I *am* here and ready to listen . . . whatever your thoughts may be."

"I just don't know who to share those with anymore. Who to *think out loud* with." I look up at the stars, knowing my mom is there, waiting patiently for me to share.

"I understand." She hooks her arm around mine. "You have to find your people. The ones who give more than they take. The people who bring you joy when you can't seem to find it on your own"—she leans her head on my shoulder—"The ones you *know* will accept that we are all human, with a complex brain full of thoughts and emotions that need to be worked through without judgment. I guess . . . those are the ones who matter . . . the people you can think out loud in front of."

I take a deep breath as we sit there. Her words swarming in my head.

I wonder if she knows that she's someone I want to think out loud in front of, that she's someone who matters to me.

Chapter Sixteen

Ellie

"So you're telling me *something* happened between you two, but you don't know what?"

Kate paces in her living room as we dissect my conversation with Benny from a few nights ago. She is animated and frustrated as we talk, and Dolly Parton, her Golden Retriever, is resting her head on my lap.

"I don't know. We glazed over the topic for a moment then got a little side tracked." I smile, reminiscing on the time I spent with him.

The vulnerability he had with me was more than I expected and the fact that I couldn't get enough of him and his life story was bewildering to me. I always try to be attentive when someone is sharing their story with me—it's literally my job. So, whether it's boring or exciting, I'm inclined to be fully present and responsive.

But with Benny, it was more than that . . . it was enthralling.

And it's not like he has this crazy life story or anything, he hasn't been to a foreign country other than his family home in the Philippines, he hasn't solved some medical mystery, no famous cousins he can brag about, just Benny. Simple, sweet Benny who lost his parents at a young age. Benny, who was average in school, but still tried. The guy who showed me his shuffle dancing abilities without any embarrassment. A guy who hasn't touched alcohol since he was twenty-two and caused an accident.

He was the tipsy designated driver for his belligerent friends. He was taking them home late after a party, and turned to tell them to calm down in the backseat, before losing control and hitting another car head on. Everyone walked away with minor injuries, but Benny still feels the burden of it.

I replay the story over and over in my head—it explains his justification for being the guy everyone calls after they drink.

"So they just call you? Anytime they need a D.D.?" I asked.

"Most of the time, yeah." He chuckled at himself. "Word just gets around that I'll pick them up, no questions asked. It seems like I condone it, I'm sure. But I make it very clear that *if* they're going to call me, they are also agreeing to a lecture on drinking and its consequences, as well as a phone call to their parents."

"Makes sense to me," I said confidently. Because it did, and he was right. The sole action of being selfless enough to help when they have no else to call. That's Benny, and he is remarkable.

His feeling of responsibility for someone else's actions, when he clearly can't control them, stem from his experience. We can't control another person's decisions and these kids will still continue making their choices, eventually dealing with the repercussions. But if they are smart enough to make a phone call, rather than make a poor choice and risk a tragic accident, Benny will be there for them.

"And usually, it happens one time. A lecture from Mr. B and a phone call to a parent is enough for them to realize they made a poor decision. But we have a handful of students who continue making poor decisions. Those are the ones who don't call me anyway, and the ones who refuse to hear me out when I try to reason with them."

He looked defeated at that moment.

I knew exactly who he was talking about: Ethan, Travis, some of the football players, even sweet Charlie Henders. They just want to rebel and eventually their poor decisions will catch up to them. But I'm sure, as teachers, you can't help but feel a little responsible. You're pouring your heart and soul into your work, trying to shape the young minds of the next generation, hoping they will come behind you and change the world.

And Benny is someone who will do whatever it takes to provide his kids that chance—the chance to change the world. Even if it means calling him in the middle of the night.

I guess he really *is* a Benny. Just an all-around wonderful guy.

Who brings the dip.

"Hello? Earth to Ellie!" Kate snaps her fingers at me. "Are you going to talk to him?" she asks, bringing me back to our conversation.

Blinking at her. "I have no idea! We haven't had time."

"You haven't had *time* to talk about your feelings?" She crosses her arms at me. "It's like a two minute discussion!"

"Pretty sure that kind of conversation needs more than two minutes of my time, and I haven't had it. Neither has he!"

"Ugh! You're just stalling!" She storms away.

Dolly Parton nuzzles my hand for pets. I *am* stalling a little bit.

I'm afraid of the inevitable rejection because a relationship with Benny isn't allowed.

"I really haven't had the time, Dolly," I whisper.

With how busy we have been at work the last few days, we hadn't really had an opportunity to revisit the discussion of us dating. It's college acceptance week and I'm on high alert for the seniors. The reassurance factory wheels were turning as a plethora of students stormed into my office to scream and cry over their acceptance freak outs, or worse . . . their rejection turmoil. I didn't realize the brevity of these decisions and how I responded to them would affect the student's mental state. Sarah had been accepted to Columbia, contingent on maintaining her grades and completing a few summer classes to graduate early. She was ecstatic, but her anxiety was on the verge of panic at the realization that she would have to move to New York before she was eighteen. Garrett Connors had received multiple rejections and was not himself *at all*, refusing to meet with me to discuss a plan. Birdie was accepted to a few four-year colleges and could care less about it if she didn't win prom queen. Students were in and out of my office all day, having these discussions, and all I wanted to do when I got home was crash on the couch.

"You have to be their guide, help them figure out next steps," Emma would tell me.

And I am.

I am elbows deep in application reviews, admissions emails, and Google searches on how best to support these students. I haven't felt so consumed with a client's success in such a long time.

The last time I felt any urgency on figuring out a plan for a client was when I had a new mom who was four months postpartum, off her medications, and dealing with intrusive suicidal thoughts. I spent weeks calling inpatient hospitals and working with her social worker to develop a plan for respite care and medication management to ensure the safety for her and her new baby. It was grueling and exhausting, but the adrenaline kept me going. That and the small signs of improvement she made each day fueled me. Finding a routine that suited her and her family, seeing her a few months later an entirely different person. An energized mom, a healthy baby and happy marriage, were the rewards I got to witness.

Did I ever think I would feel any kind of adrenaline like that as a high school guidance counselor? Definitely not.

With the mom, it was literally life and death. At the end of it, I had to accept that the outcome was out of my control and all I could do was provide support and structure. Hoping and praying they would take my recommendations. They did, thank God. But that's not always the case. And with these students, more often than not, they are refusing my recommendations. They're children, and they want what they want. Yet, I feel this urge to plead with them to let me help them, for them to just listen to me and do what I say. The continued rejection of my advice has left me feeling incompetent and like I'm unable to help them.

Surely if what I had to say was even remotely sound they would take it to heart and put it to use . . . *right?*

Dolly pawed at my hands as my petting slowed.

"What do you think?" I ask her as I scratch behind her floppy ear.

What is with these kids? Why do I feel so inept at handling these teenage life crises? And why does it feel like I *have* to figure it out? Is it an ego thing?

Or do I . . . actually care?

My head is spinning, and Dolly is panting—blowing her dog breath across my face as I pull out my phone.

I need to work through these thoughts with someone.

"Back to the party." Kate storms back in. "Don't you dare bail on our Halloween costume! I refuse to be a Thing by myself!" Dolly Parton jumps off the couch and trots to Kate's side as she sits on the floor, staring at me with defiance.

I chuckle. "You won't be a Thing by yourself!" I promise her, but deep down I am dreading this costume idea. I would rather suffer and be the third Munchkin of the Lollipop Guild with Emma and Steven than be a *Thing*.

Something about them freaks me out, maybe the blue hair, or creepy nose. At least with the Guild I can have an excuse to stuff candy in my mouth all night and avoid idle chit chat with tipsy pirates and slutty nurses.

I begged the girls to go as the three Sanderson sisters, but nope. Steven wanted to be a thoughtful husband and do a *couple's costume*.

"Good! I would hate to embarrass myself like that . . ." she says, shaking her head. "Thing 1 without Thing 2 is just humiliating." She laughs as she lays back on her living room floor.

"Yes . . . because of all the things encompassing that costume, *that's* what would be embarrassing, nothing else." I roll my eyes and lay back onto her fluffy rug with her.

"But seriously, what are you going to do about Benny?"

Gazing up at her ceiling, I avoid the question and start counting dots of popcorn ceiling.

I get to thirty-seven when she nudges me. "Answer me!"

Thirty-eight.

Thirty-nine.

Forty.

"I'm talking to him tonight, alright?"

"You are?" She throws herself over onto her stomach. "What are you going to say?"

I keep counting. *Forty-five.*

"I'm not sure. I have to talk to him about some of the kids first, then if we—"

"I swear if you say 'if you have time,' I will smack you!"

Pausing, I look at her. "If we . . . get to it . . ."

"You are ridiculous! Why are you stalling? What are you so afraid of? You like him, don't you?" She's talking fast, and sitting up now. "Of course you like him, who doesn't like Benny! You would be lucky to have him! Hell, he'd be lucky to have you!"

"Thank you," I whisper as she continues her rant.

"You guys just look so cute together! And everyone sees the way you look at each other, I bet even Mr. Clinton notices and he's practically blind! Literally . . . a bat. Worse, a bat who needs glasses! And Benny is wonderful." Her voice gets louder, and Dolly starts to run back and forth around the couch matching her energy. "He will do anything for the people he loves! Anything! Don't you want a man like that? *I* want a man like that! Why on earth is there so much hesitation?" She throws her arms up in the air and groans.

I hadn't asked myself why I was stalling or if that's what I was even doing. But I know there is something inside me resisting moving forward. The other night, with the fire, and the wine, and the coziness of his body . . . I was so infatuated with him in the moment that I just blurted out my thoughts . . . *more than coworkers.* Who does that?

But now—in the daylight—with no cozy-under-the-blanket-hand-holding, I don't have anything clouding my judgment. And the truth of the rules still remains.

We are not allowed to date.

Kate has stopped her rant and is looking at me as serious as she ever has. "Ellie, seriously. What is it?"

I sit up. "I haven't liked someone in a long time. A really long time."

"Since Liam?" she asks.

"Before that." I pause, looking back on the feelings I had for Liam—the surface level relationship we had and the inability to accept we weren't compatible. On paper, it seemed easy and expected, like we were so similar that it was ridiculous to look for anyone else.

But I did love Liam.

At least, I'm pretty sure I loved him.

I wouldn't have jumped in front of a bullet for him though.

And there were times I refused to back down just because I didn't want him to win and created more conflict. We were more against each other than we were *for* one another, viewing the world from the same lens but believing our own approaches were the best option. It was a selfish love, the love I had for Liam. But I'm pretty certain it was still love.

"You didn't like your fiancé?"

"Not entirely."

We both laugh.

"But you're still angry at him for the wedding thing?"

"Oh for sure. Do you have any idea how much money I lost?"

She starts to play with the tassels of her shaggy rug—a bright yellow and white gingham print rug with fluffy tassels sticking out in different directions. Her bouncy dark curls fall to cover her face when she asks, "Why would you agree to marry someone you don't like?"

She isn't looking at me. She knows this is a boundary I have avoided crossing with my new friends here, and I have a feeling she doesn't want to upset me by trying to get too personal.

Letting out a sigh I say, "We were both convinced we were too broken to be loved. I thought he was the best choice I had at a life with someone—that *we* were the best choice for each other. He would always ask, who could love people as dark and twisted as us?" My voice cracks. "And I believed he had a point, if no one would love someone like me, maybe I could force myself to love him. And I think he did the same."

"Did it work? Forcing yourself?"

"Mostly. I did love him . . . in a way."

"Do you really think you aren't lovable?"

I shrug. "Maybe. Who wants to love someone broken?"

"We're all broken in some way! You're a therapist, you of all people know that!"

"True, but who wants to love someone refusing to fix themselves? Someone who is so broken, they would rather fix other people than address their own issues?" I stare at her, driving my point home. "No one."

She frowns at me. "I don't believe that."

"I have yet to find a single person on this planet that loves someone like that."

"I know a person." She smirks.

"Chill out! It's not that serious!"

Is it though? Are my feelings for Benny *serious* feelings? Are his?

"If it's not serious, why would you ask him to be more than coworkers?" She air quotes with her hands. "Why entertain the idea of something *not* serious?"

"Impulse?" I wince at my own absurdity, of course it wasn't impulse. It is a thought that has been festering and building in my brain for months.

"Whatever! Don't lie to yourself, and don't lie to me. I deserve better! *We* deserve better," she says, throwing her arms around Dolly and hugging her tight. Dolly licks her face, then runs away to grab one of her squeaky toys.

"Why does it even matter? I won't be here much longer anyway! There's no need to get worked up on dating Benny when I know we have an expiration date." I feel the quiver in my voice building. Refusing to let it break, I stand up. "All of *this* has an expiration date! I won't be here after the term!" My voice is getting loud and harsh. "I'm going back to my old life, my old job, my old clients! The dirty city . . . the loud subway . . . the lonely house with the expensive rent. The place where a dark, twisted, broken person *like me* belongs!"

My body is trembling as I fix my eyes on my feet. I stand there, feeling the yellow rug tassels with my toes, holding my breath. Refusing to look up, I blinked back the tears, letting one fall to the rug. I hear the rustling of the rug as Kate stands up and walks over to me, wrapping me in a hug.

"You belong here, with us."

Dolly trots over and paws at both of our legs. I laugh and sniffle as I hug her back, holding Dolly's paw. I want her to be right, but the reality that I'm not cut out for the job is hovering over me like a black cloud. If I couldn't help these students, why would they even keep me here?

"Thank you," I say, sniffling again.

"Please talk to Benny. At least tell him how you feel. No man likes a girl playing with his emotions!"

"You're right."

"And then date him, please! The man *needs* a companion."

She releases from our hug and walks into her kitchen. I stand there, kicking at the rug tassels, giddy butterflies filling my stomach as I daydream about dating Bayani Divata.

The butterflies scurry away as reality pulls me back down to earth.

The *rules.*

"Ugh. I can't date him," I call to her in the kitchen. "I can't tell him any of this! It's against school board rules!"

She frowns at me from around the open refrigerator door. "Good point."

Laying back on her pink modular sofa I frown back. "So, what's the point?"

Walking back into the living room, eating a dairy-free ice cream bar she says, "Well, I would suggest just date until you leave at the end of the term, but I'm refusing to accept that you're leaving. So that's out of the question." She wipes the corner of her mouth. "Plus, Benny couldn't keep a secret if his life depended on it. You'd last a day before you both got fired."

"Like I said, there's no point." I throw my arms over my face and moan. "Why did I have to go and have a crush on my *boss?*"

"Ironic, huh?" she says, consuming more *fake* ice cream. "Don't therapists have to maintain boundaries or something?"

I glare at her. "Yes."

"Seems to me a boundary has been crossed, eh?"

"More like obliterated!"

She laughs at me as I scream into one of her giant purple throw pillows. Her living room color palette is a bag of skittles and she has no shame about it.

"I can't believe I let this happen. I'm unbelievable," I mumble under the pillow.

"Inconceivable!" she shouts.

"INCONCEIVABLE!" we shout in unison.

Dolly Parton howls.

CHAPTER SEVENTEEN

Ellie

"WHAT'LL IT BE?" SAM asks, smacking on his gum and clicking his pen to write down my order. Sam was a burly guy, with a less than welcoming demeanor—his bald head shining under the fluorescents of his diner.

"I'll take the special, plain, with coffee."

He snags the menu from my hands and saunters off. "You're gonna have to try something other than waffles eventually!" he calls over his shoulder.

"Just keeping it consistent," I reply.

He grumbles at me and heads to the register, mouthing my order to himself with a snarl. I giggle and look down at the table. A plexi-glass table with business cards and flyers shoved in between the layers.

Jodie's Salon, Open Monday - Thursday
Carol's Signs, Online Orders Only
Three Sisters House Cleaners, Available 24/7
Glendale Baseball Camp Happening in Two Weeks

I trace my hand over the glass, picturing each of the businesses in this corner of the city and felt the smile tug at my cheek. We were inside city limits, one of the largest cities in Oklahoma, but for the last twenty years, the ten blocks surrounding the high school had established itself as *Knight Town, Home of Glendale High School.*

"I wouldn't let Jodie go anywhere near my head, if I were you."

I look up from the cards and see Devon standing by my booth, coffees in hand.

I smile. "Bad experience?"

"She gave me a high top perm for prom last year." He rolls his eyes, setting my coffee down. "May I?" He waves to the empty seat across from me.

I nod to the seat. "You seem like someone who can pull off a perm though."

"Lucky for her sake, I can. But save yourself the trouble. Unless you wanna leave lookin' like a poodle, I'd go to the city."

"Noted"—I pour cream into my coffee—"So, when did you start working for Sam?"

"Since I beat his nephew's face in." He takes a sip of his coffee.

"Making amends, I see?"

"Mom made me." He shrugs. "Said if I wanna act like a man, I may as well work like one."

"Understandable. How are you liking it?"

"It's dumb. Wipe tables, wash dishes, pour coffee. What is there to like?"

"Getting a paycheck, perhaps? Building your resume?" I ask optimistically.

He nods in response, looking out the window.

I wait a moment, giving him an opportunity to continue. When he doesn't, I ask, "What can I do for you, Mr. Johnson?"

He sits there, silently tracing the rim of his coffee cup with his thumb before finally responding, "I need help."

Sitting forward in my seat, I look at him. "What do you need help with, Devon?"

He looks at me earnestly. "I'm having these *issues* and I don't know what to do."

I look around, ensuring no one is in earshot of our conversation and whisper, "Are these issues in your head?"

His face becomes flat as he nods slightly. I reach into my purse and pull out a sticky notepad and begin doodling.

"How are these issues making you feel?"

"Angry," he says sternly.

Angry face doodle.

"How long has this been going on?"

"About a year."

Smiley clock doodle.

"You do that with everyone?" he says, eyeing my doodles.

"Just a habit." I set my pen down to look at him. "Have you tried talking to anyone about this yet?"

"Nah, too embarrassing." He looks over my shoulder towards the door. "Hey, Mr. B."

My body goes rigid. My breathing stops, and my heart rate picks up.

My palms are sweaty.

Knees weak—arms are heavy.

Okay, Eleanor, do not *sing that song right now.*

"Hey, DJ," Benny responds, approaching the table. He touches my arm and the heat in my body surges to where he squeezes tenderly.

"Hey there," he whispers to me.

"Hi." My mind is hyper focused on his hand. He grazes his thumb in circles, sending goosebumps up my neck and behind my ears.

Fist-bumping Devon, he walks over to the counter to place his order. I'm probably staring at him like a lovesick puppy when Devon clears his throat.

"Smooth." He laughs into his coffee.

"Uh . . . I . . . ugh." Fumbling on my words, I rub my temple and try to refocus, "Back to you and this—"

"Nah, this is fun." His eyes are playful as he looks at Benny over his shoulder. "So, what's going on there?"

What is *going on there?*

"I'm not sure." I bite my thumb as I look over at Benny too.

Talking with Sam at the counter, Benny laughs and my heart just about stops. I stealthily reposition in my seat to get a better look. The top two buttons of his shirt are undone, the divot in his chest almost visible. His sleeves are rolled up unevenly, arms flexing as he puts his hands in his pockets. It's his effortlessly sexy end of the day look. A handsome ruggedness all held together by a few buttons. I want so badly to break the rules—all of them—parkour over this table and . . .

"Well, he's a good guy. Annoying as hell sometimes, but I'd trust him with my life."

"Devon, buddy I need help back here! Break's over!" Sam calls from the counter.

I blink out of my making-out-with-Benny daydream and refocus on Devon. "Come by my office tomorrow and we can talk more."

He nods, chugging the rest of his coffee, and hurrying to grab plates from the counter.

Benny pays Sam and heads back towards me, beaming. Like he's having the same daydream I was just having. *Wishful thinking.*

I watch as he weaves through tables, greeting multiple people on the way. Some students, some adults—all of them excited to see him and talk to him. I see the genuine joy ooze out of him as he entertains each person's small talk, inching closer and closer to me each chance he gets. Not once does he look at me with *help me* eyes, but instead, eyes that say, *"I'll be right there."*

I chuckle as he leaves the last table to make the final stride to our table when an elderly woman cuts him off in the aisle, hugging him at his waist. He hesitates in response, probably startled with the physical contact, and smiles at me over her shoulder.

I smirk and lift my coffee cup to him.

He rolls his eyes as he says his greetings to the gray-haired woman, gently moves past her and glides into the booth, sitting across from me.

"Finally." He exhales as he slumps against his seat.

"You're just so popular around here."

"Gotta please the people." He laughs, nudging my foot with his.

"Of course." I laugh, tapping his foot back, then placing both feet on top of his.

Just two grown adults playing footsie under the table, *no big deal*.

Devon comes back to our table, setting down our plates. His face is lit up like a billboard as he awkwardly says, "Enjoy."

I glare at the stalky lineman as he saunters away, there's no way he won't run and tell all of his football buddies about my giddy behavior. I'll never be taken seriously if he does.

"How has your week been?" he asks as he starts to cover his eggs in hot sauce. My throat is on fire just watching the red sauce splatter across his plate.

"Insane!" I pour syrup on my waffle. "I wish someone would have told me how intense college acceptance week is. I feel blindsided. Yes, one would think I would know what to expect, seeing as my entire life plan hinged on my college acceptance letter." I add a dollop of butter and Benny watches my every move with a hungry intensity, licking his lips as he eyes the concoction on my plate. "You have your own, you know." I place my chin on the back of my hand, letting my fork dangle over the plate.

"Yours look better," he says with a quiet, husky voice. Matching my position, he rests his chin in his hand, still looking at me, eyebrows dancing up and down at me. I force my eyes away from him nibbling his lips and focus on the syrupy squares of my waffle.

A long moment passes, a tense silence building. I can *feel* him still looking at me and heat splotches across my cheeks at his continued eye contact. I stare intently at the waffles sitting between us.

Maybe they will fly off my plate.

"But . . ." I clear my throat and revert back to the previous conversation. "Being on this side of things, as a sounding board for the students' erratic emotions surrounding these letters, it's an entirely other beast I wasn't expecting. *Intense* is actually an understatement."

Benny breaks his gaze, opening his napkin and buttering up his waffle, and pouring a heap of hot sauce on the side of his plate. "It's a pretty big deal. I figured Pat would have told you what to expect." He shovels food into his mouth—not in a gross way, but in a comfortable way, like he trusts me not to judge his table manners too harshly.

"She mentioned it, but I think she glazed over the high-stress-all-hands-on-deck portion of it," I say, nibbling at my waffles like a squirrel. I felt nauseous, being around Benny was always comforting and easy, but the lingering *"Define the Relationship"* conversation, or *"DTR"* as Birdie would put it, was about to make my stomach bubble over.

"What can I do to help?" He stops eating to face me, giving me his full attention.

"Well for starters, maybe you can help me figure out how to understand these kids. I am so out of my element here and I don't think I'm giving them the best support. It is so hard for me to work with their *'the world is ending'* mentality. I get that this is a huge deal for them, even monumental in some ways! But so what if they don't get into their top choice? They know there are thousands of colleges across North America, right?" I stab at my waffle out of irritation. "The amount of crying, screaming, and storming out of my office moments I've encountered this week is comparable to treating a bipolar client! This is not what I was expecting working with students."

Benny purses his lips as he studies me. "It can be a lot, for sure. College is a huge stressor for some kids, and the idea that their hopes and dreams could be hanging by a thread is enough to crumble their spirits completely. They make plans for their futures and bank on the acceptance being the key to getting to the next step." He places his hand down on the table and I can almost feel a spark from how close it is to my own hand. His eyes are softer and his tone is light when he asks, "Haven't you ever had a plan that failed because of one thing?"

I sigh, immediately thinking of Liam.

Ugh, I don't want to think about him when I'm with Benny. "I have."

"It sucks. Obviously we know there are different avenues you can take to still attain your overall goal, but these kids haven't experienced life the way we have." He shrugs matter-of-factly. "The only way to a successful life, in their minds, is going to the college of their choice."

"I can't imagine the amount of stress that puts on them."

"I've tried reorganizing how we approach college applications, but a lot of our students are influenced at home and by their friends, we can only do so much to prevent it from getting so bad." He continues eating. "It's helped a little. But there's still that cloud of dread looming if their plan doesn't work out the specific way they want."

"So, what are we supposed to do then? How can I help them if I can't make them look at other avenues?" I roll my eyes.

"We might not be able to control how they see it, but we can control how we respond to it." He smiles.

"So wise," I say, rolling my eyes again.

"Just take it one step at a time. Focus on one student individually, not the entire senior class, otherwise, you'll drown. And then I'll drown trying to save you."

I ponder his plan. "Alright, one student at a time. I think I can do that."

Surely it wouldn't be too difficult. As of right now, out of the entire senior class, I had eight rejection crises to focus on, and three contingencies. The contingencies were easy so I directed my attention to the rejections. I pulled out my notebook and started scribbling down information. I could feel Benny watching me as I went to work, jotting down a list of students in descending order of solvability. I took into consideration their emotional response to the situation, how many colleges they applied to, how attainable their goals were, and the connections I had with different admissions counselors.

Benny leans across the table, watching as I write down names, giving me important factors to consider. I try to focus on his words when all I can think about is how close his face is to mine . . .

"Now, Charlie won't want to live more than four hours from his family. And Emily Warren wants to study abroad." He taps his index finger on my paper. "Sammie Gordon is a strong volleyball player, she can probably attend tryouts somewhere." I write that down. "And Garrett . . . he *needs* football, in any possible way. He needs to be a part of the team." He gets up and joins me on my side of the booth.

Excitement was surging through me as I was scribbling and erasing all over my paper. "You are brilliant! Thank you!"

"They don't call me vice principal for nothing." He winks, taking a swig of his coffee.

I continue writing down my ideas. "I think I have a few ideas! I'll start small"—still writing, erasing, clicking my pen—"I'll call about spring try-outs at TU and ASU, then I can ask around for some open slots with study abroad groups."

"Do you think that will work?" he asks as I'm jotting down my plans.

"I'm not sure, I'll have to make some calls. But I hope so."

"Perfect. And we have another month before late enrollment!" He's beaming at me with his good hearted, shiny smile. His teeth were practically glistening.

We.

The word stuns me, and he probably didn't intend it the way I heard it. But my brain is triggered, in a good way, by that word.

"We?" I whisper in an attempt to hide the pleasure in my voice.

"We," he says so confidently, then without hesitation or reserve he wraps his arm around my shoulders and hugs me gently. Leaning down, he presses his forehead against my temple and whispers, "You're amazing." His breath is warm and spicy, swirling around me and tingling the side of my face. The moment is quick before he sits up straight, remembering we are in public.

I gaze up at him in awe. He really was so good at this job—caring for these students. And he was making *me* good at it. But more than that, he was so good at making me feel *seen* and *valued*. Without even trying, Benny was filling me with confidence in what I have to offer and what I am capable of when I have been feeling nothing but stuck and overwhelmed. He was filling in the gaps for me so effortlessly, and I knew I had a partner working *with* me. No competition or pissing contests, just putting the client first. The comparison to working with Benny and Liam hit me like a truck, it was night and day difference and I couldn't imagine it getting any better than this.

The thrill of solving a problem, with Benny as my backup, was flooding my brain and distorting any idea I had had for my future. Moving back to New York, seeing my old clients, going back to my previous life—everything I thought I needed to set my focus on—was fading.

Being a guidance counselor hadn't felt so exciting until this moment.

And something unexpected hit me . . . I wanted to keep doing it.

Chapter Eighteen

Benny

"ARE YOU FREAKING KIDDING me right now?" Kate yells at me as we walk up to Frankie's daycare.

"We just didn't get to it." I shrug, holding the door open for her as she storms in like a child.

"What is the matter with you two?" she yells.

Big Red hisses at her from his perch, his hair slowly standing up in the middle.

"She was focusing on the students. And I don't want to force her into a conversation she may not be ready to have yet." I was also terrified to admit that what was happening between Ellie and I might not be as serious for her as it was becoming for me.

"How hard is it to communicate your feelings? You see each other everyday!" she yells again. Big Red growls a hiss and stands on all fours.

"Please don't piss him off," Clark says behind the counter, without looking up from his cell phone.

"It's complicated. I don't know where she stands and for all we know, she's still heading back north after the term ends." I sign the checkout clipboard and head to the back room. "And what if I admit my feelings and she feels forced to acknowledge them because I'm her boss. Why make things awkward for her?"

Kate follows me into the playroom and sits on the couch next to Nana. "I'm sure she can handle a conversation about feelings. She's a therapist for crying out loud." A few of the cats stop playing and harassing each other to jump on the couch with her. Frankie stays perched on the cat tower, away from everyone. "And who knows, she might feel the same way you do."

"You think so?" I ask too eagerly.

She smiles at me, a little menacingly. "You're way too into this girl, aren't you?"

"What are you talking about? It's just a crush." I turn away from her to hide the red heat splotching my cheeks.

"Don't you lie to me!" The cats meow in an orchestra fashion as she snaps at me, patting their heads aggressively like they're dogs and not felines.

I can't lie to Kate, I've never been able to.

Letting out a deep sigh. "Fine, I like her." I pause to pick Frankie up off the tower. "I like her so much, it scares me."

Kate squeals and jumps up and down on the couch, completely disregarding the temperamental cat that was trying to nap on her lap. "I knew it! It's been so freaking obvious! I was honestly getting worried you were just all kinds of dumb and hadn't figured it out yet." She starts rambling in her usual excited manner. "Like how could you *not* know? The fiery tension could set a building on fire! And she for sure has a thing for you. Like major—"

"Let's not speak for her, we don't know what she's thinking," I mumble, more to myself than to Kate.

"Oh, please! She's so into you!" She sits up on the couch, cats pawing at her because she stopped petting them. "You guys would be the *it* couple! Like rule the school couple."

"We aren't in high school anymore, that's just weird."

Kate scoffs at me, "Whatever, now what are you going to do?"

I put Frankie in her carrier, adjusting her sweater and placing her catnip toy at the bottom. She scratches at the catnip frog, rolling over onto her back, flashing me her pink, fat gut—all modesty gone. I watch as she plays without a care in the world, the question Kate asked me putting a sinking feeling into my heart. "I don't know."

"Ugh, are you afraid of the rules? Is that why you're so hesitant?"

Heading toward the door, Frankie in tow. "Yes, actually. That is exactly why." The irritation in my voice is obvious as Kate follows on my heels.

"You have got to be joking. What are they going to do, *fire you?*"

We leave the daycare and turn down the sidewalk towards Wafflin'. It was a breezy autumn day, having rained just the night before, and every business on the strip was taking full advantage of the perfect weather. Jodie had her salon door propped open with a sign promoting her usual *Halloween Special - Wash and Trim 40% off.*

We walked past the salon and continued in the direction of Wafflin', waving at Jodie as she trimmed a baseball player's mullet, then at a sister from Three Sisters' Cleaning sitting at a table outside their entrance taking a smoke break, Frankie hisses at the cigarette fumes. We stop as a few students run out of Ken's Sporting Goods with shiny new cleats and pads slung over their shoulders. My heart tugging at each person I see, memories filling my brain as we mosey down to the dead end where Wafflin' sits perpendicular to the rest of the street.

"They could," I finally respond to Kate as we walk into the diner. They *could* fire me.

"I call bull. There's no way Mr. Clinton would want to lose you. Not with everything you do for him, and for that school. You are the sole reason the place is still standing," she says, picking a table for us to sit at.

"That's a stretch," I say, sliding into the booth, setting Frankie on the floor.

"I'm serious." She opens the menu to peruse. I don't know why she even opens it, she gets the same thing every time: *Vegan spicy waffle with avocado.* "And I'm confident he would go to bat for you if you wanted him to."

"What am I supposed to do?" I ask, not looking up from the menu. "Tell him I'm in love with the new hire and he should let me break the rules?" I laugh at myself. "That's insane. The man would do a lot, but that is pushing it."

Nancy, the oldest of the Wafflin' employees, approaches the table and sets down two mugs. "Hiya, sweeties. What'll it be?"

"Can I get the special, with no onions," I respond, as Nancy hands me the decanter to fill my own cup. She learned early on to just leave the pot at my table until I pay the ticket, it saves her a few steps.

"Good choice. Kate, what can I get ya?"

Kate doesn't respond. I look up after filling my cup to see she's just staring at me—like a lunatic.

"Kate? Are you alright, dear?" Nancy asks.

I widen my eyes at her to answer the little woman who just had hip surgery so she could go sit down, Kate doesn't speak. "Give her the usual." I smile at Nancy.

"Extra avocado this time," Nancy whispers to me, giving me a wink as she scribbles down our order. Her pace is slow and cautious as she walks back to the counter.

"What is wrong with you?" I whisper at Kate, who is still bug-eyed.

"Did—uh—" she stutters.

"Please don't be having a stroke. This is not the place." I cross my arms as she tries to make her brain communicate with her vocal chords.

"Did you say . . ." she whispers, leaning halfway across the table, "you *love* her?"

Oh *God.*

"Umm . . ." Flustered and mentally punching myself for not thinking before I speak, "I, uhh, didn't mean it that way. I was just, ya know."

I take a huge swig of coffee, shrugging as if this conversation means nothing to me. I reposition in my seat, tapping the table, straightening the napkins, doing anything I can to avoid making eye contact with Kate. The clear physical response of a nonchalant man who spoke too fast and meant nothing by it.

Nothing to misconstrue here.

Just good ole Benny, putting his foot in his mouth.

Just a man unconcerned with the words about his feelings he let slip out of his mouth and the reality that they may actually be true.

Nothing out of the ordinary.

"Oh my gosh, you love her!" She slaps the table as she whispers a yell at me.

All four other patrons of the diner stop their own conversations to not-so-secretly listen in on ours.

"Yes, you're right," I say robotically for everyone to hear, "I do *love* Frankie." Patting the carrier on the floor next to me.

Kate rolls her eyes at my attempt of acting natural, the rest of the diner now uninterested in eavesdropping. Frankie meows through the carrier, assuming my patting was an indication she would be joining us for a meal.

"Order up!" Devon says approaching the table with our order. Setting our food down before sliding in the booth next to me. I scoot over to make room, choosing to ignore the fact that I look like a shrimp next to the massive tank of a kid.

Devon helps himself to Kate's side of potatoes and sips on my coffee. Kate and I both glance at each other as we watch, holding back the huge grins we both have on the inside. It had been over a year since Devon had acted even remotely interested in being around us if he didn't have to. The first time he ignored us was at the after school pep rally, barely looking in our direction, just a soft head nod as he passed by with the entire football team.

"Glad to see I'm not the only one he's ignoring now," Naomi whispered to me in the thick crowd of cheering families.

Ever since then, communication, let alone just simple interaction with DJ had been slim. So seeing him gobble down our food like he was a starved bear was so exciting I didn't even mind when he inhaled half of my waffle within seconds of sitting down.

"So, what you guys been up to?" DJ asks, mouth full of waffle.

"Well . . . Ben, here, has a girlfriend." Kate smirks at me, deviously.

"I do not." I groan, throwing my head back against my seat.

"Ms. Bailey," DJ says more as a knowing statement, instead of a question, as he reaches across for Kate's plate. She swats his hand away and they both giggle, he then returns to my waffle and finishes it off.

"She's not my girlfriend." I run my hands through my hair and try to massage away the tension in my neck that has built-up. I hate having these types of conversations, and these two know it. For one, I hate not knowing the outcome, being in the dark is the worst place a person can be—especially when it comes to relationships. I want to know the path my feelings are leading me and prepare myself for the final destination, good or bad. And second, I did not want to be having this conversation with anyone but Ellie. Making assumptions about our relationship without her here to confirm or deny fills me with a guilty sensation, like it's wrong to discuss the specifics of what we have with anyone else.

Like it's sacred.

"I call bull sh—"

"No turd words around here!" Kate cuts DJ off, pointing her fork, full of vegan waffle, at him.

"I'm just saying, the way you guys drool over each other. Definitely stan." DJ shrugs as he cleans my plate with one last swipe of his fork, licking it clean. I mentally groan over the Gen Z phrase and make a mental note to Google what "stan" means in this current situation.

"Not like it's bad, everyone's rooting for y'all."

"What do you mean 'everyone'?" Kate asks before I can.

"The entire school, they all *ship* you guys."

"Of course they do!" Kate's smile is almost too big for her face.

"The entire school? And what is a ship?" I repeat back to him, my heart starting to race.

"Like relation*ship*," Kate and DJ say in unison as if that answers my question.

If the entire school "ships" us—whatever that means—then our behavior has been noticeable. This is bad. I can't be seen as the guy who can't control himself around a woman I like. I have to set an example for these kids, and if I'm doing it willingly, knowing it goes against school policy, that could be considered insubordination.

My mind lingers on the word as DJ and Kate chuckle back and forth about the entire student body and their investment in my personal affairs.

"I heard Birdie's afraid they'll make them Homecoming King and Queen," DJ quips.

"I would pay so much money to see that happen!" Kate cackles at herself.

"There's a pool going around when someone will catch them holding hands."

Kate laughs out loud and I groan into my hands. "This is bad."

"Are you kidding me? It's awesome!" DJ nudges me. "Seriously, this is the best relationship gossip I've heard since the Patsy and Bill rumor!"

"I could get fired," I mumble, keeping my head down into my hands.

"There's no way that'll happen." DJ pats my shoulder. "You're irreplaceable, everyone knows it. No way they'll fire you for liking someone."

"Loving someone," Kate retorts.

"Dudeeeeee, you love this chick?" Devon whispers, his eyes bugging out of his head.

I look out the window, watching the orange and red leaves rustle on the sidewalk, the sky a perfect blend of pink, blue, and yellow. The sight is so calm and beautiful, and all I can think about is sharing the view with Ellie.

The fear of losing my job, disappointing Mr. Clinton, creating drama in the workplace, all of that fades away as I envision Ellie and I sitting in this same booth, looking out as the breeze wooshes by and the sun sets.

Any negative thoughts I have are gone when I focus on her. She's a safe place for me, something I didn't know I was missing. Something I don't want to lose.

"I think I might."

Kate squeals and DJ hugs me. "That's awesome, man. I'm happy for you." I hug him back, not letting go as quickly as he does, savoring the moment he feels comfortable and happy enough to hug his uncle.

"Well isn't this adorable?" a voice says behind the other side of the table. I look up to see Ellie smirking at us as she's leaned over the top of the seat, eye-level with Kate, both of them laughing at our man hug.

We immediately let go and punch each other in the shoulder. DJ takes a final swig of coffee. "Break's over." He stands to hug Kate, and then back to me and whispers, "Don't be a simp." I nod as he goes to leave, noting another word I probably need to look up.

"See you tomorrow, Ms. B . . ." He shakes Ellie's hand. "Mr. B," he says, visibly winking at me, right in front of her. I might be hallucinating, but I'm pretty sure her cheeks turned bright red.

"Aww, Mr. and Ms. B, I didn't even put that together!" Kate giggles.

"Sure you didn't." I roll my eyes at Kate's smug smile.

"So, what's the emergency?" Ellie asks as she sits next to me.

"What emergency?" I look at her, feeling drawn to push back a piece of hair that's fallen out of her ponytail. I resist and focus on the side profile of her face, her soft skin light and slightly peek at the cheeks. She doesn't have makeup on today, which is a rare treat. I can clearly see the subtle freckles on her nose from a bad sunburn, and a small scar on her temple she said was from chicken pox, things she feels compelled to hide. Every inch of her is stunning, I don't want her to hide any of it.

"I thought I had a flat tire."

I clench my jaw and slowly turn to glare at Kate. "A flat, huh?"

"Yes! I was certain of it! But then I realized it wasn't even my car! HA, silly me." She fakes a laugh so unconvincing you'd think it was intentional. "Anyway, I gotta run! Thanks for coming to my rescue, El."

"Uhh, you're welcome?" Ellie looks at her confused, then at me for some telepathic information. I just shrug, acting like I have no earthly idea why Kate would text Ellie, ironically in the middle of me admitting my feelings about her, out of the blue . . . of all things.

Kate comes around the table, leaning over the back of our seat to hug each of us bye.

"You're dead," I whisper to her.

"You'll thank me later," she whispers back as she skips away—rather proud of herself, I'm sure.

"So, want to tell me what's going on?" Ellie asks, filling up Kate's mug and taking a sip.

"Oh you know, Kate is just meddling in other people's business."

"Of course." She laughs. "Well I am starving, are you up for seconds?"

Looking down at the empty plate DJ left, and hearing the hunger audibly settle in my stomach, I nod. "Nancy, get us two specials!" I call over to Nancy at the counter as I wrap my arm around Ellie's waist, squeezing her tight against me.

"Can I share something and we agree to not make it weird?" she asks me, scooting closer and resting her hand on my knee.

"I make everything weird, but yes. Go ahead."

She laughs. "I'm just sharing my thoughts, okay?"

"Out loud, of course."

"When I walked in and saw you . . ." She paused for a moment, probably afraid I would make fun of whatever she wanted to share—I would *never*. "I felt a sense of relief."

"Relief, huh? What kind of relief? Like the kind when you're on a blind date and you're afraid it's really a seventy-year-old goat farmer?" I chuckle.

"Not that kind." She giggles.

"Ahh, the other kind then?"

She gazes up at me, searching my eyes like she needs something from me.

I fix my eyes on her, hoping she can find her answers.

Whatever you want, Eleanor. It's yours.

"The kind of relief you feel when you've been lost for so long? Like you've found your way out of this huge maze." She turns her body towards me, picking up speed. "Or a pitch black storm and you finally get to a safe destination, you know?" She grabs my arm. "That full body experience where everything just releases and your breath escapes you." Her breath catches, like she realizes how excited she was getting, and she stops.

I turn my body toward her, waiting for her to continue. *Please keep going.*

"The relief you feel . . ." she whispers, "when you're finally where you were meant to end up all along."

And then, as if an inevitable force has finally pulled me to my destination, I press my lips against hers. The taste of syrup and cinnamon swirls in my mouth as she kisses me back. Any common sense I have is lost when she grabs the sides of my face and pulls me in closer, her lips curling into a smile against mine. I kiss her again and again. If it was possible for time to stand still, it would need to be this moment, so I could savor every part of her forever.

Muffled whispers start swarming around us, threatening to break our connection. An eager hum leaves her mouth when I wrap my arm around her waist, pulling her closer to me. I let the sound buzz around me, drowning out everything else. Should I be concerned for onlookers? Probably, but I don't care.

All I care about is her.

CHAPTER NINETEEN

Ellie

BENNY *KISSED* ME. IN the middle of Wafflin'.

And not just a quick peck, but an all-consuming, body surging kiss that still has my lips pulsing for more. I've never been kissed like that before. The kind of kiss that fills you with equal amounts of delight and desire. The kind of kiss you can't stop smiling about. The kind of kiss that penetrates all of your senses, sending you into a trance and making you question if it's even real life.

I can't stop staring at his lips as he leads this morning's faculty meeting. The memory of them on mine, soft and gentle at first then intense and focused as if nothing else in that moment mattered. I'm not usually one for public displays of affection, setting very solid rules and boundaries for myself, and the school policy was still very much at the center of my mind.

But the moment his pupils dilated and he entangled his hands in my hair, closing the distance between our lips, my body practically melted to the floor, taking all of my rules and boundaries with it.

I let my gaze move across him, slowly. His eyes flicker all around the room, eyebrows dancing subtly as he speaks. His forearm muscles flex as he grips the counter behind him. I can sense his fingers moving up my arms as he taps them against the granite. His hips practically dance as he shifts his weight from foot to foot.

Everything he does this morning seems to be enhanced, my altered senses on high alert.

I'm gaping at him uncontrollably—mouth wide open—the moisture on my tongue all dried up.

"We need one more person to help set up the Wafflin' tent the night before," Benny is speaking, but his voice sounds muffled as the tunnel vision I have towards his mouth clouds all of my other senses. "Sam will be out of town and so far it's just me and Malcolm. Any takers?"

"Ellie can do it!" Kate pipes in, elbowing me in the ribs.

"Ow," I whisper a growl at her, rubbing my side as she giggles at me.

"Great, thank you Ellie for being a team player," Benny says, lingering his gaze on me. My face feels red hot as I nod at him, not fully aware of what I am agreeing to.

"We need more help than that," Malcolm grumbles standing in the doorway separating us from the hallway.

"Kate would *love* to help too." I smirk in her direction and she crosses her arms, sticking her tongue out at me.

"Perfect, now that we have that handled, can we focus on more important matters?" Emma takes charge of the conversation and stands up, Benny waving to give her the floor. He turns to walk towards the back of the group, but instead of standing by Malcolm like he normally does, he keeps walking. I watch from the corner of my eye until he is out of my peripheral view, then hearing his footsteps slow as he stands beside me.

Every muscle in my back tightens as he leans his hand over onto the back of my chair, hovering slightly above my head. No one says a word, as if it is completely natural for Benny to be in another person's bubble like this.

Which it is *not*.

Benny, the king of boundaries and personal space, always standing as far from the faculty circle as possible. Benny, the man who never partakes in the group hugs and is almost on par with Malcolm and the distance he creates between himself and the group.

But now, the physical distance is nonexistent as he stands right next to me, his pant leg brushing against the armrest of my chair, sending chills down my arms and into my palms. I rub them against my jeans, dissolving the feeling, and try to focus my attention on Emma.

"Alright, the party is tomorrow night. We have our final store run this afternoon, the party is at eight p.m., and you *must* dress up." She points her pen at Malcolm, who rolls his eyes and downs the last of his coffee.

Wiping leftover droplets from his beard he whispers, "We'll see about that."

"I'm serious! No costume, no entry!" Emma says pointedly.

"The best you get from me is a bowtie."

"Better than nothing. Now are there any questions?" she asks the group.

The bell rings as everyone responds no, gathering their things and heading to their respective classrooms. Benny stays standing beside me, I can see out of the corner of my eye he shifts his weight closer to my chair.

Once we are the only two in the breakroom, he rests his hand at the nape of my neck, underneath my pinned up hair. He tugs at a loose piece before resting his thumb against my bare skin.

My eyes feel heavy as his thumb moves back and forth along the hem of my turtleneck. Traces of heat are left behind each pass. A quivering breath escapes me as I turn to look up at him.

His dark eyes are pinned on me. "Hey there," he whispers.

"Hi," my voice shakes as I close my eyes, and enjoy his closeness. He sits on the edge of my chair so my head falls against his stomach. His abs tighten as I make contact, his heart bounding across his entire middle.

"Ahem . . ."

We snap our heads to the doorway to see Garrett Connors resting against his crutches, a devilish smirk across his face.

"Mr. Connors, how are you this morning?" Benny says, his hand still resting on my neck and shoulder, unbothered that a student is witnessing him touch me. Like it doesn't matter to him if anyone sees us together.

The urge to jump out of the chair and put ten feet between Benny and myself takes over as I abruptly stand up. "Garrett, you ready?" I ask, gathering my stuff together and throwing it in my bag. Benny bends down to pick up the sticky note pad I dropped. Without even thinking, I rush past him, disregarding the pad and his gentle touch goodbye and race into the hallway, Garrett hobbling on his crutches, closely behind.

"Damn, this ain't a marathon, slow down," Garrett calls behind me as I weave in and out of students standing and gabbing in the hall.

"Come on, we're on a time crunch!" I rush into my office and throw my things down, powering up my computer. I chug my coffee and start rapidly pulling out different applications and forms to go over with Garrett as the adrenaline courses through my veins. Unsure if it's the excitement I have for the plan I've developed for Garrett, or the guilt from running away from Benny fueling it.

Garrett wobbles in, setting his crutches against the wall as he sits across from me. "Dude, you pretty much abandoned a puppy just now."

Deciding to ignore the hurt that was most definitely etched across Benny's face when I ran past him, I clasp my hands together under my desk. "That was not my intention," I respond, feeling a slight tremble in my voice. I clear my throat, gathering my thoughts and turn my focus to Garrett.

"Well you could have at least kissed the guy bye if you—"

"This is not the time."

"I'm just saying, he really likes you. You can tell—"

"Mr. Connors," I snap at him, causing his eyes to widen and shoulders deflate, irritation swelling in my chest. "This is not an appropriate conversation."

"My bad." His face changes from amused to cautious as he looks away from me to watch the other students walking by, the silence in my little office extremely loud.

"Now, let's talk about your application. Did you talk to your parents?"

Still not looking at me he says, "I did. They think it's a good plan."

"Do *you* think it's a good plan?"

He looks down at his hands. "I don't know, maybe."

The silence continues and I can tell he feels embarrassed by his comment that he's resisting carrying on this important discussion. I clasp my hands tighter, fighting back my intrusive thoughts to snap at him to *grow up,* and take a deep breath.

"Garrett," I whisper. His head is still hanging, but he looks up at me through his eyelashes, a pout peaking through. I roll my eyes. "Fine. You get thirty seconds."

"What?" he asks, confused, one eyebrow lifted higher than the other.

"You get thirty seconds to speak your mind about Mr. Divata and myself. Nothing grotesque or obscene, and I will not answer any questions. Got it?"

Garrett sits up straighter, leaning forward as if he is setting up for a sprint. Groaning, I point to the clock indicating the time and wave my hand presenting him the metaphorical stage.

"Alright, this guy is so into you. We haven't seen him date anyone since some girl named Penny or something like three years ago, and she was *weird.*" His voice picks up—he's clearly overly excited to be dishing this out. "The whole senior class wants you guys to go to homecoming and prom together, and they wanna crown you guys. Obviously won't happen if Birdie has anything to do with it, but it would be tight to see. And the guy is a saint, literally sent from the universe to protect us." A lump in my throat forms as Garrett goes on and on about Benny and what he does for all of them. "You know he stayed at the hospital with me for five hours after my surgery because my parents had work? And he took Charlie to Texas for baseball tryouts because no one would take him?" He stopped abruptly, looking at the clock.

Thirty seconds.

A moment of silence passes before Garrett whispers, "He's my hero." His voice is vulnerable and timid, like I would make fun of him for what he just shared.

I wait for him to go on, selfishly because I want to know everything about Benny and hear all of the amazing things he does for these kids. But also because I sense Garrett needs to get something off his chest.

"He's the only one who truly believed in me." He sniffles. "Outside of football, Mr. B is the only one who thought I could still get into college after my knee. He has full faith I can pull it around. My parents just laugh at me when I tell them I still want to go." He pauses, looking through the window at the empty hall. The students have all made it to class, with a few stragglers shutting lockers and high tailing it before they're tardy.

"Why do you think they laugh?" I ask, knowing full well the answer. Benny shared about Garrett's parents. About how Garrett is the youngest of five and not a single one of them has gone on to college. Garrett's dad is a warehouse manager and his mom is a librarian. Both respective jobs in their own right, but the aspect of college was never financially doable for his siblings. Football was the only way in their minds, any other avenue wasn't plausible.

He shrugs at me, refusing to acknowledge that we are probably thinking the same thing.

"What do you say we prove them wrong?" I ask.

"How so?"

"Well, I spoke with Coach Dawson at Central State and he's agreed to give our plan a shot."

"Seriously?" Garretts eyes are big and puppy-like, disbelief washing across his face.

"Seriously." I smile at him. "Contingent on you maintaining a B average in your final course load, and you have to meet requirements at training camp next month."

"My knee though." He grimaces as he repositions his boot and bandage-covered leg.

I walk around from my desk to hand him a list of training requirements. "They have scaled their expectations." He takes the list from me, reading the list carefully. "If you meet those and follow doctor's orders for recovery to get medical clearance, you'll be able to join as their second string for next fall."

The pride wells up inside me as I wait for Garrett to respond. This plan took more energy than calling about rehab placement for my frequent flyers. Calling my connections at Central State, multiple meetings with the coaches and Dean, advocating for Garrett, Benny writing a recommendation letter. He was the last student on my list of crises, and by far the most complex. The challenge of solving it was fun, but the burdening reality that it might not work out was emotionally taxing. I'd grown to adore Garrett and his quirks, his heart for others so open and accepting. I put all of his eggs in this Central State basket, not knowing if he would even be open to the idea of playing second string, let alone at a non-conference college.

It was a long shot, but I was proud of the plan and the accomplishment of orchestrating it all. Even Benny told me Patsy couldn't have come up with the idea. Which is definitely not true, but I appreciated his accolades nonetheless.

My nerves started to take over as Garrett remained silent. Watching as he slowly crinkled the paper and placed his head in his hands, shoulders moving up and down slightly. He was crying.

I let out a slow breath. "I'm sorry if this isn't what you had hoped for. I called a few other schools to see but—"

My sentence is cut off by a bear hug. Garrett had leapt from his chair, towering over me, and squeezing me around my shoulders as he sobs. Weepy "thank you's" billowing out of him like uncontrollable waves.

With my arms pinned to my sides, I awkwardly twist to pat him on the side of the arm. "Just doing my job."

"Thank you for believing in me," he whispers as he squeezes tight once more before letting go to look at me, his cheeks wet from his happy tears. His happiness was palpable.

With my shoulders slightly aching, I gingerly fist bump him before he crutches out of my office.

"Could you put that thing away and help me carry these?" Emma was carrying three large, burlap sacks full of potatoes.

I had been the worst grocery store buddy the last hour, constantly pulling out my phone to muster the courage to text Benny. I hadn't heard from him all day and was more than convinced it had something to do with my erratic exit from the break room this morning. I tried to find him as soon as my session with Garrett was over. He deserved a face-to-face apology for my behavior, but his office was dark and was nowhere to be found in the building.

Shoving my phone in my pocket, I take a bag of potatoes and hoist it into the shopping cart. "What else do we need?"

"Got the marshmallows!" Kate shouts as she rushes down the produce aisle towards us. "I got minis and extra-large, there was no in-between."

"It'll have to do," Emma says, eyeing the marshmallows, clearly making mental adjustments to whatever recipe they were being used for.

"Great! Do we have everything?" I ask, steering the cart towards the direction Kate just ran from, Kate walking beside me as she tears coupons from the Glendale fundraiser coupon book.

"I have a coupon for a BOGO bag of popcorn balls, did we get that?" she asks, tearing the coupon to show me the savings.

"Ugh, I could kill for a popcorn ball!" I laugh.

"Same! I'm starving!"

Kate and I turn down the snack aisle, leaving Emma behind to tally up her list. We each mosey along, dropping different bags of candy, chips, and crackers into the cart. Disobeying Emma's store rule of *sticking to the list.*

My stomach growls loudly as I toss in a bag of Skittles. "Why are we here when we're hungry?"

"Rookie mistake." Kate groans as she holds up two different bags of flavored pretzels, debating on which to purchase before she ultimately decides both are good options and tosses them in the cart. "So, this morning was interesting."

"What was?" I wheel the cart ahead of her to avoid eye contact. It was only a matter of time before she brought it up.

"You know *what*!" She hurries to catch up to me. "He was practically scooping you up into his lap in the middle of our meeting!"

"That's an exaggeration." I roll my eyes.

"For Benny though, that was major PDA!"

"Really? I didn't even notice." *Lies.*

"Really! He is anti-physical touch in public. He barely even hugs me unless I'm crying or just having a freak out." She pouts.

"He just leaned against my chair, what's so crazy about that?" I ask as if I am painfully unaware of my surroundings and the facts are not computing. My voice is an octave higher than it should be.

She steps in front of the rolling cart, forcing me into a sudden stop. Glaring at me, she says, "Did something happen?"

"What? Nothing . . . nothing happened." I start panicking, she'll read right through me. "I don't know. Why are you asking me?" I wheel the cart around her and try to pick up speed, but she's right on my heels.

"Ahh, no you don't!" Running past me, she plants her feet on the bottom rail of the cart like little kids do when they want to be wheeled around the store. She leans across the basket, eye level with me. "Tell. Me. Everything."

The memory of our kiss rushes back to me, causing every sensation in my body to go into overdrive, pulsating down my legs, into the floor, and back up again. God, such a good kiss.

In normal circumstances, I am a steel trap, keeping every secret detail about my life tightly closed within the walls around my heart and mind, nothing breaking through.

I'm not sure if it's Kate's hilarious attempt at intimidating eyes, the over sensory of her tapping foot, or the giddy butterflies in my stomach . . . but I can't keep it in any more. The steel trap is opening and a lovestruck teenager is about to burst through...

"Fine! We . . . kissed . . ." I whisper-squeal.

"What?" Kate yells, planting her hands on both sides of her face in shock.

Then, as if we were just told we won the lottery, we start screaming, laughing, and jumping up and down right there in front of the Doritos.

"What? What's wrong?" Emma comes rushing towards our shrieks.

"They kissed!" Kate announces to Emma and basically the entire store.

"Who? What? Oh my gosh!" Emma joins in our weird circle of giggles and nudges, hugging me so tight I feel I might crack in two. "This is so exciting! Our plan worked!"

Pushing out of her hug I stare at her. "Your what?"

"Yeah, what?" Kate asks, equally confused.

"Oh it was just a silly idea Steven had." She shrugs as if that tells us the entire story. We both look at her expectantly, she chuckles at our impatience and continues. "I had just told Steven I noticed some looks between you two here and there. He told me about Benny hitting his car—"

"Ben hit someone's car?!" Kate gasps.

"It was an accident!" I jump to defend him.

"Yes, yes, he hit the car. Accident, whatever happened." Emma waves off the details, "Steven told me we should set them up, I knew you would never go for it. So he invited him to dinner in place of paying for the damage, it was the perfect excuse." She grins at me, "I was afraid we ruined it when the wine hit and I couldn't shut up. Stupid Merlot."

"Wow." I gape at her, shocked at her sneakiness, and the fact that I didn't catch on. Emma has never been one to be sly or keep a secret, and Steven has never been one to be in cahoots with anything, let alone my love life. The length the two of them went to for me was sweet, and it almost made up for them being the tipsy loud mouths they were.

"Sorry about that by the way," she says sincerely, interlocking her arm with mine.

"All is forgiven." I smile.

"So you guys are official now?" Kate asks, bouncing up and down as we head towards the check out line.

"I guess? We haven't officially labeled it though." I wheel the cart to the cashier—a student they call Tiny Tim and he is anything but. He is a very large, dark-complected teenager who has a beard almost as good as

Malcolm's. It's a mystery if he really is seventeen or if he's just repeated his senior year a few times.

"Hi Tim, how are you?" I ask, setting the groceries on the conveyor belt.

Tim grunts as he scans our groceries and smashes them into plastic sacks. Kate clears her throat and sets two large, reusable sacks near the register, gesturing for him to use those instead of plastic. He grunts again, taking the already packed plastic bags and placing them entirely in the reusables. Kate looks at me visibly irritated, and groans, accepting the bags as Tiny Tim slides them to her without looking up from the scanner.

"You can't just kiss someone and not expect there to be an official label," Emma says, perusing the gum selection near the register.

"I know, I just assumed we would talk about it by now." I grab a large packet of spearmint gum, Benny's favorite, and toss it with the rest of the groceries.

"What haven't you?"

"Haven't had time. And I think I upset him."

"Impossible, he's too smitten. You could never do anything wrong," Kate says at the end of the check out line, reorganizing the groceries to return the plastic bags back to Tiny Tim.

"Oh I'm sure I could," I say, thinking back to the pitiful look on his face as I pushed his hand away this morning. Shame and guilt hit me down to the bone over being the source of hurt he must have felt. My mind quickly turns to panic and worry that he could be mad at me. "He hasn't texted me at all today," I say, urgently. "Garrett Connors saw us in the breakroom, we weren't doing anything! But we weren't *not* doing anything either! Nothing crazy happened!"

"What did happen then?" Emma asks.

"He was just being so, ugh, and I was literally a puddle on the floor. I didn't realize Garrett was there, I was afraid we'd get in trouble or something, I don't know! I freaked out, I ran away and now he probably hates me." My voice cracking on the word hate, fear and desperation lingering as I may have let my intrusive thoughts ruin something so wonderful.

"Benny doesn't hate anyone," Kate says, comforting me with a side hug and bringing me back to reality. "And he could never ever hate you. Or I'll disown him."

"But what if it's too good to be true?" I whisper, intrusive thoughts taking over again.

"It's not. You guys are perfect for each other!"

"Just text him. He probably thinks you don't want to talk to him or he freaked you out or something," Emma says, loading the repackaged groceries into the cart.

"Or he's realized he can do better and doesn't need a girl like me," I whisper more to myself than them.

Emotionally broken, angry, and cynical.

"Don't be ridiculous, you are wonderful and any guy would be lucky to have you. Benny included," Emma pays Tiny Tim and we start to leave the store.

"I don't know, maybe this is all too much. Maybe I should just leave it at a perfect kiss and not let anything ruin it."

"What could ruin it?" Kate demands.

I could. And I probably will.

"Anything. Our jobs, being around each other too much, we could get tired of each other—bored." I start rambling off the list of frightening realities that could ruin the perfect bubble surrounding Benny and I's wannabe relationship.

"Ellie, stop," Emma interjects, the stern tone to her voice she gets when she's at her max with the kids. "You are self-sabotaging and you need to stop. Benny is a great guy, and you don't think you deserve a great guy so you're letting your brain get the best of you. Don't let your scary thoughts win. Nothing is perfect, and things are bound to mess up somehow, especially in a relationship." She puts her hand to her heart, a heaviness lingering that she isn't ready to share yet. "But that doesn't mean it's doomed. Nothing good and worth having comes easy. Give this a chance, give something *good* a chance."

CHAPTER TWENTY

Benny

Eleanor

My reaction in front of Garrett was crappy and I hope you can forgive me. You mean a lot to me, I hope I didn't ruin this amazing thing between us

You think it's amazing? ;)

Eleanor

Don't you? ;)

Absolutely :)

Eleanor

So you forgive me?

Always

Eleanor

Can't wait to see you at the party tonight!!

Me either! I hope you're ready for my costume ;)

On the edge of my seat!

The place looks so different than it did the other night. A week ago it was just a huge, two-story house with a long driveway, and piles of leaves covering the yard and porch. There were only two pumpkins as decorations by the front door. I'm assuming they were the work of Emma's boys because one just had a big circle cut out of it and the other looked like it had been stabbed repeatedly with a fork.

Now I was basically pulling up to a professional haunted house.

The outside light bulbs have been switched out with orange bulbs and covered in fake cobwebs. Fake skeletons and tombstones line the driveway, with a full-body skeleton dangling from the second story window, while rubber bats and fake spiders cover the outside of the house, and a smoke machine is whirring a fake fog across the yard. The porch is enclosed in a black tarp with a small shimmer of light peeking out from the bottom edge that meets the floor. I put my truck in park at the end of the driveway. It's already jam-packed with cars, and I'm fifteen minutes early.

Taking a deep breath, I text Ellie letting her know I'm here. *God, I hope my costume doesn't freak her out.* I adjust the black scarf tied to the top of my head and pull the black mask over my eyes. Giving myself a once over in the mirror to confirm that yes, I look ridiculous. Ellie comes running out of the slit in the black tarp, halfway dressed in a Thing 2 costume. No blue hair, yet. I reach over to the sack sitting on my floor board, praying I got her size right. Nothing is worse than guessing a size too big when picking out clothes for your girlfriend.

I step out of the truck, smoothing out the fluffy black top Kate told me to wear, wiggling my hips to readjust the black leather pants that are clinging a little too close for comfort. Turning to face Ellie, she stops dead in her tracks and gawks at me.

"Oh my!" she yells, throwing her hands up to cover her mouth.

Yep, the costume was too much.

"Ugh, it's too much isn't it?" I throw my head back, refusing to look her in the eye and face the awkwardness I've created. "I was trying to be cute but I wasn't sure what you'd think."

"I love it!" She bounces up and down, running to meet me with a hug.

"Thank God." I hug her, relieved.

Still hugging she looks up at me. "My sweet Westley! You're amazing!"

Pushing the hair behind her ear, I stroke her cheek with my thumb and ask, "Will you be my Princess?" holding up the sack carrying a red dress Kate instructed me to purchase.

"Shut up, really?!" She snags the sack and pulls the dress out, holding it up to her like a girl playing dress up, grinning from ear to ear. I don't know if I've seen her look this happy and I want nothing more than to make her this happy all the time.

"Unless, of course, your heart is set on Thing 2?" I wink.

"Heck no! Kate will just have to deal with it!"

She takes me by the hand, interlocking her fingers with mine and leads me inside.

Once we cross the tarp threshold, it's like we're transported to a different planet. A deep blue hue of light is coming from the sconces and ceiling lights, multicolored spots of light sparkle across the walls and floor from a variety of rotating disco balls. Cobwebs cover every inch of the stairs and fireplace and black candles, paper bats, witch hats, and the like scattered across the place for a picture perfect Halloween set up.

Ellie hands me a bottle of water, knowing I won't be drinking, touches my cheek, and stares at me. Everything around us stops, I only see her, an angel in the sea of partying ghouls and goblins. Knowing full well people see us—coworkers and family—she leans in, her eyes flickering from the lights. I sense a lot of desire in this moment, but some hesitation as well.

Kissing her cheek, I say, "Go get dressed, my lady."

"As you wish!" she says, as she runs toward the stairs.

I watch as she runs into Emma, showing her the dress and pointing back at me. I do the best impression of a Westley bow that I can, they both giggle and run up the stairs.

"I hope you're happy," a voice grumbles behind me as I take a swig of water.

Turning around and simultaneously spitting out my water at the sight of Malcolm . . . with a blue beard . . . sporting a Thing 2 t-shirt. I try to stifle my laugh behind my fist and am unsuccessful. Laughter overtakes me as I cackle like a hyena.

"Is my humiliation funny to you?" Malcolm asks behind his glass of scotch before downing in a shot like fashion.

Unable to make words through my laughter, I give him a sympathy shoulder pat before snapping a selfie of our alter egos. Westley smiling under his drawn on mustache, Thing 2 refusing to look at the camera. I point at his t-shirt for emphasis on this monumental moment, sending the photo to our faculty group.

"You owe me."

"Hey, no one forced you to replace Ellie as *this*." I laugh, gesturing to his getup.

"Whatever. Just trying to be a team player." He rolls his eyes as he fills his glass with more scotch. Or bourbon? All the same to me.

"And your efforts are appreciated," I say, clinking my water bottle to his glass in his honor.

Malcolm and I wander into the living room, greeted with numerous, "hello's," "woah's," and "nice costume" chit-chat as we make our way to a table filled with other faculty gathered around it. I remind myself that these people are my friends whom I love dearly before losing myself in a fit of giggles. Bill is dressed as a giant fluffy bunny, Margaret the librarian is a poorly designed Norwal, and Ross from night school is a poor representation of Tom Cruise from Top Gun—a plethora of embarrassing, yet well intended attempts at costumes. All to appease Emma. Such troopers.

"And what are you supposed to be?" Bill asks me as he adjusts his bunny ears.

"A ninja?"

"A pirate?"

They all start spouting off answers as Ellie wraps her arms around my waist and says, "He's my Westley!"

I look down at her—long flowy red dress, hair long and wavy, with small flowers pinning pieces back. "And you're my Buttercup," I say, kissing her on the cheek.

"FINALLY!" Bill the bunny yells.

"I told you!" Ross points at Margaret.

High fives, murmurs, and the passing of dollar bills happen around the table as I stare at Ellie, smiles stretching across our faces. Instant relief pours out of me as the group hugs and congratulates us, openly supporting our relationship.

"You look beautiful," I whisper to Ellie amidst the group chatter.

Cheesing so hard she reaches up, wrapping her arms around my neck and pulls me into a kiss. Kissing her back, I wrap my arms around her waist and pull her tight against me. I kiss her lips, her cheek, jaw, forehead, anything I can without going too far, and she lets me. I'm fully aware of everyone watching us and could care less that I'll see them Monday morning.

I can't help myself.

"DJ, turn the music up!" someone yells from across the room.

Time Warp starts to play and the crowd rushes to the middle of the dance floor where the couches used to be. Ellie and I stay wrapped up in each other, laughing our heads off at everyone's hilarious attempts at dancing in step. As the music continues through a superb playlist, we watch as witches, farm animals, healthcare workers, and everything in between is jostling and gyrating like no one is watching.

Emma and Steven join, doing the sprinkler.

Kate drags Malcolm to the center, linking hands and forcing him to do the wave.

Bill does some move that is probably from his generation and Margaret follows suit.

One ghost does a slick step slide move.

Another hypes him up.

A male witch moonwalks across the floor.

Ellie watches in amazement, laughing and whooping at everyone's dance moves, bouncing along to the beat. "Can't you dance?" she yells in my ear over the music.

"Maybe a little," I yell in her ear. "Don't tell anyone!"

She lets out a full body laugh and I hear it louder in my head than the music that surrounds us, a sound I want to hear on repeat.

"Hey . . ." I tug at her arm, I can't keep my thoughts to myself anymore. She stops dancing to face me, I push back some pieces of hair that are stuck to her glistening face. *It's a thousand degrees in here.*

I cup her face, and she looks at me, mouthing, "*What's wrong?*"

Not letting go of her face, I say, "I have to say this before I lose my nerve . . ." She grabs me by the hips, watching my face, her green eyes reflecting the lights swirling around us. The embarrassment consumes me at how smitten I'm feeling. I let go of her face and look down at my pathetic black pirate boots. "I don't think I've ever been this happy."

She tilts my chin up, tracing her thumb around my lips. "Me either."

I kiss her thumb. The inside of her wrist. Up her arm. The small freckle on her neck.

"Lover boy, get out here before I put in my notice!" Malcolm yells, directing our attention to the center of the dance circle where is doing the duck dance in slow motion. Probably his form of rebellion instead of actually partaking in the dance off that's happening.

Grabbing Ellie by her hands, I throw her arms up and over my head, pulling her in for one more moment just us. "Can I introduce you as my girlfriend now?" I whisper into her neck.

She chuckles. "Gosh we're total teenagers right now!"

"Have to define the relationship, remember?" I wink, kissing her one more time.

"Of course, *boyfriend*," she emphasizes with a wink before leading me to the dance floor.

We danced for what felt like an eternity. I caved and pulled out some of my infamous dance moves, sending shock waves across the floor. Whether my moves were shockingly good or just downright bad, I'm not sure, but we were having a blast.

I lost the facemask halfway through, drenched in sweat, and was half-tempted to unbutton my pirate shirt. But I still work with these people, and needed some fresh air anyway, so Malcolm and I meandered outside to the back porch for a cigar.

"So, have you talked to Clinton yet?" Thing 2 asks as he puffs at his cigar, beard still very blue.

"Not yet. I'm delaying the inevitable." I take a small puff of my vanilla flavored cigar—it's the only way I can tolerate them, and I rarely ever finish it. But it's one of the ways Malcolm bonds outside of fishing, so I stick it out, appreciating the moments he decides to open up. "I'm hoping since we won't be working together after the term that he'll allow it."

"You sure about that? Y'all won't be working together?" He raises an eyebrow at me as he blows cigar smoke up in the air making it look cool. I cough my vanilla smoke out of my nose. "Seems to me the girl wants to stay at Glendale."

I hadn't thought about that, we hadn't even talked about her plans after term yet. I was in denial that she might actually be going back to New York in a few months, living in this infatuation bubble you start out in at the beginning of any relationship.

We sit there silently, listening to the noise of the party muffled behind us, sounds of an autumn night in front. Crickets chirping loudly, wind blowing leaves off the trees, the small table fire crackling.

"You hear what she did for Connors? Brilliant idea," Malcolm says, breaking the silence. "And Ms. Johnson said Devon seems to be responding well to their sessions." He takes a final drag of his cigar. "I'd do everything I could to get her to stay, Benny. These kids will be better off with her around," he says, squishing his cigar butt out on the bottom of his boot. I follow suit, squishing my entire cigar on my pirate boot, Malcolm chuckling at the site.

Kate slides the backdoor open. "Hey introverts, get back to the party! We're about to limbo!"

Malcolm and I share a look . . . *why us,* before standing up and reluctantly heading back inside to break our backs.

I scan the room, hoping to find Ellie with no luck, but I find Emma in the kitchen, chopping fruit and aggressively shoving it into a bowl. "Late night snack?"

She doesn't look up, just chopping and slicing like the fruit did her wrong.

"Everything okay, Em?" I ask, stepping beside her, avoiding the quick movements of the dull butter knife she is using to slice. Poor choice of utensil but not my place to bring it up right now.

"Drinks are in here. The food is bare at this point in the night but help yourself," Steven says as he leads a guy I am unfamiliar with into the kitchen. "This is Benny, Emma's boss." He gestures to me.

"Hey there," I say, shaking the lanky stanger's hand, noting his overly soft palm and inability to handshake like a man with purpose. Instead, it's just a limp noodle in my hand.

"Dr. Liam Peters," he responds and my hand freezes. "Nice to meet you."

Now *my* arm is the limp noodle.

Liam.

Steven grimaces at me and I release my hand. He leads him out of the kitchen to the party, looking back at Emma apologetically. She's still chopping, hands shaking.

"Where's Ellie?" I ask urgently.

"Outside," she quivers.

I take the butter knife out of her hand. "Will you be okay?"

She nods as tears start to stream out of her eyes, breathing picks up. "I had no idea he was coming."

I give her a quick hug and rush to find Ellie, filling Kate in on the way and telling her to keep Liam inside. Kate salutes me and storms toward them, grabbing Malcolm as her backup.

Stepping out of the enclosed foggy porch, I see Ellie yelling and stomping in the middle of the front yard. A pile of smashed pumpkins at her feet.

Approaching cautiously I call out to her as she throws another pumpkin down on the ground. "Ellie!" She doesn't respond, continuing to stomp and smash and yell. "Eleanor!" Still no response. I close the distance between us, standing close enough to make my presence known but far enough not to intrude. She slows down, no longer yelling after a few more minutes, but keeps smashing until every pumpkin in the pile is in pieces.

She comes to a stop, panting and looking up at the sky. I wait, not sure what to say or how to fix it. I could kick this guy's teeth in for showing up here.

After another moment she faces me, tears in her eyes but still not speaking.

"What do you need?" I ask, careful to respect her emotional processing. Remembering that she told me everyone processes things differently and sometimes the best thing to do is ask how we can help them instead of assuming a solution.

No response, just tears.

"Can I hug you?"

She nods and I close the gap between us in two strides, wrapping her up in my arms. She starts crying into my chest, knees almost buckling as she holds onto me. I lower both of us to the ground and hold her as close as humanly possible, letting her cry.

I want to kiss her, and tell her what she means to me—reassure her that she's not alone. But sometimes words aren't enough. Words aren't what we need. So I just hold her, knowing it's not the time for me to be the hero. I just hope me being here is healing enough, in this moment.

Her crying slows. "I'm a mess," she whispers into my chest.

"You are not a mess, that guy is just a douche and blindsided you at your own party." I stroke her hair with one hand, holding her against me with the other.

"He is a douche." She groans.

Another moment of silence goes by and I ask, "Do you want to talk about it?"

"I don't know what to say." She lifts her head, her eyes red and wet. Wiping the tears and her hair out of her face as she looks at me.

"Just tell me what you're thinking."

"You don't want to know . . ." She points to her head with both hands. "It's angry up here."

"I want to know . . ." I take her hands in my mind. "Your thoughts don't scare me. They don't define you. It's what you do with them that shows who you truly are."

"What does *that* say about me?" She gestures to the pumpkin remains scattered on the ground.

"Smashing pumpkins *does* say a lot about a person's character," I joke. We both laugh and her face brightens a tiny bit, the anger fading.

"Are you sure you want this?" she asks, her voice breaking. "An angry woman in your life? No one wants that." Looking down at her hands held in mine, tracing her thumb along my knuckles she hesitates. "You . . . you don't need me . . ."

"You're right." She looks up at me, offended. "I might not *need* you . . ." Pressing her hands up to my mouth, I whisper against her fingers, "But I *do* want you. And you want me. Angry pumpkin massacre or not, I'm in this. Period."

CHAPTER TWENTY-ONE

Ellie

"Good morning, everyone." Liam says, traipsing into the kitchen like he's not the worst thing I could possibly see first thing in the morning.

Emma and I refuse to acknowledge his presence and continue sipping our coffee.

"Gotta get the coffee," he chirps as he man-handles the coffee pot. Sloshing, clinking, pouring.

"This looks delicious!" He eyes the breakfast spread Emma prepared for everyone before helping himself to the fresh fruit and crunchy bacon, and then opening the refrigerator and cabinets, banging stuff around as he prepares his plate.

You know those people? The ones who seem to make noise with every single sudden movement? That's Liam.

Crunching, smacking, slurping . . . *breathing*.

Anger chills my spine as I watch him—disgust definitely plastered across my face.

It has been a long time since I was so easily irritated, even dealing with the student drama these last few months didn't hold a candle to the internal rage that was filling my stomach as I watched my ex-fiancé slither around my sister's kitchen like he had the right. A snake in human form.

Why is he here?

"Morning, everyone!" Steven walks in the kitchen, carrying one of the twins.

"What's up, little man?" Liam high-fives my nephew and jostles his hair as he leaves the kitchen with a plate piled high with food.

Steven joins us at the table after the little terror wiggles out of his arms and chases after Liam. Hopefully to kick him in the shin just for fun. Steven picks food off of Emma's plate, oblivious to the daggers we are both staring at him.

"What's on the agenda for today?" he asks Steven, his mouth full of bagel.

"Are you freaking serious right now?" Emma whisper shrieks at him. "What is he doing here?"

"He called me from the airport," he whispers—an uncomfortable guilt in his tone. "He just came for the weekend, said he wanted bro time." I roll my eyes and Emma huffs, crossing her arms at Steven. "What was I supposed to do? He already booked a flight." He pauses, looking at me with sad eyes. "I swear I didn't invite him. But I can't just turn him away either, El."

Crossing my arms, fighting the urge to let his puppy dog eyes dissolve my anger, I peek around the corner to the living room as I see my nephews throwing toys and cheerios at Liam, interrupting his attempt at a peaceful meal. I guess the gremlins are useful for something.

"When is he leaving?" Emma says through her teeth.

"Tomorrow morning, first thing—"

"He's here for another day?" I gape at him. The internal battle to not scream and break things slowly being lost.

"I'm sorry." Steven sounds pitiful, like he really means his apology. "I'm taking him fishing for most of the day though!"

We all sit there in silence, pondering if that's enough. What if this happens again? What if Liam thinks he can just wedge himself back into our family solely because he's friends with Steven? This can't happen, I refuse to let it.

"Yo, Stevie boy, you ready?" Liam calls from near the front door, nephews pelting him with Nerf bullets. I wish, in this moment, they truly were covered in metal casing . . . just a light layer, ya know . . . for forceful emphasis . . .

"Coming!" Steven chugs the rest of Emma's coffee, kissing her on the forehead as she maintains her irritated composure. "I really am sorry, he's gone tomorrow," he whispers to me, his sincere smile doing a decent job at fizzling some of my anger.

They head out the door, grabbing their pathetic fishing hats and cooler on the way.

"Love you!" Steven says to all of us.

"See y'all at dinner!" Liam says as he shutting the door as bullets fly at his head.

"Dinner?" I ask Emma, angry again.

Emma groans as she leaves the table and begins cleaning the kitchen erratically. Her irritation quickly changes into anxiety as she scrubs the counter. She scrubs so hard her arm might fall off, while the other hand shakes and twitches at her waist.

"How could he—why—ugh—" Her attempt at speaking is cut off with her heaving breaths and quivering chest. She grips the side of the counter, trying to steady herself.

I watch and wait, giving her a chance to process through her anxiety, at her constant request to *let her figure it out.* She's unsuccessful as angry sobs pour out of her, breathing uneven and erratic.

Swooping to her side, I grab both of her hands. "Em, look at me. Let's focus." Exaggerating deep breaths for her, long inhale and long exhale. "Let's find our five things, okay?"

Shaky, rapid breaths are coming out of her, one on top of the other. I squeeze her hands tighter as I deep breathe audibly. "What do you see?"

"A—Cheerio—by my left foot," she whispers in between exhales, hands shaking in mine.

I look down and see the Cheerio. "Good. What do you hear?"

Her breathing is still fast as she lifts her head, closing her eyes to focus. "The boys—laughing." She smiles as her hands become relaxed at the thought.

"I hear them too," I reassure her. "What do you smell?"

"Bacon and coffee," she answers quickly and confidently. Breaths becoming more stable.

"The best smell, right?" She nods and laughs with me. "What do you taste?"

"Bacon and coffee." She smirks, more relaxed now.

"Mommy, mommy! Sawyer took my truck!" Goblin one storms into the kitchen to Emma's feet. I watch as she simultaneously wipes her tears, takes a final steadying breath, and scoops him up to her in a bear hug. The panic gone, all her focus on her baby—like a super mom.

"Let's go remind Sawyer how to ask nicely, shall we?" she asks him as he hugs her like a koala attached to a tree. He nods in agreement as he waves shyly at me.

"Hi, Easton." I wave back and tickle his foot.

He giggles as Emma carries him away, kissing him all over his head, cheeks, and nose. Over time I think she's realized that's another way she can combat her anxiety, physical touch and affection from her babies.

I watch as she scoops Sawyer up in the other arm and sits down in the middle of the floor with them, leaving her worries behind as she gives them her undivided attention. The memory of their birth floods my brain.

An emergency c-section, two NICU babies, a long recovery for all of them.

After years of managed anxiety and little to no panic attacks, Emma's birth experience caused worsened symptoms and increased frequency so much so that she needed medication for the first few years of their life. Rightfully so, I can't imagine going through birth trauma the way she did.

For months postpartum was scary for her, but the boys, albeit colicky and a major handful in their own way, were lifelines for her. Tangible mercies for her own scary intrusive thoughts. And as much as they drive me crazy, I am so grateful they are around and love their sweet mama so much.

I finish cleaning up the kitchen for Emma then join them in the living room. My presence is enough motivation for the boys to race upstairs and drag their entire toy box down the steps and set it at my feet. Emma and I sit on the couch as Sawyer and Easton pull out each individual toy and present it to us in a showcase-like fashion. A pristine moment without angry thoughts or anxiety—just silly thoughts about broken Hot Wheels, orange dinosaurs, and pajama pants that are inside out.

My phone dings.

Benny

Need any rescuing today?

Smiling at the thread, I realize that even after the events of last night and this morning, I don't feel an immediate need to run away.

Things are actually going ok right now!

Benny

Oh? Is he there?

No, thank goodness. They went fishing

"What are you smiling at?" Emma asks from inside the odd-shaped circle of dinosaurs and toy cars the boys told her to *NOT TO LEAVE*—apparently it's a hostage situation.

Putting my phone away I shrug. "I don't know, just feeling happy."

She smiles at me, a warm and sweet smile I haven't seen in a long time, eyes looking a little misty and sentimental.

"What?" I ask her.

"I'm just happy you're happy. It's been a long time coming."

My phone dings again. Emma rolls her eyes, probably assuming Benny was double texting me—something she despises, but I secretly love. There's just something about getting back-to-back texts from someone, like they're

just thinking about you and couldn't wait for your response so they text
you again. Disregarding all response etiquette just for another chance to
hear from you.

I felt warm thinking about it.

Then another ding.

Followed by a third quickly after.

Okay, now we're bordering psychopath territory.

I unlock my phone to see multiple texts from my friend Duncan, the
admissions counselor from Columbia.

Duncan – CU

> I have a job for you

> Sending over details now

> They need an answer by next Friday – think
> about it

I stare at my phone so long my screensaver comes on—a jump roping
pineapple.

"What's wrong?" Emma asks. She's not even looking in my direction,
solely focused on manning the dinosaur fort as instructed, yet she's aware
something is up. That motherly intuition, probably.

"Uh—it's nothing—I just lost my train of thought . . ." I trail off,
staring back at my phone. My stomach is in knots, but I'm not sure if it's
due to anticipation or guilt. I haven't told Emma that I'm still scoping
out jobs. I haven't applied in a few weeks, actually, I only submitted one
application. But when I spoke to Duncan about some student applications
a few months back, I also told him *why* I was at Glendale for the time being

and the desperation I felt in regard to needing a job, back in New York, as soon as possible.

"Alright, well I'm gonna drop the kids off, then run to the store." She starts tidying up the living room, and, as if the twins have ultrasonic hearing, they come running downstairs demanding she not touch their things. Ignoring their hollers and screams she asks, "Liam hates chicken, right?"

"With a passion," I say, grabbing the box of toys before the boys rip it open again.

"Fried chicken for dinner it is!" she says primly. Gosh, I love her.

I cackle with enjoyment at her audacity and let Duncan know I'll get back to him before hoisting the box of toys over my shoulder and heading upstairs.

The job is Adjunct Professor in the Psychology Department, with rotations at the campus clinic.

I scroll through the department website, noting faculty members I recognize and new faces I would get to work alongside. As I review the curriculum, I am filled with a surge of exhilaration over the potential to teach and shape young minds in the field—an ever changing and adapting field.

A field I could have a major impact in if I were to take this job.

The job is more than intriguing . . . it's perfect.

It's everything I could have ever imagined in my dream job.

I immediately began jotting down information on my pad, doodles throughout.

As I scan the website I venture to other departments, taking note of what other avenues Columbia offers. I had never looked at other options before, it was always psychology. I jot down a few interesting undergraduate programs to share with Sarah Kim at her next session. Then I go to sports, something so uninteresting to me that I'm afraid I'm being possessed as

I look at it. I naturally start comparing the football stats of major players to Devon and Garrett. Then to baseball, thinking about Charlie and his tryouts coming up. And much to my dismay, I actually look at the cheerleading team and think of Birdie.

Glendale is bleeding over into my Columbia thoughts.

What is happening? I can't get these kids out of my head.

The picture perfect life I had envisioned in New York was within my grasp . . . but somehow, it is now distorted and out of focus.

Irrational anger creeps in and my doodles are becoming large, scratchy blobs as I scribble over the job notes I had taken.

Why is my dream all of a sudden not satisfying?

I have planned my entire life around New York and Psychology and the ability to make an impact in the field, and the fact that it felt less than stellar right now is infuriating. What's the point of planning out your life if your mind is just going to change at any given moment?

I groan as I slam my laptop shut and shove it on the ground, not really caring if I crack the screen. I want to just be irritated and angry and let it all out. For just one moment, I want to put the knowledge I have about the neuroplasticity of the brain on the backburner.

I want to throw a fit.

So I do.

A big one.

I kick and scream on my bed. I jump out of my bed to scream more. I take my purse and chuck it across the room—wallet, keys, and hand sanitizer bursting out on impact. I take a moving box packed with winter clothes and toss it at the wall—coats and sweaters toppling to the floor. I stomp on the clothes and scream into one of the huge overcoats I wore constantly in New York. My Glendale backpack filled with paperwork and notebooks is kicked repeatedly, doodled sticky notes scattering the floor. In anger, I crumple them up, shoving them in my trashcan.

I try to convince myself that my behavior and reactions are warranted as I throw a toddler-level temper tantrum.

I refuse to evaluate my choice of coping mechanism for one solitary moment.

I refuse to accept that our brains change and adapt due to our experiences, and the life I was experiencing right now was creating a lasting impact that would forever change my brain chemistry.

I refuse to embrace the change my brain was going through.

Out of breath from the kicking and screaming, I throw myself onto the floor—panting and heart racing, sweat drenching my face and hair.

Truth and fact penetrate through my emotions, forcing me to reflect on the unhealthy and immature reaction I just had. I throw my arms over my head, utterly embarrassed for what I just did, and drift off to sleep.

I feel something tickling my foot, jolting me awake as I go into defense mode.

"Don't go any further!" I yell, jerking my legs up into my chest as I flutter my eyes open.

A deep, familiar laugh greets me as I sit up. Benny is crouched down where my feet had been, holding a bouquet of flowers. His smile is striking, and even though I feel this may be a dream, I smile back. He's wearing a black cashmere sweater and pleated khaki pants, while his hair is a perfect blend of neat and messy as it swoops over to one side. He's freshly shaven and smells like a mix of coconut and spearmint—a glorious sight to see right after waking from an emotional coma.

"Hi there." He chuckles at me.

"Oh my gosh! What time is it?" I sit up straight, blinking my eyes focused at the clock on my nightstand. It's only five, dinner isn't for another two hours.

"Don't worry, you still have time. I just couldn't wait to see you." A shy, crooked smile peeks out as he reaches his hand out to help me stand.

He gently pulls me to my feet and I'm filled with instant regret as I brace for his reaction to the state of my loft. I glance around quickly but don't see the mayhem I had caused earlier. Everything is picked up, thrown into boxes, and set-up neatly, like they were packed that way intentionally. My purse has even been set back on my bed and zipped closed.

Did I hallucinate my freak out?

"Uhh—I thought it was messier in here?" I say to myself as I look around the loft.

"Well, it *did* look like a tornado hit for a minute, but I just threw everything in those boxes." He gestures to the boxes along the wall. "I hope that's okay?" he asks, rubbing his jaw, probably worried he may have crossed a line by *cleaning* for me. God, how was he so perfect?

"That was way too kind of you . . . Thank you." I reach around his waist and hug him tight against me—soaking in the experience that is, without a doubt, affecting my brain.

"These are for you." He kisses my head and hands me the bouquet of flowers—white, orange, yellow, and hints of burgundy flowers all wrapped in a little pumpkin ribbon. "I couldn't help myself," he says into my hair as he inhales, long and slow.

"They're beautiful, ugh. You're beautiful!" I say looking up at him, drooling over his freshly cleaned-up look.

"Me? Stahp." He dramatically waves his hand at me. "You're making me blushhh."

I giggle and wrap my arms around his neck, the flowers in my hand hitting his shoulder as I bring his face down to mine. He kisses me, deeply and passionately. For a moment I lose track of all space and time, letting my knees buckle ever so slightly. His grip around my waist tightens and pulls me closer, his hands splayed across my lower back. His lips move across mine, then to my cheek, down my neck and shoulder.

Then it stops.

Benny takes two giant steps backward and almost trips over my bed.

"What's wrong?" I ask him, feeling lightheaded and out of breath.

He clears his throat and rubs the back of his neck. "I want to be a gentleman."

I stare at him confused. "These were very gentleman-like," I joke, waving the flowers at him.

He lets out a long slow breath, "I—umm—don't know if I should kiss you the way I really *want* to . . . in your bedroom." He looks down at his feet, his face bright red.

"Ah, I see . . ." I say, staring at the bed behind him. Heat rushes through me, making my every part of me feel light. I am suddenly desperate for a drink of water. *That* physical aspect of our relationship hadn't crossed my mind . . . until now. I felt dizzy at the thought. I blink the thoughts out of my mind and focus on the strained look plastered on Benny's face. "I appreciate your self-control."

"It's not easy." His face relaxes a tiny bit as I giggle at him.

We stand there, awkward and tense, looking at practically anything but each other. The same heated thoughts running through our minds.

"So!" we both say in unison.

"What happened in here?" He shifts his eyes around the loft as he sits back on the edge of my bed.

"Where?" I ask sarcastically. I really don't want to address the chaos he walked into.

He raises his dark eyebrow at me, a smile crinkling his eyes as he tries to hold his gaze.

"Alright, I won't ask. But just so you know . . ." He pauses for effect. "I've seen worse." He smirks and we both laugh. He respects my boundaries and doesn't press for any more information and I'm grateful.

"Oh, really now?" I chuckle as I go to set my flowers on the bedside table.

"Oh yeah. Frankie got into a bag of catnip treats once. I had to replace my couch." He belly laughs at the memory and I join. The thought of that cat doing anything that isn't eating or napping is laughable.

We spend the next hour laughing and talking, and I refuse to get ready for dinner until the last possible minute. The entire time leading up to dinner, Benny never once pressures me for information about Liam or our history, and he doesn't give any indication that he is nervous or uncomfortable. It's a new side of a relationship I haven't experienced before.

A healthy side.

He leaves to let me get ready and I have to rush. Amidst the jumping on one foot to put my pants on, or as I practically rip my hair out when I try to brush it quickly, I'm in an odd place mentally. This is unfamiliar—no anger or sadness is creeping in—emotions I would normally expect as I prepare for the most awkward dinner of my life. It would be easy for me to fixate on a thousand questions: Liam was really here? Why? Was it really for "bro time"? Or something else?

But the questions left my mind quicker than they came and I felt at ease.

I assessed the woman looking back at me in the mirror, with a relaxed look in jeans and an oversized turtleneck sweater, minimal makeup and natural hair loosely pinned back.

For the first time in a long time, I feel content with what I see.

CHAPTER TWENTY-TWO

Benny

"So, IS THERE A reason you don't drink alcohol?" The ex-fiancé directs his question at me from behind his glass of pink, girly wine. His tone is not the friendly get-to-know-you type. Just the douchey let-me-diagnose-you type.

"Liam, that is incredibly inappropriate," Emma snaps at him in my defense.

"It's fine, Em," I say, opening the bottle of water she provided me. "Drank when I was young, got tired of it." I sip at my water, gesturing that I am very much done with that conversation. Just because you're a psychiatrist *Liam*, does not mean I feel the incessant need to share my life story with you.

I did *not* like this guy.

Did I usually mind sharing my past and the choices I made? Not at all. It's what shaped me to the man I am today, and most of the time I feel at peace with how things have ended up.

But did Liam have a right to know about said messed up past? No. Absolutely not.

I tend to like everyone. Growing-up Kate always told me to watch my back, because one day it'll get stabbed because I'm too trusting—something I always thought was a good thing. I just always have hope for other people to be good and do what's right.

It's rare that I don't see that in someone.

But right now . . . There's something about this chatty, blobfish I don't like. My gut feels very strongly that this Liam guy is not one to waste your time on.

"I see. Do you think you have a propensity for addiction?" He continues with his questioning, his cringey voice making me clench my jaw so hard my teeth might crack. He's clearly unaware of the social cues I've given that I do *not* want to share things with him.

"Liam, let's drop it." Steven forces a smile as he pats him on the back, probably at the awkwardness his *bro* was creating.

"I'm just making conversation," he says, shrugging as he shoves a slice of cheese down his gullet.

"A conversation some of us don't want to have," Emma whispers.

"Well what else shall we talk about while we wait then?" he asks, talking with his mouth full of cheese.

What did Ellie see in this guy?

He's taller than me, but he's lanky. Out of instinct, I stand up straighter, pushing my chest out, like a *man.* I'm not one to be overly confident, but I know for certain I could break this toothpick in half. And I'm pretty sure his hairline is already receding. I run my fingers through my hair, thanking the good Lord for my thick, Filipino waves.

The kitchen is eerily quiet as we all watch him eat half of the spread before any of us touch it. What a mooch.

My face feels tight as I watch him, slowly feeling unhinged. Being within ten feet of this guy the other night was enough to put me on high alert, but now, having to endure a meal with him, I feel territorial. Not just with Ellie, but with Emma and Steven too. They are great people, and I can't help but want to sucker punch this guy in his teeth as I watch him scarf down the food Emma worked so hard to prepare, without a simple *"thank you."*

Gentle hands wrap around my waist from behind with a whispered *"hey"* into my back. I turn to face Ellie, her hands still interlocked around me. Cradling her face in my hands, I kiss her long and steady, with a little extra passion—for Liam's benefit.

"Hi," I whisper, coming up for air.

Liam attempts to clear his throat nonchalantly, but I refuse to look in his direction. My gaze fixed on Ellie, her face still in my hands.

"Let's eat!" Steven says from behind me.

"Let's get this over with," Emma whispers next to Ellie and I.

Taking our seats, Ellie sits down, pulling me down next to her. I resist the temptation to pull her into my lap and lift a cocky eyebrow toward Liam as he plops down right in front of me. His foot touches mine for a millisecond and I make a mental note to burn my shoes when I get home.

We sit in silence as we plate our food, family potluck style. I watch as Liam fills his plate to the brim, chunks of food falling off. I'm curious if his body rejects the food he consumes due to the size of his pencil arms shoveling it in his mouth.

How does a guy his size eat that much and not look a little more . . . well . . . *healthy?*

"So Eleanor, how's the new client population? Are they opening up to you? Sharing their real-life problems?"

It might just be the preconceived notion I have about this guy but I sense a condescending tone in his questions. What does he have against my students?

"It's going well, actually. I'm really enjoying it," she says, smiling at me.

"Are you helping them find prom dresses and deal with breakups yet?" He chuckles, again mouth so full of food some of it falls out.

"Actually, I do more than that—"

"There's no way you're feeling fulfilled," he interrupts, "and actually making any lasting impact on the world of mental health. You know, the other day I diagnosed a set of adult twins with Borderline Personality Disorder." He continues talking in-between bites of food, "They've lived for almost forty years unaware of their symptoms, believing they were just born that way. It was invigorating to finally solve the puzzle. Just imagine the thrill you could get if you were still at the clinic!" He points his fork covered in chicken casserole at Ellie.

"That does sound thrilling," Ellie responds in a whisper. I'll give the girl credit, she's trying to be respectful of the guest, regardless of him being a tool. "But what I'm doing now is also thrilling in its own way." She pokes at her food as Liam laughs in response.

"No way. High school drama is just that, *drama*. There's no true clinical or diagnostic side of helping someone apply for college." He laughs so hard his face is beet red. "You think *that's* thrilling? Please!" The man is about to collapse from his laughter.

"It is thrilling!" Emma snaps at him.

Attempting to slow his laughing, he nods. "Right, sure."

"It really is. Just the other day I helped a student overcome a panic attack! And last week, I helped another mend a relationship with his parents," Ellie says confidently, sitting up straighter. Her smile says "*screw you*" but below the table, her leg is shaking uncontrollably. Unsure if she's shaking out of anger towards Liam being a jerk, or the truth that her job isn't as thrilling as it used to be, I place my hand on her thigh like before, "*I'm here.*"

"You're not living up to your potential." He stares at her.

I swallow the lump in my throat . . . her *potential.*

"Yes she is!" Emma places her hand on Ellie's hand. "Don't listen to him. What you're doing is valuable and impactful." She stares at Liam with a hot anger I've never seen from her before.

"I'm just saying"—he waves his hands up—"your growth here is limited. All you will ever be is a school counselor." He shrugs matter of factly and my heart breaks . . . he's right. The longer she is at Glendale, the less appealing she becomes as a psychologist and the more she falls under the *guidance counselor* umbrella. And last I checked, that's not what she wants.

Ellie has goals and aspirations so big that Glendale could be hindering her from reaching them.

I could be hindering her.

"What's so wrong with that? Being a school counselor is admirable!" Emma shouts at Liam and stands from the table. Steven tries grabbing her hand, but she dodges it and storms to the kitchen.

"No offense, Em!" Liam says, not turning around to look at her. "It's just the truth. With her education and experience, Eleanor could have endless opportunities." He looks at Steven for backup but Steven ignores him and leaves the table. Emma begins aggressively cleaning the kitchen and putting food away as Liam continues. Again, very unaware of social cues to *stop.*

"If you stay at the clinic you'll get more opportunities for advancement. Associates will be seeking you out and you won't be stuck at—"

"I'm not stuck!" Ellie cuts Liam off, slamming her hands on the table.

"You know what I mean, Ellie," he says, crossing his arms on the table, he gives her a look that makes my stomach drop. A look with feelings—feelings with a history.

"I actually don't know what you mean."

"If you stay at Glendale, you won't be taken seriously. Your judgment won't be valued in our field." *Our* field . . . the word crushes my heart. Another reminder of everything they have in common and what they *were.* The truth is crushing as I sit here helpless. I don't have anything to offer in *their* field. I can't help her change the world the way Liam can. I can't help make her dreams come true.

"Yes, it will! And it does not make me any less qualified or desirable!" Her voice was rising with each word and all I wanted to do was throw this guy through a window for upsetting her like this.

"Sure, of course not." He nods in an obvious, sarcastic way, like he pities her. My legs tense up as the image of drop-kicking him in the chest flashes through my mind. "Just be honest with yourself. You're selling yourself short and you'll never amount to anything by staying at Glendale."

Before I have the chance to reach across the table and wring Liam's neck, Ellie jumps up with her fists clenched at her sides, sending her chair toppling over behind her. "You have no idea what you're talking about!" She stands in place, looking ready to kick his teeth in and I feel a twinge of gratitude at how defensive she is of our school. "Glendale has a lot to offer and I feel lucky to be a part of it! And it will help me *amount* to whatever the hell I want!"

Liam, seeming to be unphased by her sudden burst from the table, sits back in his chair and sips on his wine. I'm concerned at his minimal reaction to Ellie's anger—that is directed solely at him—but he probably deals with worse on a daily basis so this could be nothing to him. For me, I have to fight back my urge to scoop her up and carry her out of here—remind her over and over that he's wrong and she can and will do anything she sets her mind to, and I will be there with her as she does it, cheering her on every step of the way. I want her to know she has everything to offer. That she is *everything*.

"Whatever you say." Liam finishes the last of his wine. "I just don't see any indication that you're going anywhere."

Emma slams the spatula she's been holding this entire time down on the kitchen counter, as Steven and I mutter "*dude*" and "*woah*" simultaneously. All three of us look at Ellie, who has gone from red to ghost white as she stares at Liam, hurt all over her face.

"I think, maybe, it's time for this conversation to be over," I break the silence and stand to Ellie's side, placing my hands on her arms, trying to look her in the eyes as she stares at the ground, blinking fast.

"I agree. Let's clean up," Steven murmurs in the kitchen, rubbing Emma's arms, probably to keep her from hitting Liam on the head with a pan.

"Sounds like a plan." Liam slaps his legs as he stands from the table. "I hate to upset you, Eleanor. But if you want another job in the future—"

"I *have* been offered another job!" Ellie yells around me, interrupting him.

"What?" Emma gasps from the kitchen sink.

My entire body goes numb. "Another job?" I whisper to her, my voice thick.

"Well, that is great!" Liam's voice sounds far away as I stare at Ellie. Her eyes look misty as she looks over my shoulder, not meeting my gaze.

"Were you going to tell me?" I whisper, waiting for her to look at me.

She blinks rapidly as she looks at me. "I don't know," she says, looking away as true tears start to slowly form in the corners of her eyes.

"Why didn't you tell us?" Emma asks.

"I didn't know how." Her voice is unsteady as she touches my chest, my heart pounding against her palm. Her bottom lip quivers as she looks at Emma over my shoulder, the weight of this decision in her eyes. "I don't want to disappoint you." Her voice breaks as her eyes land on me, tears flowing down her red cheeks. Ellie cares too much about what anyone else thinks and her leaving would impact more than just herself, and she knows that. She would sacrifice her dreams for us, for the school.

Words are lost on me as she searches my face, waiting for a response. I want to support her, tell her to chase her dreams and change the world. But I don't want her to leave Glendale . . . leave me . . .

The thought of losing her is unbearable. I want to tell her to stay and we can have new dreams—together.

Stay with me.

But she can't, not at the cost of her losing herself in the process.

I wipe a teardrop from her jawline with my thumb and, for some reason, that makes her tears flow faster. Cradling her face in my hands, she grabs my wrists, pressing my hands firmly against her cheeks and takes a slow steadying breath. My breathing picks up as she pulls me in closer, resting her head on my chest and tucking her arms against my chest. I wrap her up in my arms and hold her there in the middle of Emma and Steven's kitchen, ignoring the eyes on us as she lets it all out in gasping sobs.

At some point, we moved from standing to sitting on the floor and Emma wrapped us in a blanket. Eventually the sobs became sniffles, then light snores as Ellie exhausted herself into a deep sleep against my shoulder. Steven helped guide me as I carried her to bed, tucking her in and putting her phone on the charger. Her face was puffy and damp as I kissed her on the forehead and left.

CHAPTER TWENTY-THREE

Ellie

I HAVEN'T BEEN ON a run since I started at Glendale, but today feels like the best time to get out before the sun comes up—avoiding Liam was my top priority.

Tip-toeing into the kitchen for coffee unnoticed was unsuccessful when I arrive to find Steven was already wide awake, eating Fruit Loops.

"Morning." He smiles over his spoon before taking a bite of cereal. "Where are you headed?"

What are you, my dad?

His question irritates me instantly, but I bypass it. "Going on a run, just need some air."

He nods in understanding and continues eating, making no eye contact. I guess we're back to that. I silently curse Liam for his disruption of my life and reigniting the awkward tension between my brother-in-law and I.

I head out the door and am greeted with a cool, light rain, feeling instantly grateful for my decision to get up early. Taking a few deep breaths to enjoy the wet breeze on my face, I turn to start my run and see *him*, running towards me.

God. Of course he still runs.

"Good morning, Ellie," Liam pants as he jogs up to me in the driveway.

Ignoring his greeting, I sidestep and begin running, hoping he will take the hint and leave me be.

"Wait!" *Guess not.*

His steps speed up as he catches up to me. Damn his grasshopper legs.

"What do you want, Liam?" I pant, picking up my speed.

"Can we talk about last night?"

That is the last thing I want to do. Especially with him. Last night was the worst night I've had in a long time and it was all because of him and his absurdly loud mouth.

"Just give me a chance, El!"

"Why?" I yell as I halt to a stop, gravel from the driveway hitting my shins.

"Because I messed up! And I want to fix it!" he yells at me, throwing his arms out.

"Is that what you were doing last night?" My throat burns as I scream at him, "Fixing it?"

"Well no . . ." He rubs the back of his neck as he struggles to find words. "I just . . . I don't know when to shut up sometimes."

I cackle. "You think?"

He smiles, and I feel a sting in my chest—so many memories contained in that smile. "I know I can be a lot."

"Again, duh," I scoff as I turn to start walking.

Liam is on my heels, walking in step behind me. "I just feel like after everything we have been through, I could be honest with you about your future."

"You lost that privilege when you abandoned me!"

"I didn't abandon you!"

"Oh really?" I spin around to face him, my face hot and tense. "Then what would you call leaving me *at the altar?*"

"Alright, I know that wasn't the best way to handle it. But that was almost two years ago, are you really still angry?"

"Yes I am!" I yell, resisting the urge to stomp around to drive my point home.

"I'm sorry, alright? I am so sorry!" he yells back, stunning me with his first apology since the wedding. "I made a mistake and I know that. But you of all people know *this* wasn't working."

I cross my arms and look down at the wet ground, red dirt caked to the tops of my shoes. I can feel his eyes on me as he waits for me to respond.

He lets out a deep breath. "Aren't you tired of being angry, Eleanor?"

His words hit me like a ton of bricks. I was tired of being angry. But I wasn't going to tell him that. No way was I going to give him the satisfaction.

I turn on my heels and continue walking, focusing on the orange and red elm trees lining the driveway. The sprinkle of rain soaking my hair. Liam catches up to me and we walk in silence for a few minutes. We approach the end of the driveway to the busy road, waiting for the cars to pass before turning and walking along the curb. I glance at Liam as he stops to tie his shoe, noticing the bagginess of his pants as he stands back up. This is the first time I was really *looking* at him since he got here. He looks thin and frail—his skin is pale, and his eyes are surrounded by dark circles. They look different . . . sad. He doesn't look like the Liam I knew.

We turn down a road. "So, how are you?" I break the silence as we walk.

"I'm pretty tired these days." He kicks at the leaves along the side of the curb. The Liam I knew for so long was a ball of energy, the adrenaline of his work fueling him in ways I couldn't keep up with. But now, I can *see* how tired he is. My heart breaks for him a little. "I never leave the clinic." He pushes out a hard sigh, shoving his hands in the pockets of his sweatpants.

"Is Randy still there?" I continue with small talk, avoiding the pang of sadness I feel for him as it dawns on me how lonely he really is.

"Of course. He'll never leave. I told him I can't pay him any more than what I am but he won't quit on me." We both laugh at the thought of the seventy-year-old receptionist manning the phones and learning the complex telemedicine system.

"That sounds like Randy."

The rain slows to a stop and the sun starts to peek through the trees on each side of the road as we make a U-turn to head back. The walk back to the house is much hotter than the first part of our walk so we pick up the pace, jogging alongside each other as an eerie silence falls between us. Silence is a rarity most people don't get with Liam.

"Look . . ." He breaks the silence as we approach my sister's house. The remnants of the Halloween party—pumpkins, skulls, and fake cob- webs—scattered everywhere. "I really didn't mean to cause any problems by coming here. I'm just lonely. I miss Steven. And I wanted to make things right with you." He reaches for my hand. "I'm very sorry."

I let his words sink in as I stare at his outstretched hand—the decision to accept his apology within reach. For months I have felt nothing but bitter and resentment towards Liam and what he did. It would be so easy for me to walk away and let his words linger in the air. But what will that accomplish? How will I ever get past my anger?

Extend grace, Eleanor.

Taking a deep breath as I take his hand in mine, I say, "I forgive you." And for the first time since our almost-wedding, I feel like I truly mean it.

Giving my hand a tiny squeeze, he says, "Thank you."

His hand retreats back to his side, respecting the unspoken boundary we have in place as ex-fiancé's, but he stands there looking at his feet. Looking like he needs more than a hand-squeeze.

It may be the heat of the sun hazing my senses, or the cool autumn breeze filling my brain with nostalgia, or something else inside of me, ridding me of my anger and bitterness, because in this moment I feel nothing but love for Liam. Love for a man I know deep down is kind and passionate. A man who wants to care for people—the marginalized and stigmatized. A man who doesn't know when to shut up. A man who is *human*, just like me—messy and broken and far from perfect.

Without asking or acknowledging our boundaries, I step up to Liam and pull him into a hug. And as if it's exactly what he needed, his entire body relaxes and hugs me back.

"I swear if you two get back together," Emma shouts at us from her porch, wrapped in her fluffy white robe. "I will revolt!"

Breaking out of our hug Liam smiles at me. "I don't want to get back together, ya know."

"Me neither." I wink at him. And I mean it, I really don't.

There was never any doubt in my mind two years ago that I could have married Liam and been content. But would I have been happy? I don't really know. The life we could have had flashes across my mind and it fills me with peace knowing that's not where I ended up.

We spend the rest of the morning catching up at the kitchen table, sharing about our clients—old and new—and reminiscing on life in New York. He even welcomes conversation about the students and our term. I share the details of the Columbia job with all of them, welcoming their input and suggestions.

"I think it would be a spectacular opportunity," Liam says as he sets his duffle bag down by the front door.

"Agree to disagree," Emma whispers from the couch, holding a sleeping twin against her shoulder.

"We should let Ellie make her own decisions," Steven says, putting on his coat as he kisses Emma on the head. "Now, let's get going."

Steven heads out the door and to the car as Liam puts on his coat. "Walk with me?" he asks me. I follow him as he waves bye to Emma. "I can't tell you what to do," he says as he throws his bag in the truck, "but I think you should at least consider the job."

"I'm thinking about it." I wrap myself deeper into the blanket I carried outside. "But honestly, what I pictured myself doing long-term has changed."

"Is it because of *him*?" He refers to Benny with raised eyebrows and a slight lift at the corner of his mouth.

"Why? Are you jealous?" I laugh.

"I am, actually," he says, earnestly. I gape at him, confusion and worry surely visible on my face. "I'm jealous of your happiness."

My chest flutters at the thought.

Happiness.

"You are, aren't you?"

"Hmm?" I ask, my mind still fixated on his last statement.

"Happy?"

"I think I am." I grin sincerely.

"Well then"—he opens the car door then faces me—"I'm happy for you." He hugs me goodbye as I murmur "*thank you*" into his shoulder. "But you should still go to the interview."

"Come on, we gotta go!" Steven says, starting the car and blaring *I Believe I Can Fly* through his fancy car speakers.

"Every time." Liam rolls his eyes as he climbs into the car.

I chuckle at their absurd airport tradition and wave as they pull out of the driveway. The happiness bubbles over and I feel giddy, cheesing so hard my cheeks hurt.

"What's up with you?" Emma asks as I walk back inside.

"Just happy."

The smile stretches across my face as I finally let myself *feel* happy.

Chapter Twenty-Four

Ellie

"When did you plan on telling me about this little relationship?"

Mr. Clinton was sitting at his desk, spectacles sitting on the bridge of his crooked nose as he called Benny and I into his office before our morning faculty meeting. We were called into the *principal's office,* like a couple of disruptive hoodlums.

"Henry, I'm sorry," Benny whispers. "It all just happened so fast." He steals a glance at me before returning his focus on Mr. Clinton—who definitely saw the glance and rolled his eyes at the two love birds sitting across from his desk.

"How serious is this?" he asks, interlocking his hands and resting them underneath his chin. "Am I going to have to go to the board?"

Benny, who was holding my hand and disregarding the entire notion that we were *in trouble* for breaking the dating rule, continued to defend our case. "I don't know—"

"You don't know?" he interrupts, his eyes wrinkling behind his glasses as he frowns. "You could lose your job, Bayani. You better know what you're getting yourself into," he says, sternly—clearly irritated at the situation.

I adjust in my seat, my palm clammy against Benny's. "Mr. Clinton, I know this is all a little overwhelming. And I'm sorry we didn't come to you sooner."

"Ms. Bailey, look . . ." He pauses with a deep breath, smoothing out his blue linen tie. "I appreciate your contributions to this school. The students have grown to really like you. The faculty too"—he gives Benny a look—"but I can't risk losing Mr. Divata."

"I completely understand, I wouldn't want that either." I let go of Benny's hand, placing mine in my lap and whispering, "I don't want to jeopardize his job."

"You won't." Benny grabs my elbow. "Henry, please tell her she won't jeopardize my job here."

Mr. Clinton doesn't respond. Clearing his throat, he stands from his desk and walks over to the large window facing the parking lot, watching as cars start to pull in, students arriving for class. Mr. Clinton's office sits caddy-corner to the front doors of the school, and almost every morning the students can see the back of his head as he reads the school paper from the day before—something Benny admires about him is his consistency, never reading anything else, or drinking anything but his green tea with Sweet 'N Low.

"Ms. Bailey, can you give Mr. Divata and I a moment?" he asks, waving at the few early students walking into the school.

My stomach drops to the floor as I stand and go to leave—Benny reaching for, and squeezing my hand, as I walk out of the office.

Sitting in one of the two chairs seated near Mr. Clinton's office door, I notice a few whispers and giggles from students as they pass by. I sit up straight with my head held high, as I accept how it looks—Ms. Bailey was called into the principal's office. I block out the chatter growing in the halls as I focus on the conversation behind the office door.

"You could get fired . . ." *Clinton.*

"Do we know that for sure?" *Benny.*

"Hey, Ms. B!" Garrett Connors shouts at me from down the hall.

I ignore him and lean my head back, craning my neck to hear better. Their voices are muffled, maybe they moved further from the door?

Mumbled words come sporadically through the door—*job . . . rules . . . girl . . . love.*

Love?

"Ms. B, what're ya doin?" Garrett startles me as he slides into the chair next to me. How did he hobble over here so fast?

"Shhhh . . ." I whisper a screech at him. "I'm trying to listen." He mouths *"oops"* and gestures a silent finger over his lips as he leans closer to the door with me.

More words—*school board . . . term . . . New York . . .*

"Ugh, I can't make anything out." I groan in defeat.

"Here." Garrett leans across me and grabs the door handle. I shake my head rapidly, whispering *"no, no, no"* as he slowly turns the knob and cracks the door. The sound barrier is broken and we can now hear Clinton reading through school policies aloud.

"Interpersonal relations should be established prior to employment. Administrative staff are prohibited to partake in relations with faculty members unless—"

"I know the policy, Henry." Benny cuts him off, frustration in his voice.

"Then why are you doing this? Why are you risking it?"

"What's he doing?" Garrett whispers to me as we both listen.

"Because I have feelings for her!" Benny's voice carries into the hall. A few passersby look puzzled as they glance at Garrett and I.

"I knew it!" Garrett practically shrieks with ego as he slaps his uninjured knee. I snap a shush at him. "I knew it," he whispers back.

"What's going on?" Kate walks up to us, eyes darting between me and Garrett until they land on the cracked door. One of her eyebrows raises as she hears Benny and Clinton's conversation filling the halls. "Well, well, well," she says, placing her hands on her hips. "Finally told him, huh?"

"Told him what?" Garrett sits up, an overconfident smirk fixed on his face.

"Nothing." I groan.

Giving up on eavesdropping, I stand up and head down the hall towards the breakroom—Garrett and Kate following behind, whispering and giggling like little school girls. Their attitude towards the situation was frustrating. Benny was in trouble for being in a relationship with me and I was being selfish. I should have known this was going to happen, but I didn't do anything to stop it. I let his gorgeous face and personality captivate me, completely disregarding the repercussions that could accompany it.

I wave Garrett off as he veers towards his class. Kate catches up to me and begins her twenty questions about the current situation that has left me nauseous and dizzy.

"He can't lose his job, no way. We just have to figure out a plan. Maybe we can—"

She doesn't notice I'm trying to block out her questions as she has a back-and-forth conversation with herself. We weave through the hall as it fills up with students. The sound of locker doors, footsteps, and conversations pressing into me. The hot, sticky air coming from the ceiling vents hitting me in the face. My shoulders are brushed over and over by students rushing to class. Pictures of Benny are flashing through my slowed thoughts as I come to a halt in the middle of the hallway. Discomfort builds in my chest and shoulders.

I hear Kate ask if I'm okay, but her voice sounds like it's underwater.

My senses feel overwhelmed as I try to compute everything happening around me. I feel frozen in place.

"Hey, what's wrong?" Kate shakes me on the arm, the hall is basically empty now.

"I—I—I think I need to go," I manage to say as I turn on my heels, bolting for the parking lot.

"They ain't gonna eat themselves, ya know."

Sam towers over my untouched plate of waffles. I've been sitting, staring at them long enough for the usual mound of butter that sits atop the stack to turn into a liquid and is now dripping off the edges.

"Right." I force a smile as I cut into them with a spoon.

"You good?" he asks, eyeing me skeptically.

"Mmhmm." I shovel a bite into my mouth to avoid going into any further detail.

"Uh huh, well enjoy."

He heads back to the bar, looking at me over his shoulder multiple times knowing full well that I am indeed, *not* good.

I pick at my plate as I try to sift through my thoughts and what resulted in the overstimulated response earlier.

"There are other things to eat here than waffles, you know," a voice says from the booth behind me. Shuffling out of the booth and standing at my table, Naomi Johnson, Devon's mom, peers down at my sad soggy waffles. "You should try the tuna melt, it really isn't that bad."

My stomach turns at the thought of a fish sandwich. "I'll take your word for it," I say, cutting another corner of my waffle with the spoon.

"May I?" She gestures to the seat in front of me. I nod, mouth full of waffle. "I don't mean to intrude but . . . what's wrong with you?" She crosses her arms across her chest, her turtle sweater swallowing her small frame. Her dark complexion is smooth and flawless as she frowns at me, eyebrows pinched down in pity.

"Nothing." I shrug, another bite following.

"You're a bad liar."

She stares at me as I chew slowly and mechanically. She laughs, probably taking that as confirmation that she's right—I am a bad liar.

"So, you wanna share?" she asks as she crosses her legs and places her hands in her lap so elegantly.

"Not really . . ." I linger on my words, spoon slowly cutting another bite. I smear the bite in a pile of syrup and scoop it up.

"Fine with me"—clearing her throat as she whispers—"mind if I do?"

She wants to share? Now? She waits, probably expecting me to voice my disinterest to converse over waffles. But I see on her face she *needs* to have this conversation.

I bite down on my spoon and nod for her to continue, reminding myself that this is my job and whether I like it or not, my issues need to either be handled or put in the back of my mind so I can focus solely on the client. Naomi isn't a client, necessarily, but as I watch her shift in her seat uncomfortably, eyes moving from me to the door then down to her hands, it's clear that in this moment I need to treat her as one.

I wipe the syrup off my face with my napkin and sit up straight. "Please, go ahead."

"I want to talk to you about Devon," she says looking at the plate of waffles between us.

"Ms. Johnson, I am not at liberty to discuss what happens in a client session. If there are issues at home, I can offer to—"

"Oh no, it's not that," she says, waving her hands at me. "I respect Devon's privacy, and appreciate what you're doing for him. Truly." She places her hand over her heart, a sincere smile pulling at the corners of her eyes.

"Just doing my job." I shrug off the delight her appreciation brings me and continue, "So, what seems to be the issue then?"

"That's the thing." Her voice starts out low then as if she can't contain herself, it builds as she says, excitedly, "There aren't any!"

"Aren't any what? Issues?" I question.

Her head moves up and down in an excited nod. "That's right, there aren't any issues." She beams at me, revealing an insanely white smile. I'm almost distracted by it as she continues, "I mean, he's still a teenager. It's not perfect by any means. But for the last few weeks, things have been completely different. He comes home on time, no more fighting with his dad. He actually gave me a hug yesterday! A *hug!*" She is grinning from ear to ear. "I don't know what you've said to him and I don't want to know. I just have to tell you how grateful I am." Reaching across the table with both arms she rests her hands on the table, palms facing up motioning for me to take them. I pause, remembering that I barely know this woman, before placing my hands in hers. Her grip is strong and serious as she looks at me, tears building in her eyes. "Thank you." She sniffles. "You are making such a difference."

I don't know if it's the crying mom sitting across from me, or the stress of the morning thus far, but her words hit me like a ton of bricks. I choke back my own tears as I squeeze her hands—a wordless, *"you're welcome"*—before releasing them.

A moment passes as we both dab at our tears, giggling at our emotions.

"So" —she waves at Sam to bring her coffee—"tell me what's going on with you and Ben."

"You heard about that, huh?" Mentally rolling my eyes at Devon and his loud mouth. I guess it's a good thing he's opening up to his mom, but did it have to be about my love life?

Chuckling as she nods. "Pretty much everyone has."

She winks at Sam, who has brought a full pot of coffee and an extra mug to the table. He gives me a knowing grin before retreating back to the bar.

Everyone.

My speculation of who put Benny and I's relationship out there for the grapevine lands on Sam as well.

I feel ridiculous thinking that no one knew about us.

"Well, I guess we're dating now," I say, placing my chin in my hand, attempting to hide the giddy grin that's no doubt painted on my face. *Dating* Benny. I bite down on my lip to fight the urge to squeal with excitement like a lovestruck teenager.

"Is it serious?" she asks, while stirring her coffee. Her demeanor has changed from cheery to serious as she waits for my answer—her body language is tense and on guard.

Is she being protective? Of course, she is. The history she has with Benny and the man that he is deserves her protection.

"I think so," I say honestly, my smile hurting my cheeks.

"Good . . . please don't break his heart." Her tone is serious and stern as she reaches for the coffee pot. "He's a good guy and he loves his people—they are everything to him. I can only imagine how he will be with a *lady friend*." She lets a smile break through as she fills our mugs.

My heart swells at the thought of Benny and everything he does for his *people*. And the fact that *I* am one of those people—one of the people he wants to care for.

A lump forms in my throat. He *cares* about me, and I'm risking him losing his job.

"Are you alright?" Naomi's eyebrows furrow, mimicking mine.

Am I alright? There isn't enough coffee in this pot for me to process that question out loud. On one hand, yes, I feel alright knowing Benny and I are together, and I feel happy for the first time in a long time. On the other hand, I feel conflicted for being so selfish—selfish for allowing a relationship with Benny to happen, and selfish for not considering the implications of that relationship. This wasn't even a part of my plan. My plan was to get in and get out—back to New York, not fall for my *boss*. The absurdity of my situation lingers in my thoughts as I think it over.

How serious is this relationship? Is it worth changing my plans over? Did we even have a future?

My phone buzzes on the table.

Duncan

Have you scheduled an interview yet?

Impeccable timing.

"I'm fine." I nod, unconvincingly, to Naomi. She raises an eyebrow, clearly skeptical as I squeeze my phone between my palms.

"You sure you don't want to share?" Her gaze is steady on mine.

"I just have some decisions to make." I pause, looking down at the steam coming out of our matching Wafflin' mugs.

Nodding like she understands she says, "You might go back to New York, right?"

"Does everyone know my business around here?" I exaggerate an eye roll at her, pretending to be bothered by the intrusion. In New York, any knowledge my friends had of my life never went further than my work schedule. When I told them I was moving, they were stunned at the realization that I was doing so bad that I needed to get away. The lack of interest in my life was so bad that even the worst of situations wouldn't have been enough for them to care. Even if the people here in Glendale County didn't seem to understand personal boundaries, it felt nice to know they cared enough to chit chat about my business.

"You've just left a mark on this place, we like to discuss the probability of you sticking around." She shrugs like this is basic etiquette I need to accept around here.

"Mmhmm," I hum sarcastically, pulling my mug closer to my face and letting it sit under my nose. The dark roast plows through my nostrils and alerts my brain of its strength. I take a weary sip of the straight, black coffee and just about cough it out of my nose. Naomi stifles a laugh at my pitiful attempt to nonchalantly reach for the small pitcher of creamer.

Empty.

"Sam, could you get me more creamer?" I yell to the bar, rubbing my throat as the bitter taste works its way down.

He makes his way around the bar holding up two hand-sized pitchers. "Which one? We got a new one . . . peppermint, and then cinnamon." He holds them out, presenting my choices.

I choose cinnamon—like always.

Naomi laughs at my impatience as I take a big sip, relieved from the bitter taste. "It was nice chatting." She pulls a wrinkled twenty dollar bill out of her pocket and sets it on the table. "I'll see you at the party." She goes to leave, waving at Sam and a few other Wafflin' patrons before turning back to me. "I hope you choose to stay."

Chapter Twenty-Five

Benny

"She really is an interesting looking cat." Ellie pets Frankie as she paws at the couch.

"You can say ugly, she doesn't understand you." I laugh.

She refused to wear her sweater today so she looks like a cross between raw chicken and a gremlin as she sprawls across Ellie's lap. Ellie is a good sport, tolerating her, when I know full well she is not a fan of the feline species.

"Don't listen to him," she whispers to Frankie. "You are beautiful . . . in your own unique way."

I let out a laugh as I join her and Frankie on the couch with a bowl of popcorn and a fuzzy blanket. According to Ellie, you can't have a movie night without the two. I throw the blanket over our legs, covering Frankie entirely as she refuses to move.

I hand the popcorn to Ellie and kiss her before she can take a bite, enjoying the sweetness of her bare lips under mine. She lets out a soft sigh as I pull back, she looks happy. She snuggles herself deeper into the blanket, pulling her legs up underneath her as she leans her head back against the couch. The sight surrounds me like a warm hug after a long journey. A sight you want to come home to everyday. A sight of something beautiful and irreplaceable.

"You ready?" she asks, grinning from ear to ear.

"Into the Fireswamp we go." I wink at her before pressing play on *The Princess Bride*.

We watch the movie, munching on popcorn and commentating throughout.

"Just *once* I want to call someone a warthog-faced buffoon." She laughs.

"It would be fun to storm a castle," I say with a mouth full of popcorn.

The credits roll and we snuggle up on the couch—Frankie retreated to her tower halfway through the movie.

"So, how was the rest of your day?" I ask, thinking back to this morning when she wasn't in our faculty meeting and canceled her morning sessions. I don't want to pester her, but I can't help myself from thinking that our meeting with Mr. Clinton spooked her.

If she was spooked, she wasn't letting on, but of course I was worrying about it all day and jumped at the chance to hang out when she asked to come over and watch the movie. Any chance I get to hang out with Ellie, I want it. And after that awkward meeting with our boss I felt the need to hang out a little more, so I didn't hesitate.

"It was alright. I had to run a few errands so I rearranged my schedule. How was yours?" Her voice lingers, like she's asking about something specific.

I release a breath. "Can I be honest?"

She sits up straight and faces me. "I would prefer you were."

"I was worried about you all day," I say it fast and glance from the corner of my eye to see if I can read her expression. I don't see anything out of the ordinary. She doesn't *look* uncomfortable so I go on, "I'm afraid the meeting with Clinton upset you or something."

"Oh." She bites her lip and fidgets with the blanket tassel. *Crap*. Proceed with caution.

"I'm just—umm—wanting to make sure you are alright," I say.

No response. She continues twirling the blanket tassel between her fingers, not responding. God, how long do I let the silence go on? Why isn't she saying anything?

Alright, let's not make a big deal about this, Ben. You're just figuring it out, figuring her out. This is how relationships go, you have to learn how to communicate. Patience is key.

Another millisecond goes by. "Are you—" I stand up abruptly and ask, "you know, alright?" *Way to be patient.*

"Are you?" She peers at me like I'm a crazy man.

Honestly, I probably look like one as I pace back and forth in my living room.

"Me? Yeah—yeah, sure." I look at the ceiling, too nervous to look her in the eye. Tension is building in my neck so I rub it.

"Are you sure?" She giggles, as I stay staring at the ceiling.

A small yellow spot in the corner grabs my attention. "I must have a leak."

"Huh, maybe." She probably saw it too, or she is just really good at ignoring weird behavior as I keep stare at the ceiling.

A moment passes, then I hear the blanket hit the floor followed by the leather on my couch squeak and rub. I can see Ellie stand up from the corner of my eye and watch as she goes into the kitchen and puts the empty popcorn bowl away. Is she avoiding this conversation? Did I make her uncomfortable?

"I have a hard time sharing my own feelings sometimes," she calls to me from the kitchen sink, scrubbing the butter from the inside of the bowl. "Most days I just process things on my own, but I'm trying to not do that now."

I turn my attention away from the ceiling to face her. She's looking out of my kitchen window, bowl still in hand, covered in soap. I don't want to spook her so I wait for her to keep going. I'm crazy about this woman, but also aware of her boundaries. As much as I want to scoop her up, kiss her from head to toe, and tell her she can share anything with me, that might not be what she needs right now.

"The meeting with Mr. Clinton was upsetting for me, yes," she whispers.

"Why?" I ask urgently, not wanting her to ever be upset.

"Because I didn't think all of this through." Her eyes dart to me then back to the window. *Where is she going with this?*

"I just think—that maybe we—" *Oh no.* Is she about to end things? "Didn't think things through."

"Are you breaking up with me?" I whisper, my throat feels like acid.

"What?" Her eyes fix on me, a seriousness to her voice I haven't heard from her before.

"Are you . . . ?" My voice trails off.

SMASH!

In an instant, she drops the bowl, races around the kitchen island, and tackles me. My only glass bowl is definitely shattered in my sink, but I don't care. Her arms are wrapped tightly around me, like I'm her lifeboat and I squeeze her against me like she's mine.

"I would never!" she says burying her face into my chest.

The sigh of relief I make is so loud it sounds like a growl. "Thank God," I say into her hair. I squeeze her tighter against me, lifting her a few inches off the ground for a moment before setting her back down. Feeling dizzy from the tackle, I cling to her for support.

She kisses me on the chest over my hoodie, then on the shoulder, then the neck before landing on my lips. Leaving a trail on a map in a way, sending weird tingles to my heart with each destination. What this woman does to me feels addicting and I don't want any help getting clean.

"I meant"—she kisses me quickly, going back to our conversation—"I don't think we thought about how this was going to go with our jobs."

"Mmhmm." I kiss her again, not caring about anything but her lips. I can't get enough.

Giggling under my mouth she says, "I'm serious."

"I am too," I say against her lips.

We fall back into a rhythm, coming up for air when we need to. The fact that she is with me is baffling and I'm pretty sure my body is afraid that if I let her go, she will float away. I can't help myself as I cling tighter to her, kissing every part of her I can reach. Getting lost in the moment with me, she entangles herself against me, gripping my back and neck.

After a few minutes I feel out of breath and rest my forehead against hers, blinking away spots that are now clouding my vision. "What were you saying?" I ask, breathless.

Clearing her throat, she steps back from me and smooths out her hair. She wipes her lips as she smiles at me. "Our jobs."

"Right, jobs." I wipe my lips with the back of my sleeve. "What are you thinking?"

"Well, what did Clinton say?"

She sits down on the couch and Frankie miraculously reappears, bounding chaotically across the floor and jumping onto her lap. She purrs and paws, making a huge theatrical scene, making sure Ellie knows, this is *my human.*

Running my hand down my face, I hesitate sharing the details of my conversation with our boss this morning. It wasn't entirely bad, but it wasn't an ideal conversation either. The reality that we are breaking the rules was reiterated over and over. So much so that I found myself annoyed with Henry. Which never happens. But the guy just couldn't get past the idea of me breaking the rules.

"You've never been so foolish." Henry told me.

And he's right. I haven't been. Ever since the accident, I have been a rule-following, law-abiding employee. Now I was breaking a big one and he just didn't understand how it was possible.

But I did.

I'm a fool for Eleanor Bailey.

"He's upset that we're breaking the rules." I join her on the couch and she faces me, while Frankie lounges, not budging from her lap. "He's pretty confident our jobs are at risk and asked me to really think if this is worth it."

"Well . . ." She pauses, staring intently at Frankie's sweater. "Is it . . . worth it?" she whispers without looking up at me.

"Yes." My response is quick and unwavering with my answer, because it's the truth. It—*she*—is worth it. Her eyes are fixed on Frankie, but I see a smile grow on her face. "Is it worth it to you?"

"Yes," she says quickly in return and my chest feels light at her answer.

She stops stroking Frankie, who does not appreciate the absence of attention and lets out a hostile screech before pouncing across the couch, up the tower, then back down, before disappearing loudly down the hall. A loud thud sounds from the head of the dark hallway, followed by a few other questionable noises. I choose to ignore Frankie's dramatics.

I reach out and grab Ellie's hand with both of mine, circling a small divot near her thumb. "So, what do you think we should do?"

She lets out a big sigh, leaning her head back against the couch. "Maybe I should look for another job."

"Another job? Why?" My voice gets higher.

"Because you could lose your job, and I can't be the reason you do."

I'm immediately flustered at the thought of Ellie working somewhere else. Me getting to see her everyday aside, the improvements within our school are without a doubt because of her. Whether she wants to believe it or not, some of the kids rely on her. Seeing her every week has made an impact they couldn't get anywhere else. She is essential to Glendale now.

I stammer around my words trying to explain this to her, making absolutely no sense.

"I might look into a clinic job. Or Columbia." She glances at me, probably half expecting me to voice my debate on why that is the worst possible option.

I decide against *thinking out loud* so I can avoid coming off as an overbearing boyfriend. "I see." I clench my jaw and talk through my teeth. "Is that what you want?"

Please say no.

"I don't know . . ." Looking down at our hands, she deflates as she lets out a sigh.

I have a feeling she does know, but she doesn't want to admit it. It would seem selfish and she is the least selfish person I have ever met. Why wouldn't she want to go to her alma mater to teach and do research, *and* treat patients in their clinic? That has Eleanor Bailey written all over it. Her entire career has led her to this point, a chance to do something like this. And I can't be the one to tell her not to do it. She's telling me she can't be the reason I lose my job. But I could be the reason she never gets the one she truly wants. Who's the selfish one then?

I tilt her chin up, taking in her deep misty green eyes. "You can tell me, Eleanor."

She takes a deep breath, holding it a little too long before answering "The job is perfect." The mistiness pours over.

I force a smile and wipe a tear off of her cheek. "Then you should go to that interview."

CHAPTER TWENTY-SIX

Benny

"You told her to go?" Malcolm looks at me like I'm a crazy man. Not really validating the doubt I have going through my head right now.

"What else was I supposed to do?" I groan as I wipe up the coffee creamer I spilled all over the break room counter.

I've been whining around like a child since Ellie decided to go through with the interview. Rather than be an adult and share my feelings about it openly with anyone, I've just let it simmer and this morning it finally boiled over. The sight of Ellie's favorite cinnamon creamer just made me mad, so, of course, I knocked it over.

"Telling her *not* to go might have been a start," Malcolm says, leaning up against the counter. He eyes me as I wipe up, not offering to help. "You missed a spot."

"Thanks," I grit through my teeth, wiping the counter more aggressively as he chuckles.

"You got it bad, Ben."

"I don't know what you're talking about," I lie.

"Sure." He walks away and sits at the table, topping off his cup from his personal pot. "It wouldn't kill ya to be honest with the girl."

"It's not like I'm hiding anything." I throw away the pile of soaked paper towels and rinse off my hands. "I just don't want her to feel obligated to stay when she has an incredible opportunity."

"There's more than one option, Ben."

"And what would that be?" I ask, taking a seat in the chair next to him.

"You could go with her."

Choking on the coffee I just drank, I say, "Wha . . . ?"

He shrugs matter-of-factly, like what he just said didn't almost give me a brain aneurysm. Leave Glendale? The idea has never once crossed my mind. He's insane.

"Why not?" He downs his cup like it's a shot of water. "We could survive without you."

"Gee, that makes me feel so good." I slouch back into my chair, turning my mug in a circle on the table. The pink pug mug, Kate's old pug Hilda, looking back at me.

"I'm just saying." He pauses and lets out an exasperated sigh as if what he needs to say pains him. "Look, you've done a lot of good here and you are kind of irreplaceable."

I flutter my eyes and put my hands over my heart like I'm flattered by his amazing compliment.

"Watch it." He points at me.

He hates compliments, giving and receiving them, so much so that he will leave the room during end of term evaluations to avoid positive feedback or praise. He's a content man, who believes flattery is used to seek favor from someone rather than truly encourage them. I can see why, considering he grew up in an overly optimistic household that ended up in messy infidelity. The flattery he witnessed between his mother and father were lies.

"But you don't owe this place anything." Sitting up, he leans his arms against the table, gesturing with his hands. Something he does when he's worked up or overly passionate about the conversation. "You've paid your dues and there's nothing wrong with venturing away and trying something new. You, of all people, deserve it."

I pat him on the shoulder. "Thanks, Malcolm."

"Don't get me wrong, I would hate to see you leave"—he clears his throat and wiggles his nose, mustache moving simultaneously underneath it—"but I would hate even more to see you unhappy." He hesitates as he fumbles with his empty coffee cup. "You're a good man, Ben. You deserve a good life, even if that isn't here with us."

A lump forms in the back of my throat. *Us.*

My family.

I take my hand off of his shoulder and pull him into a hug. He hesitates before eventually hugging me back. The thought of leaving this guy, and the rest of Glendale, is something I never considered. I've pictured Malcolm and I sitting at this very table, sipping coffee and mumbling about our students until we are old, gray, and senile. The lump in my throat grows and I feel Malcolm's shoulders move up and down as he lets out a long whoosh of air.

The hug is quick and almost non-existent compared to other hugs out there in the world. We overcompensate for feeling emotional by clearing our throats and patting each other's back like *bros*.

"What's going on in here?" Kate asks, standing in the doorway, leering at us. She definitely saw our weepy man hug but she leaves us our dignity and doesn't point it out.

Clearing his throat even more than before, Malcolm stands from the table and takes his mug to sink. "Just telling Ben to move to New York."

"What?" Kate shrieks. We both jump at the volume, as Kate storms towards Malcolm, "Why would you tell him that?"

Malcolm tenses his body and drops his shoulder, bracing for impact as Kate swats at him with a school newspaper. She hits him a few times before storming over to me. "Why would you let him tell you that?" she asks, rearing the paper back and swatting me on the top of the head.

"I am innocent in all this!" I cover my head with my arms as she attempts to swat me again. "Physical harassment!"

"What are you gonna do? *Tell* on me?" She lands one more blow on my shoulder before strolling back over to Malcolm, giving another blow to him for good measure. Her small frame does no damage whatsoever, but we both exaggerate pain by rubbing the contact points over and over.

"Don't fill his brain with New York nonsense." She rolls her eyes, opening the cabinets and pulling out a plate before opening the fridge and pulling out a tub of cream cheese. She grabs a cold bagel from the counter and begins lathering it with an abnormally large amount of spread. She seems irritated as she aggressively smears the cream cheese and throws the butter knife in the sink.

Malcolm notices the tension and tries patting Kate on the back when she side steps and storms to the table, slamming the bagel down. He watches her for a moment as she huffs and puffs over her plate without saying a word. He frowns at me and shrugs before leaving the break room.

Kate tears her bagel in half, disregarding the fact that she grabbed the regular cream cheese as she shoves a piece in her mouth, a scowl plastered on her face. I try to point this out, but she ignores the animal product covering her mouth and continues to chew.

"Kate, he was just trying to help me." I lean against the table to eye level with her. She refuses to look at me.

"Whatever," she growls with her bagel in her mouth. Her face is somewhat red and angrier than I think this situation deserves.

I would expect her reaction to be upset if she heard I was considering leaving Glendale, but I would have never pictured her to be this mad. As close as we are, I was always under the impression that we had our own lives and there was a mutual understanding that both of us might not always be here. I also kind of assumed she would be the first to move on from Glendale.

"Kate?" She doesn't answer me. "Kate, are you really mad about New York?"

"Yes." She grits her teeth, still not looking at me.

"Is that all?" I ask, but I'm pretty sure of the answer. There was something going on before she got here and walking into Malcolm and I's conversation made her morning even worse. Growing up Kate was told she had attention span issues and she was always irritated and hostile about it. Like a chihuahua when you take their bone, but really they just forgot where they placed the bone. Over time she got better and less hostile, she changed her diet and found other ways to manage her distractions. Being at work has been one of the best outlets for her to concentrate surprisingly. And she usually comes in calm and prepared, but this morning feels different.

She looks jittery and unfocused as she throws her bagel down onto her plate then crosses her arms over her chest and grunts.

Yep, something's off.

"What's going on?" I ask, crossing my arms to match hers.

Still not looking at me, she stares out of the break room window at the football field. The sky is a mix of pink, blue, and orange as the sun glows across the field. The track team is cycling through their morning workout of sprints, relays, and calisthenics. The yells and "hoorahs" from the team carry all the way through the window. Kate watches them intently, taking it all in, and I can see her face go from angry to calm as the frown fades when she finally looks at me.

"I was hoping she would stay," she whispers, her voice breaking a tiny bit as she looks back out the window.

"She could still stay," I whisper back.

Bagel crumbs fall from her mouth as she scoffs at me, "Yeah, right. Did you see that job? She'd be insane to not accept." Another chunk of bagel goes into her mouth.

I try not to believe what Kate says. I'm at a weird stage of the grief cycle as I imagine Ellie leaving—somewhere between denial and bribery. I think those are the stages? But for Ellie's sake, I have put on my best supportive boyfriend face, helping her with her interview outfit, planning to take her to the airport, all the things that a good boyfriend does, even though I'm dying inside.

"We don't know yet, something could—"

"Don't lie to yourself," she says, interrupting me. "And you're leaving with her? Seriously? Then I'll be stuck here, alone." She stomps her foot and frowns like the toddler Kate used to.

"You won't be alone. And I don't even know if I'm leaving or not." I pat her leg and stand to walk over to the sink. I rinse my mug and start a fresh pot for the rest of the faculty.

"What would you do? Long distance?" Kate asks over her shoulder.

"I don't know . . . maybe?" I wipe the sink.

"You know that won't work," she says, knowingly. She's tried long distance before and it tore her apart. Being on the girl's side of things was eye opening as a man, seeing her fear and anxiety over the "what ifs." I couldn't stand to be the reason Ellie was stressed or worried or feeling anything but happy and secure in our relationship. But even the best of guys, with the best intentions, can't stop a woman from breaking their heart because they can't handle the distance. I couldn't handle that either.

I grip the sides of the back counter and take a deep steadying breath.

Maybe I could go to New York? Surely I could find a place to work that's comparable to Glendale. And our families are here so we would visit often . . . right?

I hear a knock at the break room door. "Excuse me, Mr. Divata?"

I look up to see a woman I don't recognize standing on the other side of the door. She is way too overdressed to be a substitute—wearing a gray pantsuit and very pointy shoes.

I shake off my emotions and walk over to greet her. "That's me. What can I do for you?"

"I'm Mrs. Herrera"—she shakes my hand firmly, looking over my shoulder to nod at Kate—"I'm with the school board." Her tone is not a friendly one as she pulls out a slip of paper and hands it to me. "You are required to attend our upcoming board meeting for an evaluation."

My throat closes as I take the paper, Kate is swiftly by my side reading it over my shoulder. I see spots around the paper and can only make out a few words . . .

Violation.

Insubordination.

Termination.

Kate snatches the paper out of my hands. "Are you kidding me right now?"

"Mr. Divata, it is paramount that you and Ms. Bailey attend this meeting."

The room feels like it's swaying as all I can do is nod in response. She nods at Kate and I then walks down the hallway, disappearing around the corner.

"What are they going to do? *Fire you?*" Kate yells as she steps into the hallway, looking in the direction of Ms. Herrara then back to me. We're both baffled.

Emma approaches from the opposite end of the hallway, looking between me and Kate, "What's going on?" She looks over Kate's shoulder at the paper, Kate hands it to her.

"I'll be back!" Kate shouts as she runs off down the same way Ms. Herrera left, leaving Emma and I standing in the doorway.

Emma scans over the paper, reading different points out loud, "Due to recent developments . . . interpersonal relationship . . . termination?" She gasps, placing her hand over her mouth as she continues to read. "No, no, no." She shakes her head in disbelief—the very feeling I, so ignorantly, am feeling right now.

I stay planted in the doorway as shock works its way over me. *Termination?* I feel like an idiot thinking this all was going to blow over. Pictures of my life work their way across my mind like a slideshow: graduating from Glendale, my first job here, my first promotion, everything I worked for while being here.

The first school bell rings and students pile into the hall from the front door, opening lockers, high-fiving each other, waving at Emma and I as they pass. Seeing their faces ignites something inside me, dissolving my shock and filling me with something else—something righteous.

This is my school. These are my students.

The option of leaving Glendale for New York is gone.

I'm not going anywhere.

CHAPTER TWENTY-SEVEN

Ellie

"You can't trust people wearing masks? That's a given!" Sarah laughs from across my desk. She keeps refusing to watch The Princess Bride for two reasons: it's *old* and *overrated*. It brings me physical pain to hear her utter these words, and for the last few weeks all of the productivity in our sessions has been focused on this debate.

"It's more than that! It's a deeper life lesson, the mask is also metaphorical!" I throw my arms up in the air. "Your life will change forever if you will just watch it!"

"You know what else can change your life? Sharknado . . . that's time you never get back." She blows a bubble with her gum, ignoring the disgust on my face for the comparison.

I groan in defeat. "Whatever, your loss. Now, let's focus on something else for the last"—I check my watch—*"fifteen* minutes before I have to leave."

"Are you really going to leave?" she whispers, looking down at her hands. She's painted her nails each a different shade of green, off-setting the bright yellow cardigan and yellow high tops she's wearing. "You just got here." Her voice is sad and it breaks my heart.

I've grown so fond of Sarah and her quirky, smarty-pants attitude.

"I don't know what I'm going to do yet." I force a smile at her hoping it hides the conflict I'm wrestling with. "Plus, I might run into you there eventually!"

"Eventually." She rolls her eyes as she blows another bubble. It pops, leaving a piece on her nose. She wipes it off and sprawls back onto the couch.

The contrast of Sarah now and Sarah a few months ago is subtle to others, but her comfort level around me has completely changed. She lounges around like she's in her own living room and I'm her buddy, not her guidance counselor who could actually send her to detention. Which I would never do, but it's fun to think of the authority I have at my disposal.

"Ethan and Birdie are going to be homecoming royalty and it makes me sick." She throws her arms over her face.

I was hoping to discuss her decision to stay at Glendale another year rather than graduate early, to make sure she was content with that decision, but alas, I am not so lucky. Instead, I'm dealing with, yet another, lovesick, child crisis.

She yammers on about how she hopes Bridie's homecoming dress will rip, and that Ethan will give her mono. How he winked at her in the hall yesterday, then proceeded to loop his arm over Birdie's shoulders.

Oof.

Ethan Blake is definitely one I would use my detention authority on.

"Who am I going to talk to about these things? You're the only one who understands!" she whines behind her arms, still laying across the couch with a leg kicked up on the back.

"Again, I don't know what's going to happen." I doodle a pair of high-top shoes under a cute homecoming dress. The thought of Birdie stepping on her own dress crosses my mind and I stifle a laugh, retracing the laces of the shoes I drew.

"Word on the street is Mr. B's gonna get canned anyway," she says, arms still covering her face.

"That's not going to happen," I say, sternly. How did she get this information? Last I checked the only people who know about the board meeting are the faculty and Steven.

I scribble everyone's name, scratching off suspects as she goes back to her love triangle. She continues on about Birdie and her *fake platinum blonde hair* and how she's pretty confident she wears a corset. Her jealousy comes out more snippy the longer she talks, like a slow leak before the pipe finally gives way and bursts with unnecessary insults. My ability to maintain a straight face as she becomes more animated with each remark falters more and more.

Even though my sessions with students are confidential and they have the freedom to speak as they wish, I do have to remind them that I am still faculty. Although, this has never stopped them from unleashing gossip and rumor theories to me. I've just had to reel them in a tad. But with this next month potentially being my last one at Glendale, my limits within sessions have become a little more lenient than the beginning of term.

Sarah needs to let it out, so I let her.

A knock on the other side of my door interrupts Sarah's theory on Birdie paying Ethan to date her, thank the Lord. She remains kicked up on the couch as reaches overhead for the doorknob and twists it, letting the door swing open. Benny walks in.

"You about ready to go?" he asks me but looks down at Sarah, giggling at the sight.

"Sup, Mr. B," she looks up at him before kicking her feet and throwing herself up to a seated position. She picks up her backpack and swings it over her shoulder then points a finger gun at me. "Don't suck tomorrow."

Pointing a finger gun right back. "I'll try not to."

She fist bumps Benny as she leaves my office, waving at us both through my office window.

"Amazing." Benny chuckles watching her skip to her locker.

"What is?" I start to pick up my desk and pack it away.

"You." He leans over my desk and kisses me on the cheek. "And what you do." He kisses the other cheek. "She's just a new person since meeting with you." A final kiss on my forehead, his lips soft against my skin as he pulls away slowly, his eyes penetrating my soul as he stands up straight.

"She's just growing up," I say, staring at his lips, resisting the urge to kiss him like a maniac in the middle of my office.

With the board meeting coming up, we decided to cool it on the public displays of affection. We were handling it well for the most part, until today. I leave for New York in two hours and Benny has taken every opportunity to kiss me, multiple times. I feel like I should be an adult and set boundaries, but there's something in the air between us—a tension neither of us want to address. *What's going to happen if I get the job?*

My stomach is in knots thinking about it. And by the way Benny has lingered all day, I can't help but think he feels the same.

I shove the question to the back of my brain as I round my desk, grabbing my bag and turning off my desk lamp. "Ready to go?"

"Mmhmm." His eyes seem darker as they dart down to my lips and back to my eyes. A quick kiss on the nose and his cheeks go a tiny bit red before he smiles and turns to the door.

The drive to the airport feels awkward.

"You have everything you need?" Benny asks.

"I think so."

"Ticket? Wallet?"

"Yep, got it."

Benny didn't let go of my hand the entire drive, even when he clearly needed two hands to pull into the loading zone.

"Call me when you land?" He strokes my cheek with his thumb.

"Of course." I wrap my hands around his waist and clutch onto him. I don't want to admit what this feels like.

I'll be back.

This isn't a goodbye.

Yet, we're hugging like it is.

He kisses me like I'm his source of oxygen, his hands clutching the sides of my face as he does. It feels intense and desperate—a need to get what we can while we can. My eyes feel blurry when we stop, for a split second I was lost in him.

"You're going to make me miss my flight," I joke as he rests his forehead against mine.

"I just can't get enough." His smile is weak as he kisses my forehead. "I'll see you soon."

Standing on my toes, I bury my face in his neck. "See you."

He kisses my head then pushes me towards the sliding glass doors of the airport. He looks sad when I wave back at him before I race to my gate.

I make it with only two minutes to spare—the haste and panic of missing my flight distracting me from Benny. Until take off, then all I do is think about him.

The flight is only a few hours so I try to nap it off, no luck.

I try talking to the person next to me, they're uninterested.

I cave and pay the ten dollar Wi-Fi fee.

Benny proceeds to send me a plethora of steamy selfies—one driving away from the airport, another at lunch, licking hot sauce off his thumb, and one at the gym, his sweat soaked shirt leaving me in pieces. I think the older gentleman in the seat next to me was clearly conflicted on how to feel about me and my uncontrollable giggling and feet kicking. We text back and forth about nonsense my entire flight, still ignoring the fact that I am going to another state to interview for a *job*. I feel absurd about the current situation, but I don't feel ready to address the technicalities either. Especially when those technicalities can be the end of something so good.

After I land I grab a taxi to my hotel and check-in. Once I get to my hotel room, I try to use the extra time to prepare for my interview. The view is congested, busy nightlife, with honking and yelling down on the streets. I look down from my hotel window and remember why I needed this place so bad, no room to think down there.

My phone dings from my bag.

My chest all of sudden feels achy looking at the glowing screen of my phone, Benny's name at the top. I *miss* him, and it hasn't even been a day. *I'm a crazy person.* I text him back, telling him about my long journey from the airport taxi to the inside of the hotel, then up the elevator to my room. He sends a laughing face, followed by a picture of his legs snuggled under a blanket, Frankie curled up on top of said blanket, *The Princess Bride* playing on his television.

Instead of responding, I toss my phone back on the bed and pull out my clothes and steamer for the next day. My skirt has a wrinkle down the middle that won't come out after multiple steam cycles. *Why do I even own this?* I chuck it into the trash. My face feels hot and my heart is fluttering rapidly as I pace back and forth. I *hate* wrinkles.

Anger is building up inside me and I know it's irrational, but I'm not stopping it.

I try calling Emma, she doesn't pick up.

I throw myself onto the bed and scream into one of the huge white pillows. It's like landing on a cloud, the entire bed swallows me and it makes me feel better. Placing my hands on my chest, my heart thumping starts to slow down and my eyes feel heavy. The freak out seems to be contained for the moment, thanks to Hilton New York.

What is happening?

Benny sends me a goodnight photo of him and Frankie, and I fall asleep looking at it.

Finding my way around campus is like deja vu. The campus hasn't changed at all. The buildings are twice as tall as Glendale, with the classic columns and dome roofs on top. The green patches of lawn are pristine and crisp as they lay in the center of the multicolored brick walkways. Nostalgia comes rushing back as I walk past my old class buildings and dorms. It feels good to be here, but different too.

"Welcome back, Ms. Bailey!" Duncan meets me outside the Psychology Department building, stainless steel water bottle in hand. He always teased me about drinking more water.

"Hi!" I hug him. "How are you?"

"Good, good." He hands me a manila envelope. "Take these, that is your tentative schedule and all the information you'll need for the classes. Do *not* lose that!"

"Wait, what? I haven't accepted the job yet." I stare at the envelope. *Did I tell him I would take it?* I'm only taking the interview. Panic sheers through me as we turn to walk into the building.

"Oh it's just a set schedule they already have, so you know what to expect when you take the job." He waves his hand at me.

"*If* I accept the job," I correct.

"Right! Sure." He gives me a sarcastic wink as he leads me down the hallway.

The inside of the building has been renovated since I was here last. The floors are a fresh cream tile, walls painted to match, and the doors to each office are a deep blue. A more modern look compared to the outside. As we walk, I count floor tiles, working on my breathing, white knuckling the envelope.

We approach a conference room and I can see inside a pane window by the door that there are three people seated at a table—two middle-aged women and an older man. Sweat builds on my lower back and under my arms. Duncan notices me fanning myself.

"Calm down, silly! You're going to do great." He smiles at me.

We stand on the other side of the door for a moment. I smooth out my skirt that I had to dig out of the trash because I didn't bring a spare, toss my hair behind my shoulder, and give myself a mental pep talk—*just get through this*. My nerves are a mix of anticipation and dread. I have no idea if they are going to offer me the job, and worse than that, I have no idea if I'm going to accept.

I take a deep breath and enter the room. Duncan joins the three at the opposite end of a long boardroom table, I take the single seat facing them. They are welcoming in their greetings, giving relaxed smiles that calm me a tiny bit. Each of them are previous PhD students and current faculty, one being the Director of the on-campus clinic. We spend a good portion of the interview discussing their roles in the department, their plans for the upcoming term, and even discussing their current research projects: *Human Behavior, Justice Data Science, and Human Brain Imaging*.

Their experience and education combined brings back the feelings of college orientation day, when you know absolutely *nothing* but want to learn *everything*. I soak it in as they chat, joining in when I feel appropriate. It feels very relaxed and easy to talk to them.

"Enough about us, let's focus on you," one of the women says. I already forgot their names and will have to ask Duncan to remind me later.

"Yes, tell us about yourself," the man requests.

"Well"—I clear my throat and lean down to remove my portfolio from my purse—"I graduated from Columbia four—"

"We know that, sweetie," woman two interjects. "Tell us about *you*."

"Oh . . ." I pause as they look at me eagerly.

What did they want to hear? That I fled New York after getting left at the altar? That I couldn't handle working at a clinic with my ex so I took a job as a high school guidance counselor? That I'm working in a job that sounds demeaning and absurd to someone with my education, but that I actually love the job? That I love it so much and the idea of me leaving it has pushed me to the verge of an irrational meltdown?

They sense me stumble and guide the conversation. "Tell us about Glendale."

I clench the edge of my portfolio binder, tapping it with my thumbs, as I try to connect my brain with my mouth. Talking about Glendale will definitely send me into a fit and I'm not wearing waterproof mascara.

The silence in the room is thick and awkward as they watch me patiently.

"Well, I have a few things." I set my portfolio on the table and clutch the zipper. Luckily I brought a recommendation letter from Malcolm, and a few student evaluations on my contributions to the school recently. I might as well present those so I can conjure up some type of verbal response.

Duncan walks towards my seat as I unzip the binder, pulling out a folder. I open the folder and instead of finding just the letters neatly packed inside, I find an envelope with a smile doodled on the front. Handing the letters to Duncan, he retreats back to his seat and hands them to the three. As they read over the critiques and accolades from a few teenagers, they giggle and show each other different points.

With the small envelope still in my hands, I discreetly tear the seal and pull out a stack of crumpled old sticky notes.

All different colors, all covered in my doodles.

I sift through them on my lap, some are so ridiculous I feel instantly embarrassed. *An angry goblin sitting on top of another goblin.* I chuckle under my breath as I reminisce over each silly square. These are stickies I threw away, stickies for the parts of my brain I was embarrassed to show anyone. My doodled thoughts in all their glory lay across my lap.

Among the pile of sticky notes, I see an unfamiliar folded up piece of paper. I clutch it tightly and glance up at Duncan and the three.

"So, Ms. Bailey, how did things turn out at Glendale?" None of them look up from the evaluations as the man asks.

"Umm . . ." My hands are shaky as I unfold the piece of paper instead of answering his question. I recognize the handwriting immediately.

I couldn't let pieces of you go to waste.

Tears fill my eyes as I stare down at the note, focusing all of my attention on Benny's words. Covering my mouth with my hand in an attempt to hide my smile is pointless as a small sob escapes me.

"Ms. Bailey?" The voice at the end of the table sounds faint as happy sobs flow out of me.

I trace the letters of his name, completely lost in my feelings for the man awaiting me back home. "It's everything I could ever want, sir."

CHAPTER TWENTY-EIGHT

Benny

"WHAT IS SHE DOING here?" Kate backs away from the breakroom table as I walk in carrying Frankie. She gives a soft meow inside her carrier and Kate practically loses her eyes in the back of her head.

"Daycare is closed," I say, pulling Frankie out of her carrier. She's in the baby blue hoodie with pink bow that Ellie got for her today. I'm really accentuating my manliness. "What else was I supposed to do?"

"Leave her at home! She's a *cat!*" Kate throws her head back, annoyed.

Setting her medication bottle on the table, I pull out a pill and stuff it inside a torn piece of bagel. Frankie watches as I do, believing she can't be fooled with carbs. I place the rolled up piece of bagel on the ground and Frankie approaches slowly, sniffing, pawing, then finally scooping it up by her teeth and swallowing it in one bite.

"Isn't that counterintuitive? Diabetes medication with *carbs?*" She puts her hands on her hips, judging my methods per usual.

"We do what we gotta do." Frankie licks her paws clean and I scratch her head as I make my way to the back of the room.

Kate looks at her, disgusted, as she gives herself a bath in the middle of the break room floor. When she finishes, Frankie swiftly and aggressively pounces on top of Kate's feet causing her to yelp and run away.

"I hate her," she whines as she climbs on top of the counter next to me so she can get away from the naked feline.

"You know she can hop up there," I point out as I fill my coffee mug.

Frankie meows from the floor up at Kate.

"No way, she's too fat." Kate looks down at her, shooing her away.

"You only have yourself to blame for her presence here."

"Don't remind me." She groans as Frankie stretches and rolls around the floor directly under her, taunting her. I laugh at their interaction and Kate hits me on the side of the arm, causing Frankie to meow and hiss at her.

"She'll protect me." I laugh again as I go back to the table, leaving Kate to fight this battle on her own. "Where are the others?" I just realized Malcolm wasn't the first one here today. Emma wasn't here either. And our morning meeting was starting in five minutes.

"Malcolm had stuff to do," Kate says, still perched on the counter behind me.

"Sorry, I'm late!" Emma bursts through the break room door, almost letting Frankie run free before shutting it abruptly behind her.

"Is everything okay?" I ask as she sets a box down on the table.

"Yes—yeah—just a crazy morning." She waves me off and starts to pull binders and flyers out of her box. "The block party is in two days, people. We have got to move fast!"

Emma starts handing items out to everyone present for the meeting. "Where's Malcolm?"

Kate tiptoes around the table to avoid Frankie who is now laying at the base of the door. "He's handling that *thing*."

"What thing?" I question Kate, who doesn't respond, and look to Emma for an answer.

"Just an errand." She waves me off. "Now, class is canceled tomorrow for set up. The seniors are using the day for their senior day trip and the juniors are—"

A knock at the door cuts Emma off, who is instantly frazzled at the interruption. She rushes to answer the door and Mrs. Herrera, with the school board, is on the other side, with another woman a little shorter and paler than she is.

"Mrs. Herrera." I meet her at the door. "What can we do for you?"

"Are you ready for the meeting?" she asks sharply.

"Next week? Yes, we will be—"

"No." She puts her hand up to stop me. "The meeting is in an hour."

"What?" Kate runs to my side, wide eyes and worry all over her face. "It's supposed to be next week!"

"Change of plans, the Vice Chair is having hip replacement surgery so it needs to happen today." She reaches into the folder she is holding and hands me an updated memo from the board, with the meeting date and time changed. "We will see you in an hour."

The two women go to leave. Kate and Emma look at me stunned. I pull my phone out and call Ellie, she doesn't answer.

"We aren't ready," she says to Emma in a panic as I hang up.

"Ready for what?" I ask without looking at her, and pulling up Ellie's flight information.

Of course . . . she's supposed to land in an hour. Perfect timing.

"Don't worry," Emma says to both of us. "Alright, people!" she announces to the rest of the faculty, "Change of plans, let's move!"

Everyone scatters quickly making phone calls, racing down the hall, breaking off into groups—like they're on a mission I haven't been debriefed on, and I'm a tad too freaked out about this meeting to even question it.

"We need to get you ready." Kate drags me by the arm out of the break room, leaving Frankie behind. She should be fine.

I text Ellie again as we rush down the hall.

CHAPTER TWENTY-NINE

Ellie

I WAS KNOCKED OUT the moment the plane took off. Getting to the airport at six in the morning? Not a fan.

My interview went well, and I am so grateful for Duncan sticking his neck out for me to make it happen. I left feeling very confident of my decision and now I just needed to get home and tell everyone. It was a face-to-face conversation anyway.

When we reached the tarmac, I turned airplane mode off and was bombarded with text messages. *Ding* after *ding* after *ding*. I quickly turn my volume off when every passenger around me glares at me for disrupting their off-boarding process. I mouth "sorry" to a few then sort through the messages.

A missed call from Benny.

Five from Emma.

About twenty from Kate.

I skip the stream of texts from the girls and immediately open Benny's thread.

An *hour*?

I check the time and see his text was sent forty-five minutes ago. I have fifteen minutes to get to that meeting.

"There's no way," I whisper to myself. I look up and over the seats of the plane before deciding to bolt down the aisle.

I shove past the few passengers standing in the way and rush past the pilot and flight attendant at the exit. Forgetting the fact that I left my carry-on, I race down the escalator and head to baggage claim.

I try to call Benny on the way and he doesn't answer.

Baggage claim is packed full of people, and the conveyor for my flight hasn't started moving. Thanking God for the small Oklahoma airport, I step outside to see if the Uber is here yet—no luck. I step back inside and wait for my bag, anxiously refreshing my Uber app and reading through my texts.

Get here fast!!

Emma – Sister

Be careful, we will meet you there

I check the time, the meeting is supposed to start in ten minutes. I try calling Benny again.

"Eleanor." My heart stops when I hear his voice. "Are you headed this way?"

"Almost, just waiting for my bag." I pace back and forth by the conveyor that still hasn't started *moving*.

"Good, good." He pauses for a moment. "Are you okay?" His voice is tense.

I stop pacing, focusing on his deep breaths on the other line. "Just flustered and trying not to freak out in the middle of this airport."

He lets out a deep rumbling laugh and I feel it pulse in my ears. "Please don't freak out." I can hear a smile in his voice, if that was something you could hear.

"Only because you asked nicely," I joke. The conveyor starts to move. "I'll be there soon!"

"Be careful, baby," he says it sweetly, but I hear it in a more intense way. *Baby.*

I don't have time to fixate on the first time he decides to use that word and what it does to every nerve ending in my body. I hang up without a response, and start scanning for my bag.

Bag after bag cycle through and mine is nowhere.

"Come on," I groan loudly. The desperation all over my body as I pace back and forth, pulling my hair a few times, stomping loudly, and groaning even more. A few people still waiting for their bags put a safe distance between themselves and me as I display escalating behavior in the middle of an airport terminal.

"Is someone in a hurry?" a woman's voice asks from behind me.

"Yes lady, I am!" I snap at the stranger over my shoulder as I pick up a bag that resembles mine but isn't and toss it back on the conveyor. *Freak out incoming.*

"Now that is no way to speak to your elders," the voice snaps back, closer to me than before.

I whip my head around half expecting airport security coming to cuff me when I see Ms. Patsy standing there—looking like she's on island time with a flowy, tropical kimono over her white sweatsuit. I jump at her, clinging to her for dear life, my anxiety simmering as her small frame squeezes me tight.

"What are you doing here?" I ask shocked, still hugging her.

"Someone called in a favor," she says, patting me on the back before shimmying out of the hug. She places her hands on my arms and gives me that familiar Patsy smile. I didn't realize how much I missed it.

She points behind me and I see my bag, the *last* one, finally cycle through the conveyor. My carry-on placed neatly on top.

Grabbing my bags I rush past her. "I'm sorry but I have to be somewhere. How long are you in town?" She follows behind me, hoisting a bright yellow beach bag over her shoulder.

"Not long," she calls behind me as we walk outside to the unloading zone.

My Uber is nowhere to be found.

"You have got to be kidding me!" I fuss and start to mentally freak out as I pull my phone out to find the Uber information.

An orange truck pulls up and honks at Patsy and I. Patsy takes my bag and heads to the truck where Malcolm steps out and waves at us.

"Come on, Ellie Belly! We have a meeting to get to!" she calls over her shoulder as she throws our bags in the truck bed. Malcolm helps her into the truck and I stare at them for a moment before shaking off the confusion and running over to the truck.

"What is going on?" Climbing into the backseat, I ask, "What are you guys doing here?"

"Like I said, someone called in a favor." Patsy winks at Malcolm as the truck comes roaring alive and he pulls away from the airport. He speeds around the corner and I fly back into the seat.

Gripping the seatbelt, I check the time.

The meeting is starting *now*.

Chapter Thirty

Benny

"Welcome, everyone, to our quarterly meeting. I apologize for the abrupt change in schedule, but we appreciate those of you who made accommodations to be here." Mrs. Herrera stands at the podium in the center of the boardroom, leading the meeting.

Kate, Emma, and myself are sitting towards the back of the room. Kate is locked in on her cell phone, texting like a maniac, and Emma is doing some sort of deep breathing exercise moving her hands up and down like this is a yoga class.

Where is Malcolm?

Some of the faculty have come in support, sitting around us. The room is also filled with faculty from the elementary and middle schools, with a few parents scattered throughout.

I've never attended one of these meetings in the past, but I never expected the room to be almost packed like this. There were maybe five chairs, total, unclaimed.

"Jill, can you go over minutes from last quarter?" Herrera sits down and another woman takes the stand. She's younger but dressed similarly, dark gray pantsuit.

Is there a uniform for these jobs?

The minutes are read and the agenda for the current meeting is announced.

"Divata-Bailey Evaluation," Jill ends her announcements with the reason we're all here. We're last to be discussed—I'm unsure if this is a good or bad thing. Good because Ellie can make it in time, bad because their decision, most likely, has already been made so why waste meeting time to even discuss it.

Kate reaches over and squeezes my hands that are clinched in a tight ball. I'm just about bent halfway over, trying to breathe, and my elbows make permanent dents in my knees as I crunch my knuckles.

"It's going to be okay," she whispers to me. I look back at her and her smile is confident and comforting.

Henry Clinton slides into the seat beside me. "How ya doing?"

My jaw clenches at his question. He's to blame that we're here right now. I get it, he has a job to do, and a reputation to protect, but to not even warn me this meeting was happening in the first place feels low.

"Fine," I say through my teeth. I'm not an angry person, but this entire situation was pushing me to the brink, and it is very possible I will snap at my boss right here, right now.

He pats me on the shoulder and I instinctively shove my shoulder away from his hand. I continue facing the front of the room, but I can see out of the corner of my eye that I offended him. Hurt is all over his innocent grandpa-face and I instantly regret my reaction.

"Sorry," I say on an exhale and tap his knee with my fist, "just on edge a bit."

"I would be too." He nods at a few board members as they walk down the aisle to the front of the room, maintaining his administrative composure before he leans over and whispers, "I'm sorry if you feel blindsided."

I blink at him. Is he a mind reader?

"You couldn't know about this," he whispers even lower. "It would have looked bad for all of us if you knew in advance. They want you in the dark." He looks around us to make sure no one is listening. An administrator from the middle school approaches and shakes his hand, then waves at me before they walk to take their seats at the front of the room. Henry adjusts the knot of his tie, clearing his throat. "But there's a plan in place," he's whispering so low I need to borrow his hearing aid just to hear the man. "We've got you."

"What plan?" I'm immediately shushed by Henry, Kate, and Emma. They have me on high alert now. I find myself looking around for suspicious faces before whispering, "What is going on, Henry?"

"Mr. Clinton, care to share updates?" A grumpy and overly large man is standing at the podium and has just finished addressing his points on the agenda. He looks at all four of us, eyes looking apprehensive before he adjusts his face to a welcoming smile. It was subtle but I clocked it, and now my alertness is in overdrive.

Was everyone here wary of me? Was my reputation actually ruined?

Henry pats me on the knee before walking up to the podium. He begins sharing about our recent construction plans for the cafeteria and the adjustments made to the upcoming baseball schedule. I check the agenda bulletin they handed us as we walked in, we have two more points before the *Divata-Bailey Evaluation.* My chest squeezes and my heart rate picks up. I look around quickly scanning the crowd, Ellie still isn't here.

My leg bounces faster and faster as Henry finishes his updates. He calls the next administrator up for their turn and my heart is now pounding so hard against my rib cage hard I feel it in the back of my throat.

This administrator, Sally from the elementary school, literally says, "We have no updates." She smiles triumphantly as if she is the hero of this entire meeting. Good God, Sally, if I ever needed you to share about the school's pet goldfish, the time would be *now.*

Sweat beads up on my temples and my hands feel jittery.

Is this what panic feels like?

I shake my hands out and pop my knuckles, maybe this will help me stay focused. It doesn't work so I crack my wrists in circles.

Kate reaches over and grabs my arm with a free hand, still texting like a speed demon with the other. Who is so important right now? Irritation swells inside me as I flick in the direction of her phone, she waves me off.

"Mr. Divata," Herrera's voice slices through me as she speaks through the microphone. Her eyes are cold towards me before she looks down and adjusts a stack of papers across the podium.

If it was possible to feel your soul leave your body, I'm pretty positive that's what is happening to me right now. I stand up on my wobbly knees, my entire body feeling weak as I stay planted in place, facing the podium. I can't seem to make my legs do what they were created to do, *walk*.

"Could you join us up here, please?" she snaps at me through the microphone. If looks could kill, the one she's giving my powered-down body would be the one to do it.

"Yes." My voice cracks like it did when puberty hit. Kate shoves me forward, my legs deciding to work with my brain as I walk towards the podium. My vision feels foggy, but I can *sense* the eyes on me as I approach the empty space in front of the board.

"Will Ms. Bailey be joining you?" Herrera asks.

My eyes dart around the room looking for Ellie, but it's so congested and my vision is out of focus so I can't locate her. I'm on display as everyone watches me.

And I'm *alone*.

Based on my lack of response, she says, "Alright then, let's begin." Herrera assumes Ellie isn't coming and proceeds to read off the affidavit she presented to me a couple weeks ago.

"I am Ms. Molly Herrera, Superintendent of the Glendale Community School Board. I am here today to bring attention to the interpersonal relationship between Mr. Bayani Divata and Ms. Eleanor Bailey."

I feel nauseous and dizzy as she continues reading off the memo. The words hitting me like bullets all over again as she says them aloud to me and the crowd watching.

Poor decision.

Disreputable.

Insubordination.

"Due to Mr. Divata's complete disregard to school policy, we have no other choice than to recommend evaluation for termination." The entire room gasps behind me. I look down at my shoes, avoiding eye contact with the board members as they gawk at me. A few of them whisper back and forth as they gawk at me like a little harlot. *Where is my scarlet letter?*

Part of me is embarrassed. Embarrassed to be up here looking like a fool who can't seem to separate business from pleasure.

Another part of me is just getting angry. Herrera continues discussing my relationship with Ellie openly to everyone in the room. I have to bite my tongue, remind myself this isn't the place to be a testosterone-filled chump and defend my actions.

"Since Ms. Bailey decided against joining us today" —she waits, glancing around the room. I glance behind me and still don't see her— "we will have to proceed without—"

"I'm here!" Eleanor's voice carries through the crowd as she pushes through people gently and apologetically, because of course, even under immense pressure she will still be the kindest person on earth.

She rushes to my side, and I force myself to resist the overwhelming desire to scoop her up and get lost in her right in the middle of this board room.

"Thank you for joining us, Ms. Bailey," Herrera continues.

Ellie grazes my hand with her thumb. "Hey," she whispers.

I grin down at her, disregarding the seriousness of our current situation and the eyes pinned on us. I can't help what she brings out in me. The typical Benny would keep his composure, he would keep looking straight ahead and nod at his employee like a professional. But I'm not that Benny anymore, not with her.

I'm a smitten little boy and I want them all to see what she does to me, how happy she makes me. "Hey you," I whisper back.

Her cheeks flush red as she smiles back.

Herrera clears her throat. "Can we focus, please?"

"Yes, ma'am," Ellie and I say in unison.

We pull ourselves together, out the magnetic field that seems to tug every part of us to each other and refocus on the board. We get a mix of looks—irritated, bored, and even some *"how adorable"* whispers, as they are all watching us.

"As I was saying," Herrera says sternly, visibly irritated at our presence, "we are here to evaluate your relationship and current employment status."

The dread in my stomach resurfaces and all color leaves my body, I'm sure, as she stares daggers at me.

"Normally, when this occurs, we will open the floor for objections, but as we are running out of time, I am afraid—"

"The hell we are!" an oddly familiar voice comes from the back of the room.

"Excuse me?" Herrera asks the voice.

Ellie and I turn around and see Patsy standing in front of the crowd of faculty and parents. Then,, as if Moses was parting the Red Sea himself, the crowd parts and in walks Malcolm, followed by at least twenty of our students: Sarah, Garrett, Devon, even Birdie and the entire cheer squad, Charlie and the baseball team, with Ethan and Travis bringing up the rear. They all pile through the crowd and stand just feet away from Ellie and I.

"I believe we do have *time* for some objections, don't you, Molly?" Patsy crosses her arms, looking very smug and stares her down over our shoulders.

Herrera stammers on her words at the podium before Jill takes the handheld microphone and walks to the floor. Jill joins us on the floor, standing beside Ellie as we face the group of students.

"What are you doing here?" I whisper to Malcolm. He just winks at me.

"We have some things we would like to say," Sarah speaks confidently and smoothly as she addresses the crowd. Stepping forward as she pulls out a color tab filled binder and hands it to Patsy.

"Thank you, Ms. Kim," Patsy says, taking the binder and walking towards the front of the room. Directly under the podium, Molly is glaring at her as she hands her a pile of papers. "Go ahead and pass those down."

Jill hands Patsy the microphone. "Ladies and gentlemen of the board, we are here to dispute your motion regarding the employment of Mr. Divata and Miss Bailey." Molly rolls her eyes as Patsy walks along the floor addressing the entire room now. "We are here to provide evidence of the positive impact both of these faculty members have had on the student body at Glendale High. We are also here"—she pauses and plants her eyes on Ellie and — "to encourage *full* support of their relationship with one another."

I hear Ellie let out a small whimper as she reaches for my hand. I clasp my hand around hers and feel her shaking. Or maybe I'm shaking. We're both shaking.

Herrera clears her throat at the microphone. "Ms. Strong, this is not how we—"

"Please leave my dead husband's name out of this." Patsy snaps her hand up, firmly interrupting Herrera, without turning around. "Now, we know how this is going to go." She turns to face the board. "You do not have the financial resources, or time, to replace *two* faculty members, let alone find remotely adequate replacements for these two." She gestures back to us, and Ellie's grip on my hand tightens as we watch Ms. Pat turn it on.

She's always been legendary. For years, Glendale got just about anything they wanted if Pat was backing it up. We needed a new jumbotron, not because it was broken but because it looked better, Pat convinced the board to fund it. We needed new mascot colors, Pat designed the costume and the board didn't bat an idea. Back in the 90's, the school cafeteria tried limiting their caffeine options to students, so Ms. Pat hosted a free coffee day and told the superintendent at the time to "deal with it." She was a force to be reckoned with and it was rare that she didn't get her way.

"I think it is about time we consider amending the age-old policy regarding interpersonal relationships and get with the times." Her voice was getting louder, like she was rallying the troops. Some people in the back whooped in agreement. "You cannot control who you love, and we sure as hell don't have any right to tell these two, or *anyone* they can't be with whom they want to be with!"

The crowd hollers and cheers, I feel goosebumps on the back of Ellie's hand. I keep my gaze focused on Herrera as Pat continues. Speaking louder as if she was making history in this very room, demanding justice and compassion, with the crowd matching her energy.

Everyone in the room starts to lose control in their excitement, the students, parents, even some of the board members are cheering and applauding like this is some street rally.

Pat ends with, "Let them be *together*"—another loud cheer—"Let them stay!" Like Mel Gibson in Braveheart yelling *FREEDOM,* Patsy yells again, "Let them!"

Then the entire room begins chanting.

LET THEM STAY!

LET THEM STAY!

LET THEM STAY!

I can't resist looking around the room at everyone. Malcolm and Kate . . . Emma, Steven, and their boys . . . Sam and Nancy . . . Naomi . . . they're all here with our students. The kids are chanting and cheering like they do at the football games, encircling us even closer.

My eyes start to sting as I see everyone . . . they're all here *supporting* us.

I turn to face Ellie and see she's done the same by looking around the room, then turns to face me with tears streaming down her face. I know she feels it too. These people love her and accept her, *us*. These people are her family now.

"Order, order!" Herrera shouts over the room, pounding on the podium with her fist. The volume and elation in the room starts to simmer as Herrera holds her chin up, waiting. "Ms. Strong—" Patsy coughs. "Ms. Pat." Herrera grits her teeth as she reluctantly corrects herself. "I'm sorry to say that the decision has already been made. Mr. Divata and Ms. Bailey made a poor decision to pursue a relationship that is strictly prohibited. There are repercussions for—"

"BOO!!" Devon yells from my right, the rest of the students follow suit. "BOOOOOO!!"

Herrera pounds on the podium. "Enough!" The room is quieter this time, she's pissed now. "Bayani . . ." She directs her attention to me, and I feel acid build in my stomach. "You know the rules."

Another bullet, I *do* know the rules. My throat starts to burn, I'm pretty sure how this is going to end and there's nothing I can do about it. There's nothing anyone in this room can do about it.

"I do, Ms. Herrera." Nodding as I answer, I set my eyes back on the floor as I wait for the final blow.

"Because of that, we have no other choice but to terminate you." A collective gasp and whispered refusals surround us. "As well as Ms. Bailey."

I look at Ellie, her eyes are filled with something sad. Remorse? Or worse . . . *regret?*

"Effective immediately."

CHAPTER THIRTY-ONE

Ellie

IMMEDIATELY?

I can't keep myself together when Ms. Herrera announces to the room that Benny and I are getting terminated. I could throw up. My head is spinning as the room shouts and yells opposing her decision.

What have I done?

Emma's arm is around my shoulders in an instant, Benny still holding my hand on the other side as I choke back my sobs. Ms. Herrera continues addressing the termination to the room, but I can't make out her words, they're muffled behind my own heartbeat—a bass drum pounding in my ears. My breathing is uneven as Benny responds to Ms. Herrera. His hand firmly surrounding mine, a steadying anchor amidst the anxiety that could pull me under at any moment. I sniffle and swallow the huge ball of moisture clinging to the back of my throat. I wipe my burning eyes, tears soaking my face.

The room is blurry, but I see Benny's mouth moving. I focus on his lips as they speak to the room. Emma's arm is still wrapped around me as she rubs my shoulder, Benny's hand holding me in place. They've got me.

The pounding in my ears turns to a faint ringing and I can hear Benny's words. "I implore you to reconsider this decision." His voice sounds like it's inside a wind tunnel, he keeps going. "Maybe look at the statistics Patsy provided?"

"I'm afraid we can't do that"—I hear Miss Herrera clearly now— "Rules are rules."

The room starts to revolt again, booing and yelling, I even hear a few students mutter profanities under their breath. A smile pulls at the corners of my mouth over the support they are showing us. The kids I had no intention of caring about a mere few months ago are here going to battle for me. It's an overwhelming feeling I can't think about right now.

Some students start to act out in their remarks, yelling over Ms. Herrera and Benny, building off of each other as they grow to a mini mob shaking their fists and pointing at the board.

Ms. Herrera looks over them with discontent, waiting for the room to settle before she continues. But it doesn't, the silence riles them up more. I watch the board lean over to each other whispering—Ms. Herrera not budging—until my eyes land on an older gentleman off to the left. He's been quiet throughout this entire ordeal, dressed to impress with a double-breasted suit and red pocket square. I'm just now noticing how overdressed he is compared to the rest of us. His eyes meet mine and I swear they crinkle at the corners.

For some reason, I smile at him, his eyes are kind and somewhat wise underneath his thick frame glasses.

Then, as if I called him to the podium myself, he watches me as he stands and literally glides to Ms. Herrera's side. He towers over her short petite frame.

He clears his throat and stands up straight as he watches the room, they've all noticed the mysterious man at the podium too as they instantly fall silent.

"Molly, why don't you take a seat?" He looks down at her, placing his hand on her back and guiding her away from the podium. Ms. Herrera is hesitant but eventually moves back to her seat with the rest of the board. "Ladies and gentlemen . . . and students." The man nods as he addresses all of us. "In all my years, I have never attended a meeting quite like this one." He smooths out his striped tie. "The support and comradery surrounding these two faculty members is quite encouraging." He rests his hands on the edges of the podium, relaxed and smiling at us.

"Who—"

"The President of the board," Emma whispers to me, answering my question before I can finish asking it.

The President continues, "As much as I would like to hear your statistics, Patsy"—he looks down at his shiny and expensive looking watch—"we are low on time." The crowd attempts to respond again, he holds his hand up effortlessly. "So . . ."

The crowd is silent as he lingers on the word. Benny's grip tightens around my hand, I squeeze back.

"We will just have to take your word for it." He winks at Ms. Pat.

"Excuse me, what?" Benny asks, clearly just as confused as I am.

The man raises his eyebrows as he smirks off to my right, I follow his gaze to Patsy who is smiling back victoriously. She catches my eyes and winks at me.

Wait . . .

I whip my gaze back to the man at the podium, excitement building in my chest as I hold my breath. He's looking at Benny and I over his glasses, a smile pulling at the corners of his mouth. "Consider your termination, terminated."

I let out the breath.

"Welcome to Glendale, Ms. Bailey." He winks at me. "Meeting adjourned."

The crowd goes *crazy.*

Erupting in victory screams, they swarm the floor and practically tackle us to the ground. Benny and I are squished against each other as they start jumping up and down, chanting: *GLENDALE, GLENDALE, GLEN-*

DALE, like we're in the tunnel before the football game. Benny's arms are around my waist, stabilizing me against his strong middle. I wrap my hands behind his head and bring his face down to mine.

"Well this is crazy, huh?" he tries to yell without actually yelling, his forehead pressed firmly against mine.

"So crazy!" I yell back, my smile is hurting my cheeks as we just stare at each other.

Then then students' chanting changes.

KISS HER!

KISS HER!

KISS HER!

We both look around at everyone, they're all expecting a big gesture, and the moment feels like the perfect build up. But . . . isn't that weird? I look back at Benny, telepathically questioning if we should go for it. He receives my question and shrugs, grinning from ear to ear.

Malcolm leans in from the crowd circling us. "Make it quick!" he yells over the chants, then starts to back the circle up.

The size of the circle grows as they give us space, smiling and chanting. Sarah is bouncing up and down. Devon has Garrett hoisted up off his bad leg. Birdie is leading the squad in some weird cheer claps. The baseball team is huddled together watching like it's about to be a grand slam.

I'm cheesing so hard when I look back at Benny and he says, "Oh, what the hell!"

And he kisses me.

The crowd goes wild for a moment, then I hear nothing. I see nothing. I feel nothing, but Benny's lips on mine—his hand on my cheek and the other on the small of my back, pulling me in closer to him. The kiss is tender and intense as his hand moves into my hair, sending bolts of electricity surging over every part of me. My heart is pounding, then stopping, then pounding again as if it didn't know what its purpose was inside my body.

Benny's body is controlled as he slows to a stop, smiling against my lips. We're both breathless after a very G-rated kiss, and I refuse to let my mind wander, thinking about what it would have been like if we were alone.

Everyone in the room starts to quiet down and Benny is still holding me tightly. "So . . ." His smile is curious and beautiful as he asks me, "Are you going to stay?"

Still buzzing from the high of his lips, almost rendering me incapable of words, I announce to him and the entire room, "I'll stay!"

And just like that, we were lost in the crowd again.

"Do you think we can sneak away, or will she catch us?" Benny whispers into my neck. He just pulled me onto his lap in the middle of this faculty meeting, wrapping his arms around me like he's my own personal heated blanket. I could live here.

"She will kill us," I whisper back as he kisses my neck, and I feel them all the way down my toes. Fighting back the giddy giggles I nudge him with my elbow. "Stop, you're going to get us in trouble."

"What can they do, send me to detention?" he whispers against my ear, his hot breath smelling like spearmint.

"I swear to God if you two don't knock it off, I will dump water on you," Malcolm growls at us from the floor. He left the couch the second Benny and I sat next to him in hopes to avoid our PDA.

"It's not me." I wave my hands in innocence. I wholeheartedly planned to behave, but Benny can't seem to get with the program as he kisses my shoulder and brushes a piece of my hair behind my ear.

"I mean it," Malcolm growls.

Benny chuckles against my back then clears his throat. "Fine, my bad."

"Alright, people, we have an hour until the block party!" Emma carries a huge plastic box labeled: *BLOCK PARTY NECESSITIES* into the living room, setting it on the coffee table with force. "Can y'all not do that right now?" She rolls her eyes at us and begins digging in the box.

I lean over and kiss Benny on the cheek and resist the temptation to get lost in his sad puppy dog eyes. "Yes ma'am!" I salute Emma as she starts to hand each of us block party t-shirts and clipboards. "Wha—What are these for?"

Malcolm cackles, probably at the disgust on my face as I look at the pile of papers on top of these clipboards. "You thought we'd be having *fun* at this thing?" He laughs and pats his knee like an old country boy before standing up and pulling on his block party t-shirt over his fishing shirt.

"These are your itineraries, please follow them *precisely*. Or the whole event will fall apart."

I return my eyes to Benny, telepathically asking, *"Is she serious?"* He receives the question and mouths, *"So serious,"* with a slow head nod. He makes me laugh, and I hear Malcolm scoff at us.

"Don't hate us cause you ain't us," Benny calls to him over his shoulder.

Malcolm mumbles under his breath as he walks out the front door. He leaves it open, and a cold gust of wind blows in, carrying a few crispy autumn leaves into the foyer. I watch him climb into his bright orange truck and ask, "What's up with him?"

"He's just jealous," Benny whispers in my ear before kissing it, his mouth lingering against my neck.

"And lonely," Emma says, hoisting the box up onto her hip, "Now come on!" She scurries out after Malcolm and tosses the box in the bed of his truck.

"Alright"—Benny rubs my thigh, giving it a gentle squeeze, before standing— "let's hurry before we get left."

He peels his Glendale polo off over his head and I swear the man is made of chiseled stone. His abs tighten and relax as he twists and pulls his block party t-shirt over his head. I don't know if I have ever seen such perfectly sculpted lines on a man's stomach before. My legs feel tingly as he finishes adjusting his shirt and smooths out his hair.

I'm staring when my mouth decides to try and go rogue. "You are so . . ." I trail off when he gives me an intrigued grin.

"What?" He blushes and slides his hands in his back pockets.

I wrap my arms around his waist, resting my chin on his chest. "So . . ." I pause intentionally. "Alluring . . ." I flutter my eyelashes at him before letting out a full body laugh.

His cheeks go bright red as he throws his head back and groans. "Come on . . ." He grabs my hand and drags me towards the door. I'm still laughing as we climb into Malcolm's truck and he backs down Emma's long drive-way.

The block party is chaos in the most fun way possible. The entire strip from the school parking lot down to the end of the street where Wafflin' sits is packed full of activities. From bouncy castles, to business tables, and food trucks, it was a mini state fair right there on Glendale block . . . and we were on clipboard duty.

"This sucks! I want to do the dunk tank," Kate whines next to me as we man the sports booth in front of Three Sisters' Cleaning. She keeps looking up and over the crowds of people down towards Wafflin' where the dunk tank is set-up. Malcolm and Benny are having a blast convincing people to try and knock them in the water, then swapping places, then attempting to hit the bullseye themselves. A little kid misses at trying to dunk Malcolm, Benny scoops him up and carries him over to the bullseye. I see Malcolm point at them and yell, *"DON'T!"* But Benny ignores him, the kid slams the bullseye, sending Malcolm into the water. Everyone watching cheers and Benny fist bumps the kid before he runs back to his parents.

"You're so in love with him, it's kind of gross." Kate rolls her eyes at me as I stare at Benny with heart eyes.

"We haven't said that yet." I laugh as I wave over the crowd at Benny. He's positioning himself on the dunk seat and blows an obnoxious kiss at me, which I pretend to catch then blow him one back. As soon as he reaches up to pretend to catch his, he's in the water. Malcolm is leaning against the bullseye and tips a salute to me and Kate.

"Silly boys." Kate laughs, her cheeks pink and eyes glistening as she glances back and forth to the dunk tank. She fumbles around with the pens at our table. "I hate how much I love them."

"They're the best, aren't they?" I watch Benny climb out of the tank and chase Malcolm around the tank like little boys playing tag. Just sheer joy as people watch and laugh at their antics.

"Break time, ladies! You're needed at the main stage in five minutes." Margaret, the librarian, walks up to our booth and sits at our table.

"Our break isn't for another hour." I look at my watch then at Kate, she shrugs equally confused.

"Don't ask me." She pulls out her phone and begins playing Candy Crush. "Now, go on!"

I grab Kate's hand and rush towards the main stage, immediately looking for Emma. She probably needs us for a new task, and I don't want to be the reason she is stressed more than she already is. We get to the stage and Emma isn't there, so we watch as the cheer squad finishes up their state routine, chants, and kicks. A football player, whose name I can't remember, walks onstage and sets up a microphone before taking a bow for his hard work, the crowd genuinely cheering for his efforts.

Birdie steps up to the microphone and taps it. "Excuse me," her voice is shrill and I try to maintain my composure. I'm really working on liking this kid, but it won't come easy.

"Here we go." I turn to the sarcastic voice that popped up next to me and see Sarah, standing with Garrett, both sharing a huge pink cotton candy.

"What?" I ask them, giving Sarah a side hug, and squeeze Garrett's arm, as we all watch the stage.

"Homecoming crowning." Garrett smiles at me then, back to the stage.

"We already know it's going to be Birdie and Ethan, why are we here?" Sarah scoffs then shoves a big piece of pink cloud into her mouth.

Garrett nudges her with his elbow. "We don't know that, now hush!"

"You have all voted, and now it's time to crown our Homecoming King and Queen!" Birdie says into the microphone, her voice an octave higher than what sounds natural.

"Did we miss it?" Benny asks, wrapping an arm around my waist. He sticks a thumb in my front pocket, and I hear Garrett and Sarah whisper, "*Damn.*"

That's right kids, Mr. B is smooth as hell.

"Not yet, where's Malcolm?" Kate looks around eagerly. Her cheeks look red again and I have to fight back the wandering my brain does about them two and their *friendship.*

"He's coming," Benny says at the same time Malcolm says, "Here." Drying his hair and beard with a towel as he shoves Benny in the arm. They both chuckle like little kids and the sound warms my heart. He's joined us in the crowd, towel drying his hair and beard. Malcolm shoves Benny's arm for chuckling at him, causing Benny's grip around my waist to tighten, pulling me closer to him. They're bicker back and forth behind me, and their boyish glee warms my heart.

"Lookin' good boys." Kate giggles, bumping her hip into Malcolm's. I see his body tense, a longing in his eyes as he looks at her. She doesn't notice as she turns her attention back to the stage. She laughs at something off in the distance, squeezing his arm in the process. The twinkle in his eye from her touch is subtle, but I clock it. He catches me watching him and gives me a look—*don't say a word*—before darting his gaze back to the stage. I bite the inside of my cheek fight the smile trying to break through.

Your secret is safe with me, Mr. Geer.

"I don't have a spare shirt," Malcolm mumbles, rolling his eyes, as he continues drying off.

"Careful, Geer!" Garrett says over our heads, "You're gonna let everyone know you're more jacked than Mr. B!" He chuckles when Malcolm unclings his soaked shirt from his middle. Kate's eyes do a double take on the thin layer of fabric leaving nothing to the imagination.

Benny rests his chin on my shoulder, his thumb still in my pocket as his fingers rub trace circles on the top of my thigh. A shiver shoots down my leg and reaches my toes. "Are you having fun?"

"A blast." I lean my head against his, the smile on my face pinching my cheeks. I can feel his smile against my cheek as he hugs me tighter. I *am* having fun. This is the most fun I've had in a long time. And it involves teenagers—*who-woulda-thought.*

"Your Homecoming King is . . ." Birdie directs our focus back to the stage with a suspenseful pause. Her mousey smile is on full display as she opens the envelope. "Mr. B!" she squeals, jumping up and down like she rehearsed it.

I gawk at Benny. Kate yells, "*What?*" Malcolm mumbles, "*Dude.*" All at the same time as Garrett points at Sarah. "I told you!"

"And your Homecoming Queen is . . ." Birdie stands up straighter and flips her hair subtly before opening the second envelope.

"She's gonna be pissed," Devon says as he walks up to stand beside Garrett.

Birdie goes ghost white for a millisecond before pulling herself together and reading the envelope out loud, "Ms. Bailey."

Kate squeals. Malcolm mumbles, *"Of course."* Sarah hugs me, all while Garrett and Devon high-five Benny.

Benny drags me up to the stage as the crowd claps and cheers at us. Birdie reluctantly places plastic crowns on our heads, then exits the stage. We stand there in the middle of the stage waving to the crowd like a true King and Queen. Benny is still soaking wet, I'm wearing a baseball cap underneath my crown, we look absolutely ridiculous. And yet, I wouldn't change a thing.

Benny kisses me on the forehead, respecting the huge group of grandparents watching from the crowd, then leads me off the stage.

"I've had enough applause to last me a lifetime," I joke as I remove the crown from my head.

"Not a big fan of the attention, huh?" Benny winks at me as he interlocks his hand in mine and guides me through the crowd. People we know, and people I don't recall, clapping and patting our backs, giving thumbs up and big smiles as we make our way to the parking lot.

Benny's truck is parked on the back row, far from the elation that is flooding across the strip. The walk is quiet as we walk instep, exchanging glances and smiles, but not saying anything. That peaceful silence I only get when I'm with him, where my brain doesn't feel the need to overanalyze itself and can just *be.* I inhale a long deep breath, letting that feeling fill me up and practically lift me off the ground.

"What are you smiling about?" Benny grins. We make it to his truck, and he opens the back, quickly throwing on a dry shirt and Glendale pullover.

"The quiet, it's just nice." I smile watching him out of the corner of my eye.

"It doesn't scare you?" He's sincere when he asks me. "The quiet?" he continues as he rounds the front of his truck and stands in front of me.

At this moment, I can't remember if I ever truly shared with him why I hated the quiet. Why I needed New York, or constant client interaction, or the mindless doodling. Why I felt the need to avoid it out of fear of where my mind will go.

"Did I tell you—"

"You didn't"—he takes my hands in his—"I just thought maybe it bothered you, the quiet." He shrugs and looks down at our feet. Is it crazy that he *sees* me better than anyone?

"It can," I say. He nods, still looking down at our feet. "But it doesn't with you." His eyes jump to mine, and I see myself in their reflection as they glisten from the sun behind me. They're beautiful and hypnotizing as they move across my face and slow to a stop on my lips.

"I have something for you." His eyes don't leave my lips as he pulls an envelope from his pocket. "But"—his eyes level with mine again— "if you don't like it, pretend I never gave it to you and we avoid any awkwardness, got it?"

"I'm sure I'll love it." Giggling, I reach for the envelope. He swipes it away from my reach, his eyes pleading with me. "Okay fine, I promise." I smile at him.

He lets out a huge huff of air and hands the envelope over, shoving his hands into his back pockets. He looks nervous as he bites the corner of his lip. Rolling back and forth on his heels, it's clear how he's feeling right now. *Anxious.*

I hold the pink envelope in my palm, labeled with a simple heart doodle in the center. It feels lumpy, like it's lined inside with bubble wrap. My eyes start to blur as I look at it. The fact that I cry almost anytime Benny does something sweet for me is becoming ridiculous, but I mentally digress and try to focus. It's small and precious and the fact Benny is looking at me with hot anticipation makes me feel fuzzy all over.

"What is it?" I stare at it, grazing my thumb over the wobbly drawn heart in the center.

"Open it." His voice is gentle and smooth as he waits.

I slide my finger under the seal and pull it open carefully, for some reason the thought of ruining this little envelope makes me sad. I pop the envelope open and take a peek, Benny taking a deep breath as I do. I glance at him, his face is almost as white as his teeth as he holds his breath. Letting out a laugh, I break my serious concentration and almost drop the sweet package.

"You're killing me," Benny says on an exhale, taking the gift from my hands. "Here." He turns my palm upward, and slides the gift gently out of the package, placing it in my hand.

There—between us—is a pack of sticky notes?

I squint at the paper then up at him. Confusion and a twinge of disappointment swarming my brain. I wasn't sure what type of gift I was expecting but office supplies were definitely not at the top of that list. His face is ghost white as he pins his eyes on the small gray square. I examine the paper and a giggle bubbles out of me as I read the first note he wrote for me.

I can feel my chest rise and fall faster as I fan through the stack of notes. Goosebumps forming on my arms as I read each little square, each little thought Benny wants to share with me.

August 12 – First day of class!
You seem nervous, I am too.
—Benny Divata (your boss)

August 30 – I forgot I was
trying to do this until I saw
you doodling when I was
talking to Bill. Sneaky ;)
—Benny

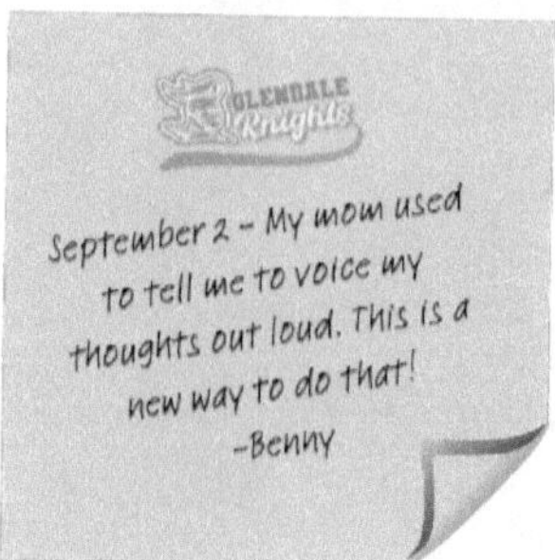
GLENDALE Knights
September 2 – My mom used
to tell me to voice my
thoughts out loud. This is a
new way to do that!
–Benny

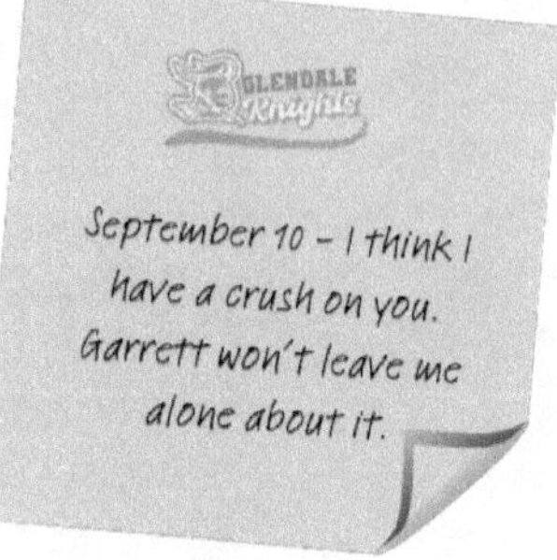
GLENDALE Knights
September 10 – I think I
have a crush on you.
Garrett won't leave me
alone about it.

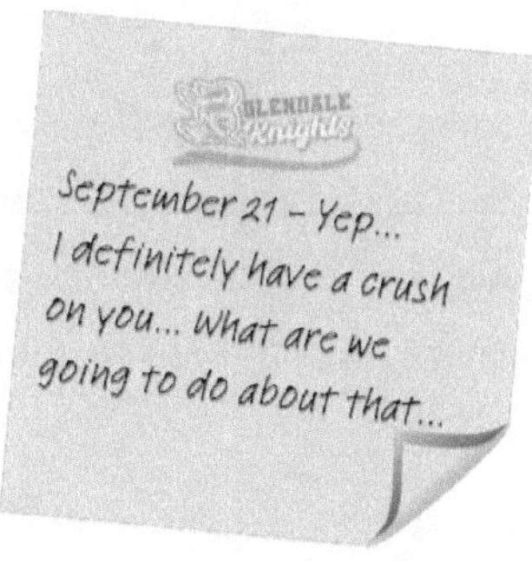

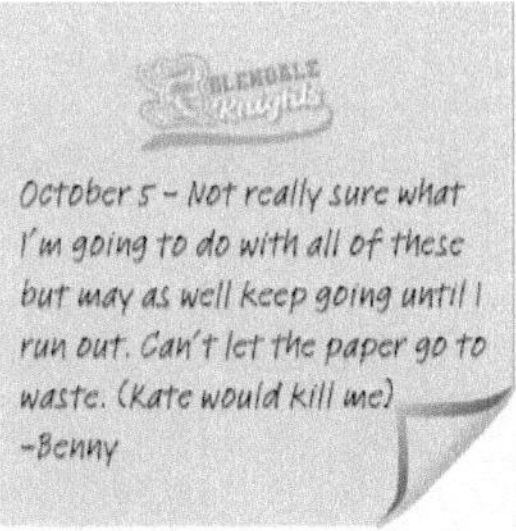

The smile on my face is hard to hide as I sift through each note, careful to not pull them away from their attached border. Reading through each scribbled out thought Benny has had over the last few months. Heavy indentions from erasing and rewriting are noticeable on a few. Others seem so illegible it was clear he was in a hurry.

I chuckle at his attempt to draw a picture of Frankie and look up at him, he rubs his jaw and shrugs his shoulders.

"This is so sweet." My voice is a whisper. I try to put the notes back into the little pink envelope and focus my attention on Benny.

He stops me with his hand, I feel it shaking on top of mine. "Please finish."

His face looks pained as he waits for me. Worry starts to creep through me as I turn my attention back to the sticky note pad.

More thoughts from our morning coffee talks, the cat daycare debacle, even a few notes from when I reluctantly led a morning faculty meeting for Emma. Just his simple words, noting even the littlest things about me. I get towards the end of the stack, just a few more pages to go until the end.

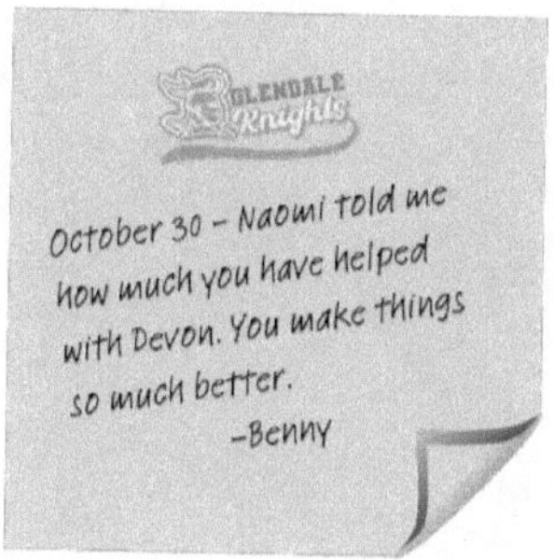
October 30 — Naomi told me
how much you have helped
with Devon. You make things
so much better.
—Benny

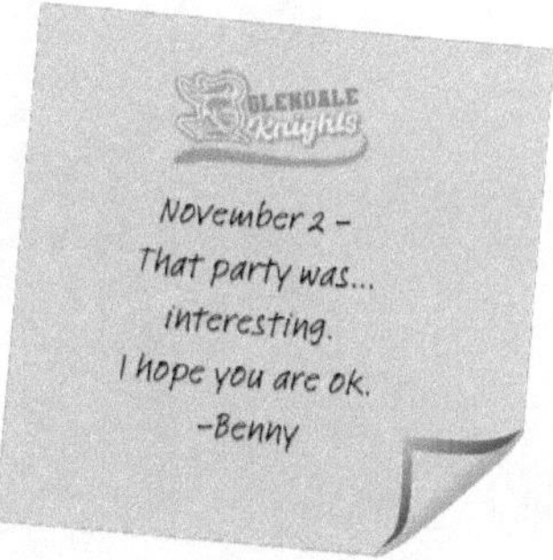
November 2 —
That party was...
interesting.
I hope you are ok.
—Benny

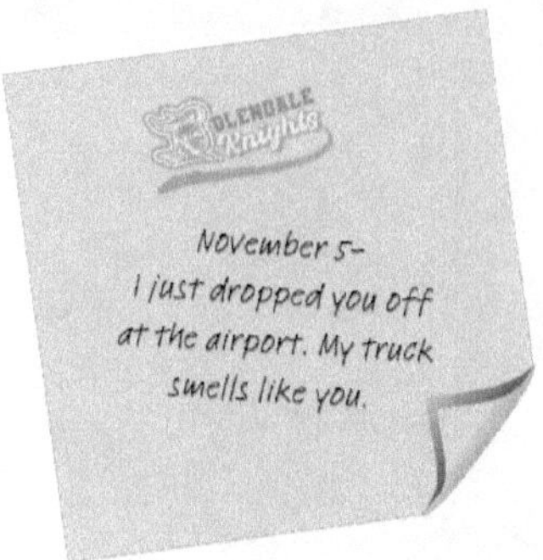
November 5—
I just dropped you off
at the airport. My truck
smells like you.

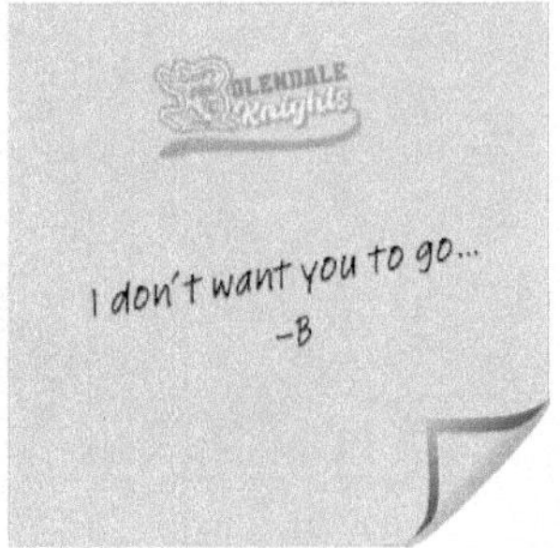
I don't want you to go...
—B

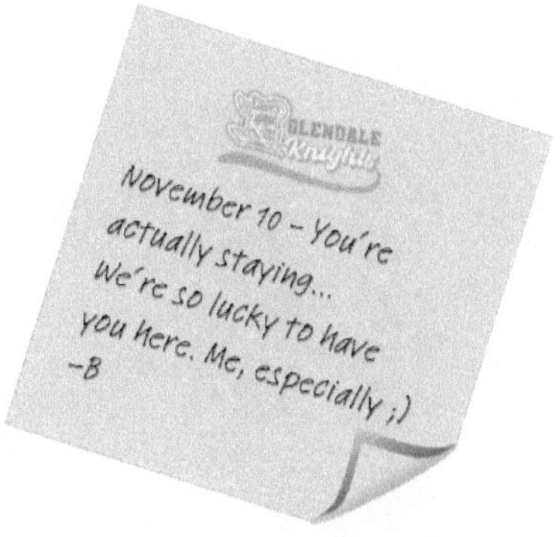

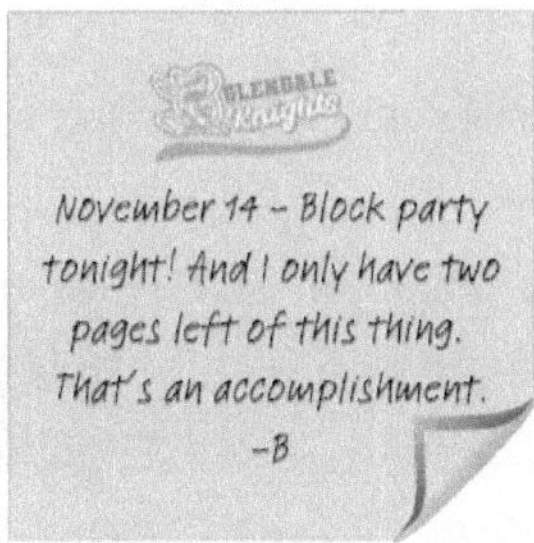

Each note I trace with the tips of my fingers, feeling the jagged indentions he left with his pen. Some notes were even in pencil, scribbles and smears confirming that these notes were not just random intrusive thoughts like mine. They were intentional, planned words. I glance back at him, his eyes pinned on the notes. I turn to the final note and choke back a cough as I read his final thought.

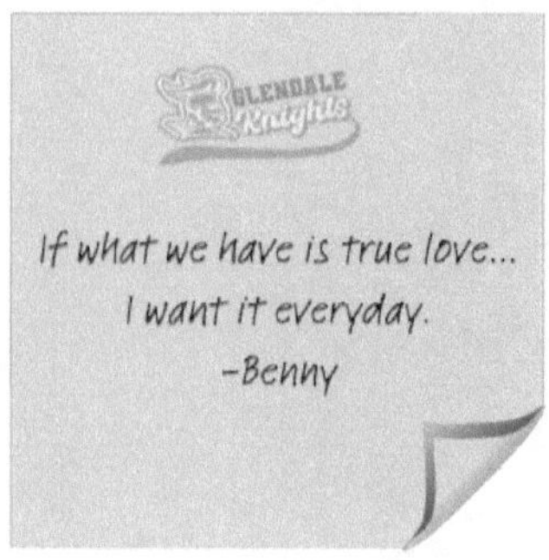

My words stutter as I attempt to register what he is professing to me. *True love.*

Benny senses my shock and quickly diverts. "It's just—you know the movie—that quote—" He waves his hands in a panic as I look between him and the written declaration that stands between us. He rubs his hand through his hair as he stammers, "It's just—ugh—please don't freak out."

"I'm not . . . freaking out," I hesitate.

He blows out a long breath and gently encloses my hand with his own, the stacked sticky notes wrinkling under his palm. His mouth opens and closes as he tries to speak.

"Benny . . . what are you saying?" I take a deep breath and hold it as I watch his eyes. They search my face with a sincere focus I haven't seen from him yet.

"The truth." My entire body releases the tension that had worked its way into my shoulders as he continues, "I'm crazy about you. I've never felt this way about anyone before, but I know it's real and it's true and I don't ever want to lose it. I don't know if you ever want to get *married* or anything . . ." My eyes widen, the "*M*" word lingering in the air like a black cloud.

I haven't thought about marrying anyone since my last failed attempt. Had I thought about a long term—possibly forever—relationship with Benny? Of course. But it wasn't ever *marriage*. Not that I'm against it, per say, rather I'm just wary of it and really don't want to endure the crash and burn again.

"And I don't want you to feel pressured to do something you aren't ready for." He levels his gaze with mine, the note pressed gently between our hands. "But I want you to know . . ." There's a soberness to his eyes—no jokes, no banter. "You are the greatest thing to ever happen to me. And I want you to trust me when I say I will never leave you." His bottom lip is quivering as he speaks. "But I am in love with you, Eleanor. I think I have been since the day you got here, and I want *this*, what we have, every day of my life. And I really hope you want it too."

The lavish altar with its white rose petals and elegant floral decor flash across my mind with his words—everyone watching as I walk down the aisle holding a small bouquet of gorgeous flowers. The scene looks familiar, like deja vu, but it feels different.

"I love every part of you and I am promising you that I'm not going anywhere," Benny continues, his hands on my shoulders now. "No matter how scary or weird you think your brain might get, I promise to be by your side and help you get through those scary things. Every single one of them." His tone is serious, honest, and every part of me believes that he's committing to be everything I want him to be. "You're it for me, Eleanor."

The altar image crosses my mind again, walking toward a man at the end of an aisle. It's just the two of us. He's in a dark black suit, accentuating his kind eyes as they are laser focused on me. His smile widens as I approach, sending a wave of peace washing over me. Peace coming from having found something . . . someone dear to my soul.

My soul loves this man.

I blink back to reality, focusing on him at this moment. I speak earnestly, meaning every word as I place my hands on his chest. "You're it for me, Bayani Divata,"

Then I reach up on my tip toes and kiss him—right there in the middle of a high school parking lot. I feel happy and safe as I kiss the man I love softly and slowly, trusting we have all the time in the world together.

Benny

One Year Later

"Alright, people! It's D-day!"

Emma barrels into the breakroom holding three small bouquets and a box of boutonnieres. I'm leaning against the refrigerator, watching as she rushes around the room, calling out orders, smoothing out ties, and tying a ribbon on Frankie's collar.

"D-day, Divata day, I love it!" Kate bounces up and down in her black bridesmaid dress—her bouncy curls looking like they did when we were little, wild and free. She started sporting the natural look again a few months after the block party. It suits her.

"How are you feeling?" Malcolm meets me at the back of the room and begins pinning the small flower to the front of my suit jacket.

"Nervous." My voice is shaky. "Excited. Ready to get started. All of it." I start to ramble and Malcolm pats me on both shoulders once he's done pinning.

"Just stay calm." He smiles, a rare Malcolm sighting. "It's going to be great."

I give him a thankful nod and adjust my tie, it feels tight and constricting around my neck, as I watch Emma line everyone up in the break room.

"We're starting in five minutes!" she announces to the room before walking up to me. "You good?" She eyes me suspiciously.

"Never better," I answer, knowing full well she will run me over with my own truck if I try to leave this wedding—which I have no plans to do—but her crazy eyes are just extra incentive to watch my step.

"Good," she says, shoving her pointer finger into my chest. "I love you, Ben, but I love her more. Do not ruin this."

I grab her finger and shake it. "I won't."

She eyes my hand then back up to my face, her stern facial expression softening. Then she hugs me quickly, the physical contact calming my nerves for a brief moment, before rushing back to the opposite end of the room.

Bill, the Janitor, joins me at the end of our makeshift aisle. Office chairs lining each side, covered in white cloth and black bows. His rusty twinkle lights strung above us in all different directions and candles set up all along the back counter.

Emma hands Kate and Patsy a bouquet, white roses and small palm leaves. I see Patsy's gaze linger on the bouquet, her eyes glistening as she brushes the leaves—a small nod to my parents and our Filipino culture.

Patsy ignores Emma's instructions to *"stay put"* and rushes up to me and Bill at the back of the room, squeezing the bouquet tight to her chest.

"They would be so proud of you, Bayani." The eyes I know of strong-willed Patsy were different today, a mixture of joy and sorrow I assume. "*I* am so proud of you." A tear escapes the corner of one eye, she grumbles as if it did it of its own volition. Wiping it quickly, she shakes her head. "Damn, these old eyes."

A combination of shuddering breath and a a chuckle escapes me as I grab her hand. My sweet, strong Patsy. I bow at my waist, kissing the top of her hand and pressing it against my forehead firmly. *Mano.*

"Patsy, come on," Kate whispers at us from the front of the room. Her face is tense as she looks at us and back at Emma who is running around like a maniac.

"Mahal kita," I say as she backs away to join Kate.

I watch as the ladies adjust their dresses, Kate straightens Malcolm's tie, and Steven wrangles the boys down the aisle. I let myself take in the scene, remember it. Everyone says you forget the small details and I don't want to forget anything. My gaze lands on the small seat at the front of the aisle housing a photo of my parents, holding me as a chubby baby. The worst possible photo of me, but the most beautiful one of them. It was Ellie's idea to have something dedicated to them, just one more thing that makes her the most incredibly thoughtful woman.

I loosen my tie another fraction, swallowing the lump that formed over their memory. Bill probably sees my emotion and pats my back as he prepares his notes for the ceremony. I had no idea Bill was an ordained minister until last month when we announced to the faculty that we were getting married—in thirty days. He jumped at the chance to do the wedding, telling me it would look good on his resume.

"Are you planning on leaving us?" Ellie asked him.

"Just always looking for side gigs." He laughed a burly, wheezy laugh.

"Crazy how life is so different now, huh?" Bill asks, bringing me back to the present.

"So crazy." I pull at my sleeves, lining them up with my wrists.

"Just a year ago I was dressed as a bunny and you were a ninja." He laughs that same wheezy laugh.

"I wasn't a ninja." I roll my eyes and he laughs again, muttering, *"Sure"* under his breath.

Life for me wasn't very different, besides the fact that I had the most perfect woman letting me love her and she was loving me right back. Outside of that, my role as vice principal remained the same, powering through the ebbs and flows of the school year. Ellie is embracing her guidance counselor role like a freaking pro, on top of accepting a remote professor job with Columbia.

There was tension in the beginning. It was hard to believe she was willing to leave New York and stay here with me, in Oklahoma no less. Her dream job was practically out the window, but when Columbia offered her a remote teaching position, with a stipend to visit campus once a quarter, she had another chance to pursue her dream while I maintained mine. Like somehow the individual desires of our hearts were being given to us.

Being with Ellie has been wonderful and more than I deserve, something I didn't see coming twelve months ago. After the block party, we were all in. But actually asking her to be my fiancée didn't happen as soon as I had hoped. I didn't want her to feel pressured into something that brought her so much pain. I couldn't do that, even if it was what I wanted more than anything.

I wanted to put her needs before my own, show her love and patience, build her trust. Show her that whatever she needed to feel safe and confident in our relationship, I would do—even if it felt like a century waiting for her to be ready. I was pretty confident I would marry her after her first day at Glendale, but I have spared her that little nugget of information.

"Places, people!" Emma shouts as she turns on the wedding music and Ed Sheeran's voice floats out of the speakers.

Well, me, I fall in love with you every single day
And I just wanna tell you I am

The music fills the room, reverberating up my legs as I close my eyes. The last year flashing across my mind like a sped up movie. In a flash I have gone from a boy, smitten over the new girl in school, to now the man head-over-heels in love, about to marry that girl.

Place your head on my beating heart
I'm thinking out loud

Maybe we found love right where we are

I hear the door open at the back of the room, followed by chairs moving and seats squeaking as people stand—my eyes still closed shut. The blinds behind me are pulled open. A lot is happening at first, then the room is silent and I hear gliding footsteps inch closer and closer. I could *feel* her closeness, hints of coconut shampoo and her special occasion perfume swirling around me. Bill taps me on the shoulder to open my eyes. I took a deep breath, and opened.

There she was—my bride.

She was mesmerizing. I sputter out a breath and my eyes sting from tears as she reaches for my hands—both of our eyes misty as we take our places on the altar. She smiles over my shoulder at the crowd of students standing on the other side of the large bay window. I insisted on only inviting them to the reception because they are chaos, but Ellie insisted harder.

"Dearly beloved, we are gathered here today—"

"Wait," Ellie interrupts Bill's opening remarks. "Can we just . . ." She pulls me around and swaps places with me, where I am now facing the window. A large crowd of our students are on the other side of the glass watching us with beady eyes and cheesy grins. "It's *your* favorite view, remember?"

I shift my gaze away from the purple and orange sky, past the football field, over the familiar faces of kids and faculty, then land on Ellie. Her dress is simple, with long flowy sleeves that gather at her wrists. Her hair is wavy, pinned back with a few pieces hanging by her face. If I were to see an angel in person, I know this is what it would be like. She practically glows with the sun shining on her back. A dusty shimmer compliments her green eyes as they watch me.

I take it in, the most beautiful view.

"It is," I say, her cheeks turning pink because she knows what my favorite view is, and it has nothing to do with that big window anymore.

Bill clears his throat and begins again, "We are all gathered here today to join these two in . . ." He pauses and looks at the room expectantly.

"MAWWAGE!" everyone in attendance cheers.

My nerves fall away as we both laugh, smiles ripping across our faces as Bill continues. He read some Bible verses, shared about marriage and the covenant we were agreeing to, then it was time for our own vows.

We talked back and forth for days about how we should do our vows, then agreed to keep them simple.

"I, Eleanor Anne Bailey, promise to love every part of you, and always be willing to think out loud with you," she said beaming at me.

"I, Bayani David Divata, promise to love every part of *you*, beautiful and weird and scary thoughts included." Her smile stretched even farther.

I cradle her face in my hands, grazing my thumbs against her cheeks. There are so many things I could promise to this amazing woman, right here in our little breakroom in front of our friends and family, but I plan to spend the rest of my life *showing* her. Showing her that every single piece of her, the good, the bad, and the scary, is worth loving. Her eyes shine brighter, if that's even possible, looking up at me, unspoken words and vows flowing between us. I let out a breath, fully embracing the clutch this woman has on every part of me.

Then the silly boy kissed the pretty girl.

Acknowledgements

Wow. We did it. You and me. We made it through a story together! To say I am all mushy about it is an understatement. I have dreamt about this since I was little and the fact that you, reader, have taken the time to read my story and are also reading this little note, means the world to me. So I must thank you first, because without you, this wouldn't be possible. I hope you loved your time at Glendale and hope you'll be back next term (wink wink)! Thank you for reading, reviewing, and sharing, you are making little girl Grayson's dreams come true!

Caitlin — my editor and friend — you are a one in a million find. I can't thank you enough for your hard work and wisdom throughout this entire process. I am not exaggerating when I say this would just be a pile of paper underneath my desk if it wasn't for you. Thank you for believing in me and my writing, and for helping make Ellie and Benny's love story as quirky and beautiful as it is! You are a national treasure.

My beta and ARC readers — thank you so much for taking the time to read, critique, and provide feedback. Your input was priceless and helped shape this story in a way I would never have been able to do on my own.

Cindy — your cover art is perfect. Thank you for helping bring Ellie and Benny to life! And thank you for putting up with me.

To my friends — Shelby, India, Bree, Tori — your wisdom, encouragement, and feedback was immensely helpful. Kenzie, Sarah, Kait, Stephanie, Ashley, and many others — you all are simply the best! Even in not knowing what the story was fully about, you being excited nonetheless kept me going. Having such wonderful people in my corner makes this journey so much sweeter!

My family — I would literally not be on this earth or at this point in my life if it weren't for you guys. I love you. And don't come at me for the steamy parts. Kenzie, thank you for making such sweet lively little boys. Please know I love my nephews and their wild spirits, dearly.

Austin — your sweet soul left this earth right in the thick of editing this novel. If I had known what was to come, I would have written an entirely new story about you and the joy you brought to my life. Maybe one day. For now, I just want it in writing how deeply I miss you.

My baby girl — life with you is so sweet. As you get older, I hope your desire to read surpasses my own. I hope you find peace and joy within the pages of books. And I hope the books that make you smile include some written by your very own mama.

And lastly, but most importantly, my husband — David. My numero uno, my biggest cheerleader, my favorite person in the entire universe. You never give up on me. You never stop rooting for me. And you never cease to amaze me. Thank you for giving us such a beautiful life, and don't be too embarrassed by the little nods to you I left throughout this book. I love you most.

Hugs,

Grayson

About The Author

Grayson Long currently resides in her home state of Oklahoma. The love she has for her family runs deep, and the love she has for Nutella might be just as strong. Her childhood dreams of writing were thwarted by a fear of failure. But turning the ripe age of thirty, she realized no better time to try than now. Grayson wrote her first novel in three months, writing in the late hours of the night, or during her daughter's naps. When she's not spending time with her family or finding time to write, Grayson can be found working in an ICU as a Registered Nurse. When you read a story written by Grayson, her hope is that you smile, laugh, kick your feet, or a combination of three. But more than that, she hopes you leave the story feeling lighter and happier than when you started. Because that's one of the great things about reading, to escape to a brighter place for a bit.

www.ingramcontent.com/pod-product-compliance
Lightning Source LLC
Chambersburg PA
CBHW021337150726
47989CB00005B/2019